I0703928

ACQUIRED LAND

Saga of the Vanishing Prairie Book 1

Cindy M. Amos

ISBN: 978-1-965352-60-1

*The earth belongs to God,
both its vast acreage
and those who dwell therein.
Psalm 24:1*

In loving memory of our
senior rancher
John Max Amos

Prologue

At the prism-edged perimeter of civilization, where the rural roads end with the letter Z, lies the open prairie in its vast splendor, unmarked by hand or time. Here, expanses of the level landform rise to the rock-strewn Flint Hills. Natural springs outcrop and drench diamond waters back toward the low places. Abundant offspring of the coyote and the badger belie both the solitude and the meagerness of their existence. Unassuming wildflowers with fleeting names like prairie groundsel and daisy fleabane bloom in sequence unheralded and unhurried by the eyes of humankind.

What may seem a placid surrender by a vanishing ecosystem toward the verge of functional existence becomes a deeply rooted hinge where the rectitude of nature heels in, garners its resources, and exerts a resurgence to regain space.

In essence, the tallgrass prairie is returning.

Chapter 1

Brittle with the passage of time, the rectangle shell of a rock house nestles on the shaded edge of a pasture on Road AA. Hedge apple and black locust trees sprout, live and—once weakened by prairie life—are toppled by the wind. Blue wood phlox and other shade-loving forbs establish in the here-then-gone relief from the sun, mimicking a flower garden around the base of the rock house. Fueled by the generosity of late spring rains and anchored with the underpinning of roots six feet deep, bunch grasses like big bluestem and switchgrass reach for the sky in exponential growth. Limestone blocks scattered about the foundation allow opportunistic animals to come and go at will. Reduced to a rock-stack memorial to a generation before, the structure is being gently reclaimed for reuse by the tallgrass prairie.

Jusdyn Linquist never recalled the prairie wearing a skirt—until today. He watched a feminine figure perched like a meadowlark on the pipe gate as he rode up from the north pond. Spellbound, he couldn't glance away from her The native grasses he'd replanted on this former crop field now reached for his stirrups as he passed, proving that early June hosted prime grazing for his herd. With his task of counting cattle hindered by the trespasser, he enjoyed the prickle of interest at the close of his morning rounds.

Riding toward a double row of pines, he realized she didn't belong here anymore than these non-native trees did. Long ago the farm foreman's home, now a solitary loafing shed broke the horizon beyond the trees. With gnarled, thickly wooded branches, this stand of trees could comb a song out of the Kansas wind that sounded ethereal. Too bad she wouldn't hear it today. As late morning stretched by, the summer sun trumped the wind leaving the pines silent. A jet contrail scratched the sky, marking the only difference between his path and one his grandfather might have taken half a century ago.

He cleared his throat to remedy an odd tightness about the same time the stranger threw her hands above her head as if to touch the sun. In less than half a minute he'd have to break her private reverie. Of all the gates on the wide open prairie, she'd chosen his only exit along this flank of the quarter section. His horse rotated one ear back as if expecting a command, but he let the scene play out the way it fell—him riding up from behind and her unaware of his company while reaching for something else. He adjusted his hat for the encounter and felt the reins stick to his palms.

The slender figure shifted on the gate ahead as if she might have glimpsed him approach. She lowered her hands to her lap, facing away. Time stood still as a cloud covered the contrail.

Duty bound to force the meet-up, he cleared his throat. "Ma'am, if you're gonna hang around here much longer, I'll have to start charging you rent." He shook the gate to accentuate the mock threat as the horse side-stepped toward the fence. He caught her startled reaction when their gazes met, an unguarded moment.

A blush stained her porcelain cheeks as she attempted to stand along the middle rung. When her boot heels slipped, she fell headfirst onto the bluestem grass of the outer pasture. A surrendering moan marked the end of her decent.

Adrenalin-flushed, Jusdyn snatched out of the saddle in a rodeo second. With a twist of his wrist, the twin gates fell open. Shouldering around the far gate, he knelt to examine the fallen figure. He cleared the soft brown hair from her face. Guilt gripped his throat. *Lord, what I wouldn't do to see her eyes flash again.*

Her unconscious state demanded his focus so he quelled the recurring specters of self-doubt and tried to think. Mayhem would not rule the pasture on his shift, even with a stranger afoot. The solid chest of his horse pressed against his shoulder as if to coax him into action.

"Water, we need water." He fished a water bottle out of the saddlebag and twisted off the cap. From basic first aid training, he knew not to move her in case of a head or neck injury. Instead, he poured a small stream of water across the crevice of her lips, shading her as he knelt. Cupping his hand, he splashed her cheeks and forehead. He paused a moment to examine her attractive features, but soon catalyzed the rescue by returning to the vitals. A woman down represented their immediate status, and he needed to remedy that dire situation.

A plan of action emerging, he tested for a breath with the back of his hand. Nothing stirred but the faintest prairie wind. Following protocol, he would need to touch his mouth to hers to initiate the next phase. He exhaled away any qualms and bent lower to get underway. In the hesitation of drawing a deeper breath, he retreated into a soul check of his true motivation, slinging his hat to the ground.

"Lord, help me do the right thing—for the right reason," he whispered with a break in his voice. Bending closer, he had no more touched his lips to hers when he felt a slight tremble followed by a certain tightening, as if she was coming to. He backed off a few inches, searching for signs of consciousness on her face. When her eyelids fluttered open, he saw the most transfixing hazel eyes he'd ever witnessed. *Too close…much too close.*

~

Blackness gave way to a mixed swirl of memory. Arie couldn't recall whether she'd finished baking the pies or not. Had smoke curling from the chimney of the little rock house given her away? Was she safe? When her head rolled, the pillow smelled like fresh grass, silky and warm on her cheek. Sunlight peeked through her eyelids and she glimpsed a cowboy hovering over her at close range. In limbo, she seemed powerless to do anything about it. A dull pain wrapped around her head. When darkness threatened to return, fear rode with it.

From nowhere, a rivulet of water came to her. The effect refreshed her throat as she pulled against the abyss to return to her beloved prairie. Pulse echoing in her ears, she willed herself to awaken and see about this stranger who had ridden up behind her on the gate. If only she could sit up, but a leaden vice held her in place. Her fingertips responded as she touched a velvety interloper that rippled against her skin. When twitching velvet transformed to nibbling teeth, a pinching sensation brought her fully into day-lit reality. "Ouch."

"Ouch?" a voice repeated. Someone touched her cheeks and forced back the blackness. A man hovered close by, his face etched with concern.

"Your horse is nibbling my fingers."

The man rose with a blown breath and pushed against the animal's chest. Clicking a command through his teeth, he backed the large horse toward the gatepost and tied it in place. "Always trying to fix things your own way, Chica." He brushed a hand down its nose.

A meadowlark called as she surveyed her situation, nestled into the prairie with a close-up of only grass—and a cowboy. A headache encircled her thoughts so she seized onto his last word like a life raft to consciousness. "Chica? So she's your girl?" She experienced the relief of his shadow as he moved closer.

"My one and only." He blinked in the sunlight. When she lifted an arm to shield the glare, he intercepted her hand and examined her fingers. "So relieved to report there's nothing broken, bruised, or bleeding here." His grip turned confining as if forcing a move.

She pulled away to shade her eyes and better assess her rescuer. "No—the axe buried in my head begs to differ." To avert the rising vertigo, she covered her eyes, but couldn't filter out the moan moving up her throat.

The man knelt at her side. "I'm Jusdyn Linquist. These cattle you're exploring around are mine. My mother is part of the McLauren clan and inherited this land you're now bunked down on. Listen, I don't know who you are or how you even got out here, but we need to get you up and maybe do a damage check." A strong arm began to wedge under her shoulder.

"I'm Arabella Henning. That's Arie to my friends—or if you're in a hurry." She clenched her teeth to brace against the dizzying motion his jostling had set loose.

"Okay, Arie. I'm going to pick you up and place you in the saddle. If everything seems intact, I'll take you back home to rest. One thing's for sure, we need to get out of this heat."

"Not on that horse," she replied in a strained tone, her throat a dry gulch. The animal responded by pawing the grass as if to sidestep any blame. She'd never survive that plodding game plan.

"Well, why not?" A gust of wind buckled the twin gates together which seemed to prompt the rancher to better state his case. "Look, you didn't do so well riding the gate, so I thought we could try the horse next." While his tone teased, his expression softened awaiting her reply. Face-to-face with only a hush of breeze between them, she lingered long enough to recognize sincerity in his eyes, and then the blackout of oblivion returned.

~

Now watching with purposeful intention, Jusdyn had neither missed the insufferable moan as he lifted Arie nor mistaken the flutter of her eyelids as she lost consciousness again. Though weakness closed in on her world by increments, he found himself strengthened by the growing conviction of a rescuer with a sure-fired plan. He turned with her in his arms and gave a command to the tethered ambulance. Chica straightened its stance and braced for the load, hastening to swallow one last mouthful of early summer grass.

"You're not going home, after all," he said to her, resolve

steadying his voice. "At least, not to *your* home." Without a doubt, she needed medical help, and he knew where to find it.

He placed her delicate frame into the saddle's protective valley, pulled out the roll of his rain poncho, and rigged a stabilizer around her neck. With the tenderness of handling a newborn calf, he strapped her in place. When she shifted position, he tightened her tether at a second point to keep her secured in the saddle.

"I'm here to help you," she babbled into the horse's mane.

A chuckle broke loose from his tight chest as he placed a reassuring hand on her back. His grandfather's favorite retort echoed to mind as he untied the reins. "Well, thunder. Here I stand bucked off my own horse by a damsel in distress who claims she's helping me." He gave his chap lips a lick. "Plus the prairie somehow tastes like apple pies this morning." The horse's left ear cocked back as if to respond, but he stood too deep in his own commiserations. "Looks like a mutiny of the first order—and I didn't even see it coming." He turned his gaze to the pine lane leading out of the pasture, his strength faltering. *Should've eaten breakfast.*

Holding the reins in one hand and bracing her with the other, he clicked a forward command to start their journey. Along the way, he marveled how a calloused work animal capable of running down a moonstruck bull could turn so soft-footed upon command. On the far vista, the prairie stretched a level flag of enduring green as if to embrace the fall victim, somehow holding the promise of healing up ahead.

Chapter 2

On the corner of Road Z and Cemetery Road, the Kentucky coffee trees hang heavy with grape-like blooms painted the faintest yellow-green. Densely wooded, this corner provides habitat for common muskrats and thirteen-lined ground squirrels. A hidden spring fills a casually meandering creek with crystal water, where barred tiger salamander juveniles spread their feathery gills among the watercress and dream of growing up. Baltimore orioles hang basket nests in forks of sturdy branches, streaking their black and orange across nearby pastures. Ornate box turtles plan their forays out into the grasslands and back with plodding precision. Here the land breaks in relief from the grassy openness of the prairie, and the tangle of a full forest canopy delights the senses with the forgiving offer of textured shade.

"At a corner just like this one, the fabled prodigal son would have made his first wrong turn." Jusdyn led the horse slack-reined toward the ranch house. "God, forbid I ever step in that direction." His hand came to rest on Arie's shoulder, though she failed to stir. He knew this stretch of land by heart, from its limestone rock outcrops to the last walnut tree where the woods surrendered to the open grass. Into the comfort of all things familiar he now brought his fall victim, knowing the next major hurdle loomed ever before him—his mother.

Muriel stepped out onto the front porch of the day cottage as the horse approached the driveway. Bending stiffly, she placed her book on the top step and headed toward them with her gait constricted with apprehension. By the time Chica stepped onto the gravel, she stood by the mailbox and stared at two boots dangling from the hem of a cotton skirt. "What we have here is young, female, and out like a light." She gave him a matter-of-fact look that demanded an explanation.

He countered with intentional directness, knowing his best bet would be a forthright rendering of the vital information, or she would launch a barrage of pointed questions. "She's had a bad fall from the top of the gate at the McLauren pasture, Mom. Couldn't manage to get her feet under her, she ended up hitting the ground headfirst. She's been in and out of consciousness a couple of times. At first, she could answer me. But that was half an hour ago."

"Sounds like a concussion. We'd better get her inside. Let's use mother's place since it's closer." She placed her hand on Chica's blaze, matching steps up to the porch.

His shame shifted deeper now, realizing that what his mother had left as a tranquil retreat moments ago she would reenter as an infirmary, a turn of fate to which even self-reliant ranchers never grew fully accustomed.

"Careful now. Every time you jar the injured area, you risk compounding the damage."

He lifted the limp rider from the saddle with deliberate slowness and turned for the porch steps. *Only a mother could pinpoint the heart of the problem so readily.* He took one step at a time, fighting back condemnation as the absolute expert at compounding damage.

She moved a layer of embroidered pillows aside. "Put her here in the front room."

He lowered the victim and stepped back to watch the nurse go to work. He had always considered her medical training a total waste, until emergencies like this came along. A couple of years earlier, she managed to keep his dad alive after a chain saw accident despite the long drive to Emporia for surgery.

She cleared the patient's face to check her vitals, borrowing the clip from her own hair. As she anchored a wave of sun-washed brown hair to one side, she made an uncharacteristic casual remark. "Goodness, she's beautiful. Is she a McLauren?"

"Henning, Mom. Arabella Henning. I'd never seen her before, never met her until today when I was checking the fence line and there she was perched atop that double gate." He noted the taking of her pulse by the trained nurse, something he'd failed to do. "Haven't seen any bleeding, Mom. She landed on some big bluestem by the gatepost. The grass broke her fall a little. Then Chica started nibbling her fingers." When the nurse raised an eyebrow, he squirmed at the recollection. "Well, that's what seemed to bring her around the first time."

She planted her fists on her hips. "So, she was knocked out immediately from the fall, and then came around with the horse biting her hand, but passed out again. That settles it for me, she has a concussion. I'll make a list of things you need to bring me from the main house. We'll need a few minutes of privacy here."

Knowing modesty would be a part of her bedside manner emergency or not, he nodded in surrender and headed out. "I need to tend the horse anyway." His hand hit the door latch in futility, feeling like an outcast.

"Listen, son. That's why they call it an accident, because it couldn't be helped. She fell and you were right there in the middle of a big, open land. Remember how long your grandpa laid in the ditch when the tree fell on him in the snow over at Blythe pasture?"

He knew his grandfather's version of the story by heart. "Halfway to tomorrow."

His mother's face animated a touch. "Truth be told, there's been no long-suffering here, so let's be thankful for that much."

He could only nod in response, feeling the choking reality coming on him like a dread. The screen door slammed with the help of the wind. He picked up the dangling reins and started around the cottage to the corral when a final confession came to mind. "Mom?" He spoke through the lace curtain, hanging his head. "She's scared of Chica now." The horse blinked at him, showing no signs of remorse.

"Well, all things considered, who wouldn't be?"

When she nodded sideways toward the big house, he stood there dismissed like a ten-year old. At final glance, the patient began to stir. Chica stepped toward the corral so he followed in numb obedience.

~

"It's time to value our friendship by making another extraordinary memory out on the prairie." Opal Litke hadn't meant for her voice to carry through the family room of Flint Hills Senior Care Facility. "The Symphony on the Prairie begins at one-thirty, not this Saturday but the next." She pointed her arthritic finger toward an invisible calendar. "Why don't Ruby and I pick you two up high noon, pay our respects at the cemetery, and head on out? That would give us more than enough time to get to the Stone Barn."

Her dear friend Vernis McLauren bristled at the invitation. "Somebody's gonna think I've gone soft." Nearby, his older brother Morrill dropped his chin to his chest.

She had the utmost conviction to stand her ground for something she believed in so strongly. "Not a single member of this community will expect you to lose one drop of venom by attending this symphony. It's never been held in Council Grove before, so it's a real honor for the townspeople. Certainly you can appreciate that."

Her sister Ruby stirred to action as if willing to aid her argument. "Why, it's our civic duty and good for the local economy."

"We'll be here at twelve for you and Morrill in two Saturdays, so don't forget." Opal set the date with certainty.

A sweet-faced attendant strolled over to the group and kissed the top of his balding head. Lettie McLauren Strom, the middle daughter of rancher Douglas McLauren, joined their collusion. "I'll remind you, Grandpa. And I'll make sure your best shirt is ironed." Lettie smiled and nodded her approval.

As if to celebrate their victory, Ruby reached into her purse and offered two large oatmeal cookies to the McLauren brothers, which the men seemed to half-expect and fully welcomed.

Vernis always tried to have the last word. "These better have coconut."

"Rode my horse to the Stone Barn more than once," Morrill recalled as he took the cookie she offered with obvious pleasure.

"That you did, Morrill." Ruby replied. "Why, I remember your buckskin horse like it came down the lane just yesterday."

When his eyes shone at the mention of the horse, Opal realized that the senior-most McLauren enjoyed recollections of his old animal companions. She also knew that a cookie in the hand was worth more than a horse story rehashed so she enjoyed watching the men savor their treat. Perhaps it might help them forget the tasteless food the dining hall served. Drawing the visit to a close, she locked Ruby's arm in hers and headed for the front door, pleased with the success of her mission.

Her blue Buick waited in the closest handicapped parking space. Never suspecting anyone in town would try to revoke her driver's license, she gave a halleluiah for her doctor who had thought some special consideration might be wise. Proud of the special parking tag hanging from the rearview mirror, she double-checked it as they approached the car. Unlocking the passenger door, she caught the reminiscent look on Ruby's face. "Sure looks like the music's already starting for some of us."

"I'm planning to sit with Morrill at the symphony."

"That'll be fine and fitting, sister." She closed the door and stepped around the car directly into the path of a tall man balancing a stack of boxes. More than ready to be the recipient of that shipment, she opened the rear door.

"Here's the pie order from Wilsey." Douglas McLauren

stooped and placed nine boxes across the rear bench seat, then straightened to hug her. "Arie's baking up a storm out there." His calloused hand dug beneath the chrome handle and opened the driver's door with courteous care.

"Well, Wilsey just got a whole lot sweeter with her ending up out there. I'll stop these pies off at the Trail Bakery before we head home."

"You're right, Miss Opal. She's brought us a little slice of heaven. And tell me, how are the distinguished McLauren brothers today?"

"Same as usual," Ruby offered from the far side of the car.

"Yes, mean as a snake and snug as a bug. Lettie's on duty and turned her head when we gave them some contraband cookies." She snickered into her fist at beating the system.

"Congratulations on the infiltration, ladies." The rancher tipped his cowboy hat. "Now it's my turn to do the charming. Hope your garden enjoyed the rain."

She watched as he turned and headed for the front entrance to the facility, sensing the rigidity of his posture as he glanced back. Engaging the gear shift to reverse without checking her mirrors, she backed the Buick until his new Dodge truck appeared a bit too close. On her traditional errand run, nothing would get in her way. A short drive down the hill past the cemetery delivered her to their next satisfactory destination, the bank.

Ruby stepped into the Farmers and Ranchers lobby behind Opal. "Why they had to go and spend all that money renovating this old building is beyond me. Just shows you how they don't mind wasting our money."

She glanced at the banquet table that had been moved into the lobby for the open house celebrating the recent renovation. "Sister, your money is safe and sound. You know the Whitehalls have always been careful with our money." She helped herself to a yellow mint. Having held the family purse for over fifty years, she was devoted to its well-being. As an act of sugary appeasement, she placed a pink mint on her sister's plate.

"My friend Pearl always thought they should have given away cultured pearl necklaces to their best customers, like Capitol Federal did." Ruby settled on the addition of a few Alma cheese curds.

"That was back in fifty-eight, for heaven's sake. Times have changed. Farmers and Ranchers Bank is trying to keep up with the technology to stay competitive. That's what keeps our money working hard earning interest, and I don't have a problem with that." Having driven home her point, she stepped over to the punchbowl.

The teller from the drive-through window approached. "Let me help you with that, Miss Opal." She filled a crystal-cut cup with lime-colored punch, slipped a napkin under it, and placed it in her hand "One for you, Miss Ruby?"

"You bet. Say, what do you think about the new vault?"

"Big enough to run twenty head of cattle in it." The teller passed her the punch cup with a girlish giggle.

She couldn't pass up a good tease. "That sure would be living up to the bank's name, wouldn't it?"

Ruby laughed with the teller. "But who'd want to clean up behind them?"

Nibbling her refreshments, Opal pretended to admire the remodeled counter with all its fretwork as her gaze swept the renovations. In truth, change was difficult to accept lately, especially for an octogenarian with a fondness for the old days.

~

Methodically turning the horse out into the back pasture, Jusdyn heaved the saddle into the tack room and slammed the door. Spotting his father as he loaded spools of barbed wire onto the flatbed truck, he dragged himself over to be the bearer of bad news. Sam, the family's blue heeler, sat under the truck in the shade until he approached. The dog stood up wagging its tail. "Hey, Dad." He threw a spool up onto the truck knowing he'd been little help all morning. Pausing, he stroked the salt-and-pepper fur of his favorite herding canine.

"I'll get these since you don't have any gloves on." Loren's muscular arms flexed as he lifted the next wire spool onto the truck bed. "How were the cattle?"

"All there." He looked eastward across the pipe corral into the hedgerow beside the farm. "Look, Dad. Something's up. Uncle Doug's niece fell off the double gate by the pines when I rode up on her, about half an hour ago. She's in and out of consciousness, so I brought her back here for Mom to look after."

The veteran rancher paused, his gaze scanning the far horizon a brief moment before making eye contact. "You've done the best you could. Doug's supposed to be in town today, so you probably saved her some major neglect by bringing her here. Your mother will know what to do. You could clean up a bit before checking back in."

"Reckon it wouldn't hurt." He lifted his hat and ran his fingers through a mop of uncombed hair. Even from his wounded state, he could sense the protective love of an understanding father. "Mom's making me a list." He followed his admission with a sigh. When a half-smile cracked his dad's serious demeanor, they shared an unspoken truth. A list always served as the first stitch in any repair at the Linquist ranch. Everything shifted to recovery mode from there.

"Make it look like a regular business deal." TJ kept his voice low. "This is merely a real estate transaction." Negotiating in the rear booth of the Rocking Saddle Café, he appreciated the rowdy atmosphere of the lunch crowd.

"I guess you're right." The older man spoke slowly as if to foot-drag a bit. Rough-handed, he fingered the rim of his hat.

He glanced around with wary discernment. "You have the Power-of-Attorney, correct?" His confidence would have to escort his accomplice through a major breach of family tradition, so he focused on the familiar face.

"Yes, everything's in order there. So you're positive it's the

Helmick quarry tract?"

"That's what my sources tell me, so we have to plan for it." He smiled in crooked reassurance. "When can you start the paperwork?"

"What about this afternoon while I'm in town?"

"Perfect. I'm depending on the element of surprise." He pushed back in the booth feeling a rush that his scheme had gained some traction.

His guest hesitated a bit. "Are you aware there needs to be a transfer of funds, even though it remains McLauren land?"

"You bet. I'll be heading to Farmers and Ranchers Bank next." TJ smoothed his moustache in his confident assertion. He found it quite satisfying that his moonlighting money would now pave the way to even greater wealth.

"Well then, guess I should say welcome to the trash business." The rancher offered his hand to cinch the deal.

He readily shook it unable to quell the smirk of satisfaction. "Reckon everybody's got to be the king of something." His actions would now launch the family down a tarnished lane while slapping a condemnation notice on the Helmick land at the same time, neither of which offended his sensibilities. *High time for sharper leadership, which is why I'm rising to the top.*

~

Jusdyn crossed the gravel driveway balancing a tray full of hit-or-miss first aid supplies and ice. Anticipating the contents of his mother's list made him realize his amateur status at medical matters. His best gamble had been the pitcher of lemonade he had found waiting by the sink. Thirsty enough to drink Four Mile Creek dry, he had brought the pitcher along out of self-preservation.

A pair of mourning doves nestled in the bare dirt of the driveway ruts trying to dust themselves solely for the comfort of it. *These doves might symbolize something meaningful.* Distracted, the tray teetered in his hand. He sure needed a dust bath of forgiveness from the fall victim, somewhere between a rock and a green place.

When he rounded the corner to the porch, he could hear two women speaking in low tones from the front room. He paused outside the lace curtain to test the waters of receptivity. "Are dudes welcome around here yet?" He hid behind the lemonade pitcher just in case.

"Come on in and let me see what else you've brought." The no-nonsense nurse soon held the screen door open, but this time, her gaze had softened a bit.

He balanced his load and stepped inside. After placing the tray on an antique vanity, he carried the pitcher to the kitchen and then returned. "So how'd I do, Mom?" He scanned the front room where a weak smile greeted him from the fainting couch. "Why, hello. Gate-rider is awake." He knelt beside the patient to drink in the sight of her consciousness.

Muriel harrumphed. "This is only half of what I'll need. Let me retrieve my medicine stash. If you're bound to hover, take this ice and make a compress for the back of her head." She handed him the ice with a kitchen towel draped over it. "Move her as little as possible."

"Oh, I got that all out of my system on the mile jaunt back home." He looked back and forth between the nurse and her patient, flashing the same off-centered grin as the boy who got caught putting a skink in his parents' bed one Saturday night after reruns of the Lawrence Welk Show. He held his palms open to declare his innocence.

"Ice pack." The nurse muttered something else inaudible as she headed out the door.

Left alone, he chose to fumble with the ice pack as a diversion, tucking the tea towel around it like a fancy napkin. *How in the world am I going to get this thing in place?* His throat tightened in the silence. Leaning against the chaise to improve his approach, he captured the patient's stare straight on. At such close range, hazel eyes dappled with flecks of gold and misting at the rims elevated him onto a plane of heightened awareness.

"Say you'll forgive me," Arie whispered. The rims of her eyes began to overflow with crystal tears that rolled unchecked down her colorless cheeks.

"Hush that talk." He attempted to quiet her, catching a solitary tear with the tip of the towel. *What a turnabout of blame.* The vice-grip of guilt loosened in his chest. "Truth is, Miss Arie, you've hit your head which might be causing you some delayed confusion about just who needs to be forgiven."

"But all this trouble, over me." Her voice cracked rendering her confession and dissipated into a humble sob.

"Let's get this into place." With the ease of a surgeon, he positioned the ice pack under her head. The sheet was edged with a delicate tatting needlework his grandmother had crafted. He smoothed the cotton against her, tucking it under with a hug to hold her snugly. The contact delivered the calming effect he had intended. "There you were sitting on the gate, pretty as a picture." He closed his eyes to better recall the scene. "While you gazed over the Valley of Serenity, a rough rancher rode in and shattered your tranquility. That's how the scene looked from horseback."

She tried to shake her head in protest, but froze and relented against the icepack with a wince.

"You know, I've ridden that pasture's edge a thousand times, and the view down into Diamond Springs valley never ceases to mesmerize me. I simply fall prey to its lure." Having attempted an adequate explanation, he gazed through the lace curtain. He somehow found her hand and held it between his. "Looking down from the pine lane, it's like a place you've always wanted to be— but can never seem to get there."

Her apprehension seemed to melt. When her eyes closed to end the protest, he gained an ounce of affirmation. They remained that way for quite some time, her in motionless recovery while he doctored by heart-felt reasoning, the only way he knew how.

~

Power-of-attorney is just legalese for long-trail-of-paper.

Doug McLauren didn't have to argue much to be convincing. With the obscene hourly charge for legal services, he kept it to the essentials—no chitchat or chewing the fat. Across the desk, the town lawyer added the last stack of documents requiring his signature.

"Your John Hancock is needed on each of these where indicated." The attorney spoke slowly as if to translate. "Of course, you are considered the 'seller' in each clause."

The rancher raised his hand firmly to halt any further comment from the barrister. He intended to read through this material with no tolerance for banter. From time-to-time, pen-scratch resonated on the oak desk like a tree limb on a rooftop. He stemmed his emotion as he worked down the stack. At last, he initialed the final page twice, and then signed in full on the first of two parallel blanks at the bottom. Standing, he towered over the attorney in stoic strength.

"The buyer will stop by within the hour." He produced a check folded into his wallet to pay the title transfer fee.

"Always a pleasure." The attorney flashed his bleached-white smile.

He paused and tipped his hat in deferred response. Exiting with a heavy heart, the door closed on the chamber of jurisprudence. It didn't take long for the familiar wave of nausea to wash over him like a bad aftertaste from these estate management visits. *I'm not cut out to be the boss.* Guilt followed him back to his truck, the usual outcome.

~

Having feigned admiration for the bank's improvements long enough, Opal and Ruby now approached the routine business of depositing their monthly checks. When the young teller dared to offer the new service of electronic deposit, both sisters became visibly appalled.

Ruby gave way to her consternation. "Father taught us to keep an eye on our money."

Opal nodded toward the charter member display. "That's right, young man. You don't get your name engraved in bronze for frivolous character qualities that stay hidden behind the scenes. Saving money has always been synonymous with the Litke name."

"Yes, ma'am." The teller relented, handing her the deposit receipt. "Have a good day."

"Well then, thank you kindly."

Ruby locked elbows with her and they shuffled toward the original front door.

A gentleman entering the bank recognized them and held open the solid oak portal.

"Afternoon, ladies. Be my guest."

Ruby exited first across the threshold. "At least good manners aren't under renovation around here."

"Thank you, TJ." Following her dear sister, Opal stepped into the hubbub of Main Street in midafternoon. Pausing to collect herself from sparring with the technology-promoting clerk, she pondered why the county's conservation officer wasn't out in the field saving the land at this time of day. Soon dismissing the tangled notion, she plunked her hand into her purse for clip-on sunglasses and popped them into place. Now, she had to find the mystifying location of the Buick so they could deliver those pies.

~

In a timeless lull, the doves cooed outside the cottage as lace curtains consented to the wind. Something began to unlatch deep inside of Jusdyn that felt like freedom. He bowed his head at the realization that his knot-tied stomach, lump-in-throat apprehension around young women had ended. His shyness vanished like an early morning mist. Maybe that had something to do with his present company.

"Tell me what kept you from falling prey to the lure of the valley today? I mean, you stayed on your horse, and I'm the one who fell." Arie tipped her head to one side as if to encourage his response.

He focused on her and discovered the glitter of sincerity in her eyes. "You did. I wasn't looking down the valley as I rode up from the pond. My gaze locked on you." He pressed the back of her hand with his thumb. "Now, no more talk about being trouble. Promise me?"

"I promise." Her assent seemed to make time stand still. The sudden beat of dove wings sealed their mutual apology as the birds reacted to a commotion outside.

Muriel peeked in as she passed the window. "What's going on in there?"

He caught a glimmer of mirth in Arie's hazel eyes as he somehow managed to pull away from their magnetic influence. "Oh, just a dust bath." His chest tightened at the return of a higher medical authority. "Mom, I really think the ice pack is working."

She stormed through the door carrying a medic's bag. "Wait until you see what these atomic ibuprofen tablets can do."

"Let me go pour the lemonade." He glanced at Arie as he stood. When she released him with a delicate smile, he sensed some healing had already begun. The medicine would be extra.

Chapter 3

Increased day length and swelling ambient temperatures bring the open prairie into full-force bloom just before summer's premier. The sweetheart of the wayside, the prairie rose, casts a spell on rural wanderers down every dusty lane. Rock ledges are draped in the soft pink of crown vetch to the momentary distraction of bees galore. Scurf pea and spiderwort join blue wild indigo to dot the meadow in colors of the sky, while upland sandpipers fly up to distract passers-by away from hidden nests. Badgers wean their young in underground chambers, preparing for their independence above deck. Brother to the bluestem, the hayfield's brome tassels out in silvery seed stalks, bowing to the wind and sun. Like the heady wheat, the brome will receive its summer cropping soon. Only the bluestem will remain unfettered in its quest for sky-high.

With fence pliers shoved into his back pocket and a bucket of fence clips jangling in the floorboard, Jusdyn rode shotgun with his father to their latest fencing challenge. Sam rested on the seat between them. The westernmost pasture contained the last of the wooden fence posts set by his great-grandfather Linquist three generations ago. Marked by a rock cage post he'd stacked as a teenager, the fence strands along this section sagged, overdue for replacing.

In the simple reasoning of the prairie, a rancher's agreement gave each neighbor responsibility for half of the shared fence line, to the right when standing at the midpoint. Under this rule of thumb, his half extended to the north, with the southern section belonging to Deke, his favorite cousin. Scanning the horizon, he could hardly wait to start the task.

"Did you know I had to go all the way to Alta Vista to keep from paying over six dollars a post at Bluestem? That can add up when you're buying two hundred at a time." His father flexed his fingers around the steering wheel.

"You're suspecting prices are creeping up because grain prices look strong and everybody thinks the average farmer might actually make some money this year, aren't you?"

"Yup, that's exactly what I'm thinking. It's a trickle-down effect when the farm economy is strong. But somebody ought to remind those merchants that the crop's still in the field."

Without fail, every year as harvest approached his father began to carry the weight of the world on his shoulders. So many variables could influence the wheat harvest at this point, including weather, wind, maturation rates, and blight. Played against these were variables like equipment readiness, fuel prices, and the time drain of endless maintenance to keep the combine operational. With grain futures predicting a dizzying seven-fold increase in wheat prices, the pressure for high production grew tangible.

"Dad, with a little hard work and some Linquist grit, we'll pull this harvest off together, don't worry. It'll all pay off, wait and see. I wouldn't trade sitting up in that combine looking out through the header tines at those golden fields for anything. It's powerful. I mean, we're feeding the world, right here from Wilsey, Kansas."

"Glad you can stay on top of the challenge, son. The older I get, the more it seems to leave me in the dust. I'm starting to second-guess my decisions and hesitate with making plans for the future. It's getting way too much for one man."

"I'm fully in this with you, Dad. Count on me. We're like two horses pulling the plow."

The senior rancher nodded his head. "Just like my dad and me."

"And like Great-grandpa and Grandpa before that. The Linquist men have a heritage of holding onto their responsibilities while keeping their heads held high. No looking back over the shoulder with regret for us."

"We keep looking ahead and plowing straight rows."

"Only with no-till cultivation nowadays, it's a little harder to see those straight rows." He flashed an unrestrained smile to accompany the joke. The truck pulled down a double-rutted lane flanked with abandoned implements that ended at a locked gate. He hopped out and swung open the pasture gate while his dad held the dog in and drove through. Jumping onto the back of the truck, he surfed across the rocky pasture edge, his feet straddling a stack of iron fence posts.

As they glided to a stop north of the rock cage post, he rapped the back cab window and pointed to a red truck rapidly approaching. "There's Deke." Genuine enthusiasm shot through his veins as the truck slowed to a halt. Sam barked until Loren let him out. The canine ran insatiably until he found the herd. Jusdyn held his arms out paralleling the fence line to embrace the challenge of the day, creating a new fence that would last through the next generation of Linquists, whoever they might be.

~

Arie awoke to the erratic sound of guinea hens pecking on the tin-bottomed screen door.

The nurse sat beside her, smiling from her vigil post in the rocking chair. "Good morning. How's the head feeling this morning?" Her host leaned forward as if concerned.

She sat up effortlessly, turned her head to glance at the peafowl at the door, and then back to her nurse. "No headache at all, it seems." The cheerfulness of the cottage revived her as she glanced around at all the quaint details.

"Let me check to see how your pupils are responding to the light. Then, we'll try to get you up."

"Yes, ma'am."

"Please, call me Muriel." She covered first one eye, then the other. "Funny thing with concussions, the snap-back motion of a rapid fall can cause a complete set of symptoms before you even hit the ground, with no impact necessary."

"I don't even remember landing. I barely remember seeing Jusdyn on his horse." The tat-a-tat of guinea hens pecking the door began again. "Insistent, aren't they?"

"Oh, those beggars are just hungry."

"Me, too." Arie rested her forearm across her empty stomach.

"That's certainly a good sign. I saved some buttered biscuits from the men's breakfast this morning. They rolled out early for a day of fencing work. We'll get you into the kitchen for a bite to eat right after a trip down the hall."

"For that, I would be very grateful." She threw aside the sheet and found the floor with her feet. When the nurse took her elbow and guided her across the front room, she came into a fuller awareness. "And when we come back, may I feed the guineas?"

"We'll do it together. Maybe that will return peace back to the morning."

~

Somewhere along the drive from Emporia to Americus, the music director transformed to social worker. Beside him, the grease-ringed bag of a fast food combo meal hinted at his favoritism. After what this child had been through, the extra effort to make a house call seemed the least he could do. This family's dissolution had brought him to tears more than once.

"Meth Amphetamine and the Music Orphan," he quipped, still grappling to understand as his car pulled into the modest drive. "Even Shakespeare could not have written a tragedy such as this." The solution-worn limestone rocks buried as stepping stones became his least favorite part of the trip. The handles of his violin case squeaked as he teetered from the stones' unevenness. Wooden steps came next, and at last, the doorbell fell within reach. It sounded with his touch and within moments, the door opened.

There she stood, his music prodigy, in rumpled clothes and uncombed hair, the epitome of neglect.

"Hello, Valor. It's time for your lesson." His bravado contrasted with the setting.

"Hi, Dr. Vorchenski. Did you bring the double cheeseburger?" She scrunched up her nose with the question. When he held the peace offering in front of her, she took it brandishing a wide smile.

"My dear, Anton Vorchenski always keeps his promises." He pulled back the flimsy Plexiglas door as far as the hinges allowed so his wide girth could gain proper entrance.

~

Highway Fifty-six east from Council Grove headed into nowhere, carrying TJ into Allen and Admire. Riding this route so many times under the mingled motivation of aspiration and desperation, the drive became automatic. Along the straightaway about twenty-two miles out, he searched for double tracks to the north along a hedgerow of cottonwood trees. Since the mid-fifties, the tranquility of the prairie here had been an astute façade for the US government's intercontinental missile silo. Now, only the massive-trunked cottonwoods at the end of the lane could testify to the frequency of visitation to the missile-extracted defunct facility.

Cleverly the least expensive pasture rent he had ever negotiated, sixteen acres wasn't enough grass to interest most ranchers. In fact, this tract had been passed over for some time. More interested in the rusty bunker anyway, he had negotiated the parcel's use as a hayfield.

Glancing down at the speedometer, he noticed his gas gauge dipping below a quarter of a tank. Passing that business expense on to the customer would be considered standard operating procedure for any heads-up entrepreneur. He laughed in a self-satisfied way thinking his customers could do very little about any unforeseen price hikes. In his sideline business, supply chased demand like a half-wit dog after its tail. *If this pace keeps up, I might have to quit my day job.* As the line of cottonwoods welcomed him up ahead, he let off the accelerator and entered an illicit, self-made world.

~

Opal startled as her sister rushed toward her in the sunroom.

"Gracious me. Morris County Commissioners have decided we need a landfill." Ruby crushed the newspaper to her chest.

She turned from her seat at the organ. "I'm almost afraid to ask. Where, pray tell, do they want to put it?"

"The article doesn't directly tell. It says they're evaluating several suitable sites, two west of Council Grove and one immediately west of the Lyon County line." Dissatisfaction spoiled her expression.

"Back in our day, we each took care of our own trash. Daddy burned trash every Saturday night. We children would watch him from the little window in the upstairs bathroom."

"We were the only ones for miles around with a genuine indoor bathtub." Ruby's tone carried a hint of pride.

She nodded, closing her eyes to recall the cabbage rose wallpaper that had trellised the room in style. The smell of lye soap stung her nose with the memory. "Then he'd stomp upstairs with soot smeared on his face to run us out so he could bathe in our bath water." She relished the fond memories of her childhood.

"You cannot get those precious days back, Sister."

"No, nowadays we've made life too convenient. Something more than water went down the drain when they turned the faucets on indoors." A silent pause filled the sunroom.

"No. Life's not simple anymore." Ruby sat and folded the newspaper into her lap.

She adjusted several settings on the organ panel and began to play a rather doleful piece, a mismatch for the youth of high noon. Holding the final chord, she relented to allow the quiet of the day to return. "I made some chicken salad for lunch."

"Yes, let's."

Opal swung her legs clear of the organ pedals. There were many happier things for them to contemplate than a dreadful landfill. After all, the symphony was approaching.

~

Jusdyn cleared the third strand of barbed wire for Deke to tighten at the far end, his mind wandering beyond his field of vision. In an unguarded moment, hazel eyes with flecks of gold registered on his consciousness which led into a daydream possessing softened edges. Minutes passed until Deke hailed him to step back from the wire strand so he could tighten it. For some reason, the field of grass stretching down to the creek didn't captivate him as thoroughly as it had last week. Taking a step back for safety's sake, he threw his hands up to signal surrender. *Fine fix I'm in.* Hollow-stomached, he attributed his restlessness to hunger, though the sensation somehow rode deeper.

Chapter 4

Courtship in the animal kingdom lofts a colorful banner in the parade of innate posturing and presentation between genders. Though misconstrued by the amateur observer to be an assertive, combative face-off among viable males of the species, the establishment of territories and advertisement of attributes equate to the age-old art of self-promotion. Those who persist are adept at perpetuating the species for another generation and can go about the business of living. On the tallgrass prairie, male greater prairie-chickens select secret dance gardens called leks and stomp their way into the females' affections before the crack of dawn. In like manner, all indigenous species pair up two-by-two in an unwritten script too intricate for words and dot the landscape with their young by midsummer.

The lower strand of barbed wire hung slack against a row of newly set posts. A hand-drawn, iron-wheeled wagon clanked over the rock-spattered gully as Jusdyn unwound the uncooperative second strand of wire past the rock cage post. Shifting barbs scratched at the cage as Deke leveraged the fence stretcher one last crank. That action allowed Loren to secure the lower strand around its new best friend, the corner post.

In response to a go-ahead shout from his dad, Jusdyn positioned the lower wire on the next iron post to a height just below his knee, affixed a fence clip, and negotiated a twist with his pliers to clamp it in place. *All works of major significance begin with one inconsequential stroke.* He stepped back to admire his new fence.

When a staccato honk sounded from the far gate, he glanced up to see his old Chevy truck rolling into the pasture. Sam barked and ran in circles, spooking the herd into a run for the safety of the woodland at the south end. Swinging north, the truck proceeded toward him at a predictable pace. Stepping seven paces down the fence line, he managed to secure another clip before yielding to the imminent break. Lunch had arrived for the work crew.

Turning from the fence, his pleasure soared when he looked up at the cab and found two smiling faces in the lunch wagon. He stepped up on the passenger-side running board and held onto the mirror for closer inspection.

Muriel steered the truck toward Loren. "Special delivery."

"You must be better, or the nurse would never let you out of the house." He noticed the color had come back to Arie's cheeks and soon enjoyed the blush his attention prompted.

"Oh, I'm a quick healer." She caressed the foil-covered pie plate in her lap. "I earned this bonus trip as a reward for being such a cooperative patient."

"And this gal knows her way around a kitchen." His mother gestured toward the dish. "We may have found us a new cook."

"Well, it's my duty to be part of that evaluation committee—before the hiring's a done deal." He reached for the foil-covered treasure. Intercepted by a swat with the paper towel roll, he offered his mother a flashy grin.

Arie laughed and snatched his straw hat into the cab, laying it up on the dashboard.

The truck's motion cooled his sweat-matted hair as he basked in the cleansing fatigue of honest hard work, buoyed by the proximity of lunch and companionship. Angling off the heavy-set corner post, the lunch wagon soon stopped for the rest of the crew.

Deke's bushy eyebrows shot up at the sight of Arie in the

passenger seat. He mouthed an accentuated *wow* to Jusdyn as he passed to take a seat on the tailgate.

"Where would you like to eat?" Muriel asked the crew chief.

Loren strode past to join Deke. "Down on the sandbar." Sam ran ahead of the truck toward the far end of the pasture.

Members of the shade-dappled herd parted long enough to allow the truck to exit through the lower gate, where a river-rock road dropped down the bank to water level. Along this portion of the winding creek, a rock-laden shoal extended away from the tree-lined bank into the flowing water. The truck stopped in the shade of a sand bar willow, a location known to all as his father's fishing spot.

Muriel handed Loren a water jug. "You men wash up while we set out the picnic." Arie met her under the shade and helped spread an old quilt over the bed of river rock. She unpacked the food hamper, arranging the lunch fare of turkey sandwiches, baked chips, and cut fruit, while her helper poured iced tea into cups. "By the way Loren, this is Arie Henning—Doug's niece."

"Nice to meet you, young lady." Loren tipped his cowboy hat. "Sorry it was a bump on the head that brought you to the Linquist ranch. We'll count that as our pure luck and your little piece of suffering."

Jusdyn smiled, noting his account lacked any of yesterday's dread.

"I'm much better now, thank you, sir." Arie dropped her gaze while smoothing the front of her skirt.

Muriel gestured for the men to sit. "Arie, this is Deke Linquist, Jusdyn's cousin and our neighboring rancher. Deke, please meet Arie Henning."

Deke reached out and gave her hand a tug. "Any friend of Jusdyn's is a friend of mine."

"Now, let's get to this food before the snapping turtles do."

"You won't have to ask me twice." Jusdyn kicked off his boots and settled in.

"Me neither." Deke gave the dog a drink from the jug and then pointed to the creek.

Muriel spoke a quiet blessing over the food and passed the sandwich platter around. A comfortable silence fell over the group as they shared a meal to the cadence of the creek. A belted kingfisher swooped across a length of riffle in a gray-blue blur, rattling a cry as it passed. Barn swallows exchanged sides of the bank, catching bugs on the fly.

Deke finished first and stretched out with a moan, covering his face with his hat.

Arie looked beyond the willow and scanned their shady nook with interest. "Is there a name for this place?"

"I call it Dad's favorite fishing hole." He reclined on his elbow, satisfied with the meal and the scenery.

Loren tore a corner off his sandwich and tossed it to the dog. "This grazing land has always been called the Bottom Pasture because it lowers all the way to the creek. This tract was original to the Linquist farm, which Deke and Jusdyn inherited from their grandfather. Deke chose the west half and lives over by a grove of trees at the far end."

"And his wife, Merrilee, is great with child." Muriel winked as she began to clean up discarded plastic wrap.

"If you'd ask Merrilee, she'd tell you there ain't nothing *great* about it when you're this far along," Deke quipped without so much as lifting his hat. "She's trying to make me a daddy by Father's Day."

He pulled a blade of foxtail grass and tickled his cousin's ear.

"That's only three days away, Deke." Muriel swatted at the foxtail.

"Which is two more days than she needs to get the job done." Deke grabbed the nuisance sprig of grass.

Arie giggled while nibbling a grape, her eyes filled with mirth.

Eventually, the women began to clear away the meal, working in tandem without speaking as they repacked the hamper. Only the foil-covered pan remained, which Muriel lifted into the air with fanfare. "And now—Arie's apple tarts." She removed the foil to reveal the treat.

Deke's lifeless body managed to fling out a hand palm-up for his portion of the offering. "Shoot me one while I'm happy." The family comedian received the usual payoff as laughter echoed across the rocky shoal.

Muriel rewarded his antics with a double portion, which disappeared under the hat.

"I'll take mine to go." Jusdyn turned to Arie and shot her a weighed glance. "Want to go creekin' with me?"

"That sounds fun." She gave a smile that set their private adventure off on the right foot. While his mother handed him several tarts wrapped in a napkin, Arie knotted her skirt hem and removed her boots, placing them beside his.

He nibbled into the napkin and made one of the sweet-smelling tarts disappear. The flavor was captivating. He winked back at his parents, offering an arm to steady Arie as she walked tender-footed across the river rock.

"No horseplay," Muriel said in an admonishing tone.

He flashed a thumbs-up sign behind Arie's back. Sam took off up the shallows splashing wildly, causing the butterflies siphoning a drink on the water's edge to flutter out of harm's way. Silence folded into the rocky shoal behind them as the creek dominated the setting with its aqueous murmur. Striding against the refreshing flow, he gazed back on the sun-glinted water of the creek downstream, wondering what lay around the bend and why the water seemed ever in a hurry to get there.

~

"Come see what I've made!" Valor tugged at TJ's arm like a three-year-old.

"This better be quick. We need to eat supper yet." His tone threatened due to the lateness of the day, but if he thought about it too long the last ounce of guilt in his emotional vault might stir. Back when they took his wife away, he had tried to compensate—

going to work late, coming home early, and dropping in at lunch to check on the girl. A plucky little thing, she seemed self-sufficient enough that he soon eased into the notion that she didn't need him around as much. After all, he had a lot of distractions to fit into his day.

He'd arrived at the point where he couldn't stand looking at the land, deciphering its features and then—forced by vocation—developing best-use scenarios. It all seemed low-tech in a truly abasing way. *I've simply grown too sophisticated for it anymore.*

"Over here!" She shook the flashlight wildly.

"Keep on the path, will you?" He lacked any parental energy to mask the exasperation in his voice. "Henry will have both our hides if you knock the brome down before he cuts the hay."

"So, what do you think?" Premature in her eagerness, she begged for input before he had stepped to the rim of the gully. Her jittery flashlight aim confused the object of her intention.

He grabbed the light and switched it off. Allowing his eyes to adjust to the glow of the waxing moon, the gully garden below began to take shape. With rows of transplanted evening primroses opening below like tiny parachutes, the child had spelled out her survival strategy in four understated letters: L-O-V-E.

He couldn't restrain his genuine reaction to her effort to gain attention, words of praise forming despite a catch in his throat. "It's beautiful, Valor, really beautiful." The truth struck him in the gut like lead shot. *I'm a despicable father.*

~

Jusdyn sat across the table from his father after dinner, sorting through bills and miscellaneous solicitations. Afterward, they compared work lists and prioritized what the following day would hold. "Hey, Dad. Did you know that Deke is planning to throw back the Blythe farm field out past the hay meadow?"

"Is that right?" Loren turned the page of his magazine. "Kind of flies in the face of the experts that are predicting over-planting of cropland due to high demands for grain, doesn't it?"

"Yeah, and according to Deke, TJ's advising against it. Says he doesn't want to have to rewrite Deke's conservation plan for a *numbskull move* he'll regret in two years."

"Well, a man's got to trust his instincts for the land over the long-term. Deke is levelheaded enough to know where he's going with this. Does he want to put the restored grassland into the Conservation Reserve Program, too?"

"I think that's his plan, if TJ will enroll him."

"That's TJ's job, son. He good-and-well better do it." Loren pushed a hefty fertilizer bill for the soybeans into his vicinity, his portion of the bill circled in red ink.

He glanced at the amount and winced, reaching for his checkbook. The high cost of doing business as a farmer made his next suggestion seem all the more illogical. "Maybe we should rest the McLauren pasture from grazing next season like CRP, Dad. Then Deke and I could walk through the restoration process together, helping each other with the annual bush-hogging and burning duties."

"You've got cattle on that grass now, son. How's it holding up?"

"Honestly, Dad, the terraces look too thin. I'm still fighting ragweed and thistles, plus the grass is struggling in the corners where the cattle congregate. What that pasture needs is a chance to get ahead without so much grazing pressure. Let the grass put down roots that will hold when the drought comes."

"Taking so much grass out of grazing rotation is a pocket-emptying consideration. I'll take the Gator out tomorrow and have a look at it for you. Then we can decide."

"Uh, Dad. I've already washed and waxed the Gator for the 'Gator Get' game Sunday."

Loren grabbed his forehead like he'd developed a headache. "Good grief. It's almost Father's Day. Well no wonder your mother brought in double groceries this week. I plum forgot about the whole shindig."

"Yeah. Better get those cane poles ready."

"And trim the grass down by the pond. Thanks for the reminder, son. We'll do the McLauren pasture drive come Monday morning. Now, where did your mother run off to?"

"She's getting things ready for Arie to stay the night in Grandma's cottage. There's some talk about letting me take her back over to Doug's tomorrow morning, if she's up to it."

"Are you planning to keep an eye on Arie when you check the cattle over there? That's a mighty lonely place for a young woman to be. Doug isn't even around half the time, it seems."

"Guess I haven't really thought about it, Dad. I don't even know where she's living."

"Well, I assumed she was staying right there with Doug in the big house. At any rate, just between an old-fashioned father and his young-buck son, keep your intentions honorable."

"Come on, Dad." He waved the bill in defense.

Loren stared at him over the top of his latest copy of *Progressive Farmer*. "There's a right way to do everything."

"And a wrong way to do most things." Writing the fertilizer check out in silence, he thought about Arie and the potential for companionship—possibly even love—out here in the remotest part of the prairie. Deke had sure gotten lucky, finding Merrilee at college and bringing her out to live on the land, happy as a spring calf. Right when he'd become half-resigned to living alone, Arie appeared under the pines. Wrestling with his thoughts as long as he could stand it, he shoved the check across the table and pushed back his chair to exit. "For me, the land's got to come first."

"Listen, God made a man's heart more wide open than the prairie. There's plenty of room for love of the land—and romantic love. They splice together for a pretty strong fence, come to think of it. Commitment to family is what keeps the farm alive for another generation."

He tried to find a rational foothold in this emotion-packed conversation. "I thought the family limited partnership is what kept the family farm together."

"That's simply a guard to keep the lands from being vulnerable to crisis or catastrophe, or even a case of rash decision-making. We're safe from losing the land if we're ever sued for damages from an accident or anything like that. For instance, I wouldn't want you to go selling off a pasture just to pay for the old folks' home for me. The FLP makes sure the land stays in the family, unless a majority of the partners vote otherwise."

"Dad, I've seen divorce rip families and their farmland in half. It's a sobering prospect for those of us looking at marriage from the outside. Suddenly, living like a monk starts looking like a peaceable option."

"Let me dismiss part of this threat, once and for all. Divorce cannot touch the Linquist land. Period. Now, if there's a deeper heart issue here, you'd be well-advised to address it."

He stood stock still contemplating what fueled his disjointedness. He'd always had a fleeting hope for a life with companionship, but had become expert at quelling that dream for fear of having to sacrifice his focus on the land. Anyway, life stayed simpler this way, a little lonely, but free from sidetracks.

"For me, it has to be the land." He turned and headed up to his room. So what if he was being hardheaded? Maybe that kind of immoveable attitude put the flint in Flint Hills. He shoved his palm against the all-too-familiar bedroom door and entered his typical refuge. Disjointedness followed him inside. *Time travels like an arrow in one direction, so let's just see where this goes.*

Chapter 5

As in the desert ecosystem, suppressive heat has charmed many prairie wildlife species into a nocturnal existence. It begins with a rising curtain of crepuscular activity at dusk, a swarm of insects, and a field-full of grazing deer. With the rising moon, the night sky fills with small brown bats and a host of disc-faced, large-eyed owls. On the water, mammals such as beaver and muskrat search for aquatic vegetation to feed their litter of kits waiting safely back at their well-constructed lodges. The land seethes with omnivorous scavengers like raccoon, opossum, striped skunk, and coyote all seeking enough here-and-there foodstuffs to exist one more day. Amid the howls, the hoots, and the twig-snapping forays up the mulberry tree comes the top carnivore feeding in quiet stealth—the widely ranging bobcat. Endeared to Kansans with the nickname wildcat and commended for controlling small mammal populations, farmers still find it prudent to lock the chicken coop at night.

Arie sat on the edge of the bed, admiring the simplicity of the iron headboard.

"The bathroom is small, but has everything you need." Muriel wrung her hands as she scanned the room. "Be sure to check for ticks before you put on your gown. You kids walked under lots of trees down on the creek."

"Yes, ma'am. But this cottage seems perfect to me, not small.

How did two houses end up on your farm?"

"Believe it or not, this house originally stood under the pines over where you fell."

"Where the little gate still welcomes no one in particular to see the most spectacular view in the county?"

"That's the spot. It was a tenant house for the farm foreman at the McLauren ranch once upon a great while ago. My mother spent many happy hours chasing chickens in that yard. The foreman had several children and they all played together. When the farm foreman's wife prayed for shade one day, my mom went home and begged grandpa for some trees. That's how the pine lane got its start. My mother helped plant and water each tree, a story she loved to retell."

"So, this was your mother's room?"

"Both Mom's and Dad's. When they reached their mid-eighties, Loren came up with a plan to have them closer to us while letting them stay independent. He hired a man to move the tenant house to our front yard and began the restoration. I painted and refinished the furniture to pull it all together. Mom and Dad lived in the house for about five years until his health began to fail. Hospitalized during Jusdyn's freshman year, Dad never got to come back home."

"How about your mother?"

"Mom lasted four more wonderful years. She still cooked and gardened, almost until the very end. You might have noticed the bright red finish on the kitchen. That was her touch. She just shined in the kitchen. I still spend a few hours most days here in the cottage because I find it both restful and reflective. That red kitchen makes me think of my mother the most."

"Thank you for letting me use this special space. It's been a delightful spot for rest and recuperation." She smiled and ran her hand across the chenille bedspread.

"What will you do back at the McLauren farm?"

"I have a little job baking pies for the Trail Bakery. Miss Opal arranged it for me. Uncle Doug takes a new batch to town every week when he's going to visit the senior McLaurens. Miss Opal canned some wonderful sliced apples last fall that I've been using until other fruit ripens. The gooseberries are just about ready."

"In that case, I'll save you some rhubarb from my garden."

"Perfect. I may have more produce than business to take my pies."

"Listen, we plan to have a yard party here on Father's Day. Please come as our guest. I could send Jusdyn for you early so you could help me cook. We'd put Mom's double ovens to good use. Would you be willing?"

"Sounds like something I wouldn't want to miss. We're at church first thing on Sunday, but the rest of my day is free."

"Sure, after church is fine. The other guests are due at four o'clock. Opal and Ruby will be here as old family friends, plus Deke and Merrilee, various other family members, and our dear neighbors. Can I tell Doug you'll be our guest?"

"Sure, why not? I look forward to a chance to pay you back for your hospitality and the caregiving." Arie locked Muriel's elbow in hers, stepping toward the door.

"Should your headache return, leave the kitchen light on. When Loren wakes me up with his snoring in the middle of the night, I'll check to see if the cottage is dark. I'll take that as your 'all is well' signal. Count on breakfast-to-go in the morning when Jusdyn takes you home."

"If it's not too late, do you think he could come over and sit with me in the porch swing for a little while? We could watch the lightning bugs together."

"If that fencing job hasn't already done him in, I'll be glad to send him over. One last thing, Arie." Muriel released her arm and squared around to face her directly. "About talking with Jusdyn, I'm afraid you may have to carry the bulk of the conversation. The Linquist men are notably brief in that particular department."

"We'll let the night speak to us if we run out of words. The prairie never loses its voice. You just have to be quiet enough to listen."

~

The thought of being in the country with the Linquist family made Opal's heart stir with appreciation. Spending an afternoon in Wilsey would be a good idea in more ways than one. She longed to see Arie and gauge how she was settling in.

Ruby glanced over before putting her knitting away for the night. "What should we take out to Muriel's for Father's Day, Sister?"

"I'm thinking about deviled eggs. Jusdyn always raves over how good they taste."

"Our homemade relish makes it special. Talk about a lot of work—plus the chopped onions water my eyes something fierce. What a labor of love on our part."

"Let's hope this year's cucumber crop really comes in prolific. I only have one more pint jar of relish left in the pantry." She made a mental note to root around and check for more.

"Ray's Apple Market has eggs for two ninety-nine a dozen. Look here in the ad." Ruby folded the paper right side out and laid it on the end table.

Peering past the marble-topped table, Opal found the quarter page advertisement. "In that case, let's buy three dozen." A big headline detailing a decision on the landfill location glared in big black letters. She shook her head in disgust. "I'm going to bed, Sister. Poor little Helmick."

~

"It's only me." Jusdyn shifted across the dark yard trailing his warning. He skipped a few steps and landed on the wood slats of the front porch, bearing the colors of his alma mater.

"Purple?" Arie scrunched one cheek and then swatted at her ankles, about the only skin she had left exposed after wrapping her torso in a sheet.

"Correction. Wildcat purple." He swiped a clawing hand

through the air like a predator.

"The mosquitoes are finding me."

"Let's try turning off the porch light." He stepped inside and grabbed his grandmother's kerosene lamp, adjusted the wick, and struck a match. Once the electric light had been extinguished, the soft glow of lamplight framed the porch. Placing the lamp on uneven wooden planks, he glanced back at Arie and caught the flame reflecting in her eyes. To survive the electric sensation moving through his chest, he trimmed the wick down slightly, discouraged a moth with the back of his hand, and knelt on one knee.

"Would the Wildcat like to swing?" She patted the seat as if to convince him.

"Only if it's safe." He sensed the lamp wasn't the only item sitting off kilter, as his breathing had grown erratic.

She tugged on the chain supporting the swing and then nodded.

A heron called from the pond, followed by the whirring fly-by of a feeding nighthawk. The beckon of the nocturnal prairie grew too hard to resist, so he surrendered to her invitation in silence. After exchanging small talk, he discovered Arie's presence to be comforting.

Gradually the night sounds replace their sporadic conversation. The swing found its rhythm, creaking with each return trip. Being beside her proved less intense than having to look directly at her as he watched the flame dance at the end of the lamp wick, a welcome distraction. The call of a great horned owl split the night, so he playfully echoed with a series of who- who-who in reply. When she smiled, he saw cute dimples appear and disappear in a blink.

"What do you suppose he's saying?"

"Probably something like, 'I'm out here, but where are you-who-who?' I'm guessing, of course, never having taken a class in old owl chit-chat." His grin pulled to one cheek, playing up the role of the wildlife expert. After she giggled, he took her cue to continue. "Now, if it were me, I'd be saying, 'Tell me something about you-who-who' so I could sort out the bad lady owls and focus it down a little." A cow bellowed from low note to high, sounding from the west pasture where his new fence reigned.

"I lived in Abilene before coming back." Arie looked over at him with vulnerability. "It's so different than the tranquility you have here. People drive around a lot at night, like they have restlessness. Dogs bark and trains pass by at all hours. Not too many twenty-three-year-olds leave the city for isolation in the country, but I couldn't take the noise anymore."

The great horned owl called again, sounding somewhat closer. He teased back with his low-pitched who-who-who for which he received a rap on the knee from his swing-mate. Maybe owl talk was under-appreciated. When Arie shifted the sheet, he refocused on the topic. "No, I totally get you. Part of the reason I couldn't stand Manhattan was the constant noise and commotion. All those sounds run together after a while, so you can't make any sense out of it. I had some favorite fishing spots out on Tuttle Creek where I could make life slow down, but that was limited refuge. Most students didn't even notice the natural world. They equated sitting through a Wildcat football game to spending quality time outdoors. Go figure."

"Fishing sounds nice." Arie placed her arm along the back of the swing.

He shifted his shoulders to avoid contact, changing his perspective. He spotted a large praying mantis working its way up the porch column behind the swing. Feeding on smaller insects along the rail, the bug cast an exaggerated shadow appearing twice its size.

A great horned owl swooped from nowhere, frantically fanning the porch swing on a quest to pluck dinner off the column, giving him a flash of unblinking yellow eyes. While Arie screamed and ducked, he instinctively covered her in a hasty attempt at protection. Seconds later, the predator-prey battle had been fought, the mantis was missing, and the owl had flown onto its next conquest.

Jusdyn regained his balance though the swing lost its rhythm and soon became achingly still. After Arie trembled from the avian attack, he reasoned that he couldn't release her to suffer alone. Slowly, the truth sank in that he truly didn't want to let go, experiencing an amazing rush holding her.

A coyote's laugh-howl bayed in the far distance. Leopard frogs sounded from the water's edge. This was the world he knew, wrapped around the farm he worked, sitting on the land he loved. "Hear the beauty of it," he whispered in tenderness through her hair.

Slowly the rhythm of the swing replaced her trembling. Her hand searched out his and stretched across it like a promise, as timeless as the prairie.

Allowing the sensation to linger as long as possible, fatigue began to win the battle over his body, forcing his surrender. "The fencing crew needs to retire." He rocked the swing back to stand. "Before I go, I have to know why you came back."

"I came back for the prairie. That's what truly brings me here." When she gestured toward their dark surroundings, the sheet fell away. She stood with him as if to say goodbye.

Every thought left his head but one. Her pure answer deserved a goodnight hug. And for once, he was standing in the right place at the right time to deliver the goods.

Chapter 6

Upon a stalk of thorny leaves, the musk thistle vaults its fuchsia shock of petals in the open heat of summer. Joined by its rogue cousin, bull thistle, a surreptitious scheme is planned to invade the prairie one breeze at a time. To further pervert the grasslands, flannel mullein hooks its taproot into the cracks of rocky ledges, infiltrating the harsh terrain with velvety leaves and a saguaro-like spike filled with a multitude of mal-intended seeds. By end of summer, the chain gang escapee Sericea lespedeza joins the assault with a tumor-like growth rate, replacing native grasses and devaluing the prairie. As a group, these noxious weeds make up Morris County's most wanted list, compelling every rancher-turned-sheriff to diligently hunt them down with hoe In hand. Any lenient enforcement by a lax landowner runs the risk of becoming a veiled threat to every neighbor, as the wind has never been a respecter of property lines.

Arie traced the edge of the red kitchen counter with her fingertips. She would be going home any second, back to the leaky rock house on Road AA that had seemed adequate only two days ago. She walked into the front room and found the sheet from the porch swing draped across the couch. Mindlessly, she folded it into halves and then quarters, looking about the cottage and its perfect detail.

She did have a life to get back to, after all. The gooseberries were ripening a little each day. There was next week's pie order to fill, and the little shed under the pines to explore. *What an unsettling thing when you walk into the presence of something more.* She hung her head, weighed by her options. The sound of gravel popping under vehicle tires motivated her out the front door to await her ride home.

~

"Me—or us?" Jusdyn forced the gearshift to grind the truck into second gear. "Seems like I made a decision for both last night." He elbowed the dog, which gained him the response of raised eyebrows. Sunlight filtered through the trees along the roadside as he pulled toward the end of the driveway. There by the scratched porch column stood the answer to his rhetorical question. "Morning, Arie." He pulled the emergency brake and slid out of the truck. "Are you ready to go?"

"Ready in some ways, I suppose." She moved to the porch edge and waited.

He reached up to ease her descent. Acting impulsive, he lifted and swirled her in midair, watching her eyes shine with mirth while the dog barked at his sudden shenanigans. "Come around to this side." He gestured to the driver's door. "Sam's a space hog when it comes to creature comforts."

She giggled and stepped onto the running board before slipping behind the steering wheel. The dog sprawled in its customary space on the passenger's seat, so she maneuvered past the gearshift and scooted only slightly toward the middle.

He hopped in, touching shoulders with Arie, and gave quick thanks for old trucks with bench seats. "I'm taking Sam with me to check the cattle this morning. He's just dying to see his old four-legged friends." He gave his canine friend a teasing whistle. The dog responded by yapping out the far window. "Calm down, boy. We'll be there soon enough. Oh, here's an egg biscuit from Mom." He passed the napkin-wrapped breakfast treat to her. "Sam will finish anything you can't eat."

The truck made its way to the end of Road Z and turned south toward the McLauren ranch. All too soon, the familiar double row of pines stretched across the horizon. In a quarter of a mile, he'd be dropping her off at the end of Doug's driveway to resume her normal life. So what was he dreading? When Arie coughed, he wondered what she might be thinking. "Isn't this where I found you?" He gestured as they passed the lane leading to the twin gates.

She nodded, but looked away toward the cascading valley.

He eased the truck to a stop at the corner of Road AA. The vista of Diamond Springs valley opened up along the passenger side window. Today, he viewed the vista from a new perspective. The background held a familiar scenic panorama, but the foreground now came with the profile of a beautiful woman. He had both, and in surreal recognition, he wanted them both.

Arie turned from the valley view and caught him studying her face. "Would Sam let me ride with you to count the herd?"

He pulled his hat lower to conceal his personal elation for the company. "Guess I could talk him into it. But understand, he doesn't take to change very readily. You see, Sam doesn't make friends too easily."

Looking back over his right shoulder for the remote possibility of on-coming traffic, it struck him how dizzying it seemed to have Arie in such proximity with her hair smelling like honeysuckle. When she gazed back at him with a twinkle of interest in her eyes, time stood still. Having only learned to drive this truck at fourteen years of age, it soon proved difficult to find reverse with the gearshift hidden in the ruffled folds of a cotton skirt. Sure as shootin' he didn't know this road they were headed down—not to be confused with the familiar lane leading back to the pasture.

~

Muriel lifted two fried eggs out of the pan onto his plate. "I want to make this Father's Day really special, Loren."

"Sure, I'm all for it. Tell me what more I can do, and I'll do it."

"You know I'm not talking about a longer to-do list, I'm talking about time spent with people—with family. That's really our gift to each other this weekend—time to listen, catch up with the latest news, share dreams, and even time to simply play together." She chopped up an orange without mercy, to the point it looked like murdered marmalade on the cutting board.

"You want me to father the whole backyard herd, is that what you're asking?" To regain peace, he removed the paring knife from her hand.

"Goodness knows some of them could use some extra fathering."

"And mothering?"

"Yes, you know I'm worried about Valor. It's not right for a child to be growing up so alone without proper supervision, or proper motherly influence." She turned back to the stove for the salt and pepper shakers, handing them to him.

"That is the darkest corner of the family right now, but I can't figure out how to help them short of literally—"

"Taking custody of the child?"

"Honey, I know you've always wanted a daughter, but that doesn't mean we have the right to take Valor just because TJ's faltering. They've been through a lot together. Shouldn't we give them the benefit of the doubt?"

"I'm willing to withhold judgment until after Sunday. Would you please try to corner TJ and talk some fatherly responsibility into him?"

"That was your cousin's job." He stabbed the egg and caught the runny yolk with his biscuit.

"And Dale wasn't strong enough to do it, was he?"

"Which is exactly how we learn from past mistakes."

"But that makes us wiser so we don't allow it to happen again." She stood directly in front of him wiping her hands on her apron.

He looked up at her for a heavy second. "Okay, I'll father the multitudes, but it's going to cost you an extra dessert on the picnic table." He dismissed his fork across the empty plate.

"You drive a hard bargain, Mr. Linquist."

Loren cleared his throat with authority. "Don't you forget it."

~

The drive to Junction City always reminded TJ of its nefarious connection to the rental truck-turned-bomb used by Timothy McVeigh to crumble the federal building in Oklahoma City. Something about transforming the innocuous into the venomous pricked his tainted psyche and turned life into a laughable game of victim and victor. He, for one, was not about to fall prey to the passively procrastinating, conservative life of the typical Midwest resident. Fortunately, he had inhaled the smelling salts of a more tenacious existence that paid better dividends, to boot.

He could not begin to express how much he loathed these community coalition meetings. Supposedly reflecting a higher plane of cooperative effort, he disdained the ploy of sharing information on which the meetings thrived. Quite honestly, he didn't want his back scratched by the other governmental agencies or local community action groups. His goal from the morning of pathetic pandering was to hook a free lunch out of the deal and then scram without further commitment of time or resources.

In stark contrast, his clandestine midafternoon meeting downtown held much more promise. Gathering with a group of behind-the-scenes businessmen that shared contacts vital to his moonlighting business really stirred his passion. The whole thing seemed like a trip to the casino where you held your breath until the dealer turned up that last card. The adrenaline rush could make or break the agent, depending on one's fortitude. He was a rock—for certain.

Entering the foyer of the public library, he headed for the rear conference room. The flash of a camera caught his eye as a flurry of activity emerged from the reference section. The balding mayor and head librarian fawned attention over an entourage emerging from the first shelf of records. His throat thickened as if he had swallowed a fishbone. He halted dead in his tracks. Across the reference counter stood an unmistakable, silver-coifed woman in a finely tailored suit.

She smiled with authentic warmth. "Hello there, TJ."

"Good morning, Governor." He extended his hand for a genial shake. With the rancor of regret, he saw his entire schedule evaporate before his eyes.

~

"Lettie?" Doug's voice rang out inside the nursing home. When a perky aide dressed in comic book scrubs threw a wave from the desk, he shifted a brown bag into the crook of his left arm to better receive her hug.

"Hey, Daddy-o. You're here early today."

"Yeah. I wanted to make Father's Day plans with Dad before running my errands this morning. Do you think he's up to coming out to Wilsey this Sunday? Loren and Muriel are having their usual get-together and we're all invited."

"I don't know about that. Uncle Morrill had a bad night. The doctor suspects he had a mini-stroke." Lettie reached for his free arm with both hands. "He's getting the best care available, Dad. Trust me on this one. But if another episode occurs, he'll have to be admitted to the hospital for further tests."

"Where is he now, Lettie?"

"Uncle is in his room, but the nurse kicked Grandpa Vernis out. I think I saw him pouting in the recreation room earlier. What's in the paper bag, anyway? Something I shouldn't notice?"

"What? This bag is full of nothing but air—with little donuts wrapped around it."

"If anyone else asks, I never saw you or that bag." She gave him a quick peck on the cheek before turning toward her station.

"What about your plans for Father's Day?"

"Sorry, Dad. We're heading for Parkerville to spend the day with my in-laws. We'll have to plan something later."

"That's okay, sweetheart. I'm always willing to share." He had become expert at keeping up the outward appearances to maintain peaceable relations, but the pull and tug between in-laws always left him feeling more than a little cheated. Resigned to play second fiddle, he confessed to an empty foyer. "And that's what I deserve for having three girls."

He walked slowly toward the recreation room to finish the lousy business of the day. A scintillating puzzle was being assembled by a group of ladies from White City in the corner. In front of the TV, a lone cast-away sat hunched in his wheelchair enjoying a catnap in the middle of "The Price is Right." A tap on the shoulder stirred the figure. "Hey, Dad. How are you this morning?"

"I got kicked out my blasted room for doing nothing," the aging man fumed straight out of a sleeper's grog. "I'm more help to Morrill than any of them could be, but every time I suggest something the nurse's tongue wagging starts up again. To have her way, she wheeled me out here and dared anyone to take off the wheel lock."

"All right, Dad. Simmer down. I'm taking off the lock right now so you can go anywhere you want to after our visit." He adjusted the chair and had to quell the building angst.

"Much obliged, Douglas. You know Morrill and I have always been a matched pair. We grew up together, farmed together, and now we're on the back section of life together. If one of us falls off the far edge before the other, someone's gonna be lost."

Having waded through this particular valley of experience as a widower, Doug tried to convey death's utter disregard for a dual existence. "Dad, you know there aren't any guarantees as to when life ends for any of us. Uncle Morrill's got a three-year head start on you to begin with. Plus, you know his love affair with bacon isn't going to serve him well."

"It's not his time to go. I can feel it, Douglas."

"That's for neither you nor me to decide. We have to make every day count so we don't live in the shadow of tomorrow. Just like with farming, Dad." He sat down on a brown plaid couch that had been generously donated by a patron. "Let's switch the subject.

I need to talk business with you for a minute."

Vernis harrumphed, seeming unapproachable.

He searched for a less damaging approach to take since his father had his hackles up. Already walking on eggshells, any step could lead in the wrong direction. "I needed to sell some land earlier this week. I can tell you the specifics if you want to know. I sold off about fifty-five acres." The truth spilled out for the first time, sounding like announcing an incurable disease.

The old man sat there with his eyes glazed over, neither nodding yes or no, just bent-shouldered receiving the unexpected news. Instead of fuming, he seemed lost in a daze.

Painfully aware that no one in the McLauren family had sold a piece of land in over four generations, he had to justify the divestment. "I sold it to a family member, if that helps you any. Dad, you know we've got to help this younger generation coming up. Times are tough in the ranching business. This will give him a leg up on the others. Call it a business investment, pure and simple." He watched as the burden weighed upon the old man, saw his concave chest heave and wondered if the old timer could deal with such a stinging departure from family protocol.

"Which tract?"

"It's a trash tract really, the old Helmick quarry. Not good for farming or grazing—just a hole ripped into the side of a hill." He sensed he was gaining some ground with the latest disclosure. A brittle minute passed without any further exchange.

"Okay, son. I trust you to do the right thing. Could you tell me who it's going to?" On the TV screen, the comedic host congratulated the latest lucky recipient of easy money.

He leaned forward and spoke the buyer's name into his father's good ear. They stared at each other for a long moment.

"He never comes to see me, you know." The old man shrugged his shoulders.

That instant, Doug could see the land deal through his father's eyes, the passing of a valued asset to an ungrateful heir. "I know,

Dad. I know." He extended the peace offering in the brown paper bag to offset the damage, but fully realized how lame the gesture registered.

~

The discovery of gooseberry bushes in the fallen windmill tower caused Jusdyn's hat to be full of tiny, ripened globes. Arie's nimble fingers plucked fruit from the laden bushes, and she revisited the hat with a delightful frequency. Sam stayed busy chasing calves from the loafing shed that overlooked Diamond Springs valley. Realizing that none of his ranch work had been accomplished yet, it didn't bother him in the least.

Their ideal corner-for-two lasted for the better part of an hour. Once his hat reached capacity, he resorted to filling the water jug with the rest of the berries. Sam found a round rock and dropped it at his feet, begging for a game of fetch.

"Let's explore the shed next," Arie suggested with child-like excitement.

He hesitated, and then remembered how snakes tend to gravitate to old foundations. Unwilling to let this outing end in trauma, he stepped into action. "Go ahead. I'm right behind you." He balanced the gooseberry crop in his hat as the water jug dangled from a finger.

She skipped over the pasture grass and found the open side of the shed. The hard-packed dirt floor reflected years of use by shelter-seeking cattle.

He spotted a tall bull thistle snuggled up to the western wall of the shed. His land management instincts shot into high gear. "Gotta get back here with my hoe."

"And I'm coming back with my broom."

"For what?" He couldn't imagine sprucing up a smelly loafing shed. Sam ran up with his rock, wet with drool.

"I might set up a little day house in here."

"You are something else, Gate-rider." A smile spread across his face as he watched her make plans to fancy-up the rather plain structure. The sound of a slow-moving car poked a hole in his reverie and jarred a forgotten promise to the forefront of his mind. "Quick, dig this note out of my shirt pocket."

"What kind of note?"

"The one from Mom I was supposed to give you when I dropped you off this morning."

She stepped toward him and fished two fingers into his shirt pocket, retrieving a folded strip of notepaper. The car approached the loafing shed corner and idled. "Arie, I have to go to Cottonwood Falls today for errands. Want to go clothes shopping with me? My treat. Muriel." Looking up, she beamed a broad smile. "Looks like I'm going shopping." She waved toward the car and started off in a carefree skip.

He fought off a sudden sense of abandonment. "Hey, what about me and my load of gooseberries here?"

"Put the berries in the refrigerator of the little red kitchen, and I'll get to them on Sunday." She flung another wave to his mother and then, in the freedom of the moment, turned and blew a kiss across the big bluestem in his direction.

The tender sentiment struck home at the same moment Sam dropped the rock-ball on the toe of his left boot. Dazed, he couldn't feel a thing.

~

Waiting for his order at the drive-through window at Dairy Queen, TJ fumed over the misallocated time investment for his day job. All the political posturing and goodwill promotion had landed with a hollow thump of a wrecking ball onto his personal itinerary for the afternoon. He'd completely missed his second meeting. How would he make amends with the cartel and still carry out his plans for expansion? At least he would be home early tonight, virtually unheard of for a Friday. Plus, he would be packing cheeseburgers, his daughter's favorite treat. Talk about winning double brownie points.

He stuck out his hand and received the white bag from the

young clerk. In eighteen minutes, he would be reheating the greasy contents for their optimum eating enjoyment as a broken family unit. Disgust over his domestic situation welled up in his throat like a rancid brew. *My life has definitely got to change.*

Chapter 7

Aquatic habitats teem with life behind the mirror of surface tension and the blur of refraction. Both serve to sufficiently detach land dwellers from pond residents, until such time a deer timorously parts the surface for a drink. Out-shying the timid fawn, sunfish and crappie wiggle down to cooler depths away from the commotion. Red-eared sliders and painted turtles, guardians of the pond edge, selectively frighten when the carnivores approach, joining the bream and the bass with total disregard to their submerged claim. Denizens of the deepest murkiness, the catfish maintains his wily vigil, ingesting whatever moves and some of what does not. With sound dampened by the water's depth, he's the last one to be made aware of the fisherman's presence until he swallows the night crawler and is persuaded to the surface by virtue of a pierced upper lip. The mirror shatters momentarily with his exit, and the food chain below adjusts incrementally.

Jusdyn took the front steps of Wilsey United Methodist Church two at a time as the second verse of "Fairest Lord Jesus" chimed from the organ. The apt lyrics *Fair are the meadows, fairer still the woodlands* ushered him to a pew behind Uncle Doug and Arie. Blushing from his hasty arrival, the music ended to provide some relief as the preacher called for prayer.

Glancing back, Doug surveyed his presence and motioned for

the removal of his hat with a hint of a smile.

Upon the spoken amen, he opened his eyes to find Arie standing beside him. When they sat down, the lavender lace of her skirt overlaid his Sunday-best denim in an enigmatic still-life moment painted by the invisible hand of destiny.

Following a sermon on leading a selfless life, the preacher challenged his congregation to go out and make a difference for the community. The men walked out hats in hand, while the ladies lingered inside to visit.

"Had a calf out this morning on the way to church. I'm suspecting the water gap west of the pump house." He relayed his fence news with hands tucked in his pockets.

The veteran rancher nodded, glancing up the road. "Tell you what, young man. Since you're taking Arie to prep for the get-together, let me stop by and run another strand of wire across that gap for you."

"Thanks a million, Uncle Doug. Mom has a task list a mile long for us."

"And just so you know, you have my permission to call on Arie any time. The Hennings are lovely people. After all, I fell for one. Besides, the more she's out of that old rock house, the better off she'll be. I told her conditions would be way too damp in there, but she had her mind set not to be any trouble for me." Doug shrugged his shoulders at the impasse.

He made no attempt to hide his dismay with the news about the rock house, but before he could explore any options, lavender came floating down the steps.

"Ready to go?" Arie's melodic voice broke into the building tension. She grabbed her tote bag from her uncle's new truck and swung it toward his antique ride.

"See you both later this afternoon. I'm heading to town to visit Dad for Father's Day. Next, I'll get the fence work rigged and then drop by the party." Doug nodded and doffed his hat.

He shifted to hold the driver's door open for his guest who

smiled and floated her colorful aura into the cab. An appreciation for the lighter shades of purple accompanied the transition, an unexpected pleasure.

~

"I can't find the paprika," Ruby called to Opal who had retreated to the sunroom still dressed in her Sunday clothes. "We can't take these eggs without a sprinkling of paprika."

"Top cabinet, second shelf to the left of the sink," Opal replied. Searching for the Council Grove Republican, she hoped to catch up on the town's latest news before the party. She heard her height-challenged sister drag the step stool to fetch the tin of paprika from the cabinet.

"There—that's perfect," Ruby soon announced.

"Would you look at this? Right here on the front page. Our TJ is standing beside the governor looking pretty important." Her chest swelled with pride.

Ruby stepped closer and took the paper into her hands to inspect the photograph. "Doesn't that beat all? It's about time something nice happened for that young man. What a shame the governor's already married." She pursed her lips and handed the paper back.

Opal recognized the hopeless romantic living inside of her sister. "Now, Ruby. Don't go to matchmaking. I'll cut out this photo and bring it to Muriel's party today. I figure TJ will be there, as much as that little girl of his loves to play games."

"You do that, sister. And I'll help you remember to show it off."

"That's a deal. Now, tell me. Where did we put those scissors?"

~

Jusdyn surveyed the backyard for the proper place for wind chimes. "Where do you want these hung, Mom?"

"I know a good spot. Let me have them. Could you go check on Arie for me?"

"Right after I get the Gator out. I want to surprise her with a tour through your garden and orchard next."

"But only if she's caught up with her cooking assignments."

"Okay, Mom." He flashed a cooperative thumbs-up as he walked to the barn. In seconds, he drove out a green utility vehicle that Valor dubbed the Two-seater Gator. His father had upgraded to the side-by-side model after Sam's hip dysplasia flared up, which had improved the dog's access considerably. Ordinarily, he considered the Gator a plodding rancher's helper, much preferring Chica or his truck. But today, Valor's Gator Get game called for the best UTV in the barn. He pulled up past the bur oak and its tables, steering for the back porch of the cottage. In three strides, he stood knocking on the back door, his expectations soaring.

"Come on in, Jusdyn." Arie bustled around the kitchen balancing a pie crust in her hands. Platters of food rested on every counter. "Promise you won't tell."

Divine aromas overtook his senses as he approached the bar. "Okay, I promise. What am I not telling?"

"My secret ingredient, of course." She lowered the crust with a wink, crimping it atop steaming gooseberry filling.

Temporarily distracted by all the culinary delights stacking up on the counter, it took him a few seconds to remember his master plan. "Can you get away for a few minutes? I have something I want to show you before the guests come." He tried to look casual, gesturing toward the door.

"Sure thing. Let me get this pie in the oven and set the timer. Then I'm all yours." After the pie made entry, she swept an array of ingredients back into the cupboard. She soon hastened to join him and took a seat in the Gator.

He glanced down and noticed a section of trim missing from her apron. "Funny thing, that bit of edging torn from your apron."

"What about it?"

"I found it wrapped around the skinned-up leg of a calf out on the McLauren pasture a couple of days before we met at the double gate."

A smile stole across her face as she diverted her gaze to the backyard.

"Well, are you guilty?"

"The evidence is against me, isn't it?" She flapped the apron hem and flour dusted the air. "Is there a punishment for chronic trespassing?"

"How about my belated thanks for beating me to the rescue?"

"You're welcome, cowboy."

"And another thing. Would you have anything to do with the prairie smelling like apple pies first thing in the morning, driving a rancher half-wild?" He stole a second glance at her.

"Guilty again, except you were already wild, Wildcat." She untied the apron and pulled it from around her neck, her hair flouncing in the sun.

He shook off a grin while maneuvering the Gator around the detached garage. After dodging the clothesline, he halted in front of a fruit orchard his parents had planted together.

As the scene unfolded, Arie's face lit with utter amazement. She slid out to stand in front of a heavy-laden cherry tree.

"Go ahead." He gestured for her to explore around the garden and stood to shadow her.

She tossed the apron aside and floated over to the fruit trees from cherry to apple and then pear. She toured the blueberry bushes and traced the blackberry vines with a delicate wave of her arm. The cut-flower garden made her expression beam. She touched the smallest blooms and skimmed the still-green pears with her fingertips.

He thought it a scene akin to the Garden of Eden, as a woman determined to live off of the land blessed it back with her pure adoration. Immeasurably glad he had brought her here before the reverie became trampled by the masses, it proved to be the perfect prelude. He waited for her at the implement garden, where his dad had retired a rustic array of farm equipment into which his mother had interspersed prairie wildflowers and garden statuary.

Completing her tour, she stepped up the slight dome and melted against him, her arms wrapping him in a tender hug. "I'm overwhelmed at the beauty," she whispered.

Having dreamed of this benediction, he held tight when it finally materialized. "I hereby invite you back to pick cherries with us next week." He pulled away, allowing a little space between them so she could read the sincerity in his eyes. "I'm in charge of the ladders," He winked about the time a car horn honked from the front drive, shattering the garden exchange. "All right. Here we go." He grabbed her hand for a mad dash toward the vehicle. When she laughed, his steps came lighter than air.

Arie jumped into the Gator like a riding pro. "Oh mercy. I forgot about my pies."

He delivered her to the back door of the cottage as Opal Litke's blue Buick halted nearby. At the driveway entrance, the Hernandez family arrived from down the road. After that, he lost track of the arrivals, his focus swept away by light banter and a river of eye-catching food. Something lingered in his mind, though, as a floral scent from Arie's hair drifted up from his shirt collar like a vague distraction. Recalling the way she touched the pears, a longing birthed for similar treatment.

~

The gooseberry pies cooled along the red countertop and a song rose from Arie's heart, being in such a wonderful place with these delightful people. Or perhaps one particular person could be held responsible for her light mood. She reflected on their spontaneous hug at the implement garden. From the back deck she spied Jusdyn down by the pond helping ready the fishing poles. Maybe he could use a little company, at least while the pies cooled. Unable to quell the attraction, she made quick work of the distance between them. "I'll hold the poles while you tie the lines." She rested a hand on the cane pole currently in his grip. She took possession and watched the resident expert.

He fiddled with the invisible fishing line until he got the tiny knot to hold. "That's right. You claimed you were here to help me, didn't you?" He motioned for the next pole. "You remember, the day I rescued you from the gate you babbled about being here to help me."

Astonishment soon gave way to embarrassment as she hoisted the end of the pole for ease of reach. Could she have let something slip as she came in and out of consciousness? How forward of her to offer help when she'd been so busy being a liability. She opened her mouth, but couldn't think of anything coherent to say.

He gave the line a final tug and set the hook free. "You've already been a help, so that initial claim is covered. Any more help will be extra. Plus. it gives me something to anticipate. How's that?" He took the cane pole and placed it against a big cooler with wheels.

She needed to find some safe territory. "Okay. I think we make a pretty good team, all things considered."

He laughed and dangled the next hook in front of her, his expression coy. "As long as I don't sneak up behind you, that is." He gestured for the next pole.

She lifted it into his vicinity with a coy tease. "Especially if I have a pie in my hands." She bobbed the pole's tip enough to give him some grief at the working end. "One should never put a handcrafted pastry at risk."

"Definitely not." He looked up from tying the hook in place. "Those treats are too rare around here, so we'd better make them count."

"I plan to." She gave him just enough time to pull the knot tight. Once the line swirled over his head, she headed for the pond's edge in a burst of speed. Work turned into fun, a lesson any hardworking rancher needed to be reminded of now and then. Almost second nature, she'd already helped him again.

~

Jusdyn glanced up from the pond's edge, spotting Deke as he lugged a heavy cooler over to the shade. He tossed the cane pole down and grabbed Arie's hand, running up from the pond. "I don't recall ever seeing you in jeans before."

"Cottonwood Falls sells everything a cowgirl needs. So how

did I do?" She exaggerated their hand swing as they came up the slope.

He glanced at her length and then hooked a rakish smile in response. "Hey there, Deke." From midway up the backyard, he gave the air a Wildcat claw.

"Just-man!" Deke dropped the cooler and threw a fist in the air. "Bring Arie over to meet Merrilee, will you?"

Loren led Opal and Ruby toward the patio set while Muriel brought the equally fragile Merrilee over for secure seating. The catalpa tree's shade became all the more genial when Deke converged on the scene with two lemonades to offer.

Jusdyn stepped into the shade, out of breath from the run, and exaggerated a reach for one of the glasses. His cousin anticipated the move like a slapstick partner in a vaudeville skit, turned sideways to deflect him, and finished serving the Litke sisters their drinks in a round of laughter. Another carload of guests arrived drawing Muriel out of the group.

"Merrilee, this is Arie Henning." He found great pleasure in allowing the two women to get acquainted. "Arie just moved back to Wilsey last month and is staying over at Uncle Doug's place. Arie, this is Merrilee, the best thing Deke ever brought back from K-State."

"Hey. What about my epic baseball jacket with my MVP badge on it?"

He countered Deke's protest with a mock blow to his bicep. "That's moth fodder out here in the real world, buddy."

The Litke sisters giggled while the younger women shook hands across the table.

Merrilee leaned closer with some effort. "Arie, I'm glad to hear you've been able to make Jusdyn stop and smell the prairie roses some this summer. It's been all cattle and barbed wire up until now. Tell me, what momentary insanity made you come back to Wilsey anyway?"

"I came back for the peace and quiet of the prairie. Found out city living wasn't for me."

"Well, I for one will be grateful for the female companionship, though we may have to chat over a crying baby before too long."

"I was a babysitter back in Abilene, so I'm used to the commotion of kids." Arie clasped her hands together, seeming excited at the prospect.

The arrival of a speeding Jeep muted their conversation as it rearranged the driveway gravel and courted the mailbox turning in from Road Z with a roar.

He grew amused by his cousin's classic redneck entrance. "TJ's here."

"Brace yourselves, everyone." Merrilee twitched her nose to one side in slight objection.

The Jeep had barely halted when Valor jumped out and ran to hug his mother by the front porch. TJ grabbed a bag of chips and sauntered down to the catalpa tree. "Howdy, folks. You weren't going to start this party without us, were you?"

He stepped toward him to shake hands. "You know it's not a full-fledged party until Valor gets here, cousin."

TJ faked avoidance and finally allowed him to connect. "She could've been here sooner if she hadn't made me stop so she could escort a red-eared slider across the road six different times." He laughed, turning to shake hands with Deke. "How's it going, Fastball? Whoa, look at you, Merrilee."

"One negative remark and you'll receive a month of dirty diapers on your front doorstep." Merrilee's lips quirked a smile, but her gaze sizzled with the dare.

A host of snickering followed until Jusdyn caught TJ eyeing Arie. Picking up on his interest right away, he intervened with a protective step in her direction. "TJ, this is a friend of mine, Arie Henning. She's come back to the prairie from Abilene and is living over at Uncle Doug's ranch." He gave Arie a shoulder hug, hoping proximity would demonstrate his growing bond and somehow deflect TJ's interest.

"Well, well. Another pretty flower on the prairie, right here in my Aunt Muriel's yard." TJ stroked his moustache which birthed a flirtatious crook of a smile.

His reactive flinch solicited a quizzical glance from Arie. He chose to hold his peace for the moment.

"Did everyone see TJ in yesterday's paper?" Opal soaked the question with admiration.

TJ strolled over to the patio chairs to embrace the elderly pair. "Hello there, Miss Opal and Miss Ruby."

"Happy Father's Day, TJ." Ruby patted his back.

"Thank you, ma'am, though I can say that I don't feel very deserving. Now, just how was I captured in the paper?"

"See? Here's the front-page picture of you standing beside our lovely governor, all important-like." Opal handed him the clipping which generated a smile.

As he passed the clipping around, TJ hesitated to read the print on back. In knee-jerk reaction, his expression fell as he turned his back to the group and muttered a swear word.

Jusdyn didn't miss the change in TJ's countenance and tried to figure out what had transpired when the article came his way. If the photo held a clue, he sure couldn't interpret any meaning. The back copy held nothing but news of another meth ring sting by local law enforcement. Stumped, he passed the clipping on to Arie.

"What a difference a page makes," TJ quipped.

Though something seemed cryptic in the brief exchange, he had a load of more important things on his mind right now and opted not to make an issue of it.

"Too bad the governor's married." Ruby's comment brought lighthearted laughter back to the group under the catalpa's shade.

Down by the fishing pond, Valor had joined his dad and acted animated.

On cue, Loren set off the alarm on his weather radio and began with an announcement. "May I have your attention, please? The Father's Day fishing contest will start momentarily. Please wander on down to the pond area and claim your pole. May the best angler win."

Several of the neighbor's children immediately ran to the water's edge as their mother shouted out precautions in Spanish.

Deke turned to Merrilee who waved him on to participate without her.

Jusdyn smiled at Arie to request her company down at the pond.

"Be down in a minute. Let me get Merrilee a drink first and set out some snacks."

Deke latched his pitching arm around TJ's shoulders and began to escort him down to the fishing grounds.

He walked abreast of his cousins trying to sort out exactly why he always allowed TJ's rogue behavior to get under his skin. In his peripheral vision, he caught TJ eyeing Arie as she leaned over the food table. He felt compelled to nix that errant interest right away. "Cousin, your dog is barking up the wrong tree." He chased the comment with a fake smile and let it drop like a lead weight. While the children made preparations by the water's edge, he felt assured that TJ had received his no trespassing message loud and clear.

When a cell phone rang on TJ's waist, he shoved Deke's arm off and took the call. As he sliced a retaliatory look Jusdyn's way, he muttered under his breath. "Better mark your territory." TJ fingered the phone, dropping back for privacy with a leer.

Jusdyn's stomach lurched in objection to the snub, a reaction that had nothing whatsoever to do with the imminent smell of fish.

Chapter 8

Nest building by the avian pair may appear as industrious vocation turned scavenger hunt. No other class of animals is as intensely aware of the realtor's credo 'location, location, location' than birds. The hunt for a successful nesting site becomes their first challenge as a couple. Once secured, the ritualistic gathering of nest-building supplies begins in earnest. Consummate recyclers, birds collect bits of leaves, grass, twigs, and twine to weave wind-resistant nesting cups. Males encumber their aerodynamic profiles transporting hay straw whiskers to the nest site, where the female weaves and waits. In short order, the nest project receives its last grass stitch and the limb-wedged sampler aptly reads 'home sweet home.'

"Five more minutes. Can anyone beat a six-inch sunfish?" The fishing judge's announcement rang out like a threat.

The outfall drain represented Jusdyn's sweet spot for fishing, but today his hook was coming up empty. Valor paced the bank on the far side of the pond, determined to find a fish with the business end of her line.

He scanned the perimeter and found Aric snipping off grass tips and tossing them on the water. She seemed content, placid yet purposeful, in beautiful balance. He thought about her a lot lately, hoping it would prove a direction—not a distraction.

Restless under pressure, he jammed his cane pole into a hole and walked up the bank behind her. Aided by the brim of his hat, he glimpsed the sandy-edged shallows where minnows darted about. A long-eared sunfish hovered in the water regarding Arie, and she appeared mutually transfixed on the fish. "Looks like you've found the perfect spot, complete with fish and everything." He knelt beside her on the bank. "Are you two conversing about anything interesting?" He gestured toward the water and the sunfish retreated to deeper water.

Arie blushed and tucked her hair back into a loose braid. "We agreed what a glorious day this is. He's a bit of an underwater philosopher, advising me to be content with the things that I have." She looked up and tossed another snippet of grass.

"Wow, what a deep message from a long-eared sunfish." He included a hint of skepticism in his tone as Valor begged fish to jump on her hook in the distance.

"Surely you're aware that the messenger rarely resembles the source of wisdom in these matters." Arie raised one eyebrow as if inviting his return volley.

Despite the cleverness of the banter, he could not help growing serious, knowing their pond-side peace would soon be broken under the judge's countdown. "Can you tell me why you've chosen to live in the rock house since you came back?" He planted a knee to wait for a valid answer.

She glanced toward the pond edge as if the sunfish would return and impart additional wisdom for her response. "Maybe it's because I like things reminiscent of days gone by—you know, simpler times." She punctuated her remark with a shoulder shrug.

He sat down close enough to touch her and casually plucked a blade of grass. Working through the difficulty of communicating beyond half-truths, he pressed the issue with tender resolve. "Remember the day you fell off the gate?" He twirled a piece of grass as Arie nodded. "Mom watched over you as you faded in and out of consciousness." When she glanced up at him with fear etched on her face, he reached for her hand and held it. "Mom told me you kept repeating an odd phrase over and over—something like 'must not take up a main space.' I'm guessing that has something to do with your choice to live in the rock house on the McLauren farm, not the ranch house." His disclosure met with silence as she seemed to drift away. "Can you tell me if that's part of it?"

"Yes, that's partly why," she whispered.

"One minute left in the fishing challenge." Loren lowered the megaphone and held up a finger.

He rose to his feet, pulling her up with him to close the gap between them. "Every now and then, we'll have to reach a little deeper to understand each other if we're going to grow closer in this friendship. For what it's worth, I actually admire the humility it takes to be out of the 'main space.' I think that mindset is part of your radiance."

"I promise to always be open and honest."

"Thirty seconds." The fishing judge's threat sounded like an alarm from the pond's edge.

The moment was about to slip away from him. He pulled Arie into his arms.

She lifted her face toward his expectantly. "I want to grow closer."

He saw the glitter in her eyes twinkle with the transparency of her admission and, like a man trying to hold a constellation in his hand, he bent and kissed her.

"Fifteen seconds." The timekeeper's warning echoed with drama.

The following series of simultaneous actions blurred together, caused by a rapid return from cloud nine. Valor called from the north bank claiming she had a big one. On the distant bank, TJ broke a cane pole over his knee in obvious frustration.

Next, Deke called for him to check his own abandoned rig which sent him running to snag the lower end of a furiously tipping pole. He attempted to set the hook, saw the flank of a long-eared sunfish glint beneath the shallows, and the line went slack. Before another second transpired, little Miguel Hernandez yielded to a monstrous tug and proceeded to fall off the bank right into the pond's depths, pole locked in hand.

"Time's up. Bring in your catch." Loren's call was immediately followed by the indiscernible screams of Mrs. Hernandez that accompanied her frantic pointing.

He converged with Deke at Miguel's fishing spot and dove in for the rescue. A murky curtain of algae-filtered pond water encased him as he groped for the missing angler. Nearby, Deke resurfaced for air, but he opted to continue.

Forcing himself deeper in the pond, he swept his arms systematically while his mind wrestled with a stark realization—the water down deep was colder that he thought. Suddenly, one touch of a cane pole with a bug-eyed boy attached brought the swimming portion of the fishing contest to an abrupt yet successful close. Clamping an arm around the boy, he reversed his stroke for shore.

Loren met him at the pond's rim, took little Miguel, and ushered him back into his mother's arms. A storm of Spanish erupted from their huddle.

Equally exhausted and elated, Jusdyn stood at the water's edge. Pond water drained off every inch of his body, turning the loamy bank into mud underfoot. Within seconds, Deke approached and slapped his back, showering innocent bystanders. Short of glory in the moment, the essence of heroism smelled like pond scum.

~

When Merrilee insisted on hanging out Deke's wet shirt, Arie went to ask the same of Jusdyn.

He paused, shirked off the damp T-shirt with a wink, and proceeded to haul the flailing catfish toward the cooler.

She strolled up toward the garden area matching Merrilee's hindered pace to where the weathered clothesline stood.

Merrilee traced the round of her abdomen with her free hand. "You may have to hang this for me. Guess my reach is a bit limited right now."

"I'd be glad to. When is your baby due?"

"The doctor says next Sunday, but I'm really hoping for earlier. Waiting is going to be my undoing if it goes on much longer than a week."

Arie wrung the excess water from the shirt and pinned it up by its hem. "Birth, death, and every day between are all a gift given by God in perfect timing. Do you have a feeling whether it's a boy or girl?"

"All along I've felt it was a girl. I'm sure Deke would like a son to carry on the farm and all, but he's open either way. I think he's going to be a great daddy, like Uncle Loren."

"Oh, I bet he will be." Arie took Deke's shirt from her.

"Tell me what you think of this place."

"I think it's a little acre of heaven. I'm truly drawn to it." She paused to snap the last clothespin in place and gazed at the fruit orchard, the flower garden, and the implement array.

Merrilee stepped closer without a break in her candor. "And what about Jusdyn?"

She swung her arms in the warm summer air to dry her hands from the pond laundry. Somehow, it felt safe to speak from the heart in such a lovely place. "Pretty hopelessly attracted there, too." She hooked her thumbs into her jean pockets and glanced down the yard in his direction. "Please don't let on though—not yet."

"Don't worry. Your secret is safe with me. Welcome to the Linquist fan club."

When Merrilee extended her arm for assistance, Arie readily took it. Walking with locked elbows, they crossed the sun-filled backyard to rejoin the party.

~

Jusdyn popped an oversized Wildcat T-shirt over Miguel's damp head. The boy grinned and tugged the whisker of the catfish on ice in Deke's cooler.

"This one's definitely a keeper," Valor said in a bragging tone.

Close by, Deke entangled himself in a similar vintage T-shirt, making an amusing expression as his bushy eyebrows reappeared like Muppets popping up from below stage.

Loren gestured for attention. "Ladies and gentlemen, I present the winner of this year's Father's Day Fishing Frolic—Miguel Hernandez with his catfish-of-the-deep." He handed the boy a modest tackle box bearing a large plank of chocolate. The winner was mobbed by his inquisitive siblings who helped him open the candy portion of the prize. Loren shook hands with Miguel's father. "Mannie, my invitation stands. Your family is welcome to come back and fish anytime."

Deke shot two fists into the air. "How about giving three cheers for a brave boy, a lunker catfish, and a rancher who pulled them both from the depths to keep the party going?" The small gathering quickly chimed in for a triple round of hip-hip-hurray in response.

To shift the focus, he lifted Miguel onto his shoulders in victorious celebration.

"Time to round up your Gators, gentlemen. The Gator Get will commence in ten minutes." Loren set the megaphone down as his carnival tone reverberated across the yard.

Muriel took Arie by the hand and bee-lined over to the food table, returning with trays of finger food to stave off any late-afternoon hunger.

On cue, Valor ran up to TJ's Jeep and retrieved a tote bag full of game props to set the next event in motion. Whether through charming insistence or dogged persistence, she had compelled her hosts to make the last challenge of the day her ultimate creation—a scavenger hunt on wheels she dubbed the Gator Get. It was an all-out race driven by a cryptic set of clues revealed one at a time. All told, the game raised quite a hullabaloo and became great fuel for good-spirited competition between the cousins.

He bit the carrot stick dip-end first and pulled away from Arie with a lingering look. "Gotta get my ride in place. You're gonna love this next event." With a running leap, he jumped into the vehicle and cranked the engine, pulling up to the hub of action. He waited for TJ to back in place before forming the fourth prong of a five-point star around a hand-made pennant marked GG flying atop a spare rake handle.

Next, Valor produced the first set of clues in her bag and walked around the contestants. "So who wants a rider this year?" The girl clutched her clue bag to her chest as if to withhold the game until they responded.

He raised his hand with Arie in mind while Loren, Deke, and Mannie indicated interest in riding partners, too.

"Okay, Dad. You'll ride solo." Valor singled out TJ with her thumbs-up approval. "Now Jusdyn, though you've been my favorite in the past, this year I'm choosing Deke, because Merrilee's not able to play. So the rest of you, go find a rider."

Having a partner to share the thrill of the race happened to be a major part of the fun of the Gator Get. He dismounted and sprinted up to the food table to snag Arie, which garnered some hoots from the spectators, led by Merrilee.

Loren came up searching out Muriel, who had wedged between Opal and Ruby. When she shooed him away like an annoying fly, he pivoted midstep.

All five of the Hernandez children jumped up and down to vie for their father's pick. When Mannie selected the oldest girl Tia for his rider, Loren tapped the oldest boy on the head and beckoned him to follow.

With the riders soon in place, Valor handed out little blocks of wood, hand-painted in primary colors. She smiled as she handed Jusdyn the purple block, so he rewarded her with a throaty Wildcat howl. "Remember, don't turn these over until I throw the 'Go' signal." Satisfied, she took her seat in front of Deke. "Is everybody ready?"

"Ready," Jusdyn called. He shot Arie a sporting glance and put the Gator into forward gear while other drivers echoed his response.

"On your mark… get set—" Valor stood and released a wobbly

water balloon over their heads, which came down and burst on TJ's rear fender.

"Get!" shouted the onlookers with insistence.

He stomped the accelerator. The Gators sped out of the start position with riders eagerly trying to determine a direction from the first cryptic clue.

Arie read aloud the script from the bottom of the purple block. "This bloom is for visitors. Okay, so wouldn't visitors come to the front door?"

"Right. I'm on it, Sherlock." He floored the gas pedal.

"What exactly are we looking for?"

"A little something we'll grab and take with us. Somewhere on it will be Clue Number Two. Think like an eleven year-old."

"A bloom… a bloom. I'm guessing some type of flower." She craned forward as if to see up ahead.

He cut sharp around the front corner of the house and approached the seldom-used front porch. In a neat line along the bricked edge he spotted five little terra cotta pots with pipe-cleaner flowers inside. "Now comes the 'Get' part of Gator Get, Arie. Go grab the purple one."

"I'm on it, Dale Junior." In three steps she had the purple pot in her hands.

He backed the Gator around to depart. "Read me the next clue."

She slid in and flipped the pot upside-down. "Hanging out in your birthday suit."

"Hanging out. Hanging out." He repeated the clue trying to analyze the inference while avoiding the front corner of the house. "What about the clothesline?"

"I like that location, but what about the birthday suit part? How do you hang that up?"

He waved to Opal and Ruby as he drove by. When Arie held up the purple flowerpot to the spectators, they received a cheer of encouragement.

She shrugged and tucked the flowerpot between them. "I don't know. Could the hint mean baby clothes?"

He guided the Gator around the edge of the garage into the garden area. They both laughed when they saw the clothesline. There dangling in the breeze hung four naked troll dolls, clipped by their rainbow-colored hair to the line.

Arie darted up and freed the one with the purple hair ribbon.

In his haste, he reversed around the garage corner, nearly colliding with TJ.

"Watch out, wide load." TJ slashed a finger across his throat.

Arie waggled the troll at him as if to ward off the threat.

He grew impatient for a new direction. "Forget TJ. Where to next?"

"To catch a drop, just stop." She drew the troll to her throat. "But a drop of what?"

"Let's assume water. There's a hand pump at the implement garden."

"What about a rain barrel?"

"We don't have one of those, but you might be on the right track with rain. Let's check Dad's rain gauge off the back porch."

"Get there, Dale Junior, and maybe give that rain barrel idea some further thought."

"Yes ma'am, Little Miss Conservationist." His teasing soon earned him a whack with the troll doll. As they sped past, the Litke sisters observed the troll flogging and let out a whoop from the shade.

Arie grabbed the front dash after they hit a pothole in the yard. "I truly have to hand it to Valor. She's made this event really fun."

"Valor's a great kid. Mom has a real soft spot for her."

"I think I've already picked up on that."

"Here's your rain gauge—and look—there's your clue." Three little turtles made from walnut shells walked the porch rail beside the rain gauge.

Arie took the turtle with a purple spot on its shell. "And then there were two."

"This is the last clue. What does it say?" He wheeled the vehicle around.

She examined it closer, knitting her brow. "Come home, cold owl."

"An owl's home is a tree—or a barn."

"No, Dale Junior. Don't you get the hint? The 'cold owl' part is the main clue. A typical owl says hoot, but what would a cold owl say?"

Recognition exploded in his head. "He'd say Brrr, of course." He swerved the Gator in a beeline toward the giant oak tree. "There's a hollow cavity in the base of this bur oak. Valor has always been fascinated by it." He stopped the Gator with a jab on the brakes.

Arie dashed out to find a purple ball hidden in the hollow. She detached the paper tag taped to the ball. "Let's roll and head for the pole."

He glanced over his shoulder and saw his mother standing alone with the rake handle in her hand. Thrill shot down his core from head to foot. They still had a chance to win. "Hang on, Arie. From here, it's an all-out race." Adrenalin-pumped, he jabbed his foot and pressed the accelerator to the floor.

She grabbed the dashboard with her right hand and danced the troll on his shoulder with her left. As they passed the Litke sisters, the high-pitched whine of TJ's Gator bore down from the rain gauge checkpoint. In an instant, Deke and Valor appeared from behind the garage with the troll doll, making their dash for the pole.

After sizing up their relative positions, he turned to his magnetic passenger. "Brace yourself. It's time for Dale Junior to use some moxie and run a little helpful interference for Deke." Yanking the wheel, he veered wide to the right which caused TJ to flank off toward the garage. Though the desperate move avoided direct collision, it landed TJ in the garden's compost heap straight on.

Deke jammed on brakes at the pole while Valor grabbed the finish line flag. Her face radiant, a spontaneous victory dance soon illuminated the backyard.

A spattering of applause heralded the winners while he circled back for damage control. Pulling alongside the compost heap, he jumped to his feet and lifted TJ's rig out by the rear rack.

TJ flicked a melon rind from his front fork, his lips drawn tight. "Classic bump-and-run move back there, wide load."

"I'd do anything for Valor, short of cheating, that is." He got in beside Arie, shifted into gear and mashed the accelerator to head in for second place when a rebel troll doll landed between the seats, headfirst. "Thanks for the tip, TJ." He drove past the admiring crowd with two dolls now dancing on his shoulder.

Arie jumped out at the pole and hugged the game's inventor. "Congratulations, Valor. Your Gator Get race was the most fun ever. I had a blast."

"That's what games are about, Arie. Glad you could be here." She clapped, happiness lighting up her expressive face.

Jusdyn swatted a high-five to his Wildcat cousin as he dismounted.

Deke cleared imaginary sweat off his brow and jabbed one finger in the air. "Hey, thanks for the fend-off on the last lap there, buddy."

The last two Gators pulled up within seconds of each other, the riders smiling and sporting handfuls of dolls, turtles, flowerpots, and balls.

"Yee-hi." Loren flapped his arms like an eagle.

Valor ran to give him a celebratory hug.

Muriel tipped the pole at the winners as the banner fluttered over their heads. "Ladies and gentlemen, please celebrate the winners of this year's Gator Get, Deke Linquist and his rider Valor McLauren."

Deke held his arms high in victory while Loren stood Valor up on the Gator seat to receive her applause. The girl wiggled her fingers skyward, shining in the moment.

Muriel brought out a pair of two-liter bottles of root beer and handed one to each of them.

He elbowed Arie to get her attention and the dancing twin trolls took a sudden break. "And that, my friend, is the Gator Get." He gestured to the winners to close out the event.

Arie wrapped the trolls around his neck in a wreath of her arms to celebrate the moment.

"Thank you, Dale Junior, for the unforgettable trip around the yard." Her dimples reappeared out of thin air.

Goose bumps tore down his right side like the electricity of cutting donuts on the victory lap. "Everyone's a winner today." He tightened the hug without hesitation and lost his next thought in her honeysuckle hair.

"Now, let's eat." Muriel pointed toward the bur oak and its underskirt of food tables.

"Amen, Auntie." Deke grabbed Muriel and danced her up to the tables under feigned protest. Loren followed twirling Valor and the Litke sisters helped Merrilee over to meet the rest.

Plate in hand, Jusdyn offered thanks for the blessing of food, family, and festivity. His much-awaited assault on the deviled eggs began in earnest upon the closing amen. *Can life get any better than this?*

Chapter 9

Survival is an all-or-none proposition in the natural world of wildlife, with shades of gray erased between milestones of black and white. Should a fledgling fall from the nest or a hatchling entangle itself in moss, there is little corrective measure the parent animal can make, and a predator happening by becomes the post-trauma cleanup crew. In truth, rehabilitation is a human contrivance stirred by a tender heart and a preoccupation for fixing the broken. Loss of the injured or compromised specimen is inconsequential with regard to the gene pool that stabilizes the population. At best, rehabilitation plumps the food chain with an additional obtainable meal. Nature neither transplants weeds to a more suitable location, nor panders to the weak or disadvantaged in an effort to neaten its order.

Jusdyn drew a cold drink from the ice tub. "Hey, look who finally made it. Uncle Doug's here right in time to eat."

The neighboring rancher balanced a silver pan in one hand and waved his Sunday hat from the crest of the front yard.

"I'm holding out for one of whatever's in that pan." TJ downed a deviled egg in one bite as if to make room on his plate.

"Make mine a double." Deke shoveled some errant traces of coleslaw to the edge of his plate. When Merrilee shot him a corrective glance, he raised his fork. "Hey, I'm eating for two here." His defense solicited giggles from the Litke sisters.

"Ladies, allow me to say that these deviled eggs are a fine offering." He held up a slippery specimen as an example. "May the cucumbers multiply like rabbits this year to fuel another bountiful crop of your sweet pickle relish."

Opal tossed down her napkin and smiled. "You bet your dancing trolls they are."

Loren and Muriel walked up to greet their guest, but were soon outdistanced by the life of the party.

The late arriver swept his free arm open wide. "Howdy, Valor. How about a hug?"

The girl leapt like a deer fawn into a lopsided embrace.

Muriel rescued the silver pan as it slipped from the rancher's grip.

"Thanks for coming, Doug." Loren started to offer his hand, but ended up patting his shoulder instead. "It seems like the family's all here now."

"Appreciate the invitation, Loren. My girls are all busy at their in-laws today."

"Not this girl." Valor placed her small hand on his chin, soliciting a bear hug from the rancher.

TJ took his turn next. "Hey, Uncle Doug. It's great to see you. Valor, hop down now and let him grab some dinner."

"Okay, Dad." The girl squeezed Doug's neck before she dropped to the ground.

"Come on over and get something to eat." Muriel lifted the pan. "What's in here?"

Doug gazed across the backyard and smiled. "Burgers cooked to perfection on a homemade grill."

Jusdyn took possession of the pan from his mother and headed for the table.

"Waiter, order for two burgers over here." Deke snapped his fingers like he was a car hop at the drive-in. After Merrilee gave him a freshness check under the table about mid-shin, he stifled a groan and flashed a hurt-puppy look.

Muriel lifted the foil off the pan. "Anyone who wants seconds has to finish what's on their plates." A matronly glow lit her face as she stood appreciating a yard full of people she cared about the most.

Loren laced an arm around Muriel's waist in a rare show of affection. "Where would the Queen Mother like to sit?" He gestured in a half-circle.

"Anywhere but on the ground." Muriel added a burger to his plate and set the foil pan on the food table. Satisfied, she strolled up the yard toward the back porch steps with Loren close behind.

Doug flipped a clean plate, making a quick survey of the food table. "Hey, Muriel. Can you two stand some company?"

"You bet. Come on up after you load your plate."

When Jusdyn handed him a cold drink, Doug nodded with genuine appreciation. "Oh, I got that fence repair job taken care of for you. I'm happy to report that calf will have to look harder to find its way out next time."

"You're the best neighbor ever." The thought swirl around until it struck him that he was standing in the finest place on earth—his own backyard.

Great food and familiar chatter filled the afternoon until the plates ran empty and appetites sat full. Restless, the children delighted in discovering lawn games beside the garage and divided out into teams to test their abilities. Ladder ball toss won out over horseshoes. When Jusdyn stepped into a heated match, he learned that he had no talent for the tossing game at all, much to the children's amusement. By contrast, Arie proved to be good at every game. Too full of good food to play the sore loser, he anted up for another slaughter at cornhole.

~

TJ busied himself clearing the table in an attempt to avoid the annoying merriment nearby. He gave half a thought to leaving soon, but a rash departure would be unfair to Valor.

Loren stepped up beside him, separating discarded drink cans into a sack. "I can't agree with the grazing being allowed in the CRP grounds this year. That ground is supposed to be set aside from grazing pressures all season long for a duration of ten years.”

“Those re-growth stands aren’t precious by any stretch, Uncle Loren. What we’ve got is a forty year-old dying dinosaur that nobody knows what to do with. That Conservation Reserve Program began to remove land out of cultivation due to a crop glut in the mid-eighties. But today there’s money to be made in grain because of alternative fuels so every farmer wants to grow as much grain and soybeans as they can. I don’t blame them, really. It all comes down to economics and keeping the farmer’s business viable. That’s a powerful bottom line.”

“But that CRP ground is juvenile tallgrass prairie.” Loren spread both arms toward the horizon. “We have enough world-class grass to graze the present-day herds without dropping the fence on that protected CRP. Did you consider the negative effect on wildlife?”

“Ground nesters should be fledged by mid-July. The rest will have to move over for the cattle, I guess. Anyway, since two-thirds of the contracts for enrolled CRP land will be expiring in the next five years, it’s not hard to understand why the program comes across as being archaic. We’re watching a farm subsidy in a death spiral. I doubt any contracts will be renewed.”

Loren crushed a can with his boot. “What about making extensions instead of renewing? Would that be feasible in your estimation?”

“Maybe, if you want to put a band-aid on a limping filly. A smart man would see a lame horse passing, take it behind the barn, and get done with it.” Though he hated to seem so fatalistic, as conservation officer, he was astute enough to read the handwriting on the wall.

Loren turned away, gazing out over the ranchlands. He turned back with unsettling emotion clouding his eyes. “Are you so ready to give up on the land, TJ? Think about matters in the long term. I know life’s not been easy this past year, but don’t get so disillusioned. You've got help right here. All these people would do anything for you and your family."

He wrestled with the offer, tightening his grip on the soda can until it popped. Whether family or farm, life seemed all about exhausting yourself to keep things going, staying between the lines only to yield a meager existence at best. Well, he'd grown way past merely getting by day-to-day. No, he needed to make peace for the fast lane he preferred.

A basic realization emerged and he had no qualms saying it aloud. "Quite frankly, I've fallen out of love with the land, Uncle Loren. Simple as that." In the instant, he felt purged. From his uncle's stunned face, the admission would be a turning point. He drained his can, crushed it, and tossed it on the ground. Like clockwork, the device on his hip sounded so he stepped away to take care of a more lucrative business. Glancing back, his uncle bent for the discarded can, visibly sobered by their conversation. A more sensitive man might have registered some remorse. *It's too late to care.*

~

"Uncle Morrill may have had a small stroke on Friday." Doug leaned toward Muriel as they lingered on the back steps. "Lettie says he's showing no further signs of complications, but he remained pretty incoherent for quite a while."

"How's Uncle Vernis taking it?"

"Like a porcupine, of course, all bristled up and ready to impale anyone who comes near him emotionally. He thinks because they lived their lives together, he has somehow earned the right for them to die together."

"Granted, those two have been very close. Living through hard times bonds the spirit, you know. They've seen the depression come and go, dustbowl days cloud and clear, and family members drown prematurely. Still, I'm sure it will take away some of his spunk if Morrill does pass first. Remember how they both went to pieces at mother's funeral? Thank goodness for Opal and Ruby, those angels."

"I've often suspected that caring for Uncle Morrill is what's been keeping Dad going for several years now. Frankly, I'm a bit concerned it will take away his will to live if Morrill passes before he does. One thing's for sure. Elder care is too much of a psychological knot-tangle for this simple rancher." Doug slouched forward under the burden.

Muriel placed an assuring hand on his shoulder. "How about I bring Valor to see her great-grandpa on Tuesday before I take her home? TJ's letting her stay with me a couple of days until her violin lesson Tuesday afternoon."

"That's the best medicine out there, if you ask me. That girl could charm a scent gland off a skunk, so a porcupine wouldn't stand a chance."

"Call Lettie tonight and tell her we'll be by on Tuesday just before lunch. And Doug, stay on the phone with her awhile to talk about the little things. She owes you some daddy time."

"Don't even get me started down that dead end, cousin." His dismissive nod said the rest.

~

Arie watched beauty transition to peace as Merrilee leaned back in her metal patio chair, exhausted yet content. Despite the lively Wildcat banter and endless chatter from the Litke sisters, tranquil repose set upon the mother-to-be. By happenstance, she saw the satin ribbon on the bodice of Merrilee's maternity dress begin to tremble, as faint as a calf twitching flies.

Merrilee awakened when the baby responded to the ribbon quiver with a visible kick to her ribs. She managed a slight smile and then surrendered to the conquering nap.

Thinking the family nurse might want to be informed, Arie stood and excused herself from the table. She started up the yard to find Muriel on the back porch.

Opal caught her arm as she passed. "Just checking in on how you're doing, honey. Are you finding many ways to help Jusdyn yet?"

She diverted her gaze to the ground. "I think so."

"Good." The old woman patted her hand. "He's going to need your help—more than you can imagine."

"Right now, Merrilee might need my help more. I'm on my way to discuss that with Muriel. We'll be right back, I promise."

"Go ahead, child. Just be ever alert, like the Good Book warns." She placed a finger on her lips as if to seal the discussion.

She walked up the yard practicing her alertness. As she approached, Uncle Doug rose and winked while taking their empty plates. The Hernandez children played badminton near the rose garden, allowing her to retrieve an errant birdie as she passed by. She paused a few seconds to let Doug drift out of earshot. "Hello, Queen Mother."

"Right. Make that Queen Mother with two aching feet."

"What a great gathering. Thank you so much for asking me to be a part of it."

"You were my first-rate helper out there, Arie. With Merrilee slowed down this year, I sure needed that extra help. You showed up in the nick of time, for more than one of us."

"Muriel, I wanted you to know that Jusdyn and I talked earlier about the phrase I was babbling during my recovery from the concussion. I must have said something about not taking up a main space. Now, he's concerned about my living in the rock house."

"Concerned might be an understatement, Arie. Listen, I want you to think about coming to live in our cottage for a while. You can accomplish your pie baking from there. The twin ovens would be perfect for that job. Here's a suggestion. Stay overnight tonight and help me clean up after the party. I promise to speak to Doug about the rest, if you're willing."

"But he's living all alone over there on the McLauren ranch."

"I know, sweetie. You're just like Valor, always trying to look after everyone else."

"Oh, that reminds me. Could you come sit with us at the patio table? I've been watching Merrilee. Her tummy's twitching ever so often. I think she might be going into labor."

Muriel's face perked up. "Suddenly, I'm in the mood for girl-talk. Bring it on." The hostess rose with a groan. She took her time, pausing to kiss Miguel on the mop-top of his black hair as they ambled down the backyard together.

Upon their arrival, Jusdyn moved Deke down and offered Arie's chair to his mother, then patted his knees to accommodate her. After perching lightly, he gave her a welcoming bounce.

"Muriel, I'm glad you came down," Opal folded her hands together. "I've wanted to talk to you about a college fund for Valor."

Muriel fixed her gaze on Merrilee's huge pink dress. "That's a grand idea."

Ruby leaned in as if conspiring with Opal. "Good, because Sister and I have been putting money aside in a Learning Quest account for her since she was five."

Deke flexed his arms. "And thus, another Wildcat is born." He spoke in deep tones as if broadcasting a new legacy in the family's collegiate saga.

Jusdyn slapped a high-five on his cousin in support.

"I wouldn't promote the Purple Cat Club so quickly." Muriel's caveat crackled under the trees. "That girl has a bent toward music that cannot be ignored. I'll be taking her home Tuesday for a violin lesson where I'll press her instructor for any possibilities to advance her potential in that direction."

"There." Arie cued the nurse with no further explanation. The satin ribbon took a quivering stroll across the top of the beach ball midsection, again ending in the knee-jerk kick from the baby. Relief loosened the stitch in her chest. *Good, I'm not imagining it.*

Muriel glanced at her watch.

Deke flinched, a bit unsteady. "Wait a sec. What's going on here, ladies?"

Muriel turned briefly from her patient. "Arie picked up on the contractions Merrilee's having. I came down to time them, that's all.

If your wife can stay asleep, there's absolutely nothing for you to worry about."

Opal leaned over her empty plate as if to make sure she'd heard correctly. "You mean Merrilee might be having the baby right now?"

Seated side by side, Jusdyn and Deke exchanged astonished looks.

"Why, that would make Deke a father right here on Father's Day." Ruby's exclamation generated an exaggerated swallow by the destined-to-be dad. "Father used to say that mid-summer births were a celebration of last fall's harvest." She began counting on her fingers.

"Yes, he did." Opal propped her chin in her palm. "I believe the soybean harvest was unusually profitable last year, wasn't it Jusdyn?"

"Yes, ma'am, it was that." He bounced Arie on his knees for each word he spoke. When she swatted his knee to have him stop, he responded by weaving his fingers into hers.

"There's another one." Muriel pointed as the ribbon went through the tectonic quiver again, this time the baby's kick knocked Merrilee's hand off her tummy and onto the metal armrest of the patio chair.

"Ouch." Merrilee's eyes blinked open as she awakened from all the internal action.

"Only five minutes apart. You're having contractions."

Arie caught a hint of queasiness in the crowd and sensed a need to shift the attention. "Hey Muriel. Deke's not looking so swell over here."

Muriel leaned past Jusdyn to take a look at her nephew. "Oh? Can you tell me what feels wrong, Deke?"

Deke turned three shades of white there under the catalpa tree. "Stomach. Breathing."

Muriel stood with a serious look on her face. ""TJ, bring me that chip bag from the food table. Deke's having an anxiety attack.

That's not terribly uncommon for fathers-to-be."

"Empathy pain is more like it," Opal clarified. "It's touching, really."

TJ dumped the chip crumbs out of the bag and ran it over to his aunt.

Arie saw that Valor had joined the adults, but stood frozen as if mortified at the scene.

Muriel pressed the bag to Deke's face after Jusdyn tipped him forward.

Arie walked over to Valor, wrapped her arms around the child's shoulders, and whispered in her ear. "Everything's going to be okay."

Stricken at the turn of events, Valor continued to watch without blinking.

After several breaths into the bag, Deke's color visibly improved, relaxing the nurse and his other attendants.

Arie saw the next ripple pattern begin on the satin racetrack. Although Merrilee tried to minimize the discomfort, the baby kicked again, resulting in a loud bone-cracking sound.

Deke shot a glance at his wife, noticed her wince, saw the dress twitch when the baby kicked, heard the rib crack, and resolutely became a dead weight in Jusdyn's arms.

She stepped up to the table quickly, but had a moment's indecision on how or who to help first.

Muriel went into take-charge mode. "Loren, wet a stack of napkins in the melt water of the drink tub and bring them over. Merrilee dear, I'd feel better if you could rest inside, just in case you labor is really starting."

"Okay, Aunt Muriel." Merrilee's tone was tinged with concern. "Jusdyn, would you stay with Deke for me?"

"Like a brother, Merrilee. Count on it."

"And I'll come with you." Arie sensed the need to go since Muriel seemed to be staying. She stepped forward and leaned toward Jusdyn, whispered thanks for the loan and slid the watch off his wrist. Doug joined her in walking Merrilee up toward the cottage's back deck.

Stiff-legged as a newborn calf, Valor began to trail them.

Midway to the cottage, a folk remedy that used aromatics flashed to mind. Turning back, she grabbed Valor's hand, relayed what plant to pick, and told her where to find it. As the child ran toward the flower garden, she launched a tiny prayer for success with the herbal application. The pulse of the party seemed to skip a beat as she trotted to catch up with Doug and Merrilee.

~

Jusdyn held Deke steady across the table while Valor raced across the yard.

Proceeding to the garden, the child appeared to be thumping bumblebees off blooming spikes. She picked the upper leaves of a tall flower stem and brought them over as fast as her legs would carry her. "Arie said to crush these leaves and rub them under Deke's nose."

"Yes, thank you." Muriel took the leaves from her junior assistant. She looked up at him, her brow raised. "It's a clever remedy, actually, and a bit more resourceful that what I have in my medic bag. Let's hope it works." She rolled the veined leaves in her fingers, and the essence of mint began to waft across the shade. When she pressed the wad to Deke's upper lip, he stirred out of his grog.

The father-to-be lifted a hand to his head. "How's Merrilee?"

Opal and Ruby held hands while whispering praises for his regained consciousness.

He planted a palm on his cousin's forearm. "Merrilee's doing fine. She's resting comfortably in grandma's cottage."

His mother took a pulse on Deke's right wrist, which Valor duplicated with precision.

Loren patted Valor on the back. "It looks like we have a little nurse in the making."

TJ beamed as some normalcy returned to the catalpa's shade.

Valor clamped her arms around Loren's waist. "The plant was Arie's idea. She had me do the picking."

Doug returned from the cottage, anxiety tightening his face. "Merrilee wants to know what's going on down here."

"Valor helped bring Deke back around with some horsemint vapors, Doug. Reminds me of something our grandmother would have done." Muriel sniffed her fingertips as proof.

"She's a musician and a medic. Doesn't that beat all?"

"Mom, maybe you should go up and check on Merrilee. Let Miss Opal and Miss Ruby care for Deke until he gets a little more pink-in-the-cheek." He nodded at the senior women who perked up at being needed.

"Okay, Jusdyn. Listen, if she's fine, Arie and I will be serving the desserts on the back porch in ten minutes. And Loren, get some help moving two tables onto the porch for us."

"Consider it done," Doug replied, surveying the distance.

"Count on me, too," TJ added.

Muriel looked over her shoulder to find her assistant. "Valor? Are you coming?"

"Coming, Aunt Muriel." Valor unlocked her grip on Loren and took her aunt's hand.

Opal and Ruby shuffled into place beside Deke, alternately patting his hand while looking keenly interested.

"Now listen here, Deke," Opal said. "Sister and I have always treasured our parents naming us for valuable gemstones. The preciousness of a child should not be trivialized."

When Deke shot him a searching look, he returned it with a patronizing smile.

After a lengthy ten minutes, the back door opened to a processional of pies, sweet breads, homemade divinity, and a towering four-layer German chocolate cake.

Deke detoured around the dessert table and slipped inside the cottage.

Muriel ushered Arie out with the last gooseberry pie and closed the door. "Just so everybody knows, the contractions have stopped." Muriel brushed her palms on her apron.

Arie caught his gaze and flashed a warm smile. "We think it was false labor, which means Baby Linquist won't be joining your family today."

He became a mixed bag of emotions, both relieved and disappointed all at the same time.

"It strikes me that false labor may be the Good Lord's way of reminding us to pray for Merrilee and the baby." Opal pressed her hands together as if to get going on her pledge right then and there.

Ruby connected with her sister by locking elbows. "And pray for Deke, too. Let's not leave the father out."

"Yeah, seems like the contractions threw Fastball a slippery curve," TJ quipped. His joke garnered only a few tight laughs.

Valor fingered a brownie out of the pan, refusing to look up. "Don't worry about Deke. He'll be ready when the baby comes."

"If he has half your confidence, honey, he sure will." Doug rested his hip against the porch railing and nodded.

"Muriel?" Loren pointed toward the towering German chocolate cake. "Is this mine?"

"Yes, it is. Happy Father's Day, Loren." She handed him the cake server.

He readily took the utensil. "You bet it is." He went for the cake's midsection, and with a flourish of the wrist, struck chocolate gold.

Considering all his mouthwatering options, Jusdyn could hardly wait his turn to be served. Pie would be first. Possibly last, too. And a slice of his father's chocolate cake would make for nice filler in between. *Multitudes in the valley of decision—and all of them first-rate.*

~

Swaying into the evening, the porch swing found its regular rhythm of squeaky song. Arie was grateful to be a guest in the quiet cottage once again. Having helped Muriel and Valor with the post-party clean-up, she had finished washing the serving platters in the neat red kitchen and then retreated to the front porch to enjoy nightfall.

Crystalline cornflower blue skies collapsed into a swirl of violet dust which settled upon the horizon. In the absence of the sun, the prairie—like the firmament above—defaulted to its passive charm of wide, empty space. Though surrounded by the elemental beauty of nocturnal nature in the comfort of familiar surroundings, she felt only partially content. A half-empty swing resonated with the sympathetic effect of growing close to someone yet not having that person nearby. The gravity of the yearning propelled the swing in motion through the hollowness of the night.

Laughter softly drifted from the guest room of the main house, as Muriel combed out Valor's hair. They were singing a silly song together which floated across the surface of the night like cottonwood seeds riding the wind. If Arie pushed the swing back beyond the corner of the cottage, she could see them dancing. *Is this my penance for not being in a main space?* The heart-prick of solitude struck for the first time. As she watched, Valor wrapped herself in the elegant sheer curtain and spun back out into the room to Muriel's soft-spoken delight.

She missed the approaching truck until its headlights shone directly onto the porch. Piercing lasers, the lights shattered her loneliness, pushing back against the hollow night. She stood by the porch column, but unlike the praying mantis, grew highly hopeful of being noticed.

As the truck slowed, the driver rolled down his window. Loren placed his shifting hand over Sam's growling muzzle. "Evening, Arie."

Jusdyn popped out over the far side of the cab. "Hey there."

"Welcome home, ranch hands." Arie drew out her words hoping to keep them a selfish minute. "How are the cattle doing?"

"They're all fine, but I still smell like pond scum," Jusdyn ran a hand through his matted hair. "Can I come visit you in ten minutes?"

"Well, it has been a little lonesome over here." She twirled a lock of hair.

He clutched his heart across the Wildcat emblem on his shirt. "That absolutely has to stop." He turned as laughter flowed from the gable of the big house.

The driver gazed up toward the second floor. "Time to get back to my girls." He released the dog to make first gear.

Barking co-mingled with old truck noises, muffling Jusdyn's parting comments. He pressed ten fingers up to the rear glass as the truck lurched down the driveway.

The stop-by visit pacified her heart-prick for the moment. The truck soon rumbled to a stop and turned off. She waited out the interim solitude by listening to frogs calling nearby.

Within minutes, a cleaner version of Jusdyn appeared running across the farmyard. "Here's a little gift from Valor to the lady in the porch swing." He hid his hands behind his back, seeming to enjoy the mysterious assignment.

She stood in the lamplight and walked to the front step, bending over him in expectation of the gift. Her loose hair trellised down. When she tried to peek, her visitor resisted.

"Nope. You have to pay the messenger first, Miss Henning."

"Oh, is that the way rural delivery works around here?" She questioned his ploy, not falling for a second of it. Though his face flinched at her initial resistance, she decided to leave room for a little more hope in the proverbial mailbox. While his messenger boy contrivance crumbled like dust against the diamond of her sincerity, she discovered an odd enjoyment in having the momentary advantage. She swept her hair up to one shoulder.

When Jusdyn cocked his arm as if to fling the token out into the night, Arie pivoted to grab the gift and planted a kiss on his lips that made the porch tremble. Locked in his arms, she realized being in a main space no longer mattered. *Simply stand beside someone who is.*

Chapter 10

Mimicry of plants and inanimate objects has been a recurring ploy of nature's denizens through the ages. Flatten a green insect laterally and it appears to be another leaf on a stem, eluding even predators of heightened visual acumen. A brown snake with arboreal inclinations becomes another branch on the tree, avoiding detection as it hunts in stealth. A speckled moth may be missed by virtue of blending in soft edges with a background of tree bark or stone. While mimicry may be the greatest form of flattery in socially defined circles, in nature it conceals the individual in a highly refined camouflage to perpetuate survival. In the purchase of tomorrow, the individual sometimes forfeits resemblance to its kind and any right to freedom of movement. When to twitch is to be caught, one must learn not to wriggle.

"Let some slack on the reins," Jusdyn stood at the corral gate and waited for Valor to respond.

"But I'm afraid she won't do what I want her to do if I let them loose."

"The only way to know is to try it and see. I'm going to open the gate, and then you guide Chica around the course I've marked."

"Am I ready for this?" Valor's voice squeaked a little as she squirmed in the saddle. Her mount bent a knee as if to move forward, anticipating the freedom of space and the ever-present temptation of grass beyond the gate.

"A true cowgirl is always ready."

"Okay. Open the gate." Her tone lacked any of her earlier bravado.

"Next, put both signals together—click and kick." He shouldered the gate and persuaded it half open.

Valor's thin legs squeezed the restless horse, her boot heels planting in its sides. She made a rookie clicking noise in her teeth, and the horse moved forward out of the gate.

"Well, now. Would you look at that?" He placed his hat over his heart as she rode past. "Rein left and walk her to the bur oak."

The girl raised her arm to neck-rein the horse, but held it a bit too long. Chica responded by completing three-quarters of a circle. "Yikes. I messed up. What should I do?"

"Correct it by reining the other way, but try to time it a bit tighter. Remember, a little steering goes a long way." He focused on her reining technique.

Her arms tightened for better control. This time around, she navigated a straight path toward the big tree.

"Pass the oak and rein left toward the redbud." He walked up the yard abreast of the horse. Nearing the cottage, he caught Arie peeking out of her kitchen window as the riding lesson moved into her backyard. His pleasure heightened when she stepped onto the porch and sat on the top step.

Valor passed Arie, flashed a quick smile, and straightened her rein-controlling arms.

Arie passed the greeting back with a minimized nod so as not to cause any trouble.

He tipped his hat to her from a distance, letting her know she had not escaped his notice, and then focused on his student. "Left again. Want the horse to trot this last length?"

Valor stiffened in the saddle. "No way. I'm good with the walking pace today." The horse's left ear rotated from front to side, as if anticipating a gait command that never came. At the catalpa tree, she freed one hand and pulled down the red bandana that marked out the end of the course. "Where to now? Do I head back to the corral?"

"No. Let's leave Chica out. I'll be riding over to check the herd this morning. Head toward Arie's porch, and I'll tie the reins for you."

"Sure thing. Thanks for the riding lesson, Jusdyn."

"You're doing great. Soon you won't need me at all." He knew that to be all too true.

She reined left and walked the horse up the center of the yard with perfect posture, like she was riding into center ring at a ribbon ceremony. The lesson ended as she pulled back on the reins, stopping the horse's muzzle at the porch railing. "Morning, Arie."

"Beautiful riding, Valor." Arie tracked a bluebird as it crossed the backyard.

"I think you're next." The girl dismounted and chased the bird a few steps.

Striding toward them, he had to tip his hat brim to hide his smile.

Arie seemed hesitant to stand. "Oh, I don't know about that."

"Breakfast is ready," Muriel called from the rear of the big house. "I need Valor in for breakfast."

"Be right there, Aunt Muriel. Are you coming Jusdyn?"

He shook his head. "Tell Mom I'll be two steps behind you." His gaze fixed on Arie while he took the reins and tied them to the porch railing.

She stepped toward the railing. "Oh, Valor. Thanks for sending the wheat weaving over last night. It's darling."

"I'm getting better at it, but some shapes are harder than others."

"Well, the heart shape should be the easiest of all because it bears the greatest message."

"I like that." She turned and ran for the ranch house.

He waited for the screen door to slam before he addressed the next issue. "Have you thought anymore about the rock house?" Determined to be intentional on this particular subject until he got it worked out, he pushed toward an outcome he favored. Immoveable, he propped a boot on the bottom step.

Arie hesitated to stroke the horse's nose. "Yes, I have."

"And what? You're still going back this morning?" His voice has an unintended forceful edge. He swallowed hard to quell it, but a walnut-sized lump lodged in his throat.

"Yes, but only to pack my things. I'll be staying here at the cottage instead."

He exhaled through taut lips. "That feels like the right thing to do."

"I have a peace about it." She upped the wattage of her smile as if sealing a peace treaty.

"How about we go over together this morning? Then Dad and I can pick you up in the truck later this afternoon."

"Okay, Jusdyn. That sounds like a plan."

"Great. Want to come over for breakfast?"

"No thanks, I've already eaten. We saved some leftovers from the party in my kitchen last night."

"All right. I'll be back for you in fifteen minutes." He checked the knotted reins and rubbed the horse's flank as he walked away.

"I'll be ready, cowboy."

He turned back to face her from across the yard. "By the way. Valor was right about one part." A crooked smile played along with his tease.

"What part is that?"

"*Your* riding lesson is next." He headed toward the big house with one more smug victory under his belt. He was gaining ground, and it wasn't even nine o'clock yet.

~

"The County's attorney has brought their first offer for the Helmick land to my office. Would you like to set up an appointment to come in and review it with me?"

"No, that won't be necessary," TJ replied. The first phase would play out his way, cold and calculated though it may seem. The attorney would have to follow his lead.

"Shall I tell you the amount of the offer?"

"No, I'm not interested. Tell them the landowner declines their first offer."

"Aha. I sense a chess game in the making."

"I've heard that planning and permitting a landfill is a lengthy process that requires jumping over a whole series of hurdles."

"Yes, that's right. Zoning changes, environmental issues, and road improvements for access. The prelude for establishing such a facility does make for an up-and-down journey, I assure you."

"So my intention is to be the city's first difficulty. The purchase offer is declined."

"Fine. I'll make the call this afternoon."

"Plan to notify me promptly when that second offer comes in."

"Expect a reply by midweek, possibly Thursday at the latest."

"That sounds good. Should it come in any later though, I'll be out-of-pocket for the symphony set up all day Friday."

"Ah, our shining musical gem set upon the rugged beauty of the prairie. I find myself drawn to it like a grasshopper to the proverbial light bulb."

"Well then, I'd better get the power generator up and running." TJ snapped the cell phone shut and tried not to think about losing two days of productivity to the performing arts. *Things will definitely be different for me by next year's event. They absolutely have to be.*

~

Much to Jusdyn's surprise, Arie stood on the back porch feeding leftover carrot sticks to Chica when he returned from breakfast. "Flatten out your hand a bit more." He hoped to prevent a pain-filled nibbling history from repeating itself.

"Like this?" She cupped her hand to cradle the carrots.

He placed his hand under hers. "Lay it out more like this." He wove his fingers into hers and flattened her palm. With his free hand, he centered the carrot treat and together they offered it to the receptive horse. "Are you ready to go?"

"Yes, I've decided to leave my things here since I'm coming back."

"I like that line of reasoning. Travel light and leave only footprints between your origin and destination."

"And the journey will bring you right back around to where you're supposed to be."

"Step over here so we can get you on the horse." He untied the reins and held them in one hand. "Remember, always mount from the left."

"Does it really matter to the horse?"

"Well, it sort of helps the animal anticipate the rider. Now, your left foot goes here." He held the stirrup steady.

"Am I sitting in the saddle?"

"Yes, you're riding solo to the end of the driveway so you can get a feel for it. Reach up and hold here and here." He placed her hands strategically on the saddle. "Now, swing up."

She straddled the horse like a riding pro. "Who gets the reins?"

"You do, Miss Arie." He handed the knotted leather straps up to her. "Tighten the slack a little, and you're ready to head out. I'll trail you a few steps so Chica has to follow your lead."

"Where's the accelerator?"

"Right here." He grabbed her left heel and positioned it for maximum effect. "Give a gentle kick on both sides."

She tried it without hesitation making the horse step away from the porch. "She's not going to run, is she?"

"Not right now." He trailed her up the sloping driveway without a hitch. "If you can move back onto the blanket, I'll take the saddle now unless you want to drive."

"Oh, no. Be my guest." She reined in the horse and stopped abreast the mailbox. Once at a standstill, she relinquished the position of authority for the passenger seat.

He mounted, throwing his right leg forward over Chica's neck, conveniently lowered in pursuit of mischief. "Uh-oh." He spotted a problem as he brought up the reins. A delicate clematis blossom dangled out of the horse's mouth. "We're sure to hear back from that mistake, Chica." When she giggled, he cued the horse forward without warning.

His passenger grappled for a handhold. "Wait. Where's the dashboard on this thing?"

"Right here, Arie." He found her arms and wrapped them around his midsection. "Now, the closer we keep our weight centered, the better it will be for the horse."

"I can scoot up." She slipped next to the cantle and tightened her hold. "Is this better?"

The surefooted horse found its rhythm on the compact dirt of Road Z as Jusdyn flushed with magnetic attraction at the proximity of his rider. Short of breath, he lowered the brim of his hat to match the rising sun. With her cheek soon riding against his shoulder blade, the prairie seemed more amicable because they journeyed together. As they turned south toward the McLauren pasture, the vista opened out to an unrestricted horizon of grass.

"Look there, Uncle Doug's handiwork from Father's Day." He pointed to the repaired water gap which boasted an additional strand of barbed wire with a shiny new fence stay laced in place.

"I like the dangling rock. It looks old-timey."

"Oh, it is, but that technique still works like a charm." After a length of mesmerized riding, the top of the pines became visible as the morning sun increased its dominion over the land. Diamond Springs valley lay hazy in the distance. He stopped the horse at the pasture lane and drank in the combination, a blend of sight and touch. Calves blinked with incredulous innocence from the loafing shed. In the pause, the horse shook its bridle.

"What are you thinking about?" Arie tapped a finger on his chest as if to prompt a reply.

He bowed his head, trying to center himself under the dizzying spell. "I'm thinking that you're beautiful." He reined the horse left onto the pasture lane. When her arms crossed his chest in a wordless hug, he responded cowboy-style by bringing the horse into a level gallop up the length of the lane.

She buried her head between his shoulder blades until the beast came to a stop in front of their favorite set of gates.

"Can you open this latch, or would you like me to?"

"Let me try." Arie slipped off the horse's hind quarters. She approached the double gates and fumbled with the constricting wire, but it failed to yield. "Looks like you'll have to after all."

He slid off the horse without effort and reached a hand toward the gate.

She refused to stand aside, as if guarding the double gates with her back. "Guess this is where it all started for us, really." She lifted her chin as if to make a point.

The plotting look in her eyes caught him off guard. "Yeah, I guess so."

"Would you do anything differently if we could go back?" She climbed up onto the lower rail as if to reenact her original perch.

He adjusted his hat in contemplation. "Well, maybe this time around I could try to get something under your head to break the fall." He slid his hands around her trim waist and set the baling wire free, enjoying the complication of her presence.

With a coy smile, she climbed higher atop the gate. "That's truly noble of you, Jusdyn. Still, if I had been looking at you that day, instead of vice versa, I think you would have been the one taking the fall."

Even at this close range, he found her impish behavior charming, but knew that he had the physical advantage of position. "Oh, is that so?" He shoved the twin gates open with moderate force. When her heels slipped off the pipe rail, she landed into his waiting grasp. "Who's falling now?" he whispered, drawing her closer. The horse snorted, impatient to enter the pasture.

She slid her arms around his neck. "You tell me, cowboy. Who is falling?" Her tease ended in a touch of lips and a hint of prairie breeze.

Something shifted full circle as he kissed her at the gate, from headache to healing, plummeting him into a flowing river of life-filled emotion. He laced his fingers into hers and then placed her hand over his heart to assure her the journey would be made together. Overhead, the pines made time stand still.

~

Whitewashed stones gleamed in the morning light, greeting the lone visitors at Wilsey Cemetery. The car stopped in the back corner at the end of a gravel lane. Valor jumped out of the passenger side and searched out the small cornerstone etched with the letter M. "I found it."

The driver moved to the trunk of the car and flipped it open. "Can you come help me bring the flowers?"

"Sure thing, Aunt Muriel." She ran to the back of the car.

"Are you remembering to be respectful where you walk?"

"Yes ma'am. I am now anyways." The child filled her hands with the little terra cotta pots that had debuted at the Gator Get, now filled with portulaca plants.

"You did a nice job painting those flowerpots by the way."

"That was part of my fun leading up to the race. It doesn't seem so bad that I'm by myself so long as I stay busy."

"Well, what if you could spend more time with us instead of being alone? Would that suit you?" Muriel took a larger planter out of the trunk and led up to the headstone.

"Oh, my gosh. That would be super. Can I put my little pots in place now?"

"Yes, go along dear."

"Where should I walk, in front or in back?"

"Always walk behind the headstone. That's part of being respectful."

"Does that mean no one's buried back here yet?"

"No, not yet. That's where your Great-grandpa Vernis wants to be buried, and over there, Great-uncle Morrill." Muriel pulled out a pair of clippers from her apron pocket and began to trim overgrown crabgrass around the base of the headstone.

Valor held a distinct fondness for the stair-step marble markers framing the ill-fated McLauren children's graves. The barely legible first initial led to her favorite cemetery game, which she called Guess My Name. She assigned a matching name to the letter which she could then use for the duration of the visit, like naming teddy bears at a tea party.

"Which one is this again?" She tapped the tallest stone.

"The oldest, she was stillborn. You know, she never lived from birth."

"Oh, that would be Olivia. Hope you like red and yellow flowers, Olivia. I've always admired the dove on your stone." She returned for two more pots. "Now, these next ones were drowned in the big flood."

Her great aunt paused to watch her act out the tender drama. "That's right, Valor. That was around nineteen-forty when the Neosho River rose and flooded all of downtown Council Grove."

"Was that before the McLaurens lived at the farmstead in Wilsey, Aunt Muriel?"

"No, I really don't think so, Valor. But we can ask your great-grandpa tomorrow."

"He doesn't ever want to talk about the old days much."

"He will, honey. If you ask him nicely, he will."

The child grabbed the remaining flowerpots and interspersed them down the stair-step monuments. "Here Lilly, Willow, Buttercup, and Anemone. Wish you could have made it out of the flood so I could have known you. We'll all play together in heaven one day. Until then, enjoy these flowers I brought you."

She patted the little lamb of stone on top of the last marker, caressing it like a real animal. Then she plucked some grass and pretended the lamb could eat from her hand. "I want a butterfly on my gravestone, Aunt Muriel."

"Oh? Why a butterfly, Valor?"

"Because they're so gentle and free. Plus, they're never far from a beautiful flower."

"That would be perfect for you. Now, help me get this big planter in the ground for Great-grandma Dottie." Muriel dropped the clippers in her pocket as Valor walked behind the stones and joined her in lifting the planter into place. "Well, what do you think?"

"The daisies make it extra special."

"Those were her favorites. Please bring me the watering can out of the trunk."

Valor broke into a run. She fished the slender-necked container out of the trunk and waddled back to the headstone. "Can I do the pouring?"

"Yes, you may, dear. So tell me, would you be willing to help me with the garden if you came to stay with us this summer?"

"I most certainly will. For now, I'm happy to water these thirsty flowers."

~

Jusdyn shifted the truck into second gear, excited about his destination.

"Talked to Deke this morning," Loren said. "The baler's out of whack, and he's got hay to cut between now and wheat harvest."

"Wow, if you add the baby coming to that schedule, he's got a full month. Were you able to get it fixed?"

"Nope, we had to order a part. It'll be here a week from Wednesday."

"Did you remember to talk about his CRP plans?"

"Oh, we talked all right. He's got his mind set on throwing back those eighty acres."

"Well, Dad. It seems like you're not totally buying into the idea," He glanced across the cab at his predictable father. "Is there something you're not agreeing with him about?"

"Nope, I think he's dead on-track with what needs to be done."

"What's the hitch then? Is it the enrollment?" He took the truck up to third gear.

Without answering, the rancher rolled his window down and crooked his elbow halfway out, then adjusted the side-view mirror.

His mind raced through the potential obstacles. "The problem is TJ, isn't it?" His jaw locked so tight his teeth hurt. The weighted silence of non-disclosure spread between them as the front tire hit a loose rock.

"Well, TJ might have expressed some disillusionment to me at the party yesterday." Loren held his gaze out of the window.

Unsatisfied, he downshifted for the intersection of Road AA. "Like what?"

"Like CRP, I mean the entire program, could be on its last leg. That's what." His father squirmed in his seat.

He contemplated the sober ramifications of ending federally subsidized conservation of restored segments of tallgrass prairie. Loss of grass, loss of habitat, and loss of wildlife all measured out as negative. "Sorry, Dad. I'm looking for the silver lining, but I just don't see one."

"I think it's all political. The new administration will come in by year's end and insist on putting their stamp on the Ag Department, clear out some dead wood personnel, and propose updates to the Farm Bill. We've seen such rash actions before and weathered it just fine."

"So where does TJ stand?"

Loren surrendered the valley view to look him straight in the eye. "TJ thinks we should take the lame horse called CRP out behind the barn and shoot it."

His chest tightened. "Just give up on conservation like it has no value to the land? Really? Is that the right answer?"

"Jusdyn, I think TJ's losing touch with what's really important. Sometimes personal trauma can do that to a man."

He pulled up to a dead stop in front of the rock house where his maternal ancestors had homesteaded. "Can you tell me exactly what he said?"

His father glanced back and forth from the rock house to Jusdyn, holding his peace.

"You've got to help me understand TJ, Dad, to keep me from flat-out hating him." Tension grew muck deep.

Loren's gaze dropped to his boots. "TJ admitted he's fallen out of love with the land."

A warning siren blared inside Jusdyn's head. Such an ominous admission could only stem from the gangrened root of selfish motivation. Losing one's love for the land equated to falling out of faith with God. Both were a bottomless pit. Considering his pivotal role in the Conservation Service, TJ's attitude could bring far more harm to the land than good, like a strategically placed double agent ready to sell out to the highest bidder. The sirens escalated with each level of sizzling realization while his father sat motionless and mute.

"Never speak against the land," a woman spoke into the truck window.

The siren in his head silenced under her message's drenching effect. He turned and found Arie standing beside her Uncle Doug.

Eyes glinting, her entire countenance seemed ablaze with righteous indignation. "One must never speak against the land." This time, her tone sounded softer as if to beg.

So halted by her crystalline delivery, he sat behind the steering wheel, unable to respond. The truth of her message echoed through his thoughts, erasing TJ's damaging rhetoric. The quenching effect lowered his pulse.

Doug broke the heaven-placed impasse with a shuffle of his boot. "Here's your baking angel, all packed and ready to go."

"Pass her over." He reached for his door handle certain he'd made the catch-of-the-day.

~

The pot lid belched under a full head of steam as Muriel checked the corn-on-the-cob. "What are you drawing in there?"

"Oh, how beautiful the cemetery looked today." Valor added a few finishing strokes to her sketch of the marble stones. "I'm going to give this picture to Great-grandpa Vernis."

"That's thoughtful of you, honey." She flipped the switch on the oven door to illuminate the foil-covered meatloaf inside.

"Is Arie coming over, Aunt Muriel?"

"Why, yes, she is. We're celebrating her tonight as our newest neighbor."

"I bet Jusdyn's glad."

"We're all glad, honey. Now, finish up and help me set the table. There'll be five of us."

~

This would be Arie's first night in her new home, one with a real floor and windows with screens. She sat on the edge of the bed, weaving her hair into a loose braid for sleeping. First the porch swing had squeaked through its fair hour of courting, and now the crickets announced bedtime from outside her bedroom window. A dry throat made her pursue a quick sip of water before turning in. She flipped a switch, and the living room light illuminated. "May I truly be grateful for this home," she prayed aloud, walking through to the kitchen. "And may the work of this kitchen—the pies that come out of it—somehow bring a glimmer of your light into this world." She filled a small glass with sweet well water.

Stepping back into the living room, she stopped to admire the small antique vanity by the fainting couch. A homemade piece, the framed mirror had been notched into the back by some novice woodworker of days gone by. She drank the water until gone, and when she lowered the glass, the silver lining on the vanity's mirror seemed to warble before her eyes. Blotches appeared next and light spots dappled the surface. For the briefest of seconds, she could make out the image of a grainy marble statue—a lamb of stone— and then the surface blurred into silvery nothingness again.

Chapter 11

For angiosperm plants, the pinnacle of growing season occurs after the showy parade of blooming flowers. Seed production is the finely appointed grand marshal of the parade and anchors the final float in crowning style. Each plant's consummate purpose is to generate seeds to assure propagation of the species, house the seed in an irresistible jacket, and stand ready to detach the pod at a moment's notice should a dispersal agent happen by. Whether blown, snagged, or eaten, the seed must venture out, hope for deposition onto suitable substrate, and settle into germination mode. Though a myriad of obstacles stand in the way of this desired outcome, nature paints the fruits bright red, sweetens their flesh with fructose, and places them just outside of ladder's reach.

Jusdyn centered his attention on the cherry tree. "I give it two more days—tops."

Muriel passed a clothespin to Valor. "You know what that means?"

"A cherry-picking jubilee is coming," Valor replied with exuberance.

Arie touched a low limb and the cherries bounced off her fingertips. "Cherry pies by the end of the week. I can hardly wait. And look how loaded the tree is."

"A little overloaded, if you ask me." Loren bent double to shove a brace board under a sagging branch.

"That's the mother lode you've got there, Dad."

"Guess I shouldn't complain since we didn't get any cherries last year due to the late freeze." Loren straightened and rubbed his back. "I've missed my cherry preserves."

"You can't dispute the orchard's promise." Muriel snapped out the next article of laundry to be hung by her apprentice.

"What promise is that?" Arie asked.

Jusdyn flashed her two fingers. "It goes something like this. What gets withheld for one spring, nature attempts to double the next. It's like the tree is trying to make up for a lost opportunity so it compensates by making more once conditions turn favorable."

Muriel picked up her basket. "I don't think I've ever seen the cherry tree this full before."

Arie spotted what looked like a deformity. "Look. Instead of growing paired at the stems, the two fruits have fused together."

Valor joined her at the tree's edge. "Yeah, like Siamese twins. We studied those in school."

"That's going to get a little tricky come pitting time." Loren kicked at the board to set it in place. "I'm always the lucky one, finding the escaped pit baked into my piece of pie."

He felt compelled to remind his father how fortunate they were. "At least you're eating pie. Hey, will we get double the pies since we have double the cherries, plus two cooks?" He glanced impishly between his mother and his new friend, sensing the win-win of his position.

"We'll sugar-pack and freeze a majority of the fruit, but eventually these cherries will turn into pies, if you ranch hands mind your manners." Muriel turned as if to leave for the house.

"I'll be thrilled to make you a pie, Ladder Man." Arie twirled in a slight tease.

"I bet you've got a secret ingredient for that, too." Engaging his brain too late, he slapped a hand over his mouth. When Arie shot him a disquieting look, guilt heated his cheeks.

"What secret ingredient?" Muriel asked.

"Oh, just a little something extra I put it in my crust to make it, you know."

Valor glanced between the two women. "Special?"

"Thank you, Valor," Arie replied. "Yes, to make it special."

"Well, everything done in secret will be made known—in due time." Muriel shifted the empty laundry basket to her other hip. "Valor and I need to head into town soon. Arie, I thought I might pick up a few not-so-secret ingredients called groceries while I'm in town. Would you like us to get you stocked up as well?"

"Would you please? I've started a short list of food and supplies. It's on my kitchen counter. Maybe I should double the sugar and flour if we're producing double the pies."

Finally, he sensed the traction he needed to claim a portion. "Now you're talking."

"Can I please come back after my lesson to get in on the cherry picking?" Valor's bottom lip quivered with the inquiry.

Muriel stole a look at Loren, who dusted off his hands. After a few moments of consideration, he gave a permissive nod, which Muriel passed on to Valor with a wink.

The spirited girl ran around the laundry basket singing a ditty. "Hurray for cherry pie. Yay for cherry pie! In two days' time there'll be cherry pie!"

"I'll call the Trail Bakery and let them know the pies will be coming at the end of the week this time." Arie touched the tree again as if sealing a pact for harvest.

"Don't plan to export all of them."

"You'll get your fair share, Ladder Man. I'll get that list for you, Muriel."

"I can run it back for you," Valor added.

"Great. And Muriel, would you mind if I cut some flowers later for the table?"

"No, you go right ahead. Spread the beauty all around."

"Jusdyn, would you like to come over for lunch?" Arie's face lit up with the offer.

"Hey, that sounds better than two bachelors cooking on a hot plate. What about it, Dad?" As he waited for his farming partner to respond, he realized that old habits were often broken across the threshold of something new—and much better.

"Nope, you two lovebirds count me out. Deke called earlier and the baler part came in early. They had one at the co-op in Alta Vista. Merrilee agreed to feed me lunch in exchange for the hard labor."

"I'd be careful using that particular term around Merrilee," Muriel warned. "Tell her I'll be back in Wilsey by six o'clock or so, in case anything starts happening with the baby."

"Will do. Jusdyn, you need to look over that Conservation Plan for the McLauren pasture. I left it on the breakfast table for you."

"I'd love to see that," Arie replied. "Could you bring it with you for lunch?"

"And take her the leftover meatloaf," Muriel added.

"Wow, meatloaf and stocking rates." He summarized his concerns. "Not exactly a real Cupid combo, is it?"

"That's how we keep it clean around here," Loren replied, his tone stern. "Work comes first, which keeps the devil's workshop at bay."

"Okay, Loren. Stop preaching and help us load the car." Muriel turned to the house leaving Arie giggling by the cherry tree.

Jusdyn shrugged his shoulders to break from his father's scrutiny. *Guilty before acting.* Some things never changed.

~

TJ arranged the canned goods to supply the cabin. *This is certainly a step in the right direction.* Okay, the camping cot could stand a little improving, but at least there was no reminder that he was sleeping single in a double bed like back home. Somehow, this place had a vacation feel despite having only traveled twenty miles. Next, he banged the Coleman propane stove onto the cardboard box.

What was the source of this air of freedom he managed to feel out here? Could it be that no one was watching him, or that no one had an expectation for part of his day? He briefly thought of a certain little someone, and then realized what he truly felt freed from the most. He was free from the guilt. Not guilt from being the black sheep of the family, as he enjoyed marching to that different drummer, or guilt of being a slacker at his job since the office staff had gradually come to expect it. It was being freed from the guilt of being a deadbeat dad, though he seemed more of a walking-in-the-shadow-of-death dad, since they still lived together.

Many times he had thought to close shop on their little attempt at family life in Americus. A scar on his timeline, it had become merely a place where his wife lived indiscreetly entwined with meth production and had been extricated from the family. At a loss about what to do with Valor, she spent way too much time without parental supervision. They lived too far from the rest of the family to link up. That's how he and Jesse had wanted it, equating distance with independence for themselves as a young couple. That unwise preference now faded into a sentence of solitary confinement for his daughter.

He produced a duffle bag full of spare clothes. *Maybe Aunt Muriel can be part of the solution.* She seemed to have a genuine affinity for Valor and wanted to have her around. She bought clothes for the girl and taught her how to craft things whenever they spent time together. That's the kind of attention Valor really deserved, someone who enjoyed her, not endured her. Would relinquishing custody be an act of sacrificial love, or a selfish shirking of responsibility? He questioned his own motivation, knowing others would, too.

Such a weighty proposition deserved more thought, but right now he had to prepare for the coming windfall, stir up a batch of product, and be done in time to show up for his day job's appointment at the McClintock farm just inside the county line. The blatant truth dawned on him—living a dual identity equated to twice as much work.

"Maybe I'm transitioning to the next rung up the ladder," he muttered to the cottonwood trees, opening the door to the bunker. An empty metallic bang echoed back up the lane, a hollow affirmation of his scheme.

~

Muriel guided Valor toward the aging men and prayed for some cooperation.

Vernis examined the lanky-legged child, squinting one eye. "Well, look here! If you ain't a whole head taller than the last time I saw you, I'll be a monkey's uncle."

"Hello, Great-grandpa." Valor hugged his neck with subdued demeanor.

"Good morning, Uncle Vernis." Muriel placed her hand over his and gave it a squeeze. "How are they treating you these days?"

"Muriel, the POWs at Delevan got treated better than they treat us." Vernis raised his voice, rousing Lettie's attention from the nurse's station.

When she shook her head at his loud railings, Muriel smiled with a knowing nod and continued her therapy session. "How's Uncle Morrill feeling this morning?"

"He's fine. They've got him over at the hospital running tests he doesn't need, filling the doctor's pockets with our retirement money."

"I wouldn't be too negative if I were you. Strokes can be tricky business. A prudent man knows how important an ounce of prevention can be."

"Yeah, well. You don't need a pound of cure if you're not sick to start with."

"Maybe you're right on this one, Uncle Vernis."

"Of course, I am."

"Look what I made for you." Valor held her drawing in front of him and waited.

"Oh, what's this?" He transferred the paper from her small hands into his feeble ones. "Why, that's Wilsey Cemetery, for sure. See these letters here?" A bent finger pointed at the McLauren headstone.

Valor beamed at his recognition. "Yes, sir."

"They're the deepest carved lettering in the whole cemetery."

"That's so people won't forget who the McLaurens are, right Great-grandpa?"

"That's a hundred percent right, honey."

"We put flowers out on Mother's grave yesterday, Uncle Vernis. And Valor here made flowerpots for all the children's graves."

"Well now, that was downright thoughtful of you."

"Could you tell me about the olden days, Great-grandpa? Tell me about those poor children." Valor pleaded with her hands folded together, just short of being melodramatic.

The old man looked into her hope-filled eyes and appeared to fade away.

When Valor gazed at her for guidance, Muriel nodded, pressing a finger to her lips.

"The first stone represents the oldest-born child who came still-born. Almost broke Mother's heart. Father said she left the cotton gowns she had sewn for the baby laying across the cradle until the day Muriel's mother was born."

"That's Grandma Dottie. Tell me what the 'O' stood for, Great grandpa. I can only read the 'O' on the headstone these days."

"They named the baby Opal just to have a name to write on the grave marker."

Muriel felt a hint of connection. "Does that have anything to do with Opal Litke, Uncle Vernis?"

"Just about everything, that's all. Mother's best friends were the Litkes in Council Grove. Mrs. Litke was about a month behind Mother in carrying her baby. To comfort her grieving friend, when Mrs. Litke gave birth to a healthy baby girl, they named her Opal."

Muriel recalled the precious stories her mother fondly retold. "And that Opal and my mother grew up to be best friends."

"Who was born next, after Grandma Dottie?"

"After Dorothy there came a string of boys."

"Were you the first?"

"Heavens no. You might find this hard to believe young lady, but I'm the baby." Vernis chuckled.

Muriel smiled as Valor absorbed this history lesson. It came as all part of her identity, the heritage of forefathers. And genealogy grew much more interesting when it could be shared out loud as opposed to printed on the page, where everyone becomes two-dimensional. When the girl inched her way onto his armrest, the old man placed his vein-ribbed hand on her knee. Muriel sensed porcupine quills being shed all over the floor.

"Now, the first boy would be Lloyd. He was a handful and a half." Vernis pointed to the second stone.

"Oops! That's the stone I called 'Lilly' yesterday."

"According to Dorothy, that kid was one hundred percent B-O-Y. Given the job of keeping him out of trouble, Dorothy found it nigh impossible to do." He thumped her knee as if to prove his point. "He liked to swing cats—by the tail." His eyes shone with the memory. His finger moved to the next stone depicted on the drawing, but then hesitated.

Valor traced a letter onto the paper. "This one is marked with a 'W' if that helps you remember. I called him 'Willow' yesterday."

"That ain't too far from being right, honey. The next boy would be Willard, born deaf he was. Since Lloyd led by only a year and a month, Willard followed him around like a shadow. Wherever you'd find one, the second would be right behind. Dorothy claimed that made it easier to keep up with them both."

"It must have been hard being deaf, never hearing the meadowlarks or water rushing in the creek." Valor's expression reflected the weight of the hardship.

"Dorothy claimed he had a remarkable way of living without hearing a sound. His eyes were keen, and he could pick up on most anything going on around him. And talk about strong. Sister used to call Willard 'the muscles' and Lloyd 'the brains' of the team."

They sat silent for a minute, he trying to remember while the child attempting to soak it all in. Muriel caught Lettie trying to approach with her medication chart and waved her off.

Lettie responded by tapping her watch and flashing ten fingers.

"That brings us to 'B' now, Great-grandpa. I know 'Buttercup' can't be right for a boy."

"No honey. Burton was next." He slid a finger to the fourth stone. "He lived to be five. Loved to play marbles and always came home covered with dirt from it. Mother would dunk him in the spring tank over Father's objections, but it worked quicker than a wink." His facial furrows aligned in a smile.

Muriel couldn't remember the last time she'd seen Vernis with such a positive countenance. *What a moment to cherish.*

"And that was our whole clan: Opal, Dorothy, Lloyd, Willard, and Burton. Then the rest you know all too well, Morrill and me, Vernis."

"What about 'Anemone'—the 'A' etched on the fifth stone?" Valor traced the lamb of stone with her fingertips.

Vernis hesitated, either struggling to recall or refusing to do so. He locked gazes with Valor and deferred. "You might have to ask Uncle Morrill, honey. After all, I was just a baby."

~

Jusdyn slid out the back door of the big house, meatloaf and conservation plan in hand. He couldn't help feeling light as a feather on the inside. Momentarily indecisive as to whether to go to the front of the cottage or hop up on the back porch, Arie helped make the decision for him with a slam of the kitchen door.

"Come back here." She set the tray on a makeshift table made complete with floral bouquet in the shaded corner of the deck. When she turned toward the steps, the hem of her white gauze dress caught the breeze and flared. "Welcome, cowboy. I've been expecting you."

Haloed by the midday sun, Arie's image turned transformational for him, like a ray of light spreads into a rainbow as it passes through a prism. Emotion overruled thought, and he halted for a moment to treasure the way it filtered through him.

"Jusdyn, come on up." She motioned for him with a hint of question. When he didn't respond, she stepped down and took the meatloaf and papers from his hands, placed them on the table and came back for him. "What is it?" she whispered, tipping her head to one side.

He folded his fingers across hers and drew her down a step toward him. Time stood still, at peace with his world and momentarily at war with the words to declare it. "Arie. I—" He had to swallow to control his constricting throat. "I'm falling in love with the girl next door, but I haven't been able to tell her yet."

Arie descended one more step. "I think she'd like to know such wonderful news."

He could see the golden flecks gleaming in a sea of hazel green. "Before you came, I had everything right here." He lifted a hand and swept past a horizon full of familiar features. "Then there you were, out on the land loving it the way I do. For that, you gained my admiration."

"Thank you," she whispered, her eyes misting. She rested her cheek on his chest a fleeting moment and then looked up as if expecting more.

He sensed her trembling and stepped up, taking her into his arms. "Something happened to me back in the garden with you Sunday. I knew it would be a special place to show you, and something in my heart-of-hearts compelled me to get you there before everyone crowded around us. Watching you there so purely adoring the beauty in the garden helped me see the grace inside you. When you walked around touching everything like you were blessing it with your fingers, I began to hope you'd come touch me too, so I would be part of the blessing like the rest."

"And I came to you."

"Yes, you came to me. And since that very moment, I haven't been able to consider the prairie without thinking about you being here on the land with me." He kissed her and whispered into her hair. "Tell me that I can be a part of what you came back to find on the prairie."

~

Arie opened her eyes and saw a man of strength who needed to move forward for the prairie's sake, but could no longer go alone. "When God drew me back to the prairie, I honestly didn't expect there would be someone like you. Sitting on that gate, I celebrated that view down into Diamond Springs valley in full adoration of the Creator who made it all."

"Then I came along and shattered your tranquility."

"Then you came along, and the Lord allowed you to take away what He only meant for a short season, my contentment to be alone on the prairie."

"Did you have to fall?" He touched his nose to hers.

"I suppose I did—away from myself and into your arms. The prairie is a life force for me, but now it somehow seems magnified when I'm by your side. For the first time, I'm only partly content—unless I'm with you."

"Do you feel something special beginning?"

"I do – with all my heart."

"I love you, Arie."

Her eyes misted with sincerity. "Jusdyn, I love you, too."

He closed the distance between them and sealed his affections with a lingering kiss. When they parted, he let out a raucous cowboy holler, making her laugh. "Now, wasn't this a lunch invitation?"

"Come over here," she replied, pulling him up the steps. "I'm dying to know about your stocking rates anyway."

~

"Good afternoon, Dr. Vorchenski. I'm Muriel Linquist, Valor's great aunt. Please come in." Muriel made a gracious gesture with her arm and the large man teetered into the doorway.

"My pleasure, I assure you." He brushed his thinning hair into place, and then glanced at his student who stood smartly dressed, her flaxen hair tamed in neat braids. "Good afternoon, Valor. You look very nice today."

"My Aunt Muriel takes really good care of me."

"Would you have a few extra minutes before the lesson begins to discuss Valor's future with me, Dr. Vorchenski?"

"Why yes, of course. Nothing would please me more."

"Valor, please go pack an overnight bag for three more days at our house."

"Yes, ma'am. I'd be happy to," she replied, disappearing into the back.

Muriel led the music professor to an untidy dinette table. A distasteful smirk stole across her face. "I'm sure you're quite use to excusing this house for its state of disarray."

"Madam, I'd come to an igloo if Valor waited inside, ready to learn music."

"Very well then. I'm assisting some old family friends who want to insure that Valor has an opportunity to advance her education at college. The financing they're making available will likely have some restrictions, but I hope to advise them on the best use of these funds, once the time comes for Valor to select a school."

"This is a very noble undertaking, Mrs. Linquist. I commend your interest in Valor, as she seems a bit lacking in care." He gave her a knowing look.

His pointed comment pierced a thin spot in her forbearance. She shifted in her chair. "I wanted to ask your professional opinion about Valor's musical ability so that I might know how to both encourage her talent and possibly channel it in the future. Could you be forthright with me regarding her ability to play the violin?"

He sat contemplating for some time, his hands pressed together on the burnt orange tabletop. He began to count on his fingers. After a time, he seemed ready to make some measure of recommendation. "I regret that I cannot help you as much as I would like to. Valor is rather young, at this point, to say what would be appropriate in the future. My deepest regret is that, by the time she is college-aged, I plan to be in full retirement. So you see, my regret is largely based on the fact that I am so old, and she is so young." His eyes twinkled with sincerity. "Even so, I have committed myself to her instruction in this interval of time, to challenge her onward, knowing this is what time I've been given."

"But does she have the talent it would take to major in music? This factor alone would greatly affect the choice of school that would be best for her. Please give me your professional opinion." Muriel furrowed her brow, not knowing what to expect, but needing some increment of expert assessment. "Dr. Vorchenski, you work with music majors every day and must see the best talent come and go. Do you sense that Valor could excel in a similar manner?"

He closed his eyes as if to draw the comparison between a mere sprite of a girl and an accomplished performer. He held his face in his hands, weighing his contemplations. At last, he turned to face her. "Valor has pure talent on the violin. As a gift, it is rare. It comes to her effortlessly, like breathing air. She takes up my instruction at a pace unparalleled by any other student. If she were not given an opportunity to receive college-level instruction, it would be a travesty to the civilized world." He shook his head as if to ward off that outcome.

Muriel's skin tingled down the full length of her arm. Having sensed there might be something exceptional about Valor's musical expression, she needed to have this conversation.

"However, I do feel some obstacles must be overcome for Valor to be successful as an adult." He lowered his voice. "When I visualize Valor on stage performing, the individuals standing with her pose no problem, but the individuals standing *behind* her are most problematic. If she cannot get the proper support during her childhood, she will be hauling a cello case full of self-esteem issues into adulthood. This travesty need not be, and those of us responsible enough to insure her well-being ought to take countermeasures in that positive direction."

"Could you write a letter stating your professional

recommendations so that I might have a record, should I need this level of support?"

"Yes. I'll draft a letter tomorrow."

"And as for schools you'd recommend?"

"Emporia State University would be privileged to have her, though I am uncertain as to whom my successor will be. Another possible consideration would be Wichita State University, with their Fine Arts Department. That would put her further from the family, of course."

"What about East Coast schools?"

"They would fall from contention. You understand why, of course. Valor must stay on the prairie as it is her other love." He spotted the girl approaching and fell silent.

Muriel beckoned her to the table, placing her arm around the child's waist. "Dr. Vorchenski, I will always treasure your superior assessment of Valor's violin skills, as I know she values your lessons. You have given her a distinguished beginning on a difficult instrument, for which our family sincerely thanks you."

"This is how the music lives on, you see. First, it passed from my mentor to me, and now extends to Valor."

She reached for her violin case. "I'm ready for my lesson."

The professor smiled. "To me, the music begins already. We'll show them Saturday, won't we Valor? Yes, we shall show them all."

Chapter 12

Only a handful of indigenous elements contrast with the pastel, placid nature of the prairie. Amid the soft-hued whites, lavenders, pinks, and yellows of midsummer comes the intense orange of butterfly milkweed. Its enigmatic chromatic ovation is both well received and frequently visited by every butterfly in the two square-mile area. As for wildlife, among the gently living thirteen-lined ground squirrels and eastern cottontails, the American badger unabashedly digs his den and establishes a territory. Measure-for-measure the most powerful carnivore on the prairie, this low-slung, shoulder-driven excavator comes equipped with recurved claws and an irreverent attitude toward trespassers. The conspicuous dirt mound left at the entrance to his burrow should be read like the skunk's stripe, an undisguised non-invitation to visit. Though some have seen the reverie of the prairie riding on the back of a bee and its clover, a more accurate representation may be a tranquility borne on the shoulders of a well-fed badger left alone in the vastness of its preferred solitude.

Arie leaned across the lunch table, trying to get a closer look at the conservation plan.

"Here we're supposed to 'restore and conserve rare declining vegetated communities and associated wildlife species.' That's what Dad calls boilerplate language. They just cut and paste it into all the conservation plans." Jusdyn's face clearly showed his frustration with the system.

"How will such a broad-brush approach help anyone know how to take specific care of their land?"

"Oh, it obviously won't. And listen to this part. 'Use environmentally sensitive prevention, avoidance, monitoring, and suppression strategies.' That's more boilerplate."

"Why would they assume every rancher needs to manage for the same set of problems when every tract of land is unique? Tell me how you can cut and paste a management plan that works for everyone?"

"When you're trying to save time, you have to resort to blanket coverage instead of being specific." He shifted in his chair, unsettled. "In this next part, they get down to the nitty-gritty."

She glanced at the photos showing a survey team establishing transects for sampling cover species. In the third photograph, a young female assisted the conservation officer by tallying the plant inventory on a record sheet. Finally, she saw something she could relate to.

"This botanical evaluation is crucial to maintaining and restoring the land as habitat and forage. Regrettably, I have to admit that I'm weak at this part. Most of my coursework in range management centered on the needs of the herd, so I opted to ignore the plants."

"Maybe that's my role as part of this team. I know most of the names of the native flowers, and some of the grasses, too. What if I taught you?"

"I think you're onto something, Plant Lady. Now, let me show you the rest. It's pretty impressive. Here's where the animals come in. 'Graze at a stocking rate which will maintain or improve the quality of desirable vegetation.' Get this—that stocking rate is really a mathematical calculation based on years of research at K-State."

"That's the real Wildcat power." She angled to get a laugh out of him and it worked.

"Ranchers around here typically go with either a cow-calf operation or raise yearling steers. The foxy term AUM—for Animal Unit of Measure—differs for each group."

"So, the math helps you figure out how much pasture to allow for each member of the herd, right?"

"Give the pretty lady in the front row an 'A' for today's lesson."

"You know that pasture on the northwest corner of Wilsey Road and Highway Fifty-six that looks so beaten down?"

"Right, the landowner has severely overstocked that ground. You can see how the land takes a direct hit under range mismanagement. Economics makes you want to manage for the short-term, but the land must be managed for the long-term for the best possible outcome."

"Something tells me I'll need a little practice on this transect thing."

"Let's go over to the west pasture where I'll show you our grazing cage. Who knows? We might even get to see Deke cutting his hay next door, if we're lucky."

"I'm up for it. Maybe I'd better put on some jeans for this assignment."

He descended several steps before turning back to her. "Let me look at you one more time all dressed up."

Unabashed, Arie twirled around the deck like an evening primrose in full bloom. When he patted his chest and left, she tucked a tiny bloom into her braid to savor the tender moment.

~

Opal glanced over the top of the newspaper while her younger sister lost herself in a scrapbook of remembrances. Ruby's fingers slipped silently across the torn and re-taped pages, looking back over their many years as good citizens of the town of Council Grove. Regret pricked her heart as she lingered over the page featuring the wagon train reenactment at the Last Chance Store in the era of the Santa Fe Trail. There on the store porch sat a youthful Morrill McLauren with ruggedly handsome features, holding a jug of molasses in his hands.

Opal recalled Ruby's role of clerk in the reenactment that day, warming right up to Morrill when he entered the store. Authentic to his part, Morrill had charmed Ruby onto his wagon so she could experience the prairie schooner's passage through town. But the charade had ended there, leaving her unrequited love an unspoken jewel of faith, like an engagement ring never summoned from its box. Thinking a distraction might do her a world of good, she glanced back to the newspaper. "Here's the first good news from the proposed landfill in Helmick."

"What kind of good news?"

"Headlines say 'Land Acquisition Stalled: Commissioners Work through Hurdle.' I personally hope they left their jumping shoes at home."

"There's got to be a better place than the old Helmick quarry to put that stinking pit. We ought to research that."

"You're not forgetting about our big date at the Symphony on the Prairie, are you?"

"Opal, the heart never forgets a date. I am still at a loss as to what to wear."

"Let's make it a day to remember." She closed the newspaper and shifted in the chair attempting to stand.

"The Lord will grant us a day for remembering." Ruby smiled down at the clipping in her lap. "I'm sure he will."

Opal exited for the kitchen, sensing it might not be the perfect day for romance. But she conceded that only God knows a man's heart. And he held the future in his hands.

~

Jusdyn's truck bounced over the uneven ground of the west pasture. The grass grew thick and high, dotted with flowering forbs in a natural array. "Dad and I have chosen to under-stock over here this year, putting in fewer head per acre than the formula allows." The validation of walking lightly on the land flooded his spirit.

"The grass looks thick and healthy to me." Arie craned her neck to help spot the cage.

"And that's our reward. Grazing the short season will have these cattle out of here by end of July. Then the grassland will have the remainder of the growing season to recover."

"The badgers can have the land back."

"Prairie grasses will contend with the native deer, not cattle. Where'd we move that grazing cage?" He steered the truck into a right angle turn when someone appeared in his rearview mirror. "Good grief, there's Deke. He looks a little frantic. We'd better double back." He whipped the truck around a stand of Baldwin ironweed coming into bloom. "Don't need those flowers anyway. Ironweed indicates overgrazing if it grows widespread in the pasture."

"Well, I think you managed to plow down the only patch in sight." She glanced to the south. "Hey, whatever this is about, we have plenty of time to help Deke."

"I probably should have called him before we left the house. Dad was over there so I assumed he had all the help he needed." He picked up her hand and kissed it in gratitude. As Deke climbed over the gate, he eased to a halt. "What's up, cousin?"

"I'm struggling to get this haying done, Just-man." Deke wiped his brow and inhaled.

He could read the worry etched into his cousin's face. "How about we get it done together? Let me go back to the barn and bring the tractor over to cut alongside you."

"What are you planning to swath with? I've already borrowed your dad's swather."

"He fixed grandpa's old swather last winter. I might have to baby it a bit, but she'll do the job. Go back and cut a center line for me. Then I can cut east of it."

"And I'll cut west."

Arie leaned across him to address Deke directly. "Speaking of baby, do you think Merrilee might like a little female companionship this afternoon? I could help her cook dinner."

"You're a saint, Arie." Deke flashed a boyish smile. "You both are."

"Naw, man, you know a Wildcat can't be a saint. Now, open the gate for us, will you?" He gestured at the latch and dropped the truck into gear.

Deke loosened the chain and guided the gate back into the pasture, then mounted his tractor and headed back across Road Z.

After passing through, Arie surprised him by jumping out to chain the gate shut.

Once she returned to the cab, he needed to ask another favor. "Ever drove a tractor before?" Out of the corner of his eye, he didn't miss her jaw drop at such a daunting prospect.

~

"Will Uncle Morrill be back at the nursing home by now?"

"He should be, Valor. Remember, we have groceries in the car, so we can't stay long. He may not be up to much visiting, depending on what they did at the hospital."

"Is he sick, Aunt Muriel?"

"No, honey. He's just old so the caregivers are being cautious, that's all."

"Does his brain still work okay? I mean, he understands me, doesn't he?"

"He understands you just fine. Uncle Morrill never liked to talk much. Now that he's older, he goes days without talking. Some people think that's how he copes with all the activity at the senior care facility."

"You mean he kinda shuts down on the inside to deal with the outside?"

"Exactly. Here we are. So it's five-thirty. We have to keep our visit under half an hour because they need to eat supper at six o'clock. Plus, we need to get back to Wilsey."

"I'll carry our secret in. No one will stop a polite child with such an innocent-looking package."

"Good plan." Muriel eased the car into a parking spot in the shade. They walked through the automatic door of the care facility without notice. Residents had been rolled into a commons area to await the opening of the dining hall. They found the McLauren brothers side-by-side in matching wheelchairs.

Muriel stooped so the aging man could recognize her face. "There you are, Uncle Morrill. I've brought little Valor back to see you."

Vernis reached across Morrill and placed his hand on Valor's arm. "Hey, hon. What kind of medicine are you toting in that white bag?"

"I can't say it out loud, but I can hand you one if you want." Valor slipped the cup out of the bag without fuss and handed it to him.

Morrill sat in silence, staring ahead. Then his hand rose ever so slightly.

Valor knit her brow to ask permission, and proceeded once Muriel nodded. "Great-grandpa, did you show my picture of the cemetery to Uncle Morrill?"

Vernis nodded. "I sure did, just like I promised. He took it into his own hands and looked at it real close. But Morrill ain't likely to answer any questions because they ran a tube down his throat for a while during his hospital lock-up."

"Oh, I'm sorry, Uncle Morrill," Valor melted across his wheelchair, sharing his trauma. "That storytelling about the lamb of stone can wait until another time. I hope you like that chocolate milkshake."

Morrill stopped drawing a sip through the straw and regarded the child for the first time. "Good," he said, a little scratchy but as plain as day.

"There you go, Valor. I think he likes our frozen treat."

The girl's eyes shone in response. "Uncle Morrill, how about we come back to see you and Great-grandpa Vernis on Friday when I come back through town?"

Vernis touched her arm. "We'd like that a lot."

"Good." Morrill eased his free hand up to his shirt pocket and brought out the folded drawing of the map, extending it to her.

Valor took it and pressed it to her chest. "I love you, Uncle Morrill. Love you too, Great-grandpa." She hugged both men around the neck.

Muriel pulled her away as the interns approached to roll the residents into the dining hall. Shaking their heads, the staff members took possession the treat cups though the brothers gained one last sip. Muriel fought to hold back a giggle as her accomplice escaped through the exit.

Valor settled into the passenger seat for the half-hour drive back to Wilsey. She unfolded the drawing and traced the line of headstones with her finger. "Aunt Muriel, it seems Uncle Morrill liked my drawing after all."

"How can you tell, Valor?" She eased the car out onto the highway. When her passenger flashed the image in her direction, she saw several new marks on the page. Four stones were marked with the letters 'Mc' above, but the lamb of stone bore a separate marking etched in jittery pencil.

Valor tapped the last stone. "It says right here, he thinks it's good."

"Very nice. How about we pray for everyone on the way home? I'm getting a little worried about Merrilee, so that's a good place to start."

"And the baby."

"Yes, Merrilee and the baby." One glance in the rearview mirror reflected where they had been, not where they were going. With a baby in the mix, the future was anyone's guess.

~

Sweat trickled down Jusdyn's back as he waited for his dad's verdict.

"Okay, the baler's good as new." Loren exited the machine shed with his pronouncement. He cradled the fingers of his right hand, wrapping them in his handkerchief.

"Dad, what did you do to your hand?"

"Oh, I managed to get the entire way through the job injury-free, only to bang my knuckles when closing the housing. Muriel will be home soon, so she can doctor me up."

Deke wiped his forearm. "Uncle Loren, thank you for getting that baler off the injured reserve list. I plan to tow it around come Friday and decorate the landscape with rectangular art."

"You've got your work cut out for you, Deke. It took both of you over five hours to get that hay meadow cut today." Loren glanced from Deke to Jusdyn.

"We saw a family of prairie chickens fly into the south pasture, Dad."

"Yeah, your grandpa used to talk about hearing them courting on the lek somewhere between here and the creek every spring. That's part of your heritage—if you can manage to keep them here."

"Yet another vanishing part of the tallgrass prairie well worth saving." Jusdyn felt this potential loss a little closer than most. Those bird sightings had grown pretty rare.

"I ought to give them back the brome field and save myself this workout." Deke stepped back toward the machine shed.

Loren turned toward him. "I'm ready to head home. Reckon Arie's ready to come back with me?"

"Let me go back with you and get cleaned up."

"Then you'll have both the truck and the tractor over here. How's that gonna work?"

He tried to reason through that scenario, but saw the immediate hitch. "Arie can drive one back home for me, and I'll drive the other."

Deke raised his heavy brows, adding comic relief to the moment of decision. "I'll put the swather away, and let the ladies know you'll be back in a few. But I'm not going to mention the driving dilemma to Arie. Merrilee would rather walk the distance than learn to drive a tractor."

He opened the passenger door. "Well, Merrilee has her own set of challenges ahead of her. They're bound to make driving a tractor look like a picnic."

"She's read all the natural childbirth books, if printed knowledge is worth anything."

"We'll see when the time comes. Experience is the real teacher." Loren favored his injured hand getting behind the wheel. "You're one day closer to fatherhood."

Deke pumped his arm in a power fist. "Bring it."

He cranked the window fully down as the truck started. "I'll be back in fifteen minutes for Arie."

Deke made a thespian bow as the vehicle exited the U-shaped drive and then disappeared through the back door.

"Dad, I know Deke's right about one thing. We've got too much brome growing for the amount of hay we need. Something's out of balance there that we could tighten up a bit."

"For starters, your grandpa probably overwintered more of his herd than we do now, so he needed a larger hay meadow. Plus, he had more horses to feed." Loren turned up the dial to hear his talk radio station.

He sat deep in thought, grappling with the problem as the sun lowered on the horizon. "Dad, what does it look like to throw back brome to native bluestem?"

"It's an all-out battle of the grasses. The brome doesn't want to give up—it's hardy."

Though his father shook his head as if to dissuade him, he spent the rest of the drive home searching for a way to sabotage the unwanted brome while building an alliance with the bluestem. Undeterred by the tough prognosis, he reveled in the challenge.

~

Arie looked up as Deke walked into the house. Lights were dimmed and soft lyrics crooned in the background as she massaged the swollen feet of her hostess.

He stopped dead in his tracks. "We're done at long last. Jusdyn went home with Uncle Loren to get cleaned up, Arie. He'll be back for you in fifteen minutes."

"Getting cleaned up sounds like a great idea, dearie." Merrilee shifted from her reclined position of total tranquility. "We're having dinner together, so go wash off the prairie."

"Hope there's some hot water left."

"Probably not. Arie's done three loads of laundry, changed the linens, made dinner, and now she's working on me."

Arie smiled up at him while folding the throw onto the sofa's back.

Deke snapped the light switch on with a mumble under his breath. "Water hog."

She locked gazes with Merrilee and giggled in conspiracy. A gain in order always came with a cost, so she launched a fleeting prayer that the water heater had recycled.

~

Jusdyn entered the darkened room, his eyes blinking like an innocent fawn. Lit candles floated in a cut-glass bowl at the center of the dinner table. Wonderful aromas drifted out of the open kitchen. Deke and Merrilee sat at the table, holding hands across the corner.

"Come on in, Ranch Hand." Arie crossed the dimmed space, sporting a borrowed apron with a serving spoon in hand. A quartet squeaked out a melody from the living room.

He halted, refusing to enter much beyond the welcome mat. "What's going on in here?"

She placed an encouraging hand on his folded arms, trying to ease him into the setting.

"Come on in, Dude." Deke gestured to his seat. "You'll like this setup. It comes with mouth-watering food."

Merrilee giggled. "We're having dinner together as two romantic couples."

"But I need to talk to Deke about my great idea for throwing back the brome field." He allowed Arie to lead him into the double date with measurable resistance.

Deke shook his head. "Switch gears, Just-man. We'll get together after dessert."

He leaned closer to Arie. "And exactly what's in this for me?"

"Herbed flank steak, garlic mashed potatoes, tender English peas, and a peach cobbler."

"Okay, I'm in." He sat like a gentleman at a fine restaurant. Her apron was printed with a provocative suggestion which sounded like a great idea. "May I kiss the cook?"

"That really depends." Arie walked back into the kitchen to tend the meal.

"On what?"

"On how well you can switch gears." She lifted a pot lid to stir the contents, looking beautiful with a face full of steam and a head-full of romantic diversion.

"Oh, I can switch quite well." He wiggled his eyebrows to catch their attention. "So very lovely of you to have us over." His polite tone rang a little insincere.

Merrilee tried but could not hold back the belly laugh so Deke braced her abdomen to protect it from bouncing through the outburst. In delayed response, a potholder flew out of the kitchen and landed squarely on his head.

"Strike one," Deke called, playing umpire while enjoying the lively courtship game.

Arie brought in an impressive platter of herb-speckled steak, trimmed with carrots. "Let's try to get through this meal without making Merrilee's water break, shall we?"

"Oh, I can turn serious as a heartbeat." He launched into playing the goof by tucking his napkin into his collar. When Merrilee guffawed and Deke again held back the labor levee, a second potholder sailed across the table, arriving on target for his midsection.

"Strike two!" Deke displayed his count with two fingers on his right hand.

Arie approached and retrieve the potholders. "Were you going to swing the bat tonight, Mr. MVP?" She tugged his homeboy napkin out of his collar and let it drift into his lap.

"Lady, tonight I'm swinging for the fence." He caught her by the waist, dipped her back, and planted a cook-appreciating kiss squarely on her lips.

Deke and Merrilee cheered from across the table.

"Well, well." Arie straightened, flushed at his advance. "That was a home run, for sure."

Jusdyn pulled out her chair. "Allow me to bring in the tender English peas."

"By all means."

After she rewarded him with a tightly tucked smile, he proceeded into the kitchen. The aroma of the succulent food overwhelmed him so he began to reframe the evening. *Maybe dating is better than killing brome.* Suddenly, he was starving.

Chapter 13

As a treeless plain, the tallgrass prairie bears a low-centered profile, its strength lying in its soil and the plant roots that hold it intact as a substrate. In cross-section, big bluestem touts a root system that can tunnel to a depth of six feet seeking hydration. Not only drought resistant, these roots anchor the plant in place, come what may, for the ambient atmospheric conditions above ground. In a typical weather pattern of wind with more wind expected, the slender blade shape minimizes desiccation, the basal meristem keeps the growth zone out of harm's way, and the length of the roots ties the whole bundle to the prairie's rooftop. Thus begins the endless highway of grass blown by the volume-less, variable wind. A truce is held between plant and air until the excessive combination of heat, wind, and evaporative condensation drops a hook, which starts to spin as a rotating cloud of sky trouble. All bets are off on the verge of a storm, and six feet deep takes on an entirely different meaning.

Arie blamed the late dinner on her inability to catch the mourning doves' first stanza of the morning. Nonetheless, she would be happy today because the cherries had ripened and the family would pick them together. Even Valor seemed to sense the pending fun and gained a reprieve to be included in the fruit harvest.

She finished her breakfast without sitting, hoping to have a few moments in the garden alone for her morning quiet time before the commotion of aluminum ladders began. Brushing through her hair quickly, she took the white satin ribbon into the front room where the lace curtains allowed the early light to suffuse. Laying the ribbon on the vanity, she worked her hands down the furrows of a braid. She brought the end in front of her shoulder and reached for the ribbon, knotting it in place then looping it in a bow.

One parting glance into the mirror proved to be her undoing. The mirror's silver backing rippled again and brought with it a strange sensation. She strained to receive a communication, like a sound in the night might prick one's ear. Once she gave a discernible nod to beckon it onward, the center of the mirror opened up to white. When the image sharpened, she could see some type of pail balanced on the shelf of a ladder. Cherries began falling into it from above until they spilled over the edge. All at once, the ladder angled and the pail began to tumble in slow motion. Though no longer able to see the container, she heard a distinctive snap. Then the image went blank, leaving the mirror to reflect a pale-faced onlooker.

Outside, aluminum ladders clattered against one another, bringing her back into focus for the day. After all, it was the much-awaited cherry picking day at the Linquist ranch. Determined to enjoy every minute of it, she grabbed two enamel bowls from the little red kitchen and exited the back door full of expectations. Should forewarned be forearmed, she would watch for tipping cherries and try to catch them as best she could—before the snap.

Cradling the bowls on her hip, she crossed the yard to the orchard. Two mourning doves perched on the seat of the sharpening stone in the implement garden took wing as she drew closer, punctuating the quiet morning with their crying wing strokes. The dew hung a heavy drape of liquid droplets on the cut flower garden and sewed sequins onto the spider webs.

She decided to pray with her eyes open to this magnificent expression of creation's glory so as not to miss even the tiniest butterfly. A fluid prayer of adoration and thanksgiving poured from her lips as she spoke aloud over the flowers and their rusty counterparts. She offered the confession portion in humility. Next, she launched her petitions for others.

In this portion, she had placed Jusdyn first on the prayer list since the day they had met. As he worked through decisions about the land, she would pray all the more fervently—for both discernment and protection. Praying for Valor, she touched a stem of horsemint as she asked for a balance of energy and a fullness of love to surround the child. She finished the prayer with a soft amen.

"Double amen," a deeper voice echoed from the far corner of the garage. "Good morning, Arie." Loren carried over a handful of cut-off milk jugs under his arm. "That was quite a prayer. As a father, I appreciated every word of it."

"Good morning, Loren. I admit that some places make me feel closer to heaven than others. This spot is certainly special to me."

"Muriel and I are fond of it, too. Somehow, a flower garden doesn't seem like as much work as a vegetable garden."

"The rewards sure are different. There's no pressure for yield here, because dinner doesn't depend on it."

"That's a major part of what separates the two." He walked up to the cherry tree to inspect the crop.

"How does it look to you?"

"Like a promise fulfilled, kind of like you have been." He turned to her and smiled, his gray eyes twinkling with the admission. "I've been watching the transformation in my son since you arrived. Part of him seemed to be tucked away, a part he chose to ignore. Living out here on the edge of civilization made it easier for him to retreat away from people and relationships. Part of his cover was to hide behind his devotion to the land."

"But there's nothing wrong with being devoted to the land."

"No, but he could accomplish so much more if he didn't always opt for the comfort zone of the familiar."

"You want him to look at the bigger picture? Like something beyond this ranch?"

"Not that I don't appreciate the help, but sometimes he seems to be hiding his candle under a bushel basket out here."

"Jusdyn needs to live like he believes all things work together for the good for those that love the Lord. If God wants him to step beyond this barbed wire perimeter, he'll lead the way."

"Well, no matter which direction he chooses, there's a place for you with him. That much, I'm certain about."

"Thank you. Your approval means a lot to me. Now, do you think I could pick some cherries for a breakfast cobbler?"

"Pick only what you need and then let's allow the dew to dry on the rest. Jusdyn will be back from the head count by midmorning. I'll have Muriel and Valor ready by ten o'clock, so let's plan to meet back here around then."

"Did he take the horse this morning?"

"You bet he did."

"I'll leave him a note about the cherry cobbler down by the tack room then."

"You're gonna make his day with that note."

Arie smiled as the first pair of cherries yielded to her touch. "I hope so."

~

Reins slackened against the neck of a horse meant the animal operated on autopilot. Jusdyn surveyed the stretch of pasture extending beyond the water gap, contemplating how wonderfully treeless the land rolled, deep in big bluestem and unscarred by human hands. The remnant tallgrass prairie carpeted the mid-continent in the wake of a former inland sea, once grooved by the retreat of ancient glaciers, charred by nomadic Native Americans, and wallowed upon by vast herds of bison. Now, almost nothing remained of these once rampant forces or the mighty grassland—except the expanse he owned right here.

A catch filled his throat like a half-hitch knot as he deliberated the prairie's decline, a constricting range brought about by the manifest destiny of a free country. Ease of plowing for stretches without the entanglement of tree roots proved too fortuitous for homesteading settlers pursuing the American dream. Freedom to shoot bison from the window of a passing train for the fun of it provided a mere preoccupation for those restless to pass through its great flat expanse. After a hundred-fifty years of ingress and egress, use and abandonment, alteration and degradation, only a backbone of tallgrass prairie remained unaltered within its natural range. Experts estimated that remnant at less than five percent of its original expanse.

He gazed across the horizon at the deceptive vastness of the prairie stretching before him as he rode. Though the bison had been replaced by cattle over time, the seed stock for the grass remained unaltered. Almost all of it existed right here in the Flint Hills of Kansas, rooted solid and thriving.

What if this grass becomes the hub of recovery? Could I somehow halt the prairie from vanishing? A fire seared through his core at the realization that he could make a difference. By rote instinct, he found the reins and pulled the horse back under his control.

"Enough condemning the prairie," Jusdyn shouted, unable to repress the coursing surge of purpose rising inside. Digging in his heels, he compelled the horse to respond, negotiating a barrel turn onto the home stretch of Road Z with a pulse of newfound determination. Embracing the revelation, he regarded the dense woodland on the corner. "The tallgrass prairie will return—so help me God."

~

"That settles it. I choose the peach chiffon." Ruby led Opal around her canopied bed. She placed the cameo-carved carnelian brooch in the valley of the deeply cut bodice with a flourish of her hand and smiled with satisfaction.

Opal touched the sheer cuff of a billowing sleeve. "But this powder blue brings out your violet eyes."

"No. That dress won't work. I wore it to TJ's wedding."

"Well, this lemon and raspberry brocade is stylish for a suit."

"Yet hardly feminine enough for the occasion."

Opal stood in front of the fussy peach chiffon dress with pleated skirt that bustled in back, falling into a mock train. "Then I predict the bluestem will positively relish tearing this hemline to shreds." How had her sister even gotten a hold of a fancy number like this?

"Go ahead and let it try." Ruby posed at the mirror, practicing a French twist hairdo.

"Tell me what's gotten into you. You're acting like a schoolgirl gussying up for the prom." Her sister hadn't fussed over her looks like this in quite some time.

Ruby finished anchoring the twist with hair combs and turned toward Opal. "I have a date this Saturday, and I plan to knock his socks off."

"You never stopped trying with Morrill, did you?"

"I don't believe the Good Lord ever told me to stop trying, now did he?"

"No, not that he told me, anyhow." She softened her gaze in sympathetic truce. "Guess that means I can't wear red."

"Absolutely not. That's an obvious clash with peach." Ruby smoothed the fabric with the back of her hand.

Opal snickered, cracking her defiant role as wardrobe critic. She pushed the brocade suit over and perched light as a bird on the edge of the bed.

Ruby came and stood in front of her, taking her hands and folding them into her own. "We've had a beautiful life here together in our lovely home. Don't suppose for one moment that I haven't appreciated it or failed to enjoy your company. Still, there's this call from deep in my heart that has gone unanswered."

"Morrill is no longer a young man, Sister."

"Nor am I a maiden. I may be having more than a little desperation over the lateness of the hour."

"Hence the frivolity of the peach chiffon dress."

"Think I can carry it off?"

"Better wear some extra rouge so the light color won't wash out your features."

"You're a real dear for going along with all this."

"Guess it's my turn to find something that doesn't clash with peace chiffon." She stood and walked toward the door.

"The governor is wearing red to the symphony."

"She can have it. Mother never thought highly of women who wore red." Opal clucked as she headed to search her closet for something a bit more functional that trailing chiffon.

~

Jusdyn slowed Chica to a walk at the top of the driveway, stroking her neck in reward for the hasty return to the ranch. Valor ran from the back door of the big house as he passed, which rousted Sam from a midmorning nap. Obligated to escort the returning rancher back to the corral, the blue heeler barked through their gleeful reunion.

Valor stopped and picked up the lower end of a ladder being carried by his father. Connected, they made a promenade to the blushing canopy of the cherry tree, ripe for picking. A plucky blue jay flew from the highest branch, pinching a scarlet fruit in its beak.

"Consider that your last one." Loren shook his fist in mock threat. When Valor giggled, he focused on his ladder mate. "Go get your pail, honey."

Dismounting, he swung the corral gate open and tied the reins to the pipe rail. With a strong grip, he tugged the cinch loose, unfastening the saddle. Yanking the saddle and pad off, he cradled it on his forearm, stepping toward the tack room.

"Lord, show me where to start," he whispered. "I'm claiming your promise that you'll direct the path of those who stay right with you. Here comes my first step." He reached for the familiar tack room door and discovered a small white note. *Cherry Cobbler in Cottage.* It was signed with the letter A encircled with a heart.

"Guess nobody said that first step couldn't be a sweet one." He slung the saddle onto its stand and returned to the corral long enough to unbridle the horse.

"Jusdyn, the birds are beating us to the cherries," Valor yelled through cupped hands. Sam echoed her excitement with a bark.

"Be right there in two blinks of an eye." He ran toward the cottage, took a power lunge up the deck steps, and crashed into the little red kitchen.

Across the counter, Arie lifted a lattice-topped cobbler from the upper oven. She stood with it balanced squarely in front, her cheeks dimpled. "You weren't planning to pick cherries on an empty stomach, were you?"

"No, not with an angel watching over me from the kitchen." He rubbed his hands together and detected the scent of leather. He stepped toward the baker, wishing the counter between them would disappear into thin air.

~

TJ walked out of the conservation office to take his private call. It seemed like he had to do that a lot lately.

"I haven't heard anything back yet, so there is no second offer to report." The attorney paused as if to offer him some space.

"Not terribly surprising, given the way this symphony thing has set the whole town on its narrow end."

"You're right about that. Who can work when there's so much play? Anyway, the paper says the planning committee has hit a hurdle."

"Can you imagine that?" His tone came laced with so much sarcasm, he hardly recognized his own voice.

"Disappointing, I'm certain, since the town generates trash daily and elected officials can't think of anything more efficient to do than to truck it out to a neighboring county."

"Let me get back to you first of the week. We'll see if they're ready to come to the ballpark by then."

"With hats over their hearts, most likely."

"I just want their wallets out, that's all."

"I read you loud and clear. Enjoy the symphony."

"From the cheap seats, maybe. Lucky me, I've drawn security duty along the perimeter."

"Then my advice is to listen for the silver lining."

"Right, I'll check in Monday." TJ sliced his thumbnail through the end call button. *What can possibly be worse than an attorney who butchers his adages without any sign of remorse?*

~

Arie held a basin half-full of cherries from the first round of picking. Close by, Loren worked on the upper canopy from the ladder rung labeled *Not a Step*. Arie noticed he was a Type A cherry picker, while Jusdyn seemed more placid, plucking fruit here and there. Valor liked to pull the branch way down and view the cherries from above, a technique made easier by perching oneself high on a ladder. Everyone had been tasked with Muriel's pick-by-the-stem rule which suffered mixed compliance.

Valor directed Jusdyn with a sweep of her hands. "Over this way a little more."

On the back porch, Muriel established a pitting station where she provided the elbow grease for a new hand-cranked cherry pitter. With the devise clamped to the patio table, cherries could be loaded into the top and pitted at a mere turn of the crank. The cherry flesh fell out into a bowl, somewhat torn but edible. The pits spewed from a trough at the far end of the pitter's muzzle to be collected for convenient disposal.

Arie walked the basin of freshly picked cherries over to her kitchen, refrigerating them in her dishpan for hand-pitting later. Though agonizingly slow, the cherry flesh came out more intact by the process, making for better presentation in a pastry shell. Though old-fashioned by comparison, it provided less opportunity for a pit to sneak into a pie.

Three hours into picking. Jusdyn had grown tired of the repetitive harvest. He brought a half-filled milk jug of cherries to her basin, dumped them in, and kissed her kerchief-covered forehead. "I need to run over to the Hernandez place and pick up grandpa's old baler to use at Deke's tomorrow. With rain in the forecast for Saturday, we'll have to get the hay wagon loaded and over to the barn all in a working day's time."

"Tell Deke he can count on me by midafternoon for loading," Loren added from the upper branches of the tree canopy.

"Thanks, Dad. We'll appreciate some fresh help by then."

"Friday morning I'll be baking pies for the Trail Bakery. Muriel and Valor have kindly offered to drop them off for me on their way through town."

"Please don't make me have to stick my thumb through the top of one of those exported pies to get my portion." He feigned desperation by grabbing the basin in her hands.

"Oh, the Ladder Man always gets what's coming to him."

Muriel took the cherries from Arie. "Jusdyn, can you make sure Merrilee knows I'll be running Valor back home Friday afternoon late?"

"About what time, Mom?"

"Tell her around six o'clock tomorrow evening—if the creek doesn't rise."

"Break time's over." Loren's feet appeared on a lower rung of the ladder. "I need to dump my cherries."

Muriel walked a basin over to the ladder and a shower of cherries rained down into her arms. She maneuvered the basin around to catch a majority of the red droplets while Valor retrieved most of what missed.

She accompanied Jusdyn to his truck, enjoying a little more time in his company. "Will you be deciding what to change about the hayfield with Deke today?"

"Stewardship starts in your own backyard—or in this case—in Deke's. Grandpa left that hayfield to both of us. Still, if I can't convince my own cousin to buy into a plan for native grass restoration, how in the world can I expect to influence anyone else?" He opened the truck door and slipped in, accentuating his question with a door slam.

"Surely you recognize the win-win resolution of what you're about to start. The rancher can maximize use of his land while moderating his workload. And the prairie regains ground."

"I'm convinced it's time to start tightening down our management." He cranked the ignition and the engine fired.

"Ask Deke if he thinks the baby should get a peek at those prairie chickens for herself." She leaned in with the challenge, hugging his neck.

"Restoration is not an act of retreat, after all."

"Not at all. Restoration is our reconciliation with the land."

"You try to keep the harvest taskmaster happy."

"Sure. Give me the easy job." She waved as the truck pulled out. As she turned toward the cherry tree, she noticed her shoulders had grown sore.

"Arie, we're out of empty buckets up here."

"Coming, Loren." She ran to bring him more storage capacity, wondering how much fruit was enough.

~

Doug softened the strike of his boot soles on the gleaming tile floor down the back corridor to the familiar room. "Dad?" The rancher peered through the cracked door. He found the elderly brothers sitting at a table in the corner, alertly evaluating a stack of papers pulled from a file folder. "Howdy, gentlemen. What exactly is going on in here?"

Morrill stood and shook hands like they hadn't seen each other in years. "Guess you could say we're planning our escape from this place."

"A man just can't sit in the old folks home and wait to die." Vernis touched the pencil to his cheek and then scribbled on the paper in front of him.

"What brought on this change of heart, Dad?"

"Oh, it was probably when your cousin Muriel brought that delightful Valor to see us earlier in the week. She drew us a picture of the McLauren plot at the cemetery there in Wilsey, wanting to know all about the names of the kids on the stones and such.”

Morrill retook his seat and motioned him closer. “I couldn’t even talk that day to answer her questions, bless her heart.”

Doug floated into the room, totally bewildered.

“Yeah, that innocent little sketch got us motivated to do a whole lot of soul-searching. That it did.” Vernis regarded him with a piercing gaze.

Morrill took his chin in his hand and stretched the wrinkles from his face, making him look twenty years younger. “Vernis and I have some unfinished business. I’m finally seeing some things with a clarity I haven’t had in a long while.”

“Better sit down, son. We need to go over some legal matters with you.” Vernis kicked the spare chair out from under the table with authority.

Doug felt like he had just walked into a boardroom meeting as an unprepared member of the opposition. His body surrendered to the seat of the chair while his mind grappled with his father’s resurgence.

“To start with, Douglas, we’re planning to retract the Power-of-Attorney from you.” The authoritative tone Vernis used didn’t beg for further discussion.

“It’s for the best right now,” Morrill added, his tone more considerate.

His feet started to sweat inside his boots. The sudden urge to jump up and run away washed over him. “Can you even do that?”

“The rescinding paperwork has already been filed. We met with our lawyer yesterday.”

“We’re calling a family meeting for the entire McLauren clan, Sunday afternoon at two o’clock.” Morrill handed over a piece of paper with names all printed in columns. “We’d appreciate it if you could call everyone on this list.”

“Consider yourself officially notified. This is a come-hell-or-high-water invitation.” Vernis raised his graying brow to make the words sear deeper.

His blood ran ice cold in his chest. "Yes, sir." He took the list being offered, all the while trying to rationalize the believability of their exchange. "Can I possibly ask just one more question?"

"Certainly, Douglas." Morrill leaned toward him, alert and attentive. "Go ahead."

"What did you gentlemen eat for breakfast this morning?" He shook his head as the boardroom erupted in congenial laughter before launching into the next pressing agenda item.

Chapter 14

Nature often plays the numbers game in powers of ten, where six inches of rain may bring sixty bushels per acre of grain that in turn feeds six hundred blackbirds along the road to the grain elevator. Whether arithmetic or exponential, the strategy to multiply by seed or offspring is fundamental to each viable species. Plants react to prime temperature, sunlight, and precipitation by growing in profusion from every possible germinating seed. Subsequently, wildlife responds to an abundance of food supply, often doubling the litter size to take advantage of times of plenty. The prairie knows neither glut nor waste, with everything re-used, reduced, or recycled in a balance weighted toward the supply-and-demand of seeds and seedeaters. Opportunistic feeders are known to get it while they can with respect to ripening food sources, but must strike while the harvest is hot.

Making another trip toward the back deck with a bowlful of cherries, Arie considered the distinction between a bumper crop and glut, with the weight on the scale fully skewed by the weariness of the harvester.

Valor stood by Muriel on the back deck, waiting to collect yet another pail full of cherry pits. "I doubt the compost heap can hold any more of these." She stood mesmerized at the lava flow of organic stones streaming out of the pitter, swiping a mosquito off her cheek while the final pit dropped.

Muriel swatted across dusk's dimming light. "Loren, that's enough for today. The skeeters are starting to come out. Here, Arie. You keep the rest of the cherries. I'm shutting down the pitting station. Valor, go dump those last pits so we can close up shop."

Arie contrasted the success of the day against the chronic ache in her shoulders. Having fresh fruit for her pie-making venture meant a great deal to her, but now she would have to complete the first round of baking while stiff and sore. She gathered the collection of pails and buckets, consolidating the fruit into her basin and trying to decide where to store it. The refrigerator stood chock full and cherries plastered the red countertop edge-to-edge. She eyed the contents to make sure they would fill a crust. "Guess you'll become the first pies of the season."

Valor passed with a dripping load of pits. "Already planning your pies, Arie?"

She turned to reply and heard an odd sound—a wood-against-wood scraping as the brace board began rejecting its role under the tree. The release ended in a slap against the ground, jostling the aluminum ladder on its way. The jiggled platform shook the crew leader out of the canopy. In short order, Loren fell into view, his legs entangled in the ladder's frame while showering cherries all around.

Setting her basin down, Arie managed one step toward the unfolding scene when it came—the unmistakable snap of a bone breaking—just like the vision had warned.

Loren hit the ground with a moan and the ladder clattered down next to him.

Valor screamed in disbelief, releasing the bowl of pits like spatter art onto the yard.

Pinned under the ladder, Loren doubled over in pain, clasping his right leg.

Arie ran to his side. "Dad, let me see if I can help." She touched the twill of his khaki pants around the spot already reddening with blood.

"Easy does it." His warning came through clenched teeth.

She delicately traced the jagged edge of a protruding femur with her fingertips. A sober realization drifted into focus. Nothing in the garden could remedy this severe an injury. "I'm going for Muriel's help, and we'll get you into the car. Try not to move that leg." She stood looking for help. "Valor?"

The child seemed frozen in place as if undone by the injury.

Arie stepped over, put her arm around her shoulders, and led her over to his side. "Uncle Loren has broken his leg so we need to get him to the hospital. Can you help me by keeping him comfortable and still while I go get Aunt Muriel?"

Valor stepped toward him, unblinking with the grim assignment. "I'll take care of him."

Arie broke out in a run for the nurse. Her inability to have avoided the calamity despite the mirror's warning began to crowd her focus all the more. She knocked and opened the back screen door in one motion.

Muriel stood at the counter, sugar-packing a plastic container full of pitted cherries destined for the freezer. "Has something happened?"

"It's Loren. The brace board gave way and knocked him off the ladder. Too high to control his fall, he came down twisted in the ladder." Arie could barely catch her breath. The back of her throat started burning, and she tried to quell the feeling of bitter guilt.

"Where's he hurt?" Muriel turned her back, tossing the container in the freezer.

Trailing her actions, Arie's gaze arrested on the cemetery art clipped to the refrigerator where she noticed the hand-drawn lamb headstone. A void of consciousness opened under her like a crack in time, and for the briefest of moments the sensation of invisible floodwaters rushed around her. In a blink, she landed back in the kitchen where she'd been standing.

"Arie, please tell me. Where is Loren hurt?"

"His right leg—above the knee. I felt a jagged edge poking up through his pants leg."

"Compound break." Muriel wiped her hands on a dishtowel. "Any bleeding?"

"Yes, ma'am, I'm afraid so." Her voice trembling, she fell apart from the inside out.

"That's the worst case scenario all right, which Loren is particularly good at. Time to circle up the ambulance for a trip to town. Let me get the keys."

"So sorry this had to happen." She held the door for Muriel to exit, grateful to have someone else take charge of the rescue.

Muriel broke into a trot heading down the yard. "Can you drive?"

"Only the tractor." Arie sped up, suffocating as the guilt came back full throttle.

~

The cabin resonated with noises from the laboratory as another batch of product simmered into existence. After a duty-free week, the time had come to go back into babysitting mode. TJ felt the dread coming on him already. Tomorrow he would be an upright citizen and pillar of the community. He would stagecraft, tent-pitch, sound-check and set up folding chairs ad nauseam. By nightfall, as he reached the hypocritical pinnacle of this alter ego existence, he would tuck in the guest violinist and recite some meaningless prayer-poem over her.

With his hands busy doing the measured work of a chemist, he tried to imagine a life without her. Many passing through a life storm would say that having a dependent was what literally tethered them to the dock of life. Others would claim that hangers-on were what fouled the lines and brought the ship down amid the tempest.

The pure truth glared at him. A child did not belong beside a man who chose the crooked road. The notion held an irreconcilable wrongness about it. He turned off the overhead light, allowing the chemical reaction to run the full length of its course. Standing there in the dark, a line of detachment tore through his heart in a perforated rift of separation.

"What will any of it matter?" TJ threw open the cabin door to greet the empathy of midafternoon. The cottonwoods answered back with resounding unity, rattling their heart-shaped leaves in the wind.

~

Arie rounded the corner of the garage and found Valor sitting on her knees with her head against her great uncle's shoulder blade, her arms around his neck.

Muriel padded up right behind her out of breath from the sprint. "Loren, tell me what I'm dealing with." Her tone held a clinical detachment.

She glanced at his flower-filled lap, saw his fully extended right leg, and noticed his relaxed expression. A wave of astonishment rippled over her, extinguishing the guilt burning down the back of her throat. Even the stain drying on his pants leg more resembled crushed cherries than blood.

Loren cleared his throat. "Well, I had a bad couple of seconds there when I first hit the ground. I could have sworn I broke my leg, but when Arie touched it, the pain started rolling back. Then Valor said she would fix it with flowers, and the more she piled on, the faster the red-hot bump went away."

Clearly not assuaged, Muriel pressed for more information. "Can you move your lower leg?" When her husband flexed his right foot side-to-side and then back and forth, she straightened up and harrumphed. Next, she cut her eyes at Arie with a smirk.

"Wait. I most definitely touched the jagged edge of a clean bone break." To better prove it to the quizzical nurse, she knelt and pointed to the site of infraction. Her skin tightened with goose bumps as the obvious became apparent. The mirror's vision had been less of a warning, and more of an announcement.

Muriel stooped to inspect the injured limb. "I'm certain you thought you did."

She gravitated toward Valor, smoothing her hair. Though the girl added nothing to her recounting of the accident, she sensed

God's unmistakable grace scattered all around, like the cherries on the ground.

"Muriel, as best I can tell you, when I hit the ground this leg did break just like Arie said. It hurt worse than when the old mule backed me into the feedbox. But my leg is fine now." Loren accepted Valor's hand as she tried to hoist him from the scene of the accident.

Arie caught his other arm and a definitive power surge linked them.

The once-broken rancher came off the ground as spry as a young man in his prime. "Thank you, Lord." He flexed to tiptoes and back, hugging them both at once.

Muriel peered at him with her over-the-glasses, no-nonsense glare.

"Listen. What we've had here is nothing short of a miracle." Loren spoke as if throwing a gauntlet down in front of his dubious wife.

Caught up in their search for truth, she failed to notice Jusdyn until he stood between them and the cherry tree.

He gestured toward the ladder. "Will someone please tell me what's going on here?"

"You're not going to believe it." Muriel turned and stomped back up to the house while Loren scratched his head.

"Well?" He stared at his father.

"We were quitting for the evening when the brace board decided to go AWOL and take my ladder with it." Loren pointed to the culprit. "Before gravity could deliver me squarely to the ground, I discovered a painful new way to bend my right leg—about mid-thigh."

"You mean you broke your leg?" His voice rose a note or two.

"That's right, son. Then these two angels touched it and the pain stopped, the bone repaired, and the bleeding stopped—all within a minute's time. I'm calling this my garden healing. And I was especially touched that Arie called me 'Dad' when she came to my rescue. In fact, that may have started the healing process."

"Love does cover a multitude of sins." She blushed at the admission of her error, which earned her another shoulder squeeze from Loren. When Jusdyn's expression warmed, she sensed the bond between them strengthening.

"Yeah, like the sin of standing where the ladder warns you not to." Valor swatted at his pant leg to punctuate her reprimand.

The rancher bent and kissed her hair.

"Loren?" Muriel stood on the back porch with her arms akimbo. "Come on up here and let me get a closer look at your leg."

"That'd be our Doubting Thomas." Loren raised his eyebrows. Though Arie stifled most of her giggle, Valor didn't seem to try. He winked at their collusion. "Yes, dear. Be right there."

"Hey, I could use a little of that double hug." Jusdyn held his arms out for a transfer of affection.

She obliged and once Valor played along, they became bookends of admiring support for the young rancher.

The girl squirmed out of formation. "I'm hungry as a bear."

"Come on over, girlfriend." Arie retrieved her bowl of cherries and led the way.

~

"Hello, Lettie, it's Dad. I'm calling to officially announce that Grandpa Vernis plans to hold a family meeting for all the McLauren clan on Sunday afternoon at two o'clock in the Cordiality Room. Seems like we have some major changes coming, just so you can anticipate what the meeting is about. Hate to ask you to show up at your workplace on your day off, but it's a mandatory meeting. Talk to Jeff and see if he can watch the kids. Plan on sitting with me. I'll see you there. Love you, honey." Doug hung up and made a check mark beside another name on the list, coded with M for message.

His gaze moved around the perimeter of his eat-in kitchen. Dishes cluttered every conceivable surface, even on top of his refrigerator. He couldn't remember how long they'd been out like that, or even tell if they were clean. He hung his head at how low he'd stooped. It's one thing to hide out from society to dodge the colossal mistake you've made that cost your wife her life. It's quite another to abase yourself by living in outer squalor to match the inner pain.

What would his father say about the present condition of things? He would surely be critical of the state of the ranch and its manager. Rightly so. Somehow, matters needed to turn around, at least on the surface, for his father's sake. For starters, he'd clean this pigsty of a house from top to bottom.

"Let me make one more call first." His fingers worked to enter the seldom-used number. Again, an answering machine clicked into service. "Hello Laynie, it's Dad."

~

A walnut sleigh bed dominated the no-fuss bedroom at the right of the stairs in the Litke home. Crisp white linens were covered by an eyelet-edged white down comforter. Opal laid a pure moiré silk suit in a rich lavender color against the snow-white background. "How might this look beside peach chiffon?"

She'd grown a bit bothered to be bound by color restrictions set by her sister. The symphony would not be ordinary by any stretch of the imagination. The flute would sing where the cow typically bellowed, and that deserved a touch of lavender silk, most assuredly. "Sister, can you bring that peach thing in here so we can tell if we'll clash?" She opened her jewelry case to search for coordinating accents.

"Why certainly." Seconds later, Ruby came swirling into the room like a hummingbird on a peach hibiscus, sweeping its petals atop the silk suit. Both hovered over the bouquet of color for the critical moment of analysis. "You've done a remarkable job of blending the delicate with the exquisite, Opal. Now, what will you wear for jewelry?"

"I'm thinking about pearls, Ruby. Pearls can hardly steer you wrong. Nature's art for the performing arts, you know."

"Perfect selection. I have white pearls if you need to borrow them."

"No, I'll wear the cream strand from Capitol Federal."

"And what about adding the mother-of-pearl brooch to your lapel for a nicely thought-out finish?" Ruby fidgeted with the pin's closure.

Opal shushed her hand away. She picked up the peach chiffon dress and handed it to her sister. The brooch idea had somehow pushed her sensibilities past the line between accessory and obsessive décor. The need to take a stand rose with her blood pressure. "Let me think about the brooch." She escorted Ruby to her bedroom door.

"Opal, won't it be grand to hear Valor play along with the symphony?"

"It's a considerable amount of pressure for such a young girl. All in all, I wouldn't expect her performance to come off perfect."

"She'll do just fine. Now, don't forget our hair appointment in the morning."

"I wish I could." She exited the room mindful to find something more productive to do than primping.

~

The porch swing suffered from its tether with the pitting bowl. All-thumbs, Jusdyn tried to pry each pit from its nature-given position, but couldn't get the knack. When Arie handed him the pincer-like pitting utensil, he pretended it was fencing pliers, producing only modest results.

His neck cramped after a short while making him impatient. Surely they could return to the good old days of a free-ranging porch swing. "Can't we call it quits for the evening?"

"Let's get this one full." Arie tapped the edge of the plastic container. "I'll need it in the morning."

Five more cherries found their way into the tub. "Can we talk about what happened to Dad this afternoon?" He softened his expression and glanced up at her between cherries.

"Your mother doesn't believe me that his leg was broken."

"Well, let's say that I do. Remember that day down by the fishing pond? You promised me you would always be honest and open." When he brushed her juice-stained knuckles, her eyes beamed with validation. He grew hopeful that it reflected the progression of her heart down the lane of well-founded trust.

"I only saw it happen out of the corner of my eye. Loren came down awkwardly, half on and half off the ladder. His thighbone broke before he hit the ground. I remember hearing the snap before the ladder clattered down."

He tossed a handful of pitted cherries into the tub. "Then Valor touched the leg and it healed?"

"No, I came to him first. Valor, poor thing, froze in place and screamed from the shock of seeing Loren hurt. He sat up clenching his teeth because of the pain. Blood stained his pants leg right away, so I didn't have to search far to find the break with my fingertips. A jagged bone had ripped through his skin on impact, and that's what I touched."

He clicked the pitting tool at her. "When did Valor enter the rescue picture?"

"I had to run get your mother, but dared not leave Loren unattended."

"Good strategy. He's such a tough nut he probably would have tried to walk it off."

"Valor had retreated into herself so I had to coax her back out. I put my arm around her, walked her over, and asked if she could keep him still." She picked up several more cherries.

"Was she crying?"

"No, actually her confidence returned right away, and she assured me she would take care of him." She finished the cherries in her hand and sat upright, shrugging her shoulders.

He paused, contemplating the only plausible explanation. "Arie, do you sense that God in his mercy may have healed Dad through either you or Valor?" He clicked one last cherry into the container.

"There's no two ways around it, Jusdyn. Your father received a miracle. What's more, he fully recognized it. As for me, I didn't feel anything unusual at the time."

"That would leave Valor—or maybe a combination of the two of you." He tossed the pitter into the empty basin.

In silent agreement, Arie snapped the lid onto the container and wiped her hands on the towel under the bowl.

He pushed the porch swing free of the pitting station, glad to be done at last. They sat in shared silence for several minutes, letting the prairie speak of its own mysteries. Somewhere in the night, violin music added its slow, sweet reverie.

She exhaled and laid her head on his shoulder. "I do think the Lord tried to warn me about the pending accident."

"How so?" he whispered, turning toward her.

"This morning when I was tying the ribbon in my hair in front of the vanity's mirror, a vision appeared. A shower of cherries rained down and then the ladder fell—followed by the sound of a snap." She moved away as if her words had created an impasse between them.

He sat forward and searched her face, a forthright soul reflecting deeply in her eyes. "Do you mean this ribbon?" Moving slowly, he reached up and untied the bow, releasing her hair from the braid in an attempt to unfurl the strain of a tumultuous day. As his fingers caressed away the last twist, the distance between them melted away.

Kissing her in the music-filled night, he embraced the truth. A faith walk comes complete with the inexplicable, a promise of constancy from a never-sleeping shepherd, and the sanity-imposed quota of one white elephant per day. For this particular day, he would accept the uncountable multiplication of cherries. *Plus one miraculous healing.*

Chapter 15

A weary female coyote pads her den beneath a slow-rotting tree trunk which has fallen across the conservation easement, awaiting the moment that will set her free from her abdominal burden. The gestation, begun in the mild wetness of early spring, plays itself out as a swelling crescendo in the dry heave of midsummer. As a living organism, she looks like an emaciated, mangy specimen. To her pups, she will appear a fortress of protection and a well of knowledge from which to drink. The hour of birthing nears and her hind legs weaken. In a stalwart display of fortitude, she abandons the life-sparing shade of the den to quench her burning thirst at the nearby pond. Dragging her hind limbs back to the hideout, she has successfully allowed herself enough water to survive the fluid loss of live birth. Now she waits in contracted spans for the coolness of dusk to accomplish her miraculous feat.

Arie scrutinized Valor's rolling pin action across the red countertop. "Try to roll the dough toward the edge a bit at a time."

"Like this?"

"Yes, that's right. Now, roll in another direction all the way to the edge." From the sink, she continued the never-ending process of cherry pitting, taking solace in the bounty of pies cooling on the glitter-topped dinette table.

"This one's for Jusdyn." Valor bit her bottom lip, working to flatten the crust.

"He will simply love it." She stepped over to stir the cherry filling thickening on the stovetop. "After this, maybe we should take a break and bring Jusdyn some lunch." With her thoughts wandering to the haying crew, she poured the pie filling into the bottom crust.

"Finished." Valor dusted the flour from her hands, sending it everywhere.

"Now loosen it from underneath with the spatula like I showed you, and then I'll help you place it on."

Her apprentice worked the circle free from the counter's surface with all the precision she could muster. "Ready already."

"I'll crimp the edges if you want to cut some decorative shapes from these scraps." Arie folded the crust over the rolling pin and lifted it into place.

"Oh, yes. I want to embellish, as Aunt Muriel calls it." Valor found a set of petite cookie cutters in the shape of fruits and leaves. She soon brought over a sheet of wax paper bearing a dozen stamped shapes.

"Okay, dip your finger into the water bowl and paint the back of each shape. That's the glue to hold each cutout onto the crust. Let me cut in the vents first." Arie sliced three ellipses radiating from the crust's center. "Now, she's all yours." She donned mitts to clear the bottom oven. Two more cherry pies debuted in sugar-touched perfection, which she transferred to the range top for cooling. "Whenever you're ready, we'll put yours in."

"Right about—now." The girl gestured toward the masterpiece.

She popped the oven mitts onto her hands. "Great job with the prep, now in it goes." She pulled the oven door open.

With great concentration, the girl slipped the glass plate into the heat-wafting oven and then closed the door. "Pie baking is the greatest!"

"Yes, it is. Now, would you run ask Aunt Muriel if we can borrow the Gator to take Jusdyn his lunch?" Arie wiped a smudge of flour off the girl's soft cheek.

Quick as a wink, Valor dropped the mitts and skipped away. "I claim the driver's seat." She unlatched the screen door, tossing her a smile.

"Fine. Be my guest." She wiped a pile of pastry crumbles off the countertop to make way for the next kitchen project—a picnic lunch.

~

"Mr. McLauren, this is Rita Fieldcrest from the health care facility. How are you this morning?" Her crisp voice reverberated across the phone line lending life to a dull scene.

Doug halted, knee-deep in housekeeping chores. "About fair to middling."

"Your father and uncle have come to my office this morning requesting discharge papers from the facility. You understand, of course, how unusual this circumstance is for us—though they have made a fully plausible case for discharge."

"Yes, ma'am. I bet they have."

"Technically, we have you listed as the admitting agent for the family. That would require your signature on the release form before I can allow them to be dismissed."

"I'll be in town on Sunday afternoon for a family meeting in your Cordiality Room. Could you possibly leave the paperwork at the nurses' station for me?"

"Sure. That would work nicely. Let me mark the signature lines for you."

"Much obliged. Rita, Can you possibly shed some light on what sparked this turnabout?"

"The head nurse speculates that the deep brain stimulation Morrill received earlier in the week somehow reconnected some misfiring synapses in his brain. It's a terribly complex organ."

"And what about Dad's improvement?"

"Physiologically, it defies explanation. But you realize that those two have a connecting life-thread, don't you?"

"Always have and always will." He overheard the sound of a

tapping pen resonating through the speakerphone as the administrator seemed to contemplate her recommendation.

"Here's my suggestion. Take this resurgence as a gift and make the most of it. You don't know how many people would like to turn back the stream of systems failure in geriatric care. Such reversals are virtually unheard of. It's a bit miracle-like really."

"Here's my real quandary, Rita. I've got to get this ranch house ready for dad's return. Right now, it's a little below par. What release date are they asking for?"

"Monday morning, first thing. But you could take them Sunday once the papers are signed."

"Oh, brother. This place is a wreck. I've been a widower for two years."

"Listen, Doug. I have a niece that does domestic work. How about I send her out to help you? Would you want her today or tomorrow?"

"Yes and yes." He hadn't intended the response to seem so desperate. "And could you have her bring out some groceries, too? I'll reimburse her, no questions asked."

"Consider it done. And best of luck to you all."

"I certainly need it." Doug couldn't miss the laugh teasing down the phone line before it disconnected. He glanced around at the disarranged collection of a half-attempted existence. "Be careful what you pray for." Regarding the massive clutter on the kitchen counter, he threw his hands up, abandoning the cleanup effort to go feed the horses.

~

"The governor's motorcade enters here." The planning chairman wiggled a laser pointer's red dot on a mock-up of the event setting. "Who has the north gate?"

TJ raised his hand. "That'd be me." Regret would be far too weak a word to describe what swept through him as he agonized through the pre-event logistics session.

"Good. Best to have someone the governor knows and trusts at the post." Pausing to study his outline, humorous murmurs erupted from a row of mixed clergy.

"I didn't mean 'know' in the biblical sense, gentlemen. I meant someone she recognizes and trusts." The speaker turned his back to regard the diagram.

TJ rewarded the hecklers by smoothing his moustache with both hands, then raising a flirtatious eyebrow toward them. Several elders rumbled in mirthful response.

"Look you guys." The chairman leaned forward to dramatize his frankness. "Let's not mess this up. Having the governor present for Symphony on the Prairie is a real privilege for Council Grove."

"But we're Republicans." A different heckler decried his party lines from the back row and a second round of laughter followed.

"Last time I checked, the fine arts were non-partisan." The chairman snatched his glasses off, gesturing with them until the rumble subsided. "Now, to continue the briefing." He donned his glasses and picked up the pointer. "She then proceeds to the front row of the patrons' tent approximately fifteen minutes before the performance begins. Her entourage will flank her, seated here and there." The red dot floated in an arc around the center seat.

"Are they on duty to swat the bumblebees off her—or what?" a heckler jested.

"Nonsense," the chairman shouted over the incoming tide of snickers.

TJ raised his hand to be recognized by the chairman, providing a legitimate distraction. "Just what *are* these guys meant to protect her against?"

"It's mostly just standard operating procedure for them to be present. We'll actually be doing most of the security work to protect her." The presenter hedged a bit, leaving his explanation open-ended.

Unsatisfied, he wanted more of an answer. "Protect from what, exactly?" He shifted forward in his seat, demanding to know. The ensuing pause seemed to set members of the elder row on edge. A floor joist creaked, setting his nerves on end. Had he just heard the lid of Pandora's Box pry open?

The chairman mopped his brow with a crumpled tissue. "Seems the weather forecast is not all that favorable tomorrow." He spoke the disclosure with some reluctance. "A front is churning off some rain bands up from central Oklahoma toward the north and east."

A bony elder stood, his eyes widening. "That's the classic Tornado Alley track."

"A little late in the season for that, Mack," one row-mate replied.

"But the weather patterns are coming in late this year," said a short bald man. "My wheat harvest is nearly two weeks behind schedule."

"Gentlemen, gentlemen, please. Let's not get carried away." The chairman attempted to restore order above the directionless murmuring.

TJ stood and held up both hands demanding quiet, then sat back down when it arrived.

"Thank you, Mr. McLauren. Please know that we do have a contingency plan in place for inclement weather. The patrons' tent is equipped with side panels that can be lowered for a passing squall. There will be other canopies flanking the sitting area that can shelter some of the rest of us from the rain."

He had to expose the weak spot in the plan. "What if the winds are up?" A sobering truth settled on the room making him fight the sudden urge to spit. If the winds picked up beyond tent strength, the contingency plan would become thinner than the paper it had been written on.

"Well, at that point, we'd have to seek shelter in something more substantial—like the stone barn. I'll use the P.A. system to announce our course of action: Code Yellow for rain tarps and, if necessary, Code Red for the barn. Any further comments?" The chairman tamped the pointer into his palm.

Along the back row, the elders' ridicule fell silent.

A mile short of pacified, TJ acknowledged the tenuous situation. "Just titanic."

The Catholic priest reciprocated by tracing the sign of the cross over his chest as if to shoo a hell-bent albatross away from the invisible horizon of tomorrow.

~

Jusdyn checked the alignment of the baler against the row of raked hay, and then engaged the PTO to start another endless line of rectangular hay bales. He battled the sun today, and the rim of his hat proved insufficient to fully protect him. Glancing back at Deke, he spotted a man possessed. Merrilee could only migrate from the bed to the couch this morning, leaving Deke to insist that the baling job be history by nightfall.

A tattered band of clouds across the far southwestern horizon promised some welcome shade for an overheated tractor operator. A change in weather set fine with him as long as the clouds didn't spring a leak while overhead. Rain would make for wet grass, which led to moldy hay, a worthless end product. In truth, neither the hay nor the drying wheat needed the rain right now, so the neighboring soybeans would have to do without.

For the second time that morning, he wished his father would arrive to join the team. He'd never known anyone who could outwork that man. Loren was organized, efficient, and stronger than most men twenty years his junior. The camaraderie of matching up with him stroke for stroke pushed him through some of the most monotonous, dirt-flinging jobs at the ranch.

Checking the eastern horizon once again, he caught sight of the Gator approaching to bring his lunch. As the end of the grass row neared, he broke off turning west where he baled the outer row right up to Deke's machine shed.

Valor dropped off Muriel who disappeared into the house. After a brief pause, she jabbed the accelerator and pulled up under a wispy grove of honey locust trees beside the shed.

Arie sat astride a cooler in the bed of the Gator, balancing a container in her hands.

He cut the PTO, switched off the tractor, and hit the ground running for some sustenance and the opportunity for sweet company. "I can't rightly say which one of you I'm happiest to see." He flexed his legs in celebration of being off the tractor.

"That'd be me." Valor poured a K-State stadium cup full of lemonade.

His parched lips met the cup rim, and he drank the liquid revival gulch dry.

"Or me." Arie played the greeting game to perfection by uncovering the picnic lunch, one culinary enticement after the next.

He crossed his gritty hands over his heart. "I'm hopelessly hooked."

"Come on, Catfish." Deke locked him in a wrestler's grip and hauled him into the oily depths of the machine shed. "Be right back after we've washed up, ladies."

He flashed a mawkish grin as he pried off his cousin's half-Nelson grip. Clean hands sounded like a good idea. He licked his lips, and they tasted like lemons.

~

"Valor, can you help me with the corners here?" Arie struggled to unfold the picnic blanket, her thoughts drifting to the hayfield. How much of the grass would be hay no more? When Valor took the opposite corners, she angled the blanket under the remaining shade. Dividing the food onto four paper plates, she placed Valor's cherry pie as the centerpiece.

The girl had a mischievous look on her face. "Let's see how long it takes one of them to peek under the foil after the prayer. I bet it's more than a minute."

"And I'll guess less than twenty seconds." She grabbed a handful of napkins and spread them over the plates to ward off the flies. Their progress across the hayfield was evidenced by randomly placed rectangle bales. When she glanced back, the men were returning.

"Wow. What's all this fancy food?" Deke eyed the ample spread. "Are our days of eating bologna on white bread a thing of the past?"

"Oh, I think we're allowed to make little improvements here and there. Shall I bless the fancy food now?" Arie bowed as she gave thanks, which ended with a collective amen. When she opened her eyes, Jusdyn's hand had already pried up the foil.

He lifted the edge to peek at the contents. "Hope I know what's under here."

"I think I win, Valor." She shook her head at Jusdyn.

He gave her a guilty smile. "Pretty predictable, right?"

"Maybe we should have prayed longer." Valor pressed the foil back in place, but soon released her pouty grudge.

Deke attacked his rolled flatbread sandwich chocked with smoked turkey breast and fresh peach salsa, stopping long enough to wash it down with a current of ice-cold lemonade. "So good. This is killing me." He took a huge bite as if to fight for dominance, leaving the group in stitches.

Jusdyn forked a heaping pile of potato salad down his hatch, savoring it like a kid eating cotton candy at the county fair. He waved his up-turned fork at her. "Is this Mom's?"

She nodded in confirmation and drew the turkey wrap into biting range.

Deke tested the colorful veggie chips, sounding like a horse munching on oats. "What in the world are these things?" He exaggerated his jaw action in protest.

"Hay bales for humans. They're good for you." Arie picked up the bag and showed him the organic label.

"Good for me maybe—say if I had a gizzard." He stuck his neck out like a chicken, sending Valor rolling back giggling. "Think my gizzard and I will stick with the apple slices, but thanks just the same."

"It's all good. Thank you both so much, for saving our stomachs and our sanity. That tractor is getting the better of me today. Next year, we might even be done baling hay by lunchtime." Jusdyn chased the news with a little grin.

A certainty rose in Arie's spirit. An important act of restoration must be in the works. "Oh, how's that?"

"We're putting exactly half the hayfield back into native grass, the entire western half." His hand hovered over the pie plate, chopping down its equator in illustration.

"I'll keep the brome against the house here and some along the road, ending at the far end of the gate." Deke's sure tone reflected his commitment to the transition.

She beamed back her validation for his plan. "That's an incredible plan. Congratulations to you both for such an ambitious restoration." When Jusdyn reached over to hug her across the picnic spread, she tingled with inspiration. "It's starting. Right here, right now," she whispered into his ear. They savored the rest of lunch in relative silence as the smell of sweet hay blew across their shady haven.

Deke tapped the top of the centerpiece. "When can we unveil this foil-trapped thing?"

"That's the cherry pie I made for Jusdyn." Valor loosened and removed the cover.

Jusdyn's eyebrows shot up in approval as she inched it toward him. A little wreath of maple leaves formed a heart in the center of the pastry, soliciting a whistle from Deke.

She rummaged through the hamper and found the pie server. "Although it's a bit messy for picnic fare, we just couldn't resist."

"Okay, we'll try our best—" Jusdyn began to pledge.

"To eat the whole thing," Deke added.

Arie passed the pie server to Valor, who extended it toward the rough-handed ranchers.

Jusdyn gave her shoulders a squeeze. "Almost too pretty to eat."

"Yeah. Almost." Deke blew a kiss toward the child and then wrangled the pie front-and-center.

"Oh, go ahead." Valor took one last bite of her lunch. "That's the trouble with edible art."

"Yeah—it's too edible." Deke seized the server and scooped out the first piece. When part of the filling plopped out before he found his plate, Jusdyn scooped it up from the tablecloth into his mouth.

"Maybe you should let me do that." She took possession of the long-promised pie.

Jusdyn held his plate under the pie tin, begging like an orphan.

"Big or little?" She rotated the server's blade a few degrees in each direction trying to get an idea of what he wanted.

He gave her a serious look. "Remember, I'm making up for a two-year drought here."

She angled the server out a few extra degrees and notched the blade into the crust right through the maple leaves. Her lips parted as she placed the generous slice onto his plate. Locked in his appreciative gaze, being generous suddenly took on new proportions.

Valor folded her hands under her chin in anticipation. "You're gonna love this, Jusdyn."

"I know I will, because homemade means it's sealed with love."

Arie could only imagine the celebration his taste buds were having as the first forkful entered their deprived domain. Overhead, a gust of wind made the branches of the honey locust dance. For an instant, her thoughts drifted to Muriel, hoping Merrilee could stay comfortable.

~

A second load of wayward dirty dishes filled the racks of the seldom-used dishwasher. Doug loaded the soap powder, forced the door closed, and then pressed the normal button having no idea what the setting meant. The countertops had grown almost visible again, but not the baseboard trim. Miscellaneous boxes of mail and piles of paper capped the perimeter of the kitchen. Only one space remained open at the table, the rest engulfed by nonessential clutter.

The rancher turned to regain his perspective, hoping to find a job small enough to tackle before lunch. He noticed a mountain of dirty laundry cascading out of the utility room. He could sort through the mound and diminish it with relative ease. Too bad he hadn't given the task equal consideration last week. In short order, he had the clothes separated into two piles, soiled ranching denims and bleachable whites.

"What a simple life." He began to take some comfort in the work, selecting the whites and jamming them into the washer. "Everything's either colors or whites, taking the guesswork out of it." He knuckled the hot water button, and then remembered the soap and bleach which he added without measuring. As he closed the lid and shoved in the setting knob, the washing machine clicked on with a reassuring hum.

A solid knock reverberated from the front door and startled him. Visitors on Road AA came few and far between. One step away from the door, it occurred to him that Rita had promised to send out help. He opened the door to the piercing brightness of day and there stood a petite woman wearing white-rimmed sunglasses, carrying two heaping bags of groceries. He automatically bent and retrieved the bags from her, stunned speechless by the stylish female company.

She slowly raised the glasses, tucking them into her wavy auburn hair. "I'm Darlene Cosgrove. You know, Rita's niece?"

Something unrecognizable moved in his chest when he looked deep into her honey brown eyes. "Gosh, where are my manners? Please, come inside." He shifted to one side of the doorway. As he pinched the daylight back outside the door with his foot, a sneaky suspicion washed over him that the choices had just gotten more complicated than whites or colors.

~

Sherry's Styling Salon had been operating at maximum capacity, so Opal felt privileged to keep her regular Friday appointment with her sister in tow. Bringing the symphony to town proved to be the perfect excuse for some necessary self-improvement. The operator had brought in two guest stylists to keep up with the demand.

Sherry stepped to the check-in counter, sweeping and neatening the end station of errant curlers and clips as she approached. "What'll it be, ladies?"

"The regular for me." Opal had not changed her hairstyle in over twenty years and didn't feel compelled to do so today.

Sherry sat her in the first chair and fastened the black cape securely around her neck. Without notice, she collapsed the seatback and began the torture session, adjusting the water to the normal scalp-burning temperature. Slathering shampoo onto her fingertips, she proceeded to bury her acrylic nails into the tenderest scalp in the county. The scalding rinse water came as sensory relief of a different kind.

"How about you, Miss Ruby?" The jovial owner shut off the torpid splash. Conditioner smelling of lilacs poured over Opal's burn zone introducing a thirty-second ceasefire.

"I'm going for an up-do. A French twist, I think." Ruby motioned to a poster on the wall.

"She has a date for the symphony." Opal allowed the tradition of shop talk to free her speech. What was a trip to the salon for anyway?

"So who's the lucky fellow?" Sherry brought Opal's rinse water up to a cauldron-boil on the back of her hand. Lilac essence filled the basin as the ceasefire ended and the conditioner retreated down the drain.

"We're taking the McLauren brothers," she confessed in self-defense, setting her jaw to survive the towel-drying phase. A row of pink curlers joined the pointed end of a teasing comb for the next round of the assault, as Sherry used the divide-and-conquer technique to accomplish the latter portion of a wash-and-set.

"Morrill's my date. I'm wearing a peach dress that has a sweeping hemline like this." Ruby flashed the fashion magazine page at the operator, who halted digging Opal's scalp a moment to examine the skinny model trailing a pleated skirt.

Sherry leaned over and tapped her comb handle against the revealing neckline. "She needs to take some of this—and put it up here." When Opal laughed, the last mutinous curler unfurled.

Sherry pushed her head back down, recaptured the escapee, and clipped it back in place. "On to the drier with you, Miss Opal." The hairdresser swiveled her chair around and offered a sturdy arm for the trip. They walked to the far wall adorned with faded advertisements. "Now, let me get this thing cranking." A garnet-red hood began spewing a dried plastic smell that intensified as the dryer heated up.

Opal nodded at Mildred Spruill under the second dryer, envious of her portable oxygen line for the briefest of moments. She sat down to accept her drying phase without protest.

"See you in twenty minutes." Sherry snapped the hood in place and its blowers muffled the rest of the world.

Opal settled in and picked up the latest issue of Readers Digest as pain management for her incarceration.

While Sherry stopped to dabble with the perm of another customer, Ruby took the chair and fastened her own cape. Returning, the stylist laid the chair back and started the next round of the torture cycle. Eventually toweling off Ruby's clean hair, she sat her bolt upright and thundered a rumor down gossip lane.

"Ellie Roper was in this morning. You know her daughter is the dietician at the nursing home." Sherry snatched a comb through Ruby's long hair in preparation for blow-drying. "Anyway, Ellie says those McLauren brothers are causing a ruckus wanting to check out of the care facility after this weekend. Seems they don't think they need to live there anymore—or some such nonsense. Well, if they're moving on, you might make the most of this farewell date."

Opal happened to glance up from the "Comedy in Uniform" page to see how far along her dear sister had progressed under the throes of the beautification attack. It mattered not that the dryer made it difficult to hear any of their conversational exchange at that point. She could see Ruby's countenance in the mirror, and her hollow eyes were those of the young woman running from the Last Chance Store, fearful of abandonment once again. For the life of her, she couldn't figure out anything to do about it beyond the lifeline of prayer. In the physical realm, she was losing the current skirmish, hair-locked in a curler stockade.

~

Arie came out from visiting Merrilee with Valor trailing and saw Jusdyn on the tractor weaving his rectangular crop when Loren drove in with reinforcements. Mannie Hernandez and his daughter Tia exited the cab, waving at their hosts. Jusdyn swiped his hat through the air in response, letting out a cowboy whoop. Deke stood and punched his fist into the air as if to lead the charge. Loren gestured to the machine shed, soon formulating the game plan for loading the hay bales. The men hitched trailers and hay wagons to the Gator and truck, which were driven out onto the hayfield for loading.

Arie taught the girls how to lift a bale together and swing it onto the low trailer platform behind the Gator. Valor and Tia took turns easing the gas-powered workhorse down the row, stopping abreast of the next grouping of bales. With the baling twine cutting into the palm of her leather gloves, she felt gratitude for the modest protection as she swung the awkward load onto the trailer. Eventually, Muriel came out and drove the truck for the hay wagon team, advancing bale-by-bale toward the empty hay barn.

As the afternoon ebbed away, the storm clouds steadily advanced from the southwest. Jusdyn surrendered the antique baler to the machine shed, leaving Deke the western edge of the hayfield to bale on his final round.

Her heart leapt as he ran out to join their team, staring skyward as if to gauge the storm. "Hey, good-looking." She flashed him a welcoming smile across the trailer.

"Come here often?" He loaded his first bale.

She struggled to lift her rectangle, feeling soreness developing under her gloves. "Not too often, but I may have stayed too long." She propped up the next bale half onto the trailer.

"How so? Hard work getting to you?" He took her bale and slid it into place. When he clicked for Valor to move the vehicle, she picked up on his command code and floored it.

"Not the hard work so much as the soft hands." Arie winced as she removed her right glove. They walked forward shoulder-to-shoulder to the next line of bales.

"Ouch. That line of blisters looks red-hot. I'll bring some Utter Balm to the porch swing tonight and doctor you up. Hey Valor, can you come help Arie lift bales for a while?"

"Will do, Jusdyn. Your turn to drive, Tia." After Valor jumped out, the quiet neighbor shifted into the driver's seat. She ran back and grabbed Arie's hand to get a glimpse of the blisters brewing. "Holy cow. We're harvesting all kinds of crops this week." Her fingertip glided over the translucent ridges on Arie's palm.

In matched effort, they balanced the baling twine and hoisted the next bale in place. She flashed Jusdyn the okay signal to register the vast improvement. Once they had stacked a third layer of bales, he took the driver's seat and gave the crew a memorable ride back to the barn.

The other team of men stood waiting to assist with the unloading. As the girls scampered up the stair-stepped hay pile to chase the barn cat, she made her way over to Muriel in the truck cab. Overheated, the driver sat fanning her face with a straw hat.

"Would you care for some water?" Muriel's inquiry held a hollow politeness, but she affirmed the offer by tapping the lid of a cooler on the seat beside her.

"Yes, please. That would be great."

She placed a water bottle into her waiting hand.

The ice-cold bottle relieved the fire left by repetitive lifting. Arie perched on the edge of the seat, grateful for the break. "So, how do you think Merrilee looks?"

"She looks like a woman in the final day of her pregnancy to me. Loren says the barometric pressure is likely to drop when this storm rolls through. That might be the push her body needs to start the labor."

Arie unscrewed the cap from the water bottle and took a long drink.

"Me, me, me." Valor ran up to the open door with Tia right behind.

Muriel popped two water bottles out of the cooler and passed them across Arie. The girls took the bottles and ran off to continue their exploration.

"I thought Merrilee looked a bit sallow." Arie gazed back toward the house.

"It wouldn't surprise me if she's a touch anemic here at the end. Hard to tell what her skin tone looks like inside a house with so much dastardly green in the décor."

"Well, you know what they say. Little girls rob all the beauty from their mothers while they're being carried."

"Deke and I feel pretty confident it's going to be a boy." Muriel placed the hat back on her head and glanced in the side mirror at the work crew.

Arie conceded for the sake of non-argument, appeasing her with a nod. She began to watch the men unload the hay bales, but soon got distracted by the brooding sky. "If Loren is right about a drop in pressure, we won't have to guess at the baby's gender much longer. Thanks for the water." She slid out of the cab and allowed the bale stackers access to the watering hole.

Deke approached and stuck out his arm without a word. Muriel placed a water bottle into the young rancher's hand, waggling it back and forth. He unscrewed the lid and downed the entire contents in one long drink.

"It looks like we have less than an hour." Jusdyn gestured at the sky with his water bottle.

Arie stood beside him, gazing at the ominous bank of dark

clouds. The countdown crimped her next breath. They needed to work faster.

~

"Saddle up and hit it hard, folks." Loren shoved into the passenger seat and moved the cooler into his lap. "Mannie?" A fraction of a second later, his neighbor appeared and slipped quietly into the cab for the last trip out. He opened the cooler and brought out the last two bottles. "Water, you can't live with it." After tipping a bottle skyward, he took a long drink.

Mannie accepted his water bottle with a grateful nod. "And you sure can't live without it." The team rode out onto the hayfield in silent anticipation.

A line of bales was slung out along the eastern perimeter of the field like corks on a seine net, and the teams crossed the ocean's interior with prudent haste. About midway out, the wind shifted from the southeast to match the approaching squall, bringing the stench of exhaust into the truck's cab. Loren and Mannie exchanged looks and quickly finished their water break.

Muriel grew uneasy having missed the clue. "What?"

"Wind just shifted to match the storm. It won't be long now." Loren pointed at a row of rectangles up ahead.

She pressed on the accelerator heading for the furthest bales. "Let's work from the back forward. If the sky rips open, we'll take only what we have loaded and make the shorter trip in." She glanced at Loren who raised a grimy forearm in her direction.

"Fair enough." He patted her no-nonsense arm attached with firm purpose to the steering wheel. "Glad I got a woman who can keep her head under pressure." He stole a look in the rearview mirror. Mannie added a thin smile and nodded without speaking.

~

The Gator crew took the road edge portion of the field, Jusdyn having duly noted the wind shift. All members worked together now out of sheer necessity, the guys tossing bales from the outer rows while the gals loaded the closer ones. Occasionally, he would step onto the trailer and rearrange the bales into neater arrays for level stacking, ever checking the sky. At four bales deep, the stacks became difficult to manage so the driver had to ease up on the speed.

"I just felt a raindrop." Valor touched her nose where the sprinkle hit.

He climbed atop the four-deep hay bales and could see a curtain of heavy rain coming over the soybean field south of the house. "Everybody get on. We're heading in. Deke, you drive." He caught one last bale and stacked it as his cousin leapt into the Gator.

Ousted, Arie shifted the girls over to the second seat and perched on a double stack of bales in the rear cargo bed.

"Hold on tight." With the warning, Deke eased the vehicle forward.

When the stack flexed on the trailer, he lowered his center of gravity by riding on his stomach. Arie reached up from her stack and laced her fingers into his, bracing for the ride in.

Having once touted their independence, the sprinkles also began to hold hands. By mid-field, his sleeve was speckled with drops. He repositioned his grip and pressed the hay bales in place using his weary legs. The energy of the storm surged against them.

The first lightning strike forced the truck crew into retreat from the disappearing rim. A quick count revealed fewer than a dozen bales remained in the field. The truck seemed to hesitate at the next line of bales, but a second boom of thunder pounded it into forward motion. Jusdyn could sense his father's angst across the field. *The storm is gaining ground and we're retreating. Yet another brilliant reminder of why it all depends on the weather.* Gazing down on his faithful crew, he doubted they would make the barn's shelter before the bottom fell out.

~

Arie looked up from under the front ledge of the hay barn where Deke had angled in. The girls scampered up the dry haystack and huddled together for protection. She jumped out of the Gator to join the team as they began the process of unloading with due haste.

"Put those top bales over to the side and let them dry." Jusdyn dropped bales one-by-one to Deke, who turned to set them behind the main stack.

She looked up as a sky-ripping flash turned the soybean field blue. Within seconds, thunder rattled the countryside. When Jusdyn pitched the first bale of dry hay, she took the heavy rectangle with a wince, but completed the lift.

"Valor, can you go check on Merrilee for me?" Deke's voice filtered down from the stack, a worry tied to it like twine wrapping a bale.

The child glanced at Muriel, who hesitated but nodded her permission. "Sure thing, Deke. Be right back." With a parting hug for Tia, she bounced down the stacked bales and flung herself face-first into the quickening rain.

The crew worked feverously, unloading the bales with the carelessness of haste. Under the weight of each hay bale, Arie felt the blisters tear open beneath the gloves as they filled the barn with the bumper brome crop. A mandate flashed into her thoughts, reminding her of a key element of her charge. *No deed of sacrifice is unimportant.*

Amid the downpour, her thoughts turned into prayer. "Please hold back the rain." For the next few minutes, the rain appeared to slacken, allowing the harvesters to complete their task.

"That's the last of it." Loren passed a lopsided bale to Deke who shoved it into place. The bottom tore out of the cloud overhead, trouncing the tin roof of the barn in a great clamor. Rain cloaked the meadow like a shower curtain rimming a bathtub.

Arie moved into Jusdyn's gritty arms for shelter. Mannie leaned on the tailgate beside Loren, looking thoroughly exhausted. Tia stepped down from the stack and placed her slender arm around her father. Deke sank a knee into the hay bale where Muriel sat and they exchanged a weighted look. With only the drum of rain breaking the silence, she acknowledged the grace that had allowed them to finish such a monumental chore.

"Aunt Muriel!" Valor's shrill call echoed across the tumultuous downpour.

Reacting on pure instinct, Deke took off for home in a mad dash.

Muriel followed mere steps behind him, moving as fast as her aging joints would allow.

Without needing to check any instrument panel, Arie knew the barometric pressure had just shifted. As Jusdyn pulled her closer, she felt his heart pounding inside his chest. *Labor's final day comes amid untold exhaustion.* The surrounding hay smelled sweet as a thunderclap rolled up the valley.

Chapter 16

Physical processes smooth and shape the natural world, occurring with a routine status of nonentity. As such, their sleight of hand may continue unnoticed for long lapses of human attention. Within the normal range of daily temperature fluctuation, seasonal variation, and average precipitation, the indiscernible forces of weathering and erosion take place. Also ushered in are the paired associates of chipping/cracking, siltation/sedimentation, and accretion /deposition. Inserted into the interstitial spaces of such everyday processes—at intervals unknown to its inhabitants—are catastrophic forces of nature. Collectively held in the 3-D composite of death, doom, and destruction, these devastating forces of immense alteration have the power to flood entire valleys, char mountainsides of vegetation to soot, and tectonically fold the earth's surface from ill-fated epicenters. When time and tide turn catastrophic, land dwellers respond with adrenalin-bolstered raw instinct, maneuvering to somehow survive the falling cataclysm.

Jusdyn banged out of the back door on his way out to an early head count as Loren examined the orange-tinged sky. Honest to a fault, the rain gauge read a mere quarter inch. The first front through had only been a warning.

His father paced, seeming uneasy. "Take the truck and make it quick." He gave him a terse look while emptying the glass cylinder to reset the rain gauge.

He nodded and scraped his boot sole on the edge of the top step. "Any word from Mom?"

"Nothing yet." Loren slid the calibrated tube back into position.

"You reckon she got Valor home all right last night?" He knew plucking cockle burs from a coyote's coat was risky business, but unanswered worries could be equally as menacing.

"I can tell you that for certain. TJ called around nine o'clock saying Valor had arrived back home. Deke had to drive her to Americus so Muriel could stay at the hospital. Guess you were over at Arie's when he called."

"Dad, I need to talk to Arie about the storm shelter."

"Her kitchen light just came on. I'm going down to prep the storm shelter—in case we need it."

"The world seems on the verge of spinning out of control. Can you feel the turbulence coming?" He studied the worry lines in his father's face trying to get a trustworthy read.

"Stay close to the land, son—and watch the sky." He stepped toward the shelter doors. "Wish we could have our women back in Wilsey."

He ran to the back door of the cottage, words tumbling in his mind. He knocked before walking right in, pressed by a lack of time. Back to him, Arie stood like an unsuspecting angel, still dressed in her nightgown and a thin robe. Her domesticity struck him like the most natural thing he'd ever witnessed, and when she turned and smiled, a blessing rained down.

"You're worried about me should the weather worsen, aren't you?" She set the milk down on the counter. Her countenance radiated like a thousand candles contrasted against the approaching storm. Tucking her free-flowing hair behind a shoulder, she stepped around the counter right into his arm.

He wrapped her in a powerful embrace, lending a moment of comfort amid the brewing uncertainty. "I need to know you'll be "safe if a storm comes." He spoke through wisps of her hair, apprehensive to allow her to see how much he cared. "I have to move the cattle into the loafing shed under the pines for cover. Dad's prepping the storm shelter just beyond the back porch. He's eaten up with worry about Mom."

She nodded and placed a hand over his heart. "I'll get dressed and go help him."

"That'd be great." When emotions caught in his throat, he swallowed the fear and touched his lips to her cheek. "Go shine a little light into a dark place. And stay close to home."

"We'll be fine." She held him in her gaze, her eyes aglow with coppery flecks. "The arm of the Lord is not too short to reach into the wayside places to protect the faithful."

"Jusdyn?" Loren called from the backyard. "Better get going."

As Arie ushered him to the door, he discovered that her peaceful spirit had already been contagious, a miracle of companionship that he'd never experienced before. "I love you beyond the horizon." He glazed her lips with a kiss that couldn't last. With a bang of a boot on the aluminum screen door, he released himself into the orange haze of a day charged with hazards unknown.

~

The hospital room was marked with a frenetic busyness surrounding an inert core of matter. Merrilee lay shivering on a maternity ward bed, waiting for the next contraction to appear on the monitor.

Muriel tried to refocus her patient's mindset. "Are you trying to relax like a rag doll?"

Merrilee fell back on the pillow. "How can I when it's so blasted cold in here?"

Overhearing the remark, a nurse intervened and retrieved a heated blanket from the far end of the room. Five seconds later, a contraction began to buzz the monitor.

"Here we go. Try to relax under the heat wave so the

contraction can do its work." Muriel prompted her well into the throes of the contraction.

Merrilee lasted like a rag doll for all of eight seconds, and then clenched her fists to match her teeth at the upper elevations of the mountain cresting on the monitor's screen.

Muriel straightened as the contraction dissipated, beckoning the ward nurse. "Would you check her again?" Full of hope, she squeezed Merrilee's fist.

The delivery nurse came over, checked the patient's dilation, and faced Muriel point blank. "Still stalled at seven. We can start a drip to remedy that, if you'd like."

Muriel looked down at the wet-faced mother-to-be, now fallen slack against the bedding with eyes closed. How long she could keep this up was anyone's guess. But all signs indicated that time was not on their side.

"We're trying to do this naturally." Merrilee repeated her birthing mantra.

"Give us another half-hour," Muriel added with a pat of her hand.

The ward nurse nodded and left to attend her other patients.

"Aunt Muriel, I need Deke."

"I'll go get him, honey. It might take a few minutes to get him scrubbed up." The labor coach faded out the birthing center door on a dire mission. She had to fetch a husband out of hiding and surrender her station in the swap-out. Though it seemed like a demotion, Merrilee needed her soulmate for support. Maybe she could grab a decent cup of coffee in the transition.

~

Deke sat head down with hands laced across the back of his baseball cap in the maternity ward waiting room. He could have delivered half a dozen calves in the time it had taken Merrilee already. Why didn't someone come out there and give him an update? He never planned on being on the perimeter. Things just sort of fell out that way.

Suddenly, Muriel stood in front of him, long faced. "Deke, Merrilee has hit a plateau in her dilation progression."

From deep left field, he drifted amid the labor lingo she had tossed out. He cocked his brow, looking quizzical. "Shoot me that in other terms, Aunt Muriel."

"She's only seven out of a possible ten right now. But she's stalled out, like the pitch clock got hung up. The baby's got to have a ten to step into the batter's box. Do you get me?"

"Yeah. Okay, so what do we need to do to get her there?"

"She's asking for a conference at the mound right now."

"Me?" His voice squeaked. "Merrilee's asking for me?"

Muriel nodded in slow motion. "You go through that door right there to let the staff get you cleaned up first. I'm going down the hall for coffee."

He stood and tossed his cap in the seat. "But I'm only trained for pulling calves, you know that."

"Just remember, that's your beloved wife in there laying everything she's got on the line." Muriel turned away with heavy steps.

As if shepherded by the Lord's hand, he walked the opposite way down the hall. Merrilee meant more to him than being his partner. She'd become a part of him, adding depth to his life.

Reconnecting his prayer from a baseline of obedience without knowledge, Deke pled for the Lord's favor to face extra innings in the land of the unfamiliar. Equipped with faith and love, he came striding through the birthing room door, catching the attention of the ward nurse. She pointed to the corner sink and met him there to attempt to sanitize his calf-puller exterior.

Nearby, Merrilee lay motionless, her eyes closed. The whirring technology hooked up to her warned of a coming assault. Slathered by the sink, all Deke could do was watch from afar and notice the progression of things as the mountain built up to Merrilee's arched-back reaction to the peak of pain.

Drying his hands on the move, he arrived by her side before the monitor returned to the valley. "I'm here, darling wife." He stroked her arm to connect. "Tell me where you are."

A solitary tear rolled from the outer corner of her eye. "Deke, thank God you came." Her chest heaved under the blanket. "This labor's got me straddled over a fence. I'm too exhausted to go forward, but the baby's too far down to go back. I can't seem to move one way or the other." She sobbed at the helpless confession.

While he braced her shoulder, a recollection flashed across his mind by divine orchestration. Encouraged at the thought, a new direction let him heel in and catch traction in this uncharted territory. "Listen close, Merrilee. Do you remember back when we were dating and I brought you to the ranch for the first time?" A great sense of calm fell on him. When she managed a faint smile, he took it to heart. "You were out there in your fancy glitter-pocket jeans, and when we stepped through the strands of the barbed wire fence to walk the pasture, you got hitched up on the top wire and couldn't move."

She gave a small nod before falling back in exhaustion.

"Look at me, Mer." He leaned closer with all sincerity he could muster. "I promised you from that day on, I'd get the top wire if you'd get the bottom one. That's how we cross life like a team— together under the Lord's hand. Now, you've got to tell me how to hold my wire to get you off this fence because the truth is—the baby's coming out, one way or the other."

"My back shakes from the pain by the end of every contraction. Can you somehow push against my legs and wedge my hips against the bed so the contractions can do their work?"

"You've got it. Let me know when." A faint whir started nearby. "Wait, does this mean one's coming?"

"Yeah, here we go." Merrilee squared her shoulders and motioned to her legs.

He stepped around to get in position. Alternately studying the monitor and the mother-to-be, he pushed pressure against her knees, bearing down more as the mountain built toward its summit. Though

Merrilee grimaced through the peak, no back arching or shaking accompanied the contraction. Once the monitor gave that round of fence-crossing a respite he let up, encircling her knees in a hug. "How was that adjustment?"

Merrilee relaxed, taking a deep breath. "So much better."

"See. We're doing it, Mer. We're doing it together. What do you say we do it again?" He let out a war cry of Wildcat enthusiasm.

The ward nurse looked up from tending another recent arrival as if to assess his unorthodox technique.

Deke swabbed Merrilee's forehead with a corner of the blanket, flashed an irrepressible grin, and got set for the next round of tightening. His gaze darted to the monitor, awaiting its cue like the flashing fingers of a catcher calling the next pitch.

He watched the mountain begin to etch its path across and up the monitor. "Here it comes. This one's going to get us off the fence. We're getting ready to have a baby here." This time he worked with the natural force instead of opposing it. As the contraction waned, Deke looked down for a sign of progress and spotted the unmistakable evidence he'd hoped for. He smiled and kissed Merrilee's kneecap, then scanned the room for help. "Nurse?"

Muriel reappeared through the door.

The nurse shuffled over, took a quick look beneath the blanket, and immediately hastened her countenance. "I'll summon the doctor." She reached for the pager and sent the message coded baby-on-the-way.

Deke drew Muriel closer and revealed the evidence. "She's off that fence, for sure."

Muriel fought back tears. "You're about to be a daddy."

"Bring it on. I'm beyond ready."

~

As Arie stepped into the opening, Loren tossed several rusty soup cans out of the storm shelter doors. "Tomato soup was never my favorite." She eased down the first two steps.

He glanced up from his shelf-life assessment, on the verge of rejecting some split pea soup next. "Morning, Arie." A static-stifled radio babbled in the background. "How are those hands feeling?"

"Not too bad." She positioned them for the catch just as he tossed the split pea castoff to her and then assisted the can out to the yard. "Utter Balm is fast-working, I'll have to admit."

"We haven't kept this place up like we should have. Muriel usually stocks the canned goods." He stared vacantly at the food stored in the hybrid root cellar turned storm shelter.

"You know the hospital will have an evacuation plan—if it comes down to needing one."

"Who knows if Merrilee could even be moved at the time a twister might drop down?" He snatched another can from the shelf—green beans gone bad. "Don't even try to imagine how anyone could keep a multitude of music lovers safe over at the county fairgrounds. And there's our Valor smack dab in the midst of it. Curse that symphony."

She could sense that he was eaten up with worry, playing the what ifs, a losers game. She reached past him and cut off the radio, bringing an element of peace back into the little alcove. *Seems Loren has a knack for playing king of the worst case scenario.*

Here to make a difference, she decided to confront the matter. "Guess I could offer you some replacement cans to restock your shelves, but I don't think a full food supply is much of a remedy for the quivering faith of a worrier." She paused to let her words sink in. "You can't forget whose mighty hand makes the weather and spins it into place. That same hand shields the sparrow and then plows under the lilies of the field, all as he wills."

"Right. One will be taken, one will be left." Loren found a can of baked beans that had to go and tossed them to her.

"Yes, but let's not confuse divine mercy with the folly of man." She pitched the can out to the grass. "We have to live our lives dependent on the sufficiency of God's provision—that he gives us a safe place in life's storms, much like he gave Moses a cleft in the rocks when his presence passed by. Then it's faith or folly what we do with that security."

"Here's my folly. I allowed my wife to go into town where I can't protect her." His voice grew gravelly with emotion. "I've always felt like God put us out in Wilsey as part of our safety net, which is why I'm so unsettled about Muriel being in town. If I had even half a reason, I'd be heading in to fetch her back home right now."

"Well, if that's your hesitation, I can give you a dozen reasons to go. My pies got left behind last night in all the excitement of Merrilee's water breaking. They still need a ride to town for delivery to the bakery as promised."

"Consider it done." Standing too soon, he struck his head on the low overhang. "But what about you? I can't leave you here alone."

"Don't worry about me. Jusdyn will be back any minute. I'll get the replacement cans and tinker around in here until I hear his truck. Maybe I'll clean up a bit while I wait." She stepped back up the stairs into the muted light of day.

Loren emerged from the shelter with quick, purposeful steps, walking like a man with a new mission to recover his wife and orchestrate her return to Wilsey, safe and sound. "I'll take Muriel's car to keep the pies nice and clean. Let me pull up beside the back porch of the cottage, and we can load up from there. Do you think anyone will be at the bakery this early?"

"Go to the back door and pull the rope of an old-fashioned bell hanging there. Someone will hear it and come." She started toward the cottage as Loren disappeared into the garage, his gaze fixed on the sky.

A dusty orange cast tinted the sky above the catalpa tree making her realize more than the large-leafed trees and sugar-crusted pies would be vulnerable if the storm should escalate. She slipped through the screen door and let it slam with a bang, as if the aged cottage could provide any security at all.

~

"Confound cattle." Jusdyn turned his head to spit a bug off his lips while standing under the pines. Their song came as more of a warning this morning, with erratic winds slicing through the slender needles without mercy. Sam worked the remainder of the herd from open pasture, bringing them to the gate. Somehow the process had taken twice as long as planned, and he half-expected to see his dad drive up ranting with worry at any moment.

Sam doubled back to gather a foursome that were dog-shy and not too savvy when it came to rescue plans. This group included the little calf with the gimp leg. He could have called the next move like an eight-ball aimed at the corner pocket. When his herding dog put the heat of nipping at the calf's rear, it bolted up the pasture toward the pond—one hundred-eighty degrees in the wrong direction. Working with the three teachable bovines, he brought them in to a rapidly closing gate.

He fastened the gate with haste and reached for the door of the truck. "Kennel Sam." The dog heeled, leaping into the seat wild-eyed and panting. "Good boy." He slid in behind the dog, striking up the ignition to depart. He swung the truck around to exit along the pasture road while Sam pointed his nose out of the far window and began barking nonstop.

"No, we're leaving gimpy out there." He shifted to second gear. Sam wandered toward him, lurching to nip at his arm. "Who's being pig-headed? That calf's the one that went the wrong way—so let him stay out." The dog whined, half-crying for a second chance. With a swift glance at the angry southwest sky, his gaze shifted to the northeast horizon now marked by the retreating hindquarters of a solitary wayward calf.

"Oh, all right." He wheeled the truck around to the north. Sam lifted his muzzle and yipped, then sited on his target. "When did you get to be such a Lassie?" In the side-view mirror, he saw the southernmost pine tree lose a weak limb to the wind. "Lord, please let me borrow some time to finish this roundup." The blue heeler rolled his eyes back to regard the driver, and then fixated on its prey once again.

~

TJ picked up the emerging toaster waffles bare-fingered and dropped them on a plate. "That dress doesn't really need pants under it."

"I've got lots of time to kill before the concert, Dad. I plan to go froggin' over on Big John Creek to make the most of being in town." Valor held up her hem and did a little two-step move to drive her point home in drama queen fashion.

He smiled at the innocence of her sidetrack, having considered a few diabolical ones of his own. Today he would clearly be straddled by duty, no two ways about it. He poured the imitation syrup over the crusty stack. "Okay. Breakfast is ready." He slid the plate onto the dinette table. "Oh great, I forgot to pick up any milk."

"Fine. I'll have what you're having, Dad."

"It's not decaffeinated."

"Neither is this syrup. No worries, Dad. I'll play it all out, one way or the other." She mimicked holding her violin bow, and then prayed with her fork hovering over the waffle stack.

"Don't forget to pack your violin case, or you will be playing an air instrument."

She cut into the waffle stack. "It's already in the Jeep."

He set a steamy cup of black coffee in front of her and flipped a couple of creamer packets against it. Not a good substitute, but she didn't seem to mind.

"Watch out bullfrogs, here I come—full of this high-octane fuel." Valor tore the packets open and turned creaming her coffee into a chemistry experiment.

TJ stood in the middle of his kitchen and called to mind some of the toads he'd be teamed with for the day. *What good could come of this trying day?* Trapped by duty, he took a long draught of burning coffee to redirect the pain.

~

Opal brushed the remains of her early-morning toast from the table. Funny how morning meditation could make the crumbs of life disappear. Maybe the focus of one's attention could become real for that moment. How she loved to read through the book of Proverbs, which she considered the heart of God's word for right living. However, the close of the second chapter had lent her some discomfort, given the weather forecast.

"For the upright will live in the land, and the blameless will remain in it; but the wicked will be cut off from the land, and the unfaithful torn from it." Opal traced the words with a bent finger as she read. She contemplated the verse—both the upright and the unfaithful—on the wide open land she lived upon. She closed her Bible and folded her hands over it.

"Help me, Almighty Lord, in this oh-so-ordinary life. Help me be obedient whether my steps fall in the valley, on the mountaintop—or across the prairie in between. Advance the good work begun by your merciful hand to bring the tallgrass prairie back in the fullness of your grace to mankind. Continue to help us when we do not know how to help ourselves. Remind us of your unfailing love as we live in a world that often forgets how to love in return. And lastly, thank you for the splendor of this day. May we fully enjoy and remember it fondly. Amen."

Ruby stepped into the breakfast nook. "You might have prayed that your sister not make a fool of herself today."

She started to respond when the telephone rang. "Hello? Why yes, Vernis. Good morning to you also." She stood to remove her plate from the table.

Ruby followed her into the kitchen, taking the plate from her hand and rinsing it lightly in the sink.

"We can certainly do that. Thank you. Not at all, we'll be ready early and come by for you both at eleven thirty. See you then." She moved in slow motion returning the receiver to its resting place.

A silence followed making Ruby knit her brow. "Well, what on earth is it, Sister?"

"The McLauren men want to take us to lunch at the Hays House before the symphony. Vernis claims they want to celebrate our friendship over the past sixty years."

Ruby found the glass of orange juice poured for her. "I'll drink to that."

Opal sensed an electricity of something beyond anticipation running through her soul, making her leave the kitchen with a heightened expectation for the day. This would be a day over which the Lord would manifest his sovereignty. For her part, she would maintain her spiritual discernment on high alert to see what he had coming.

~

This time Doug welcomed the sound as someone knocked to disturb his day. He left the sparkling kitchen and enjoyed the cleared path to the front door. When he opened it, his helper smiled and handed him another bag of groceries for the pantry.

"Good morning, Darlene. Maybe I should have called you and canceled on account of the bad weather." He took the bag and gestured for her to enter.

"But we're not done yet, are we? Oh, my. Could that be coffee I smell?"

"You bet. Cowboys still enjoy their coffee in the morning." He opened the door wider for her to come inside. "Would you join me for a cup? It might lend us a spare minute to decide what task to tackle first."

"Great. I think I may have brought something to go with a good cup of coffee." She led him into the kitchen with a smile. After he set the bag on the counter, she began to rummage through its contents.

He diverted his attention to finding matching cups, poured their coffee, and then delivered it with satisfaction. On the small table by the front window, a tray of oversized cinnamon rolls caught his eye. "Well now." The sentimentality of a comfort food touched him. "I can't tell you the last time something like that was served at this ranch."

A weighty pause filled the room. "Listen Doug. Your farm

accident affected us all. Some have dubbed it the day Council Grove cried." Darlene slipped her fingers through the mug handle and inhaled.

He stared into the black liquid circled by his cup rim, wondering how he would keep from sliding back into the cesspool of guilt that always covered him when this topic surfaced. "I suppose Loretta had a lot of friends in town." He took a scalding sip, cleared his throat, and finally gained the courage to look his cleaning partner in the eye.

"Somehow, I don't think we were crying for Loretta." She tilted her head as if to regard him in a different way.

Unable to bear up under the honesty of her gaze, he diverted his attention to the corral east of the barn. The horses ran restless against the orange-tinted sky, tossing manes as they darted the length of the fence. Something in his core ascended out of the dark abyss, and with it came a sensation of warm feelings where stone cold numbness had resided before.

"Beautiful, isn't it?" Darlene gazed out on the wild splendor as she held the cup in both hands.

He focused on the panorama of wild sky and fleeting horses, Darlene's profile in the foreground softening the hurried feel of it all. "It's too beautiful for words." His voice grew husky at the disclosure.

She slipped her hand across the table and covered his in a moment of tender human compassion.

He responded by saying grace over the shared breakfast. When she slid the tray toward him, he readily encompassed the circumference of the bakery delight with his undeserving hand.

"We may have to get the horses in, should the weather worsen." He raised the delicacy to his lips and took a sample of pure heaven.

"Sure. I'm glad to help. I kept horses all through high school and have a few ribbons to show for it." Darlene sipped her coffee and stopped to add more sugar.

"You're as handy as a pocket on a shirt. Guess Rita knew what she was doing by sending you out here. I sure hope your family doesn't worry about you being out in the storm."

"Nobody's waiting for me at home." Her answer came without hesitation as she selected a cinnamon roll. "I thought I was married once in another lifetime, but evidently he didn't think so. It didn't last out the year. Maybe I wouldn't have been good at it, I don't know."

Doug hastened to return the rescue with a sliver of masculine insight. "Oh, I doubt that." Between the coffee, the confection, and the pleasant company, he somehow regained lost ground over breakfast. While angry skies raced past the running horses, he thought a part of the storm had already passed, in ways too intricate to trace.

~

The on-call obstetrics doctor pushed through the birthing room doors, veered left, and made a beeline to Merrilee. Pulled into his wake, both Deke and Muriel bobbed up on either side of the bed. Picking up the blanket edge, the doctor addressed the delegation with a recitation of policy. "Only one birthing coach allowed per patient. Hospital rules."

Retreating under the reprimand Deke automatically headed for the door, only to find Muriel right behind him.

She held the door closed with one hand and placed the other across his forearm. "I need to leave—and you need to stay."

"Are you sure?"

"Positive. I'm going down to admissions and call Loren to give him an update. We haven't talked since last night."

Deke set his heavy brow and turned back into the room. Walking into the setting that would make him a father, he found it sweetly exhilarating.

"Make her breathe through the pushing," Muriel called through closing door.

Deke stepped up to the doctor's side, ready for duty.

"Ever done this before, young man?"

Deke spread his stance to better hold his ground. "Yep, but most of my patients are the four-legged kind."

"Fair enough. Now, we're going to ride these peaks in waves. You're going to have her push right at the crest—but only at the crest. Merrilee, are you ready to have this baby?" He snapped the clipboard back onto the footboard and gave her a sharp look.

"Yes, sir. I'm beyond ready." As she spoke, her fists clenched the sheet into wads.

Deke heard the monitor whir and launched a rally in the bottom of the ninth. ""Here we go. Get ready to push down and dirty, Merrilee. Get mad if you need to." He positioned in left field while the doctor took center.

Merrilee pushed through the peak and its accompanying pain, and then came her ear-splitting expression of stretched-beyond-maximum body parts.

Deke read the monitor to confirm the peak had subsided, though Merrilee remained tense under his supportive grip.

"Mercy. Look at all that dark hair." The doctor sounded a bit distracted.

Deke wanted to know why. He shifted to glance at evidence of his firstborn, feeling giddy to meet the first time. A dark-haired baby had emerged, but the shoulders had snagged.

"I need to push," Merrilee insisted through her teeth in a very unladylike tone.

"Not yet." The doctor motioned Deke forward. "Hold her off until the mountain peak comes back."

Duty-bound and love-tied, he bent and looked into her pain-glazed eyes. "This next mountain has a sign at the top." He crafted each word with care, weaving his spell over her. "You know what that sign says, Merrilee? It only says one word. One beautiful, magnificent word that all mankind has been built upon for ages. It says *Mother*. That's going to be you, Merrilee, when we get to the top of that next mountain. All you have to do is wait—and push from the peak—and you'll be there." He stroked her hairline until she nodded and then he bent to cap it with a kiss. In the background, the monitor started its ascent.

"Here we go." The doctor lowered on the stool. "Get ready and start—now."

"That Mother sign is right there. You go for it, babe." Deke locked his arm around her left knee and anchored her to the delivery table. On his cue, Merrilee pushed deep and low, releasing a low howl to chase the pain down the prairie. Deke's gaze gravitated back to the doctor and spied him cradling their baby in his hands, first in part—and then in whole. As he cut the umbilical cord, the ward nurse stepped in with soft cloths to clean fluid from the baby's ruddy face.

The doctor turned the baby upright. "Let's hear her mew like a kitten first."

"Her?" Caught between a laugh and a cry, Deke's heart split wide open.

Exhausted, Merrilee fell limp, freely shedding a river of tears when those first vocalizations erupted. The doctor handed the baby to him like the prized home run ball. The nurse worked on making her presentable from the fortress of his arms. By the time he positioned the raven-haired baby on Merrilee's stomach, tears of joy drenched his face. He placed one hand on both of them, connecting his little family.

The doctor held a protracted pause, writing notes on the clipboard. "Ten fingers and ten toes. She looks perfect."

The nurse stepped away to check on her other patient and returned, giving the doctor a look filled with expectation.

"Next, I've got a little clean-up work here on some tissue tearing for mom while the baby heads to the nursery for tests. As for the new dad, do you have anybody you'd like to call with the great arrival news?"

"Only half the county. I'm on it." Deke ran through the swinging doors of the maternity ward, his heart bursting with joy.

~

A new line of soup cans peered at the occupant of the storm shelter as Arie bided her time. Her cleaning cloth swept past the food supply and focused on the emergency radio, coated with dust. Hitting the on-off switch by accident, she riled the static monster to life. Interested in the synthetic-voiced weather service alert, she fine-tuned the transmission.

A prickle ran down her back as Chase County to the south was placed under a tornado warning for the next thirty minutes. Surely Jusdyn would be with her in the shelter by then if the situation shifted north. Though dreading the news, she dared not turn the radio off again and sever her only line of communication with the outside world.

No surface lay immune to the cleaning cloth's influence, and she had circumnavigated the small space within half an hour. Moving a small wooden crate filled with flashlights and batteries, Arie spied a little ring-necked snake trying to live in the shelter.

"This will never do for you." She captured the worm-like snake and brought it into the storm-tinged light of day, celebrating the beauty of a work in miniature. Jet-black scales braided down its length came broken only by a red-orange band just behind its dark diamond eyes. "The implement garden is the perfect spot for you."

Upon returning from the critter's release, it struck her that the shelter would make an admirable nook for her morning quiet time, so she ran to the cottage to retrieve her Bible. Thoughtlessly, she stroked her hair as she entered the back door and was rewarded with the discovery of a cobweb. Stopping by the vanity mirror to assess the weightless stowaway, she bowed and glanced at her reflection. In an instant, the mirror's silver lining shivered from solid to quivering gas, and an image progressed from hazy edges into razor-sharp focus.

There seemed to be a tube, a rock tunnel of sorts, crowded with children. Harried and frightened as they crouched in confinement, their numbers were added to until the tunnel could hold no more. In the last pair of children shoved into its core, Arie clearly recognized

Valor, who carried her violin, refusing to discard it. Sobbing shuttered from the interior, which Valor tried to quell like an angel of mercy. A wind-strafed curtain of debris then sealed off the tunnel. Afterward, the soft strains of the violin could be heard crying out in a transcendent S-O-S.

"I hear you, Valor." Arie stirred into resolute action as the silver resurfaced the mirror. She snatched the oilskin bag from the vanity's drawer and dashed out into the backyard, weighing her transportation options. She had to get to Jusdyn and convince him to take her to the symphony grounds in town. Instinctively, she headed toward the barn where the vehicles sat.

"Help me, Lord." She stepped toward the door where they parked the Gator. As if beckoned, Chica galloped from the back of the corral and dug its hooves to a halt fronting the gate. They regarded one another under the compelling truce of duty, and she relented with weak knees in favor of speed over stability. She climbed the fence rail and slid the gate latch open, then slung her right leg over the horse's bare back. "Take me to Jusdyn, girl." She lowered on the horse's neck and laced her fingers into its halter. Chica exploded through the gate and up the driveway, galloping faster than Arie thought possible.

~

Jusdyn's vintage truck rambled up from the pond with its tailgate down, a thick-headed calf at the far end of a hemp rope lead line. A dark gray cloud line scarred the southwestern horizon, its gauze lining barely holding back an orange-tinged gangrene of violent wind. Any sky watcher recognized this as duck-and-cover weather. He risked violating some unspoken outdoorsman trust by even being out here in the wide open.

"This will be our version of the ninety and nine safely in the fold." He nodded to the dog. Sam must have missed the reverent relevance of the analogy, dipping his muzzle under Jusdyn's elbow to get the reward he truly wanted. He moved his hand from the steering wheel and placed it on his faithful pet's head. "We got him, didn't we boy?" Sam answered with a dry bark.

The wind directed its stinging rain to the earth's surface as the truck approached the pasture gate. Jusdyn darted out into the sudden downpour and fingered the tether loose from the tailgate. He led the uncooperative calf into its safe haven, unlatched the gate, and turned to experience first-hand the rushing sound of decimation's locomotive.

Glancing skyward, he spotted a ropey twister snatching its way east through the farm field on the far side of the McLauren ranch house. Unnerved by the raw strength of this natural force, he slapped the rump of the unrepentant calf, latched the gate, and stepped onto the running board of the truck, lead line in hand.

Panicked for the first time, he checked his only escape route— a short stretch of dirt lane between him and the road that led home. How he longed to get there, plunge through the storm shelter doors, and retreat into the comforting arms of the woman he loved. He jumped into the truck cab, jammed the stick shift into reverse, and angled out of the access road. Alongside, the pines objected angrily to the rapacious winds as if determined to stand guard over the herd while attempting to stay off the fence. Purpose driven, he refused to look in his rearview mirror as he left the complications of the herd behind.

"Lord, the cattle on a thousand hills are yours. I've done all I can for this herd. You'll have to do the rest." A low whine came from deep within the dog's throat as the rain pelted the truck's cab.

He inched forward on the seat to wipe the foggy windshield with a bare hand. The gravel road loomed ahead, and with it the freedom of racing north away from the tornado. The light gray of the road lay just beyond the hood when he discerned a sudden movement against the pale rock. In reflex, he hit the brake when a horse appeared carrying a rain-drenched rider. The dog's whine erupted into a full-throated bark at the same second he recognized Chica.

Lunging, his shoulder forced the door panel open against the tearing wind. Low-slung and limp, Arie's body contoured to the horse's back. Windborne debris strafed them through the pelting rain as he caught the horse by its halter, slinging his other arm around the rider. Once abreast the truck door, he eased Arie off and placed her across the bench seat, where Sam filled the role of medic and began applying a licking compress to her forehead. Blinded by the rain, he grabbed the hemp lead line and tied it to Chica's halter, then fastened it to the tailgate.

He denied the tornado any satisfaction from a spectator's admiring glance, focusing on his world now condensed down to a truckload of earthly treasures. He managed to find first gear and turned the wheel to the right, quickly feeling the gravel slip under the tires. When Arie stirred, he dropped his right hand down to connect with her, finding a saturated shoulder to bond with. Only after she straightened would the gearshift find the room necessary to make second gear. The horse loped to keep pace with the energized truck, while the canine medic gazed out of the back glass at its corral companion.

Arie rose to lay her head against his wet shoulder.

He kissed her hair and pulled her closer to him on the bench seat so nothing would separate them on this rain-whipped escape route to safety. An overwhelming urge to survive pulsed through his veins as he pushed the truck into third gear. When Sam objected with a bark, he glanced back to see the galloping horse's eyes flash white from behind the tailgate. Visualizing the storm shelter, his hands rehearsed throwing the safety latch across the doors from the inside, safe and dry. At last Road Z appeared, so he took the left turn in haste, refusing to sympathize with the riparian woodland cowering in the corner.

Arie began to sob against his shoulder, searing a raw swag across his heart. The mailbox post marking the driveway entrance appeared before the downpour obliterated the view once again. He timed his turn-in and was rewarded with gravel under his tires before the next swipe of the windshield provided the visual evidence he longed to see—the safety of home. He pulled up to the back edge of the house and slipped into the curtain of rain to tend the horse. Despite being drenched, the trip back to the truck blazed with an unquenchable fire to gain safety.

Arie's somber face halted him. Vivid coals of fire flecked her hazel eyes as she sat rigid on the seat. She seemed to shrink back from the opening.

"C'mon. We made it." Jusdyn leveraged a hand on the truck seat to counter her resistance. "Let's head for the storm shelter." When he tried to pick her up, she rebuffed him with a stiff arm of refusal. The angled rain made the separation between them seem like a country mile. Sam whined in the background.

"Valor needs us." She folded her other arm to support her shivering diaphragm. "I saw Valor in a vision. There's a tube of huddled children crouching in fear with the wind raining down all around." She wiped the rain from her brow and stared at him.

He had to make a decision. As a portal of unknown challenges opened beyond him, he realized in an instant that the eight steps to the safety of the storm shelter would somehow never happen. Immobilized, he stood begging God for direction.

She pressed a burning palm to his chest. "Don't you see? We have to go to her. Your dad was right. The tornado will touch down on the symphony grounds in Council Grove where no one can be protected. Before the vision ended, the children cried out and violin music floated above them into a shearing wind." She sobbed and pleaded with her eyes.

"Go get dry clothes on, then cover yourself with the rain suit from the front closet. I'll change and grab mom's medic bag. If the kitchen light's turned off, head straight for the truck. Is that clear?"

Trembling, Arie nodded as she slipped out of the cab and into the rain.

Jusdyn called the dog and strode up the rain-slicked back porch, glancing down at the unoccupied storm shelter, now rendered useless by circumstances beyond his control. "We're in your territory now," he shouted skyward, his words beaten back by the rain. "Send us where you need us." The back door gave way at his insistence and he stepped into his boyhood home with panicked detachment, as if it could be his last visit.

Chapter 17

The atmospheric instability of two fronts colliding in mid-air becomes more than just a bully on the playground with a victim in sight. Condensation is shoved to its saturation point, hail is tossed into the upper atmosphere with the regular repetition of balls in a spiteful juggler's hand, and the wind is siphoned from its straight-lined tendencies to be spun around the perimeter of the collision. Angered by the coercion, jets of wind organize into vortices, gain weight with precipitation, and drop out of the anvil-bottomed thunderstorm resembling a scorpion's tail. Below, the level prairie waits in equanimity like the deck of an aircraft carrier, hoping beyond hope not to be snared by the lengthening tail-hook. From dancing rope to stovepipe and plowing wedge, tornados drop down in rampant animosity, leaving the surface of the land marred by the complication of swirling skies.

Arie let herself in the kitchen door to find her twin slicker-clad counterpart on the phone. Muriel's medic bag rested on the counter. She placed a hand on it, waiting for him to complete the phone call.

"Norm, this is Jusdyn Linquist, Loren's son. We've just had a tornado on the ground south of the McLauren farm at the intersection of Road AA and Road Nineteen hundred." He looked up at her and held her in a loving stare. "What's that? Six so far?"

She moved beside him and wrapped her arms around his waist. She could hear the bombastic weather service coordinator elaborating further as the receiver reverberated from the conversation. The dog whined and knocked its tail on the linoleum beside his empty food bowl.

"How does the forecast look for the east side of Council Grove?" He folded his arms on the counter.

Arie searched and found the bag of dog food, placing three generous handfuls into the cow herder's bowl. She lifted the water bowl and replenished it as well.

He shook his head at her, as if the caregiving was unnecessary, all things considered.

"You're right, probably too early to tell. Hey, we've got a situation here and I sure could use some help getting a message to my dad. Know anybody at WIBW? Just tell him to ask Loren Linquist to meet his son at the symphony grounds, that's all." He hung up and smiled down at her as she rewarded the dog with a back scratching. "Mom would have gotten to that when she got home."

She beamed back a sincere smile despite his somewhat callous demeanor. "No act of love is insignificant."

"Which is one of the many lessons you were sent here to teach me." He met her halfway across the counter for a quick kiss. When the phone rang, she slid a hand under the receiver and placed it up to his ear.

"Hello. Deke? What's the news? A little girl? You did? Well, then where's Mom?" He drew her closer. "Things are coming down out here, man. We've had a small twister touch down south of Doug's place. I got the cattle in and managed to lasso Arie who picked a fine time to be out doing some horseback riding. Yeah, she's a little concerned about Valor, so we're driving into town to check on her. Hey, if Dad comes there to pick up Mom, will you hold him at the hospital until we get there? Okay, see you in half an hour, Daddy Deke." He lowered the receiver.

"A pure blessing tucked within the curse of the storm." She

grabbed the medic's bag and headed around the counter for the door.

"Isn't that the way the Lord always works?" He flipped off the kitchen light and opened the portal out to the pelting rain.

She raised his hood to shelter his cowboy hat and out into the madness of a rescue they stepped.

~

"Where are we?" Doug's voice echoed in the place of refuge where he lay.

"Safe for now," a woman whispered. "We managed to make the corncrib."

"Darlene? What happened out there? I feel broken in half."

"The tornado ricocheted from the soybean field as we locked the horses in the barn. After starting to the house, you turned back to find me, and the hayloft doors flew off like graham crackers from a gingerbread house. One panel hit you squarely across the shoulder blades, and then it struck your head. You've been passed out ever since."

"How'd we get in here?" His breath turned shallow, but he needed the blanks filled in. The sweet, dusty smell of corn surrounded him like a natural narcotic.

"I had to drag you through the mud, but didn't know where to go. The barn was out of the question. I'm not sure it's even standing anymore, Doug. Then I saw this silo, shining in the storm like a silver lighthouse, dug in my heels, and brought you in with me." She made a tiny sound like a whimper somewhere to his right side.

He would have agonized more over their predicament had the pain not been piercing him front to back. "Can you tell if it's letting up?" He could still hear the rain thrashing against their metal shelter. "May need to have this back looked at."

"I'm a first responder and substitute for the EMT crew in town, when they need a warm body. If we could get to the house, I could take the first crack at treating the injury. I don't mind a little rain. It's steady, but not whipping like before."

"How long has it been?"

"We've probably been in here the better part of twenty minutes." She made the whimper again, but this time it wore more emotion.

He needed to come up with a plan. "We've got to make it to the house. Closest way is through the laundry room." He wanted to elaborate, but lost his breath wheezing.

"Doug, your difficulty breathing tells me you may have a rib poking through your lung. I need to check it out before we think about moving you." She shifted on the pile of corn kernels until her knee pressed against him.

"Left side." He moved to assist her and regretted it right away as a red-hot shot of pain made him freeze.

Her fingertips took an educated walk down his shoulder blade and onto his ribs, finding a fire-filled zone by the third bone down.

He grimaced at the pressure. "Bingo."

She continued down his rib cage one more finger-step.

"Double bingo." He was grateful when her hand lifted from his premises. Mentally tracing the distance through the farmyard to the ranch house, he knew it would be magnified by the pain in his upper torso.

"Given the house is still there, I can clean you up while we wait out the storm. But we'll have to head to town at some point. You need to be x-rayed and treated at the hospital."

Regret began to fill the corncrib, fed by the auger of endangerment and his lack of foresight. It rankled him stem-to-stern that he was laying here disabled and had placed Darlene at risk, to boot. She'd flat out saved his hide once and would likely be pushed to the limit of doing it again before the day was over. "Way beyond the call of duty," he muttered into the corn dust.

"How dare you say that." Darlene's attempt at control failed to cover the sob that escaped her lips. "No one came to Wilsey this morning out of a sense of duty." She sniffled in the dark.

Doug lowered his head onto the corn pillow, allowing the miracle of being the object of someone's affection to flow over him like being immersed in a healing pool. He yielded to Darlene's arms as they folded across his chest, her occasional sob anchoring him from slipping out of consciousness. Here—in the meekest of places amid the tumult ransacking the prairie—his innermost prayer was being answered. Now, all he had to do was survive to enjoy it.

~

After hanging up the phone with Jusdyn, Deke realized that he literally stood at Information Central. With a whipsaw storm flailing the county and a contact list in his hand with all his friends and family on it, he could orchestrate some weather-linked peace of mind and get the word out about the baby at the same time. When Muriel stepped out of the coffee shop, he beckoned her over. "Jusdyn and Arie are on their way into town."

"Whatever for? They should wait out this storm before coming to see the baby."

"Jusdyn just rode out a tornado at the McLauren ranch. When he called it in, Norm told him that six twisters had been documented so far. He claimed Arie had a sense of something bad happening to Valor, so they're coming into town."

"Well, why didn't Loren call Norm?"

Deke pointed to the main entrance. "Because Loren's right there."

Muriel tracked with his gesture as her husband came striding through the front doors. "Call Doug next to make sure he's okay. I'll stall this bulldog until we can get some answers. You reckon Merrilee would be up for some company by now?"

"Yeah, why don't you two go see the cutest baby in the world? She's the one with the black mop-top laying inside the nursery window."

Muriel stepped toward the visitor's station to intercept Loren and redirect him to the maternity ward.

Deke dialed the McLauren ranch and let the phone ring longer than normal. After a full count of unpromising rings, he surrendered the receiver toward disconnect when he heard an unfamiliar female voice respond.

"Hello?"

"Hey, this is Deke Linquist. I'm calling to check on Doug. We heard the weather had kicked up out his way so Aunt Muriel wanted me to call and make sure he's all right."

"Is Muriel there?"

"No, Loren and Muriel just went to the nursery to see my new baby."

"Wait. You're calling from the hospital?"

"Yes, ma'am. I'm calling both to check on you guys and to deliver the good news."

"Deke, this is Darlene Cosgrove. I'm out here helping Doug get the house ready for his dad's return. We were rounding up horses when a twister dropped down and started, well, rearranging the ranch."

Certain Muriel would want to know details, he'd been up all night so his three-second memory no longer existed. He began to scratch notes in the margin of the call list, his illegible penmanship contrasting with the rounded flowing font of his wife.

"Is everybody okay?"

"Doug is injured and it looks serious." Her words hung like weights on the phone line. "He took a strike from the hayloft door right across the back, about shoulder blade high. With the way he's rasping, I'm pretty sure he has broken ribs and a punctured lung."

"Good gravy. We've got to get you guys some help."

"Listen, I could use a little medical advice. I need you to stop the next staffer you see, wherever you are."

"In the lobby." Deke looked up from his post like a sniper ready to place the crosshairs on someone. A middle-aged woman in scrubs entered striking distance, busily untangling some kind of tubing from a coil. "Here comes a nurse now."

"Tell her you have an EMT on the line that needs some assistance."

Deke read her nametag while cradling the phone against the call list. "Excuse me, Nurse Mabel."

The white-footed scrub nurse halted and sized him up. "What do you want?"

"A tornado touched down in south Wilsey leaving Doug McLauren injured. The EMT tending him is asking for some assistance."

"How'd that call come in on this line?" She snatched the receiver from Deke.

He responded by shrugging his bony shoulders in the internationally recognized *I couldn't possibly know* signal.

"Mabel Proctor here. Who's this and what do you have?" The furrowed skin of her brow folded like a Shar-pei as she ascertained the name, rank, and serial number of the caller.

Loren and Muriel came into view all smiles, so Deke stepped away from Information Central.

Loren extended a congratulatory handshake. "She is something else. That puts an end to the drought of expanding the Linquist lineage." His other hand clamped on Deke's pitching shoulder.

Muriel crunched the stats and glanced up. "Seven pounds, five ounces and mostly hair." She smiled as she reported in.

Deke jotted the birth weight like an ERA onto his call list margin.

"Sounds like it," the nurse replied into the receiver.

"Who is she talking to?" Muriel seemed a bit irritated that he'd relinquished the phone.

Deke tapped his call list. "Darlene Cosgrove called from the McLauren ranch." When Muriel raised one eyebrow, he matched her gesture, suspicion for suspicion. "She's had to go from maid to medic, as I'm afraid Doug's been hurt." He checked his notes. "Punctured lung with broken ribs."

His recitation of medical condition must have pushed Muriel past the point of restraint. She took a brassy step forward and held up her hand for the receiver.

"Right. I'll start the paperwork. You get him here STAT." The nurse handed over the receiver, pointed at Loren, and then motioned him toward the admissions counter.

Knowing his uncle to be a diploma-bearing graduate of nurse obedience school, Deke watched as Loren followed the floor nurse to address the blanks riddling an admissions form.

"Hey, Darlene. It's Muriel. Yes, it's been a long time. Are you okay?" Muriel held her temples while her acquaintance added details to the dilemma.

Deke circled the name Doug McLauren on his list, tapping it with his pen tip.

"Tell me about Doug. What does his back look like?" Muriel closed her eyes. "Probably imbedded bits of wood then. You could remove the splinters before you wrap the gauze."

Deke circled Jusdyn's name and scribbled *fine* in the margin.

"Darlene, could you possibly hold the phone to Doug's ear? I'd like to assure him the rest of us are okay. See you at the ER within the hour. And Darlene, thanks for everything."

Deke wrote in Arie's name beside Jusdyn's. When Muriel paused to understand the connection, he framed it with a heart and gave Muriel a nod.

"Doug, I just wanted you to know that Jusdyn has Arie and they're both okay. They're coming into town, so we'll all be here waiting for you."

Deke overheard Doug trying to muster an objection followed by Darlene cautioning him to be still.

"Listen, Doug." Muriel's voice began to waiver. "This storm's a real threat. Yours was the sixth tornado reported and it's far from over yet. Loren is here with me and the kids are on their way, but I won't rest easy until you and Darlene are here with us."

As her voice collapsed into a tremble, Deke rescued the phone and added his two cents. "And Doug, when you get here, I'll introduce you to the newest sweetheart of Wilsey. Merrilee had our healthy baby girl not half an hour ago. She's a real heart-stealer. We're all going to be praying for you, so hang on and get here soon.

Bye now." Slipping his free arm around his calling partner's shoulders, he attempted to buoy her spirits.

She squeezed out a pained smile as the receiver found its cradle.

Deke involved her with a necessary diversion. "Who next?"

His aunt closed her sleepless eyes, pressing her fingers to her forehead. "Call TJ. "He'll be able to give us an update on Valor so we can relay to Arie that she's okay."

Deke dialed the cell phone number as directed, hoping to be brief.

"What is it?" TJ barked into the phone.

He took a direct hit in the eardrum, but was set to deliver the message. "Deke here, TJ. The baby came about half an hour ago. It's a healthy little girl."

"Oh, sorry Wildcat. Didn't mean to bite your head off. I've been working with a direction-challenged crew this morning." TJ's voice softened on the line. "Hey, tell Merrilee good job for me. Little girls are lots of fun."

When Muriel motioned for the phone, he began to surrender the receiver. "I'll do that. Here's Aunt Muriel."

"TJ, when was the last time you saw Valor?" Muriel pinched the bridge of her nose.

"Oh, I'd say fifteen minutes ago. She's up to two bullfrogs now. When she wanted to put them on my Gator for safekeeping I told her absolutely not."

"I need to tell you the weather's been a little uneven out Wilsey way. Doug's place took a hit. He's been injured, but he has medical help who can bring him in to the hospital. Loren and I will be waiting for him here so we'll keep you posted. Six tornadoes have dropped out of the sky with this front, and Council Grove hasn't been cleared by the weather service yet. Be sure you know where Valor is at all times."

"Geez, the orchestra just walked out on the grounds for picture-taking. They've been holed up in the community building for practice. I'd better go, Aunt Muriel. Thanks for the update on the weather. I'll keep an eye on the sky, for sure."

"Love you, TJ." She rushed her last words before the line went dead.

Deke took the receiver and placed it back on the wall.

She glanced at her watch. "We've got about ten minutes before Jusdyn should arrive. That gives you enough time to call your father."

Deke knew not to protest. Better to simply do it and get the awkward exchange over with. He tried to calculate the time difference between Kansas and California, but then realized it didn't matter. He found the number at the bottom of the list and dialed. As usual, the voice mail option rolled up.

"Hello, Dad. Merrilee had the baby this morning. It's a girl. She's seven pounds and five ounces. Haven't named her yet. Give us a call when you get this message."

Muriel waited for him to hang up the phone. "You two haven't named the baby yet?"

He shook his head and took another look at the list.

"Go to Merrilee this instant and don't come back until you have a name picked out. I mean first, middle, and last. Then we can tell everyone what to call her. Now shoo."

"But Jusdyn's not here yet," Deke objected.

Muriel pointed down the corridor with resolve. "I'll send Jusdyn and Arie down the minute they walk in." She folded her arms across her chest and then walked over to the admitting desk to join Loren with the paperwork.

The talk radio station defaulted to its blaring warning system. Out of nowhere, prickles shot up Deke's back.

Loren settled Muriel into his lap. "This isn't going to be good news."

As the synthesized voice of the weather service took command of the airwaves, Deke broke into a panicked run to reunite with his precious little family.

~

Having four of their longest-lived patrons in for lunch came as an unexpected treat for the Hays House staff, and Opal appreciated the tide of dining room help that ebbed and flowed from their corner table more than anyone. Vernis and Morrill had made an impromptu game out of remembering the year each staff member had been born. A plump redhead stepped forward as their next target.

"You came the year of the potato glut, remember that, Vernis?" Morrill snickered, buttering another biscuit. "There were so many spuds that year, the farmers came and dumped huge piles in the shade for any family that would let 'em. Your father came by and announced your arrival while he shoveled our load under the elm tree out front. I told him to call you 'Tater Sack Annie' which he shortened and sweetened to 'Annie Mae.' I'd guess around nineteen and sixty-four, is that about right?"

The blushing waitress flexed her ankles, looking like a girl again. "Yes, Mr. Morrill."

"And your mother was the best quilter I've ever seen." Ruby chuckled and laid her napkin by her empty plate. "She ought to have her work in a museum somewhere with stitching that even."

"Well, Miss Litke. I have a closet full of samples if you ever come up with the museum part." Annie Mae leaned close, clearing their plates away with a wink. One-by-one, the staff made parting comments and went on their way.

"Did anyone want to make a drive through the cemetery before the concert?" Opal picked up the bill out of habit and waved it across the table. "The weather's fussing to throw a fit out there, but we might be able to spend a little time paying respects before the tantrum comes."

"I sure wanted to." Vernis pulled the bill from her loose grip. "But Ruby ain't exactly dressed for walking through a storm."

Ruby attempted to cover her blushing neckline with her napkin, reacting to his critical comment.

"Nonsense." Morrill stood, cutting an impressive figure. "Why, you've never looked more beautiful than you do today, Ruby Litke.

And I don't give a jackrabbit's ear who hears me declare it." A light patter of applause echoed from the wait staff around the room's perimeter. "I'd be more than happy to hold your arm every step of the way if you really want to go."

Ruby stood opposite him. "Well, now I do."

Opal grew pleased as punch when Morrill stepped over and extended his arm. Her sister moved regally as she linked arms with him, her extra hemline laced across her free arm. Morrill surprised them all by leading Ruby through a few sweeping dance steps, swirling her around the worn wooden floor.

"Where have you been these sixty-odd years?" Ruby asked.

He took her up into his arms. "I've been locked away in the empty vault of myself. It's been a hell-on-earth for me, not being able to remember the combination to let myself out."

"What matters now is that you are out. And you're not by yourself anymore."

"Thank the Good Lord. And Ruby, thank you for waiting for me. I don't know that I deserve it, but I'm grateful."

"Sometimes, we get better than we deserve." She clutched his arm as he began to lead her around the floor again. The cash register bell sounded its transaction to interrupt their dance.

Vernis opened the old oak door and let in a gust of wind.

Opal clutched the front of her lavender suit jacket and waited for the others.

"You guys be careful out there," Annie Mae called from the dining room as the foursome exited over the foot-worn threshold.

"Just another adventure in Council Grove waiting to be retold." Amused with the morning's events, Opal stepped down onto Main Street wondering what would come next.

~

"You look great, Dr. Vorchenski!"

"And look at you, Valor. Why, you're heavy with amphibians, it would seem." He smiled at her childish pursuits, as the third bullfrog of the morning kicked hopeful to loosen her tight grip. He held out his violin bow and pretended to be-knight the bullfrog. "Perhaps someday he will become a tall prince and carry you away."

"Guess that would be fine and dandy, as long as it's not too far away."

"Everyone knows, for her true happiness, Princess Valor must remain on the prairie."

"That's right, sir. It's the land that I love. These critters just sort of come with it—like a wiggly bonus."

"Hey, Valor." TJ rode up on his Gator, his tone full of impatience. "No more frog hunting. We're running out of time. Go wash up and make yourself presentable."

Valor twitched her mouth to one side, then turned on one heel and started back toward the parking lot.

"Where is she putting those things anyway?"

"You really don't want to know," TJ squeezed the thumb throttle and continued his route.

The music genius stood his ground, squinting across the distance. He watched as the long-legged creature was folded into something resembling a violin case.

"Wouldn't be the first time." He gave a chuckle, remembering the playful immigrant youth down by the river in his boyhood memories. Next, he began the agonizingly uneven trip back to the 4 H building across the ageless prairie to await the concert and the duet of a lifetime.

~

Jusdyn walked up the front sidewalk of the hospital where he was born, hand-in-hand with Arie who seemed to have difficulty maneuvering against the wind. When his mother spotted them first, she jumped to her feet and heading for the front entrance with his father following behind. The automatic doors opened and allowed their yellow rain slickers inside.

"Are you both okay?" Muriel encircled them with open arms.

He nodded, shucking his raincoat and taking Arie's from her, piling them by the door.

Loren nodded. "Council Grove just got added to the tornado warning area by the National Weather Service about five minutes ago. What did you see driving up?"

"The entire front is shifting east, no two ways about it." Jusdyn glanced between them as his objectivity started unraveling. "Appears to still be south of Four Mile Creek yet, probably staggering its brimstone through Helmick right now."

"Is Uncle Doug here?" Arie's face brightened, her countenance laced with hope.

Loren placed his arm around her shoulder and shook his head. As the wind worked on the metal roofing of the portico, the little group fell sullen under the dire circumstances that had led them here.

Muriel's face paled when she glanced at the brooding skies beyond the lobby windows. "At least Valor is okay. Deke just spoke to TJ over at the symphony grounds."

Jusdyn saw a spark in Arie's eyes on an otherwise darkening horizon and smiled in appreciation of some good news. When Arie knelt to pray, he readily joined her in the posture of humility. They clasped hands and came to the Lord together.

"Father, please sustain the weak, the wounded, and the helpless as the storm bears down on Council Grove. We especially ask that you get Uncle Doug to the hospital where he can receive some help and where we can surround him with our love. I ask your hand of protection over Valor and the children attending the symphony, that no child would be hurt by this whirlwind settling upon the county. In the power of Jesus Christ, we make these requests."

"Amen." Deke's familiar voice provided the benediction. "Now, who wants to meet the most beautiful baby in the world?" A smile erupted on the new father's face that failed to carry any concern beyond the nursery.

He lifted Arie in a sweet embrace, making it impossible to suppress a smile.

"She even has a brand-new name," Deke bragged, "to be announced once you meet her."

"Unless somebody has a problem with it, we'll all go down together. No one's been able to stop a Linquist before." Muriel's spoken dare echoed down the hall. A wall of tension released as the group shared a laugh in a rebound of tenacity.

Loren placed his hand out to corral Muriel. "So why would they even try now?"

Deke locked shoulders with Jusdyn and Arie, leading them down to the nursery. By the time the entourage arrived, no babies remained in the viewing window. He stepped into the cry-filled room and returned to the hallway with a real sleeping beauty.

"They're calling her 'The Angel of the Nursery' because she's such a good baby." Deke shifted a fold in the blanket down and a tiny infant emerged.

Unable to resist the delicate bundle, Arie reached up to take her little hand with one finger. The baby grasped on, stirring her tiny head chock full of pitch-black hair. Arie beamed a smile toward Jusdyn.

His mother cleared her throat. "And tell us. What are you calling the baby?"

"I'm ready for you this time, Aunt Muriel. Her first name is Beryl which means 'green gemstone.' I got to thinking about what Miss Ruby told me that day at the picnic in your backyard. She and Miss Opal always held it special in their hearts that their parents wanted to name them after something treasured. That hit a soft spot with me, so Merrilee dug out some names of semi-precious stones and this is the one we picked."

"Didn't have anything to do with it being green, did it?" Muriel got a few laughs at the obvious maternal connection. Merrilee had a penchant for decorating everything in green.

"There's actually a deeper meaning, when you put it with her middle name." Deke threw a meaningful glance his way. "Her full name is Beryl Leigh Linquist."

Moved at the pronouncement, he dropped his head in humility, his eyes misting with sentimentality. The baby would share a bond with him, no question.

"Jusdyn's middle name is Lee," Muriel confided to Arie. "It means meadow."

He took possession and cradled the newborn against his chest. "Hello there, little Beryl Leigh Linquist." His voice turned candy soft. "You're a green gemstone meadow, like the ones we have in Wilsey." The baby opened her mouth as if to reply, but could not break her bond with sleep. "It's me, your Uncle Jusdyn."

"He's a cowboy, but a cute cowboy." Arie giggled, toying with her tiny fingers.

His heart grew tender as the new baby became the apple of his eye within moments.

Muriel fidgeted beside him. "My turn next." She reached for the infant.

He passed the fragile bundle crowned with hair to his mother so she could properly dote over her new grandniece.

"You know, babies are contagious." Deke teased, winging him with his elbow.

Arie blushed beside him.

Caught off guard, he dropped his gaze to the floor, speechless.

Loren patted the blanket in Muriel's possession. "We're ready to have a passel of grandchildren, believe you me."

Arie slid her arm around his waist seeming at peace with the conversation's course.

He shuffled his feet trying to get comfortable with the idea. "Guess we wouldn't want the cousins too far apart in age, would we?"

"Hey, you." An authoritative voice boomed down the nursery hallway. The larger-than-life floor nurse came down full force as if to pounce upon the Linquist family reunion.

Deke stepped out front to protect the rest as Arie shouldered behind his shield. Muriel dodged into the nursery with the baby while Deke straightened his spine to confront the disgruntled staff member.

"Is this yours?" She hurled a dark object toward the new father. When Deke snagged the item out of mid-air, he held his tattered K-State baseball cap. "I found it in the waiting room. Must have been a long night."

Deke placed the relic on his head. "Much obliged, Nurse Mabel."

A panic button sounded from the nurse's pager, which she glanced at and punched off. "Uh-oh. Incoming wounded." Mabel reversed her steps back up the hall.

"Uncle Doug?" Arie reached out as if to catch the nurse.

Jusdyn placed a hand on her arm at a lost as whether to follow the hospital icon or wait.

Loren stepped toward the nursery door. "I need Muriel with me from here on out."

"Better let me, Uncle Loren," Deke disappeared into the nursery and soon both returned.

"Which way to the Emergency Room?" Loren asked Muriel.

Muriel led with confidence. "Follow me."

When his father locked his arm around his mother, Jusdyn pulled Arie tight and noticed her lips were quivering. *This is how the storm becomes personal, when the broken and battered emerge for help and you recognize their faces.* The group made it halfway down the hall before he remembered to breathe.

Muriel took a sharp left, halting the group just inside of the main ER entrance. At that same instant, the door gaped open and a gurney slithered through the crack, pulled by the hospital intern and pushed by a mud-swathed rescuer.

Shock rocked him as he assessed the mass of man laid out on the rolling bed, shirtless and crisscrossed with white gauze soaked through with blood. When Arie sobbed at the initial scene and fell back against his chest, he could only wrap her in his arms to stave the hurt off them both.

A double door on the left wall swung open enough to engulf the gurney and its attached personnel. Muriel managed a consoling hand on the helper's shoulder as she passed. Darlene responded with a haunting stare that more than adequately summarized their rough round with nature's fury.

Muriel folded her arms across her stomach. "Lord, please help us."

"Well, if that's what's coming our way, he'll have to." Loren slid his arm around her.

Feeling like he'd just sized up the storm's potency, it pegged out beyond formidable.

A gust of wind caught the back door that had failed to latch, flailing it open. Before he could mitigate the vulnerable breach, the tornado siren at the base of the hill began to sound a warning, piercing the hospital interior. Adrenaline pulsing, he grabbed the door handle and forced it to latch.

Nurse Mabel came down the hall from the nurse's station. "Everybody head downstairs."

"Here we go again." He tried to guide his family down the corridor to the stairs.

"Not without Deke's family." Loren broke away in a full run to the maternity ward.

He caught Arie's arm and led her down the stairs behind Muriel, feeling her tremble as they descended.

Her face blanched pale. "What about Uncle Doug?"

He glanced at her, and then at Muriel. "Stay together." He shot back up the stairs. Retracing his steps from the ER, he took a breath, and then shoved open the double doors to locate his wounded neighbor. A whirring click preceded Darlene's reappearance from behind a leaden curtain.

"I'm just getting his pictures done before we head down."

"Is there an elevator?"

The intern busily detached an IV line. "At the far end of the building."

"No, I've got a quicker way. Help me roll this thing to the top of the stairs." He grabbed the near end as Darlene took her position as the pusher.

The intern scrambled to get the wires and tubing free from the ER station. After a protracted second, he gestured for takeoff. "All set to go."

The double doors bounced off his back as he pulled the gurney to the emergency exit. "Bring his lines." After drawing a fortifying breath, he bent to lift Doug. "Get his arms across my back."

"Try not to jostle him too much," Darlene added, supporting his legs.

He completed the hoist of a fireman's carry as Doug stifled the moan accompanying the jarring transition. Next, he began the agonizing descent, one weighed step at a time.

Down below, Muriel had a line of stored cots opened and stretched along the far wall of the cluttered evacuation room. Arie systematically searched for sheets and covers to drape the mattresses. They looked up as he negotiated the last of the stairs, balanced by the intern in front and Darlene in back.

"Over here, son." Muriel motioned him toward an alcove of sorts. She helped ease her cousin off his back and laid the patient face down on the cot. The intern set at once to improvise a flow through the IV and then checked Doug's vitals.

Winded, he perched on the edge of a derelict wooden chair to catch his breath.

Darlene stooped beside the cot on the bare concrete floor, still holding Doug's hand. Her fortitude failed about the same time her knees did, and she collapsed against Doug, weeping unconstrained.

"You go ahead, honey." Muriel smoothed Darlene's mud-streaked hair back into its clip. "Let it out. We're all safe now."

"Almost all." Jusdyn passed the women, moving toward the stairs.

Loren appeared with the first of three clear-sided isolets, each bearing a bracelet-clad baby from the nursery. The third portable crib was empty, but the baby followed right behind, cradled in the crook of her father's pitching arm.

He intercepted the isolets from his father, placing them one-by-one on the foldout cots.

Arie stood and took possession of Beryl, freeing Deke to return for Merrilee.

Two maternity ward nurses arrived paired with a new mother and descended the stairs. The parade came staggered by obvious pain. Nurse Mabel guided the last of the mothers down the stairs—more accurately a mother-to-be—looking poised to make the transition in fairly short order.

Loren dragged a mattress off the last cot and Muriel joined him in making a blanket-topped pallet on the floor for her labor.

The small noises in the room became a microcosm of keen awareness. Doug exhaled a pain-filled moan that set one of the newborns to crying. Darlene's rhythmic sobbing blended with the shushing appeasement of the crier's mother, after which the mother-to-be responded to her latest contraction with a gasp.

Muriel knelt to coach the young Hispanic woman through her birthing pains.

He grabbed Arie and drew Beryl toward Deke where Merrilee reclined.

Loren surrendered for a rest, sitting on the cot beside Arie.

"We'll all be fine." He took stock of the situation while Arie leaned on him, exhaling audibly. As if to beg otherwise, a thrashing of wind leveraged against the building and threatened to pry off the roof. From the safety of the hospital basement, the lights flickered once and then extinguished, delivering them into total darkness. *Blinded by a blackout.* Jusdyn blinked, but it didn't make any difference.

Chapter 18

Nature has been planned in the binary code of paired choices. Working through a dichotomous key, one may sort inorganic rock from organic being, dividing further between plant or animal, cold-blooded or warm-blooded, and male or female. One infamously paired choice associated with animal behavior is the stimulus-response mechanism of hunker or flee. Fueled by the proximity of a hungry predator or unexpected threat, prey species have a split second to choose a route for survival. The fleet of foot and swift of wing often select for flee, hedging bets on a burst of adrenaline, an explosive wing clap, and an advantage for knowing the local terrain. The less impulsive, the plodding, and the well-armored select for the other choice, opting to hunker in place, motionless and breathless, until the menace passes. While denying the thrill of escape-through-motion, the heroism of hunkering cannot be overrated. Someone must be left post-trauma to observe the dawn's early light, assess the damage, and—for tool users—bury the dead.

Peach fabric billowed in the wind, wrapping Ruby's hemline around Morrill's suit. The silkiness of it moved him in a visceral way, standing there amid the vacant stares of previous friendships marked by gray headstones. He squeezed the delicate arm that entwined his.

Ruby touched the solitary rose embellishing the stone in front of them. "Look. Here's dear Pearl, a best friend if ever I had one."

"There was a time back in high school the two of you were inseparable."

"If I had stayed closer by her side in those days, maybe she wouldn't have married the likes of Rolf Good."

"No one could have seen that coming, Ruby. We all thought the world of his brother Reed. And when Rolf moved back here after the military, we thought destiny had brought him to stay and become one of the upright pillars of the community."

"How could a man be so ready for marriage, yet be so in denial over raising a family?"

"How so, Ruby?"

"Six months into the marriage Pearl found herself expecting a baby. But Rolf didn't want family responsibilities that soon." She pressed her fingers to her lips.

"Are you implying that Rolf had something to do with Pearl's untimely death?"

"What I'm saying is that the butcher over in Admire wasn't just a meat cutter. Rumor had it he kept coat hangers in the back room for dispensing of the otherwise unwanted. Well, you can imagine the rest." She dropped her gaze as if unwilling to trust him.

Morrill mulled over the inference. The cakewalk of life sometimes included going barefoot over shattered glass. When a chilled wind sliced through the cemetery, Ruby shivered against his side from overexposure. In the distance, Vernis walked Opal back to the Buick to escape the bluster.

He slipped off his suit jacket and drew her closer under its shelter. "My dear Ruby, such are the flawed decisions common to man. Can we choose to let forgiveness unburden our hearts today?" He lowered his face to hers and smiling ever so faintly. They stood in the piercing wind as she worked through the surrendering of a long-held bitterness, eventually allowing the absolution of a lesser emotion for a greater one.

She looked up at him with a nod. "Love bears all things."

"Yes, and love endures all things—like a sixty-ycar wait, for example. But I won't let it wait another unnecessary second from here on out. Know that I love you, Ruby. I always have, and I always will." He shut out all else but her sparkling violet eyes.

"Because love hopes all things, it never arrives too late." She rose to her tiptoes and placed a kiss on his lips, allowing it to linger until the overcast sky split open.

Rain began to pelt the land without mercy. Opal's car pulled alongside the family plot and the horn sounded. He tucked Ruby into his side, and they dashed to the rear. He opened the door and followed her inside with haste, laughing as they tumbled in together.

Vernis peered back at them in the mirror. "You two kooks deserve each other."

He handed Ruby a handful of wet peach fabric in a swap for his jacket.

She tucked loose strands into her hairdo and giggled like a young woman with a secret. Soon, her sister couldn't help but join her.

Morrill raked his wind-whipped hair back into place and punched his brother's shoulder. "Must be this tipsy weather."

Vernis turned away to check his side-view mirror, but a smile soon reflected in it.

Opal drove out of the cemetery failing to employ either the defogger or the wiper blades, though the storm had picked up considerably. With a premature turn on the far corner, a torrential sheet of rain led them on a bumpy detour. Built to an extra height, this distinguished plot connoted the banking family's prominence in the community. After a protracted screech from the undercarriage, the car jerked to a complete stop atop the Whitehall plot's cornerstone.

With the Buick high-centered on the granite stone and listing heavily, Morrill realized that symphony on the prairie would no longer be the destination of this ticket-holding foursome. "Looks like we're trapped here, at least until the rain lets up." He tried to wipe the rear window clear with his sleeve to no avail.

Vernis scowled at the rain and tried to sit erect in his slightly tilted seat. "I never wanted to go to that symphony show anyway."

After a quick tug to join her on the downhill side of the back seat, Ruby caught the giggles again. Her merriment offset any potential for disappointment.

Morrill placed his jacket across the rear deck as the rain increased in intensity. "The prairie doesn't need any fancy music to gussy it up anyway. We've got the real party on the prairie going on right here in this Buick." Sensing God's hand in it all, a peace beyond understanding fell on him as their outing teetered on a mere cornerstone.

~

Arie sat upright in the darkness, only to discover Beryl's soft-as-spring-grass hair tickling her right arm. When she reached out to caress the baby's head, a shower of sparks lit the darkness. Suspecting a connection, they needed to be closer. "Loren, may I hold the baby?"

She maneuvered her arms under his for better positioning. When he passed the child without a word, she loosened the swaddled blanket to locate a tiny arm to hold. The contact birthed sparks vivid with contrast, the particles slow-moving as if trying to arrange into an image. She rested her open palm on the infant's chest to spread the connection, her pulse matching the tiny heartbeat at her fingertips. Under increased surface area, the vision coalesced into the bottom portion of a moving image.

She blinked to refocus in the dark basement, unsure of what she saw. One thing became certain. The pastel colors matched those from the vanity mirror, with Beryl now serving as a link for the transmission. The moving image portrayed feet shuffling, all moving in one direction, but not in unison. When Arie lifted the baby to her shoulder, she jostled against Jusdyn.

"Are you two okay?" His tone carried a note of concern.

She watched as the image expanded to full screen, showing

people running amuck in total mayhem. Out of nowhere, a flash of red lit the pastel scene. Then the entire image vanished. She cradled Beryl's head and shifted the infant across her lap. "The baby helped bring me another vision."

"What could you see?"

"Feet moving in one direction across the grass, and then racing in all directions." She tucked the blanket up under the infant's chin, hopeful Beryl would continue to sleep in peace. "The closer I held the baby, the more I could see. Toward the end, people ran in total chaos. There was a flash of red before the image went dark." A fragile silence followed her revelation.

"The governor's in danger." Loren's voice cracked the quiet, husky with apprehension. "Last week, the newspaper reported that the governor would wear red to the symphony."

Jusdyn bumped her as he stood. 'We've got to get to the east side as soon as possible."

"Nurse Mabel Proctor?" Loren spoke in a commanding tone, making the baby startle.

"Present," the nurse replied from across the black abyss.

"Do we need to throw a lever to get your emergency generator to fire up?"

"No. It should switch over automatically to maintain life support systems—at least that's how the system was designed."

Arie scanned the perimeter of the basement until she detected a pinpoint of orange light on the far wall. "Loren, I think I see a dot glowing on the back wall to the right." She nudged Jusdyn with a finger.

"Let me get this." He departed to make his way over to the light. His frame soon eclipsed the orange dot. Within seconds, a whirring sound led a cavalry of galloping gray incandescence overhead. The faint illumination strengthened within seconds.

"Hallelujah for small miracles," Merrilee said, reaching to connect with her daughter.

Arie passed the newborn back to Deke, who lowered the

precious bundle to her mother for a kiss. The intern snapped into position at Doug's side, checking the drip from the IV with Darlene assisting. When Jusdyn passed in front of her, a sense of duty compelled her to follow. She rose and kissed his shoulder to seal their togetherness.

"Wait." Loren stood, visibly hesitant. "We don't even know if it's safe out there yet."

"I think Arie's supposed to help me, Dad." Jusdyn locked his fingers through hers. "Plus, we have the rain suits, so let us be the first ones to venture out."

Muriel stood up as if to rally in Loren's defense.

A permissive nod reflected his change of heart. "I stashed some raingear in the trunk of Muriel's car. Would you mind throwing that bundle into the foyer before you head out?"

"You've got it, Dad."

"Be careful out there." Muriel's caution chased them from the safety of shelter.

They climbed the stairs at a frantic pace. As the basement door clicked shut behind them, a subtle delineation fell between the safe and the at-risk. When Jusdyn forced open the emergency room door, Arie caught a glimpse of the destruction outside and began to tremble.

~

"I honestly cannot believe this cursed event is going to get off the ground." TJ pulled the symphony program out of his back pocket and gave it a glance. Stationed at the main gate, a posse of cowboys on horseback awaited their cue in the third score. For visual effect, they were scripted to approach the herd, round up the cattle near the northern ridgeline, and then run them across the open prairie to emulate the days of old. He checked for Valor and found her on the second row of violins seated beside her music mentor. Much to his relief, she had even removed those tacky pants.

He drove the ATV over toward the familiar cowboys. "Hey, Keeter. Heard you guys had a funnel cloud out your way. Doug

McLauren got injured and had to be brought to the hospital."

"First I've heard tell of any bad weather in Wilsey, TJ." The cowboy stroked his beard. "I'm unplugged right now since I never carry my cell phone when I'm on horseback. They just don't go together, if you know what I mean." Several members of the posse laughed at the insider's joke, making rowdy comments until the appaloosa in back squirreled around, fighting the rider's attempt at control.

"Better keep your distance, Junior." Keeter flipped his reins to the north. "You can wander up the fence line and check TJ's perimeter—since he ain't doing it. That way you can still fall in with us about halfway out to the ridge."

"Sorry, Keeter," Junior replied. "He fidgets something terrible whenever it thunders. There's nothing I can do about it but ride out the storm." He spurred the appaloosa, reined left, and headed north of the symphony along the fence line.

"Oh, hearken to the woes of the lonesome cowboy," TJ joked behind him. "That detached duty will likely pull some heartstrings in the crowd today."

"Right," Keeter agreed, turning to view the amassing crowd. "Nobody needs to tell the rest of the story, that the appaloosa's spooked by mysterious thunder nobody else can hear." The posse got a good laugh out of that admission, loosening attitudes in the spirit of the occasion.

TJ spied the adage-fracturing attorney waving his symphony program while heading his way. "Well, I better go. Give 'em a good show, fellas." As he downshifted into avoidance mode, a black Lexus with official state plates caught his attention. "Uh-oh. Here comes the big boss now. I'd better return to my post." He swung the ATV around and headed to the north gate. Up ahead, Junior steered the appaloosa away from the thunder of a black Lexus chomping at the bit to gain entrance.

He squeezed the brake and quick-stepped to the gate chain, releasing the lock and swinging the barrier wide open. The luxury car slinked onto the prairie like an urban mistake, the rear window sliding down in electric smoothness until it no longer mirrored the grass.

A well-coifed woman appeared in the frame. "Howdy, TJ."

"Welcome to the tallgrass prairie, Governor." He swept his hat toward the big bluestem.

"The weather's not going to come down on us this morning, is it?"

"I hope not, ma'am, as that would downright ruin the show, now wouldn't it?"

"Would for me, that's for certain. Got any pointers to heighten my enjoyment?"

"Yeah, don't miss the junior violinist in the second piece. She's a chip off my old block and can make that fiddle squawk pretty good."

"I'm sure she's a darling. Come find me at the dog-and-pony show for dignitaries afterward. I'll have a picture taken with your little musician."

"That's a deal, ma'am. You folks enjoy the show." He tapped his hat back into place as the window retraced its fitting. The Lexus pulled toward the patrons' tent, met by a cacophony of strings and woodwinds tuning up. He secured the gate and sat idle to guard the restricted entry. From his remote vantage point, he watched as a red swatch exited the car to a smattering of applause. The patrons' tent stood stark white beneath the darkening sky, making him realize how much the gala failed to blend in.

He traced the lay of the land with his eyes, following the gullies down to Big John Creek. A great blue heron sat in the tallest tree overlooking the creek, a storybook picture of tranquility. Funny how the landscape used to move him, making his heart yearn for the vast open spaces. Lately, the rural horizon represented nothing but an unproductive wasteland, a meaningless distance between two fences with a herd of cookie-cutter cattle trapped in the middle.

What a peculiar happenstance to have fallen out of love with the land. Such a stance left him like a man without a country, listless with no comfortable port to call home. In truth, he had given up on a number of things simultaneously, and now it became difficult to separate the significance of one forfeiture from another. What a ruse of a life to change so much on the inside, yet try to maintain respectable outward appearances. He couldn't figure out who he was anymore. How fitting to be stationed on the perimeter of the largest gathering of his people, watching like an outsider from afar.

~

Jusdyn's senses sat on edge as he maneuvered the old truck down Main Street Council Grove. Washunga Day banners flailed and jerked in the wind, longing to be freed from their moorings on the light poles. The small-town setting looked anything but festive.

"Erie, isn't it?" Arie craned to peer down each empty street they passed.

He reached over and put a reassuring hand on her knee. "Not a great commentary on our first date in town, is it? Look, I want us to stay together no matter what. Do you understand?" Her nod provided a bit of relief. "What's in that hamper, anyway?"

"More significant acts of love waiting to happen."

"You packed some emergency food, didn't you?"

"Maybe. It never hurts to be prepared."

"Whoa. Would you look at that?" He braked to a stop midway on the bridge over the Neosho River. "The Corps of Engineers must have opened the gates on the dam." The spectacle of rushing water moving down the river's course in foam-crested chaos left quite the impression.

Arie squeezed her eyes closed and dry-heaved, her hands clamping over her mouth.

"Crank the window down." His suggestion barely landed in time.

She pitched ashen white toward the door. The window handle could have popped off in her hand, she turned it so violently. She navigated the brief tempest of nausea. Recoiling from the window, she groped for the hamper, flipped open the lid, and grabbed a napkin from the top.

He attempted a boardinghouse reach to crank the window closed and caught an eye-full of the seething sky static bearing down from the south. The atmosphere seemed absolutely aquiver. The outer dark gray band contrasted with ricocheting bolts of lightning, like a pulsing vein on the temple of a madman. "Oh, thunder." His breath ran short. "A tornado is coming up Dunlap Road—and we're too early for a rescue."

Arie covered her eyes as wave after wave of rushing water slapped the bridge pilings below. "Or too late. Can you get us off this bridge?"

He released the clutch and forced the vehicle to advance, though their eastward progression wasn't the direction his instincts demanded. They should be fleeing in the opposite direction. Rain found the hood in half a block as they passed the Madonna of the Plains statue.

Quelling a growing desperation for cover, he began to scour familiar terrain. The Post Office Oak historic site appeared on the left, and the Apple Market on the right. Relying on gut instinct, he forged ahead one driveway at a time, evaluating potential shelters. Finally, he spotted the combination he needed—an alcove for the truck under the Farmers and Ranchers drive-through ATM with the town park anchored next door. He wheeled to the left and jammed the truck under the overhang. "Are you in any shape to run?"

"I'll be right with you." Arie pulled her hood up and stared out at the rain.

"We have three choices inside the park—the cowpoke calaboose, the train depot, or the old red caboose. Got a preference?"

"The closest one."

"Get ready to go to jail, then." He coaxed the door open, grabbed her hand, and pulled her out of the cab behind him, hitting the ground at a run. He set a vigorous pace across the narrow side street and lifted her onto the porch of the two-celled jailhouse. A humble respite for incarceration dating back to Santa Fe Trail days, the calaboose stood solid, a square of flat-stacked lumber built sturdy to resist ruffian breakouts.

He touched the rusted metal grate barring the entrance to one of the twin cells. "Number one or two?"

She stepped left on the creaky floorboards. "Away from the tornado."

He grabbed the metal bar and forced open the latch, letting Arie enter. "Take the back inside corner." He slammed the barred door closed. Slipping to a crouch beside her, he faced away from the storm and wrapped her in a shielding embrace. "You've got to admit. This date's getting a little memorable now." He pressed his nose against her cheek.

"Totally unforgettable." She shifted her crouch in silence, listening while the hounds of hell rode churning winds up Old Dunlap Road. "We should pray right about now." She started to beg for protection, her voice shaky but reverent.

"Yes, God help us in our time of dire need," he added. Too frightened to breathe, he leaned against the jail cell's innermost wall as the storm sheared up the east side of Council Grove. *Hunkered and helpless.* His discernment blanked out as the deafening locomotive sound approached the old train depot a mere stone's throw away.

~

Just in time to have music soothe the savage beast within TJ's rebellious heart, the symphony began to play. One note on a thin edge pressed against a blade of grass and then a second joined in. The highly refined met the lowly natural by the end of the first bar, and the two struck up an eclectic acquaintance. *Simply mesmerizing. Imagine the effect from the front row.* He quickly found the music to be an intermediary on some higher plane, an escape from the schism that frequently robbed him of peace. He sat behind the crowd in motionless surrender.

A flock of oboes ended the first piece on a rich hovering note that lingered on his ear. When he realized the audience had begun applauding, he joined them with vigor. Mildly shocking, it represented his first genuine reaction all day. He craned to see, if by the remotest of chances, he could spot Valor being antsy for her entrance.

A strong solitary violin explored the grass next, like a mother cow looking for her calf, surefooted on the Flint Hills. The calf then echoed the same call as Valor launched into the piece in absolute perfection. He held his breath, unsure whether out of fear of flaw, or forgetting his wellbeing in deference to hers. The entire section of violins carried the next bar forward atop the hill in resounding support, reveling in a thousand wildflowers along their way.

His eyes misted, wholly transported by the moment. The song resonated far and wide, so ethereal it transcended time or place. Then, as a solitary violin echoed the lingering refrain once again, the music vanished into the air. Applause roared like a thunderous bison herd back upon the prairie once again. He shook his head and pinched the tears out of his eyes. The conductor paused to acknowledge the soloists with individual bows, which apparently Valor feigned some reluctance to do. At last he made visual contact as Vorchenski picked her up like a heroine, causing the audience to laugh with delight until unchecked applause swept the hillside again.

The cue for the cowboys came like a firecracker over the megaphone a good measure too early, its amped volume startling him. The conductor seemed caught off-cue, though the cowboys' round up began in earnest. The musicians started playing somewhat out-of-sync, as if trying to catch the cowboy's galloping horses.

Too jumbled to be planned, TJ strained to assess the situation. When he gazed up on the ridgeline and spotted Junior trying to control his rearing appaloosa, a chilling dread trickled over him. A solitary wisp of smoke caught the next gust of wind, hinting of a lightning strike on the power pole housing the sound system. Within a split second, thunder ripped across the low-ceiling of storm clouds above the event.

To their credit, the symphony members held their ground attempting to play out the piece. The appaloosa streaked across the ridgeline with its throttle stuck on maximum speed, converting Junior into a pony express rider lacking any mail to deliver. Keeter and his fellow cowboys worked the herd into a tight group, but failed to make the beasts move in unison against the aggravation of erratic winds.

An absence of microphone now thwarted the ascending warning scale as planned, so he never heard the code yellow directive rendered. When the orchestra finished the piece, portions of the crowd had already left their seats for the shelter of the close-by vendor tents. Uninvited, the rain arrived in drenching sheets as the event coordinator gestured for movement into shelters for a weather delay. Viewing the mayhem from the perimeter, he gritted his teeth in disgust.

The orchestra members dispersed and blended with the audience, exiting toward the tents with their instruments. Confused and wetter by the second, the crowd capitulated to chaos, moving in a tangled exodus.

Dry-mouthed at the apparent lack of leadership in the situation, TJ cranked the ATV to life and headed for the northern flank of the crowd. Up ahead, Keeter led the cowboys around the western flank, herding the concert attendees back toward the historic stone barn. *At least it's a plan with a roof overhead.* Speeding ahead, he drove straight into the rain. At the edge of the swarm, he pulled out his rain poncho and snatched it over his head, circling his arm in exaggerated motion toward the stone barn.

An extended flash of blue-tinted lightning blazed to the south and struck the HVAC system of the 4-H building nearby. The ensuing explosion deafened him momentarily, soliciting shrieks from the chaos-bound crowd. Gunmetal blue gleamed from the door panel of an escaping Lexus. He cursed under his breath as the car slinked toward his north gate, knowing full well he had secured the lock and the dignitaries would be trapped. Standing on the foot pedals, he searched for Valor one last time in the crowd, gave up with a growl, and then jerked the handlebars hard left to go pacify the antsy Lexus.

~

"Together." Valor insisted on the coupling though the press of the crowd knocked against her instrument. She squeezed her instructor's hand and pulled him along the uneven ground toward the stone barn. Pelting dirt made it difficult to see so she followed the general movement of the crowd. Unable to hasten, Dr. Vorchenski tried to let go, but she refused. Swifter runners passed them on both sides, but the storm wasn't kind to the slow. She lifted her face into the rain in time to recognize one of the cowboys pressing down on them.

Rain rolled off his hat brim as he dismounted. "Children are being evacuated to safe shelter." He grabbed her shoulders. "I'll take the girl from here."

Dr. Vorchenski nodded, relinquishing her hand to the rescuer.

A wave of fear collapsed her insides. "No—I can't leave you!" She fought for freedom as the cowboy lifted her onto his saddle. During the struggle, her instrument slipped from her grasp. The sidestepping horse crushed it into the mud.

As the cowboy mounted behind her, her music mentor appeared off the horse's front flank. "The music lives on—and now must go with you." He handed over his violin and bow.

She grasped them in a blur of tears. "Bless you, Dr. Vorchenski." Her heart ached for him as the horse turned deeper into the storm. Unable to take the worsening commotion, she shut her eyes and clutched the precious violin. She felt the cowboy's arm lock around her as the horse broke into a hasty gallop.

~

The north gate stood stalwart, impervious to the pelting rain, the raging wind, and the sharp horn blasts of an impertinent Lexus. TJ fumbled with the chain, found the lock with the key, and threw open the gate. Wincing under the responsibility of having to

236

evacuate VIPs in the heat of total chaos, he took on the responsibility of someone else's job in the spur of the moment, a bitter outcome.

Inflicted with a slight hesitation, the driver lowered his window, only to have the rear window immediately follow. "TJ, can you make a recommendation? Should we just stay here in the car?" The governor's imploring tone replaced her typical all-business demeanor.

"No, ma'am—at least not here in the open." He looked over the car's roof and saw the unmistakable profile of the 4-H building, now released from its foundation and hurtling through the skies into a vacuum of death-gray.

"Dear Mother of God." His exclamation turned to gravel in his throat as he stared at the dreaded atmospheric phenomena he'd only read about. The right side windows on the Lexus floated down in silent query. As far as the eye could see east to west, a gray-green vortex both filled the sky and cleared the land. The eerie modulation of a wind-filled wedge struck next, like the slicing of a deafening scissor symphony, followed by the ripped-from-the-roots sound of the land receiving it.

A possible escape route occurred to him in a panic. "No time to waste. Follow me." TJ mounted the ATV in a burst of adrenaline. He tore through the gateless opening, turning a hard left toward the north pastures. Having stomped these grounds in the idleness of high school mischief-making with buddy Jimmy John Wilson, he had a couple of ideas where to hole up with his burdensome entourage.

The pipe gate to the Metzgers pasture sat closed but not chained, so he throttled the ATV to open the gate with brute force, allowing entrance for his small parade. He kicked the pipe gate open further as he passed, the Lexus following shadow close. A rock-strewn hill rose off the fence line to the east where raindrops had just begun to color the limestone darker yellow. Within seconds, the refuge he sought came into view beyond the barbed wire fence.

Only a wire gate and fifteen yards of amicable prairie stood between the escapees and adequate shelter. He shouldered into the gatepost, loosened the wire loop that held the post in place, and flung the wire gate open. He advanced the ATV toward the foot of the hill. Rocks abounded everywhere, and the Lexus had to pull up short to avoid the blocky foundation remains. To the right, an arched entrance to a root cellar frowned from a grotto in the hillside.

"End of the road," TJ shouted, beckoning the occupants out. Three men and the governor abandoned their escape vehicle and stood frozen at the atrocity occurring on the horizon. He pointed to the hollow interior of the root cellar. "Give me two in here."

The driver and a guard turned to the governor who motioned permission to take cover. The two men stumbled up the hillside, hastening to beat the advancing tornado.

"Governor, you're with me." TJ tore off his rain poncho and covered her red suit. "Get on the ATV. There's an old dry well shaft just ahead. You'll be safe in there." When she hesitated and nodded toward her husband, he shot out an option. "Let him run the distance—it's not far." He angled north, searching like a madman for the spider hole he and Jimmy John used to pitch rocks down ages ago. Years of plant growth had altered the appearance of the gully, and heavy rain began to cloak the landscape even more. The couple attempted to hold hands, but the ATV's rapid progress pulled them apart.

He began to zigzag, first through rocks and then through relics of dismembered farm equipment. The wind and rain pitched against them, pushing up from the south. As a panicked sense of failure wedged against his sternum, the old well opened up right under the ATV. With half a tire's width holding him onto the prairie's surface, he locked the hand brake and slid off.

He lifted his petite passenger and pulled her to the lip of the shaft. Seconds later, her husband joined them at the precipice. Even with big rocks littering the bottom, it easily represented a fifteen-foot drop.

He regarded the governor, now looking merely mortal—and frightened at that. ""He goes down first. Then I'll pass you down to him to lessen the risk."

Her devoted partner already sat on the slumping edge of the well's casement, ready to be lowered to secure entry. He reached up and they locked forearms. That rain-slicked grasp lasted a fleeting second and ended with a premature vertical transfer. The rocks below held a hostile reception for the visitor who howled on impact.

Desperate and down to one, he turned to grab the governor who already had his profile fixed in her gaze.

"You're coming in with us, right TJ?"

He set his grasp and began lifting her from the rim. Nearby, a warning cry from the guard pierced the prairie. Upon glancing over to find the rock arch now under assault, he slid the governor into the tunnel's opening with haste. They locked gazes for an infinitesimal moment, a real gut check. "Remember me to Valor," he managed, releasing her down the well hole.

He fought back to the ATV, the storm now breaking over his head like a punishing reprimand. Crevasses in the limestone ledge offered his only salvation now, so he headed for the cliff rim like a man possessed. Lowering his profile in the wind, he set his arms like steel on the handlebars, straight-lining toward the crumbling ledge.

"Want me to cry out for your help, don't you?" he ranted skyward. "No way. I refuse to give you the satisfaction." The ATV wheeled onto the limestone ridge leaving him a split second to pick a launch spot. He steered hard right and went airborne, setting the adrenaline deeper.

At the last second, TJ recognized the protruding nose of Sulking Bull, Jimmy John's favorite rock formation, and kicked away from the ATV in midair. His free-fall aimed at a deep crack in the face of the limestone landmark. Landing headfirst, the impact proved brutal. And then the world went black.

Chapter 19

The nuances of transition for wildlife can be comprehended as much more than a superficial makeover of external characteristics, though many extremities may be rearranged in the process. In the case of the Woodhouse toad, metamorphosis will require the underling to grow limbs and absorb its tail, seemingly counterproductive for continued agility in the aquatic environment. Seldom is the tadpole forward-thinking enough to understand that it is being equipped for life as a terrestrial amphibian, which it will enjoy quite thoroughly as soon as its taste buds adapt alongside. In the complete metamorphosis of the monarch butterfly, the transition to adult phase is much more stagger-step, and the caterpillar never imagines itself the ornate, aerially acrobatic butterfly until he stops and surrenders to the pupa's motionless chrysalis. The inevitability of change through time should thus be considered the honing of a creature to its highest state, and the time of acclimation truly savored.

Jusdyn couldn't be certain how long the slatted hull of the calaboose stood as their gauntlet against the pummeling winds. By his best reckoning they had missed the brunt of the dark gray core, but continued to catch its slanderous edge. At least they were fairly dry, as beneficiaries of the build-to-last philosophy of the State Historic Preservation Officer's commitment for solid roof construction. They would wait out only the destructive winds because pressing concern for the unsheltered would not allow them to wait out the rain.

"Hey, we may be walking into a world of hurt pretty soon." He squeezed his eyes closed, imagining what the symphony might look like turned upside-down. He had never arrived in the fresh wake of a disaster before and couldn't begin to fathom the unnatural order of it all.

Arie slipped her hand between his and drew a weighted breath. "Well, whatever the Lord leads us to, we have to look on the situation with compassion."

"You know, entering a tunnel trailing death's shadow isn't exactly a path I would have chosen in the past." Though he couldn't visualize life's upcoming horizon, he sensed an urge to step toward it with her. A world larger than the fields of Wilsey opened before him, dissolving his crutch of dependency on familiar surroundings. His gaze rested on a rusty lock frozen on the jail door, and then dropped to her face.

Arie gave his hand a squeeze. "Maybe the real reason I came back to Wilsey was so you wouldn't have to face your new path alone."

Each honest word seared deeper into his soul, affirming a divine gift of immeasurable consequence. "Together and forward, then?" he whispered, his heart searching for hers. In the silence that followed he heard the wind lash a final swirling barrage against the calaboose and quit, leaving only rain. Somehow, the jail cell seemed less dim at the prospect.

"Yes, together and forward—on the prairie and for the prairie."

Jusdyn stood to leave, offering her a hand up. He'd been given a helper because the Good Lord knew he needed one. The trip back to the truck would be telling, given the destructive power of strong winds. They had a mile to navigate before reaching the symphony grounds, a tattered route at best.

~

Loren returned to the lobby from delivering the last of the baby isolets to the maternity ward. Though far from clearing, the skies appeared a familiar shade of overcast gray, without the orange-tinged anger of encased wind. The portico roof lay strewn across the hospital's front lawn, along with other debris brought uphill by swirling winds.

Loren noticed his rain gear rolled against the front glass of the main entrance and headed toward it. "This is going to be a royal mess."

"You aren't kidding," Mabel replied, following him into the lobby. "I need to set up an emergency admissions process that can streamline our check-in."

"You might consider what you really need to know and boil it down to the essentials." Oversensitive, he'd just gone through the tedious paperwork for Doug. "Try name, phone number, and next of kin."

"Our billing department may skin me alive over this." She turned and walked toward the admissions counter.

"Not if I have anything to do with it." He shoved open the grit-bound door and reached down to pick up his roll. Coming up the hill, motion caught his attention so he straightened to behold a scene blown in from the past. "Mabel, you have your first aftermath customers—and they're riding in on a workhorse of the ages."

The floor nurse walked midway out into the lobby to spy the antique tractor making traction on the rain-slicked road. "You mean those broken people on a hunk of junk?"

"Funny, I see them as our first storm survivors riding in on a classic Farmall M tractor in desperate need of medical help. I'll clear the front entrance and try to get them to pull in here."

"Let me get the abbreviated forms ready. Send them to me at the admissions desk."

"Will do. And Mabel, here's something to think about. As Christians, we're challenged to put on the garment of love. I always equated that with the comfort of cotton, like a favorite T-shirt, easy to wear and soft from lots of everyday use. But today that covering might look more like the cotton scrubs a nurse wears, so give a thought about what love looks like on you."

She stood wordless at the desk, blinking as if his words had struck a nerve.

He walked out and began to clear the front entrance of the hospital for the incoming walking wounded. The M pulled into the front circle drive, guided by his beckoning. He lifted a frail farmer's wife off the contraption and escorted both refugees inside.

Mabel met them halfway out with a clipboard in her hands. "Your names, please."

"Erskine and Viola Newcomb," the elderly man replied. "I think her arm is broke."

"We'll get to treating her right away, I promise you." Mabel's tone dripped with compassion. "All I need is the name and phone number of a loved one, in case we need to contact them."

Loren faded behind the couple, flashing a thumbs-up on the speedy check-in as he headed outside to resume clearing the entrance of storm debris.

~

Valor blinked as her eyes adjusted to the dingy darkness of their safety tube. Children of every size were crammed into its length, making for tight quarters. She had been next to the last in rescue order and now stood crowded by the final addition of a boy who'd been reluctant to part from his mother. She reached out and touched the protective barrier rolled in place at the culvert's end, the millstone used each year to crush sugarcane at the Fall Festival. Repeated volleys of dirt and debris jetted through the cracks left by the stone's imperfect seal. When the boy sobbed, she felt compelled to act. "Hey, my name is Valor. Why so much fuss?"

"I'm Bobby Dean Hale. My face is bleeding."

"Show my finger where the hurt is, and I'll make it go away." When he lifted her hand to his forehead, she felt the sticky mat of blood beneath a considerable gash of flesh. Needing the direct contact, she traced the length of it with her finger. Seconds passed in numbness, leaving her to wonder if the boy would be reluctant to let off his sobbing. "Does your head feel any better yet, Bobby Dean?"

"A little, I reckon." The boy didn't seem to embrace improvement as another sob escaped. More forsaken children began to despair at their abandonment as the full length of the tube filled with moans and sobs.

The idea of a musical remedy came to her. "Don't stand up too tall, Bobby Dean. I'm fixin' to play right over your head." She angled the full-sized violin to her chin and freed her opposing arm to pass the bow over its strings. Another round of grit spattered into the tunnel, but she set her heart to bring peace inside the tube over the storm's objections.

Amid sobbing cries, Valor launched into her featured score, the notes rippling down the corrugated tube. A hush soon fell across the group, lending a sense of fragile peace. She recalled the symphony performance when their world was more in order. How she wished the occupants could be consoled by familiar faces once again. She played Dr. Vorchenski's final refrain with reverence. When the last note vanished, the haven remained quiet.

"Water's flowing into my end of the tube," an older boy said in a shaky voice.

"That's okay." Slow water didn't pose a threat. "That's just nature's way of showing us she's already recovering and putting the rain where she wants it to go—downhill."

"But what if I spoil my Sunday shoes and get in trouble?" a young girl asked.

"Okay, anyone who wants to can take off their shoes and socks." To set the example, she soon had hers off, giving her more items to carry. The next instant, the tube filled with wiggle worms becoming barefoot in the storm. Somewhat exposed, she pined for her froggin' pants while the gusting wind seemed intent to blow the whole world away beyond the stone.

~

Loren peeled off the rain jacket and crossed the lobby toward the admissions counter where Mabel regarded him heavy-faced. A radio show buzzed with chatter in the background. When the emergency frequency tone sounded over the air, they both paused to listen. As the bulletin ended, he opened his mouth to comment, only to be silenced by Mabel's shushing finger and a tacked-on plea from the radio announcer.

"We understand our friends down in Morris County are taking a wallop being dished out by the weather right now. The management here at WIBW wants you to know our thoughts and prayers are with you all. Stay hunkered and tuned in, folks. We promise to keep you updated with the latest Doppler readings and area warnings." Mabel nodded in appreciation.

"In that light, we are making an exception to our long-standing rule of no personal communications being aired from this frequency with the following message. It goes out to a noted weather spotter from out Wilsey way named Loren Linquist. If you're listening— and I feel certain that you are—your son is requesting assistance over at the symphony grounds."

Loren stared wide-eyed across the counter at Mabel.

She ran a hand across her thick neck and rested it across her carotid. "Time for you to go. Here, take this." Her hand slid into a front pocket and pulled out her cell phone. "Hit Memory One followed by Send, and I'll be right on the other end." She nodded and made him accept the device.

Loren swallowed the technophobic lump rising in his throat. Tossing aside the last vestige of his isolated world, he clipped the phone to his belt. "I'll go over, but I need Muriel and Darlene with me. Remember, any help arriving for you here has to approach town from the west. Make that crystal clear to anyone calling in."

"Right, chief."

"Any word on a doctor for Doug yet?" He looked back for her response, walking toward the ER to gather his entourage.

"On his way from the west side of the lake." She held up a finger as if to keep score.

As he departed, the talk radio babbled its inconsequential repartee as the rest of the Midwest enjoyed a routine summer's day.

~

With every nerve ending in his face firing with acute pain, TJ clutched the rock ledge like a gargoyle in a suicide crouch. He'd have little to lose should he submit to the tornado's thrashing. Call that a fitting end to the good years he'd allowed recent circumstances to tarnish. Death would vault him from hero to martyr, a celebration always held without the guest of honor. Another strafing of flint rock pummeled his exterior making an animal-like grunt escape his throat.

The new wave of pain provoked an unescorted thought. If he could survive, there might be a crack in the storm's aftermath through which he could slither unnoticed. At first, the idea appealed to his depraved side, fed up with maintaining the façade of decency in a nine-to-five existence. Pushed by pain, he began to fan the dark flame of hope with a renewed finger-grip of determination. Valor's face flashed onto his mind's eye for an involuntary instant, but he quelled it by planning his clandestine exit, step-by-step. *Be gone dual existence.* From the cocoon of Sulking Bull's lap, a menace would emerge—with all honorable strings severed.

~

Jusdyn's drive into the symphony grounds ended at the trunk of a large black walnut tree lying across the only access road into the site. Exiting the cab, he climbed atop the fallen log in the pouring rain, surveying the ravaged landscape to the north. That walnut tree once stood as sentinel for the riparian woodland flanking a draw between the 4-H building and the rodeo grounds. When Arie's hand slid into his, he pulled her up by his side. Even through the rain he could see that the valley beyond had been sheared to ground level. "Lord, have mercy."

He scanned the path of the tornado for any signs of life. The only motion came in the form of incessant rain. A wet blackness descended on him as the first rescuer on the scene. Downcast at the decimation, only the touch of Arie's hand seemed to buoy his spirits.

An ethereal, out-of-place sound emerged over the drumming rain. Of distinct human origin, it floated like a melodic harkening over the desolate scene. As the lilting promise of life continued, he took heart and pushed back against the arresting shock. "Could that be our Valor?"

He leapt from the log and followed the signal's beckon to its source. Violin music wafted up from the depths of the creek bed, which currently performed its purpose as a water conveyance feature. After splashing into the ankle-deep water, he discovered the grinding stone capping the culvert pipe. He dug at the stone to widen a crack. "Valor? Are you in there?" He peered inside, hope quickening his heartbeat.

Valor's big blue eyes soon appeared in the gap. "Yes, I'm in here. Hey, everybody. We've been found!" Multiple voices responded from inside the tube celebrating the news.

When a hug glanced off his slick shoulders, he turned to find Arie, now wet-footed in the trenches with him. "Help me roll this stone onto the creek bank." He took a stance on the closer edge to maximize the push while she joined him a bit lower.

Flotsam from the wind combined with runoff from the rain to add resistance, but he would not be denied. The millstone rocked and fell back in place twice. But then on the third heft, he forced the rock wheel into compliance, dropping the stone flat into the mud. The tube entrance filled with living, breathing children eager to end their captive phase.

"Praise God above." Arie collapsed on the opening to take the first child.

Jusdyn reached past a chubby boy to evict Valor, violin and all. When she squeezed her bony limbs around his frame, he fought the burn of honest tears, kissing her tousled hair.

"None of us have our shoes on." Valor clamped hers under one arm.

He laughed and hugged his precious second cousin, more like a little sister to him than anyone else on the face of the earth.

Arie bent and picked up the sullen first boy, who kissed her cheek like a long lost relative.

"We'll carry you back to the truck." He turned to ascend the bank, clueless as to how many shoe-toting children waited in the culvert. As he navigated the slippery slope, Valor held the violin over her head like an umbrella.

Arie took a wider swing and met the downed walnut tree further along its length, setting the boy free atop its deeply grooved bark. The boy scampered and met Valor up the log where he grabbed both and transferred them to the truck cab.

Exhilarated by their discovery, he hopped the fallen trunk in one fell swoop and caught Arie's rain-slicked hand, turning her toward him for a personal celebration. "How are you doing now, Miss Henning?" Towering over her, he grinned.

"On top of the world, Wildcat."

He lifted her chin and kissed her like an exuberant sailor just returning to port. A heartening cheer came from the tube below. He slid down the bank, turning his attention back to the children. "Okay. Who's next?"

"Me, Jenna Baker." A freckle-faced elementary-aged girl put her hand in the air. She tiptoed to the pipe's edge. Though her expression seemed rimmed with worry, a flicker of relief shone in her blue eyes.

He moved with care and lifted her with a prayer for her relatives, wherever they might be.

"Next is Tucker Marshall," an older boy said, standing back to wait his eventual turn. "He's only four."

Arie moved in and lifted the small boy into her arms.

The little tyke grew chatty. "I only liked part of the concert."

"Oh? Which part was that?"

"The part where the cowboys saved us by putting us in the

tube." He jabbed his thumb back at the refuge as they progressed uphill.

When Jusdyn shot an askance glance as she set the boy on the log bridge, she responded by shrugging her shoulders.

He grabbed the boy and delivered the two children to the cab as Valor opened the door. "Tell me. Did the cowboys pick you out of the crowd to save you inside the culvert?"

"Don't know about the rest of them 'cause I was near 'bout last." Valor licked her lips as if trying to recall. "Mr. Keeter came and picked me up, and then his heavy-footed horse stepped right on my violin. That's when Dr. Vorchenski told me the music needed to live on and passed his priceless violin up to me. I'll never forget that moment as long as I live."

"About how many cowboys were in the show?"

"I'd say three. No, maybe four. One couldn't keep his horse still so he left early and went up on the ridge. His horse had a speckled rump."

"That's Junior Yates. He and Keeter are both from Wilsey." Jusdyn drew a deep breath. "Remind me to thank them a million times over for collecting all you precious kids and keeping you safe in this tube corral."

Arie clapped for his attention. "Hey. I could use some help down here."

The older boy now waited with a set of twin girls identically dressed and standing shoulder-to-shoulder in front.

Energized, he hurdled over the walnut's trunk, slid down the mud bank, and stood in front of the culvert to pluck one of the twins.

"You're going to run out of dry storage space." The teenager leaned sideways to reveal at least a dozen more faces awaiting freedom.

Arie laughed. "What a delightful problem to have." She reached for the second ribbon-tied girl.

"Problem? What problem?" He lifted the first girl while contemplating a possible solution. From the bottom of his heart, he wished more help would arrive, witness the euphoric rescue of these children, and bring him about twenty seats of available space.

~

Coasting down the hill from the hospital, Loren found himself hankering for his utilitarian truck. The family car had such low clearance that if any debris littered the road ahead, their arrival on the east side would be hindered.

Muriel sat beside him, giving him an evaluative look. "Sure could use my medic bag today. So, what's with you?"

"I've got a perfectly good storm shelter at home completely going to waste."

"That wasn't how it fell out for us today, was it? Maybe the townsfolk need us."

"Maybe so."

"I've used my nursing degree more today than I have in twenty-five years."

"Granted, a silver lining lurks in there somewhere." He pulled left onto the highway, easing into the residential portion of town. Certainly not the damage zone he had imagined, almost everything remained intact, minus a few brittle elm branches. Once the wipers cleared his view, he spotted a smudge of blue up the hill amid the white headstones of the cemetery. "Good grief. Is that Opal Litke's car sitting in the graveyard?" He wrenched in his seat.

"Sure looks like it. Turn in for Pete's sake." Muriel gave his shoulder a shove.

He slowed to get a better look and could tell the car sat tilted, its front bumper nosing into the large Whitehall monument.

"Looks like she's got herself stuck, but we've got a higher calling right now." He loosened the cell phone from his waist. The car veered sharply as he attempted to focus on the dial, so Muriel snatched the phone away. "Dial Memory One, then Send."

She completed the sequence and held the unit to his ear.

"Mabel, Loren here. Get Deke and have him take the M down the hill to the cemetery. Opal Litke's blue Buick is hitched up on a cornerstone, and she's going to need some help. They're probably right inside, riding out the storm." He paused for her response, continuing into town. When the nurse questioned the instructions, he got flustered. "The M is that rusty heap of tractor out in your front entrance, that's what. How about we use what we have and be glad for it? Okay, we will." He dismissed the call.

Muriel closed the flip phone and laid it on his lap. "Jeepers, you act like you could get use to that thing."

"Well, an old dog learns a new trick when he has to." He smiled without meaning it, positioning the phone back in place. "My son sent me an S-O-S message over the radio, and I don't plan to stop for any diversions until I get there." He glanced in the rearview mirror to check on Darlene and found the dark green Subaru shadowing their inept rescue vehicle.

Muriel looked over at him with a tinge of fear on her face. "Can I tell an old dog how much he means to me before everything starts getting squirrelly?"

He reached across the plush seat and took her hand. "We have each other, right? Whether we're in Wilsey or not." He could only hope that togetherness was enough. When Jusdyn flashed to mind, he sensed the distance between them closing though he still had a river to cross.

TJ's legs felt like he had been adrift at sea for days as he stood in the driving rain. One glance south along the tornado's route was all he allowed, lest there be some damsel in need of rescue or other such hindrance to his plan. Nothing familiar remained which he took as an omen to head in another direction. With a simple phone call, his plan would be set in motion. He flipped out the phone, confident that his associate would be ready, willing, and able to help.

"Hey, it's TJ. Come pick me up at the corner of Highway Fifty-six and Five Hundred Road. I'll be up the dirt road a ways, just to lay low. Get going." He folded the phone closed and then dashed it against the rocks to cover his tracks. Now, all he had to do was make it over to his rendezvous point and catch a ride back to his cabin.

Shoving off the rock protruding from Sulking Bull, he stepped into the open. An odd sensation emanated from his mouth. Reaching up to smooth his mustache, he discovered the ill-chosen consequence of diving headfirst into a rock ledge. His upper lip was so deeply gashed, half of his moustache dangled free.

Lifting his face into the rain, he washed the blood from the wound and tore a swatch from his shirttail, applying pressure to staunch the blood flow. One touch of the compress brought a thousand pricks of light into his vision which soon flared into an explosion from each jangling nerve ending. He cursed under his breath because of the happenstance of the injury. In the thrill of breaking away, he had made little provision for any mortal complication.

~

Jusdyn discovered the teenage boy now held a toddler in tow while a boy about kindergarten-aged waited under the culvert's awning for the trip up to safety. He lifted the older child without a word, still trying to resolve his space problem.

Arie's lips moved in silent prayer as she picked up the toddler and turned to ascend the bank. Once he'd crossed the trunk, she launched the toddler up to him. Valor opened the door to receive the small children out of the rain, but it became evident they were running out of room behind her. The first boy had assumed the driver's position and was steering the heck out of the wheel.

"Move over, Bobby Dean." Valor swatted at him behind her back. The five-year old walked across laps attracted by the instrument panel while Valor locked the toddler in her lap.

One glance at the packed interior of the truck left him with dwindling hope. They simply needed more room. As he turned to brainstorm possible solutions with Arie, the sound of a child crying raked across his heartstrings. He reached across the walnut trunk to guide her over. "What will we do with all the rest?"

A man cleared his throat from upslope. "Well, you could put

them in our car."

"Uncle Loren!" Valor squealed through a crack in the door. "Saved by a cowboy again!"

Elated, Jusdyn closed the distance between them and extended a mud-streaked hand which his father readily shook. He could hardly rein in a canyon-sized smile at his rain-soaked redemption. "Man, are we glad to see you guys."

"And just in the nick of time." Arie added, sliding across the tree trunk to join them.

"I've got another two rows of seats to fill," Darlene offered, "if there are that many children." She stopped her descent to share an umbrella with Muriel.

Arie stepped under the umbrella's shelter. "Miss Cosgrove, I didn't get to thank you for bringing my Uncle Doug into town earlier." She wrapped her in a hug, wet rain gear and all.

He gestured down the embankment. "Let's get loading then." The men took turns descending the creek bank and brought the children up to the women, who walked them along the tree trunk and then placed them into Muriel's car. Once sufficiently loaded, they started filling the Subaru. On the last trip up, the teenage boy accompanied the Linquist men.

Jusdyn appreciated the youth's help during the evacuation. "What's your name?"

"I'm Virgil Sinclair. My mom's in the symphony. We're from Emporia." As the teen lost traction coming up the bank in his dress shoes, his father caught him and braced his arm.

"I'm Loren Linquist, from Wilsey." He paused to shake hands. Having reached the downed tree, the trio stood there for a moment of assessment. The rain had lightened considerably as the storm progressed to the northeast. "I reckon you might have just left your childhood behind in that culvert, young man."

"Yes sir. Coming out on the other side has a different feel to it, for certain."

Jusdyn took a giant stride over the log and waited for them on the other side "Say, if you're up for it, would you consider joining up with us when it's time to come back?"

"Be glad to." The youth took a leggy leap over the tree trunk.

Loren negotiated the barrier next and then they walked over to join the women.

Muriel wiped mud from a pair of Sunday shoes, her expression taut.

Darlene made a final head count with exaggerated finger motions. "Twenty-two." She glanced up and spotted the teen standing with the men. "Make that twenty-three."

Arie reached for the hamper stashed in the truck bed. "Is anyone hungry?"

"Yes, oh, yes. We're starving," the twins replied in unison.

She opened the hamper and handed foil-wrapped packages to each woman for their carload. Then she brought the last package to the old truck and opened it to reveal tiny cherry tarts for everyone.

From their eager reception, he realized that not one part of Arie's effort had the least appearance of insignificance about it, lifting the heaviness off the children for the moment.

"Oh, Muriel. Here's something else for you." Arie pulled the medical bag out from behind the cab.

The family nurse met her halfway with a look of utter gratitude on her face. "Saints be praised." She slid her fingers through the handle. "Now I can medicate the wounded on the go."

"Let's thank the Good Lord we don't need treatment for these children." Arie held her hands over her heart. "There doesn't seem to be a scratch among them."

The first boy released the steering wheel to touch his forehead.

"Scoot over, Bobby Labonte." Jusdyn tapped his shoulder, ready to take the wheel.

The boy inched toward the middle where he checked his forehead in the rearview mirror.

Loren appeared through the far door. "Any suggestions as to where are we headed? Guess we don't need the hospital."

He hadn't thought that far ahead and paused to consider their options.

"How about the nursing home?" Muriel gestured with her bag. "There's room enough, and plenty of food, too."

Valor sniffed her cherry tart. "I bet Uncle Morrill would love some company."

"The nursing home it is then." Glad for the decision, he sensed the logic of the choice. "That would put them close to the hospital, in case the wounded and non-wounded need to visit and reconnect."

Loren flipped out the cell phone and began punching the keypad. "I'll call the hospital and have them coordinate our arrival so the nursing home staff can be expecting us."

Muriel walked up to the cab and removed Valor to make room for Arie.

Seeing how lovingly the girl melted into his mother's embrace, he realized for the first time that those two souls truly belonged together. He started the truck and glanced across the bustling cab as Arie settled in. She looked like an angel perched in subdued happiness, tending to the children and feeding them leftover pieces of crust. A sudden multiplication of the reasons why he loved her so much flooded to mind. When she looked over at him, her gold-flecked eyes simply shone. The driver-boy scooted so he could operate the gear shift as the rescuer vehicles departed the trauma scene one by one.

Reversing the truck, he regarded the fallen tree. "We'll be right back." The stillness on the horizon ahead lent a heavy foreboding. The next trip out might not be quite as lively. *Lord, help us, because this rescue isn't over yet.*

The driver-boy looked first at Arie and then Jusdyn. "Has anybody seen my mother?"

Arie patted an empty spot on the seat. "First, let's get you back safe and sound, sweetie. That's the way your mother would want it."

"Okay." The boy checked his well-being in the rearview mirror one more time as if to make sure it was truly there.

He nodded as the boy took his seat with a smidge of reluctance. The children were safe and sound. *What a miracle.* The drive through town lasted long enough for him to formulate a healthy list of folks to thank for that particular round-up.

~

Deke didn't mind the diversion at all. The baby needed to sleep. So did Merrilee. The power outage wouldn't matter in the least to those two, destined to sleep away the storm to their mutual benefit.

He'd never driven a Farmall M tractor, but managed to get it cranked and put in forward gear. The clutch seemed a bit worn, but the wheels dug in with the gumption of a younger tractor and made the trip down the hill to the cemetery in fairly short order. Punchy from his lack of sleep, he found it funny that the graveyard laid a mere stone's throw away from the nursing home. They both seemed peaceable now, and with the rain easing, it proved an enjoyable ride altogether.

The blue Buick's tipped state became highly visible from the main entrance. He hooked a strong left, elbows flying above the oversized steering wheel, and directed the tractor towards the cemetery's west side.

Two elderly men exited the car and waved him down as he approached.

Deke couldn't have been more surprised. "Hey, Morrill and Vernis. Who knew you guys would be hanging out around here?"

The Litke sisters emerged once the rain slacked off, adding color to the merriment of the reunion.

"What puts a Linquist out in these parts?" Morrill asked.

"The baby came this morning in the height of the storm. You're all invited up to the nursery to see our precious daughter, Beryl Leigh Linquist."

Ruby could barely suppress a smile. "Isn't beryl some sort of gemstone, Sister?"

Opal nodded to acknowledge the inside connection. "Why yes, I believe it is."

"A little birdie once told me that naming your child for a treasure showed how much you cherished them so who am I to argue otherwise?" Deke followed his confession with a sheepish chuckle, making the elderly sisters hug with delight.

Morrill seemed to have a growing interest in the tractor as he patted the maker's plate. "Know what you're doing on this thing, young man?"

"No sir, I sure don't. I've been like Christopher Columbus up here. You know, searching for something until I land upon it."

"How about I give it a try? It's been awhile, but we're of similar vintage. That way you can hook the chains for me."

"That's a deal." Deke scrambled down, leaving the tractor idling as his feet rediscovered the soggy ground.

Vernis motioned to the high spot under the car. "Reckon the banker would like his cornerstone left intact."

Morrill hitched up his pant leg to make the bottom step. With a helping hand, he climbed right up to the driver's seat without further difficulty. "We put in more than a few good years, didn't we Vernis?" His hands made reacquaintance with the control levers.

"You bet your buckskin we did. And it was worth every minute of aggravation."

"Thought I'd go for the back bumper first, lift her up, and then swing her around."

"Go for it." Deke clapped to cheer him on.

Morrill brought the antique tractor around like an old pro, pivoting and squaring up with the Buick's back bumper. He lowered the PTO mechanism as Deke waited below to secure the chains around the frame. The ensuing metal moans sounded like a battle of the ironclads, with the Buick finally submitting to the lift power of the tractor.

Deke motioned Morrill back as Vernis dropped to a knee to gauge their clearance over the cornerstone. Once past it, Vernis gave a thumbs-up so he transferred the signal up to Morrill, who moved the car off the plot and back onto the road. The rear wheels touched down with kid-glove maneuvering, making him appreciate the bail-out. He worked the heavy-linked chains loose and then signaled for the PTO to be lifted.

Morrill obliged and backed the tractor off the car, then pulled alongside. "Mind if I run her back up the hill?" The antique operator peered down at him, obviously having a ball at the helm.

Happy to be shed of the contraption, he relented. "No, sir. Please be my guest."

Morrill extended his hand toward Ruby. "Would my sweetie ride along with me?"

The sudden realization that something romantic might be going on with this senior set caught him off guard. The wind could have knocked him over with a mere puff.

"Who could say no to that?" Ruby replied, her pleasure far too apparent.

He escorted her to the tractor and helped Morrill hoist her up, flowing peach hemline and all. Once perched on the wheel well, Ruby waved at Opal like a parade queen. He assisted his passengers back into the Buick and trailed the tractor out of the cemetery and up the hill.

The scene framed by the windshield looked like something right off an antique tractor calendar—a pretty girl, a stalwart driver, and a Farmall M series tractor that the storm chose to leave behind. He could hardly wait until he could tell Merrilee about this latest development since she always appreciated a good romance story.

~

The trek from Metzgers over to Jed Wilson's pasture took longer than TJ anticipated, probably because every footfall managed to fire up the pain on his face. When he approached the five-strand fence ending Metzgers pasture, he took it one-handed, mindful to keep pressure applied to his wound. As his left leg attempted to clear the top strand, the bottom of his boot-cut jeans caught on a barb and hung up, knocking him off-balance enough he fell. Lying eye-level with wet clumps of big bluestem his temper flared—both at his fallibility and the low-tech landing mat that had softened his fall.

"I'll never walk this forsaken prairie again if I can help it." He spat, trying to diffuse his anger. He dug his knees into the mud and slowly regained his feet. Thoughts of the exodus of Israel came to mind as he continued his trek eastward, remembering how Pharaoh hardened his heart against God and managed to call down his own demise. He didn't see any plagues lying about, only pathetic grass—and lots of it.

~

Approaching the nursing home, Jusdyn noticed the antique tractor pulled to the side with Opal's Buick trailing it. He stared in amazement, recognizing a flowing Ruby Litke and his glowing Uncle Morrill atop the Farmall, waving as he passed. When he caught Arie's gaze, her eyebrows wiggled at the innuendo behind the odd spectacle.

The parking lot at the nursing home sat empty due to the storm, so he pulled in parallel to the front curb. The other vehicles parked likewise, until the tractor arrived and claimed the handicapped access plus half the sidewalk.

He hurried over to help the elderly couple down. "No one's going to miss you two on that relic."

Muriel grabbed Valor by the hand and ran to join them. "The tornado came up the east side, Uncle Morrill," she said. "Jusdyn and Arie found these children. All of them were kept safe and sound inside the culvert under the access road."

"Not even a scratch on anyone." Arie added, maintaining a tight grip on driver-boy's chubby hand.

When Deke clamped an arm around his shoulder, he paid him back with a twin girl. He picked up the matching child and scooped up the toddler for balance.

"We're all present and accounted for." Darlene had the children from the Subaru arranged in ascending height order, with lanky Virgil Sinclair punctuating the end like an exclamation mark.

Vernis came up behind them, escorting a slow-moving Opal

Litke onto the sidewalk.

Freckle-faced Jenna Baker looked over the premises with caution. "Is this going to be our new home?"

"Just for awhile, until we can match you with your family." Muriel tried to satisfy her with a bit of diplomacy while Arie looped her arm around the girl's drooping shoulders.

"Nobody lives here too long, anyway," Vernis said. "I'm leaving tomorrow to live with my son, so some of you can take my room."

At the reference to the injured rancher, Muriel sent him a wary look.

The toddler in his arms squirmed for freedom, forcing him to prioritize his tasks. "Uncle Vernis, we need to talk to you about Doug. Can you give us a few minutes to get the children situated first?"

"Count on me to help, Jusdyn. You know we had three boys underfoot and managed to survive that peril."

"That's the McLauren spirit." Morrill stepped toward the entrance and walked right into Valor's hug. "And the lunchroom has Jell-O, so how bad can it be?"

The four-year old boy walked up to the tractor driver who stood a mile tall in comparison. "I take mine green." The whole group laughed, gathered in an informal semi-circle around the M.

An intern appeared through the front door accompanied by other staff coming to usher their new occupants into the facility. Arie found a place by his side as they waited to enter, took the toddler from his arms, and set the driver-boy free.

"Hope they have cable here," the chubby-cheeked boy said.

Vernis placed a bent finger of correction on the child's shoulder. "There's more to life than watching TV."

Opal chuckled a bit and drew a deep breath to recover from her walk from the Buick.

Noticing she leaned on Vernis beyond what seemed companionable to make the trip inside, Jusdyn realized the day had already taken a toll in a multitude of ways.

~

Mabel stared at the taffy-green cast on Viola Newcomb's right arm as her husband brought her into the front lobby. "You're officially discharged, Miss Viola." She checked the color under her nails one last time. "If you don't mind me asking, Mr. Newcomb, do you have much of a home to go back to?"

The old man straightened his stoop for an instant and then exhaled back into a defeated posture. "Seems like the twister dropped down right on our front porch." He closed his eyes as if to block out the memory. "We were lucky to have made the storm cellar, all things considered."

"Let me see what I can do." Mabel began dialing her own cell phone number. "Say, Loren. I've got Erskine and Viola Newcomb here, ready to discharge. Since you've got their wheels over yonder, I thought we'd just invite them over to join you for now. Yeah, not much left down Old Dunlap Road. Meet you halfway then."

She looked up with a sparkle in her eyes, locking Viola's good elbow in hers. "We're going to have you join the good folks over at the senior care facility for a hot lunch, how does that sound?"

Erskine gave a chuckle "Sounds like we're being thrown back into the briar patch."

"Half his checker-playing buddies live over there," Viola added.

Mabel laughed so hard her scrub-clad bulk jiggled. They were in recovery mode, and it felt therapeutic, case by fractured case. Bones could heal, and the community would rebuild.

~

As the El Camino crept across the gravel toward him, TJ stood up out of the ditch and approached the familiar vehicle, his shirt blood-riddled down to his jeans. The driver fixated on his traumatic state, his jaw dropped in disbelief.

"Henry, you might not want to play any poker if you can't screen your reactions better than that." TJ stepped to the passenger side and rattled the door handle.

Henry lunged over to unlock the door. "Hey, I came for you, didn't I?"

Weary, he plunked down on the custom plush upholstery, arriving successfully at his first checkpoint. "Yeah, you came for me. How much is that going to cost?" He pulled down the visor and checked his facial wound in the mirror. The damage repulsed him. "Looks like I'll have a little more personal baggage to bear, thanks to the tornado."

"Well, wherever you're heading, you might want to pick up some first aid on that lip along the way." Henry gave his whiskers a stroke. "Hey, my wife's a good seamstress."

"Get me there," TJ had a strong inkling there would be a hitch-up before he could get to checkpoint number two. As he eased his bruised head back onto the seat cover, he tried to rationalize the extra stop to his advantage. "Guess I could grab a few more things from home anyway." The highway soon slid under the El Camino's wheels, and he yielded to the marred circumstance at hand, embracing the diversion for its best possible outcome.

~

Loren stepped around the water collecting in the drainage swale between the two health facilities. Less than twenty yards out, Mabel led the Newcombs from the pavement of the front drive and started across the saturated lawn.

"Thanks for the loaner on the tractor, Erskine." Loren greeted the old timer with a firm handshake. "She's everybody's favorite set of wheels now."

"It sure looks good up on that front lawn. Maybe they'll let us keep it there for now." He navigated around the puddle's edge to keep his shoes dry.

Loren took the frail-looking Viola in his arms and lifted her across the standing water like a porcelain figurine. She'd already dodged enough peril for one day.

The old man grew emotional as his wife joined him on the

nursing home lawn. "I'll never forget the way everyone's been so kind to us while we're down to the shirts on our backs."

Viola reached with her good hand as if to comfort her husband.

Circumspect, he motioned toward the building. "Life's a short walk on an endless prairie. It sure means more when we stop to help one another along the way."

The old timer nodded and threaded his bony arm through his wife's.

Loren tossed a questioning look Mabel's way, telegraphing his inquiry.

"The latest report has the tornado over Richey Cove, heading northeast. That blocks the highway from Manhattan, leaving us completely cut off from the east side."

"Call the coroner and put him on standby. I looked out over the symphony grounds and didn't see another living soul." A shiver ran down his back as he delivered the news.

"What? There must have been a thousand people there before the storm. Are you trying to tell me they're—"

"Gone. Yep." Loren's throat thickened. "There'll be victims galore, I'm afraid."

"We have the miracle of the children, for starters. I'd count them as a blessing."

"Twenty-three shoeless blessings at that." He jogged to catch up with the Newcombs, her bright cast reminding him the recovery was well under way. Turkey red wheat survived winter much the same way, holding on through bad weather with the hope of better days ahead.

~

Doug labored to inhale, once again igniting the soaring inferno in his chest, but fulfilling his desperation for the air. He was down in a foxhole, fighting for his life. His swirling train of thought ran tattered through the pain, and came up with a vision of his brother Dale dressed in desert fatigues under fire in Iran. A legion of robe-wearing infantrymen crossed the sand on full attack, infiltrated the allied trench, and ridded it of all life.

When the enemy departed, Doug stood in the trench with a teenaged TJ, headstrong and resistant to any assistance, the sand swirling all around. The vision faded, chased by the usual haunting shadow of regret. He exhaled only because his lungs required it. A hand reached down from the gray lighting overhead, tapping his shoulder to beckon him back to a conscious state.

A slight-built man wrapped in scrubs hovered over him speaking through a surgical mask. "Hang in there, soldier. We're going to let you take a nap and then rebuild that rib cage of yours. See you on the other side."

Doug blinked to accentuate the limited head nod, giving way to the nosecone bringing with it a fresh breeze of oxygen and sickly sweet anesthesia.

Suddenly, a saintly nurse stood by his side, rendering the angelic news that the children had all been found safe at the symphony grounds. Relief washed over his body. As he received the blessing, he felt somehow released from the tether of this world and rid from all its cares. Freedom became his last conscious thought before the darkness won.

Chapter 20

The presence of light powers the greatest motivation in the plant kingdom. Even from a seedling, the leaf buds gravitate upward and outward in a positive phototrophic response, while the root tips are most content in their positive geotropic tendencies downward. Consider the bastion of the prairie, the cottonwood tree. Where the prairie runs to an abrupt end at the shores of Lake Michigan, the cottonwood tree maintains its vertical vigil, towering high above the grasses in its attempt to capture sunlight. Unable to migrate out of sands shifting from the near-shore dunes, this fortress of flora refuses to surrender to the heckling wind. Denied the light it once revered due to sand accretion at its base, the tree reconfigures its buried branches into roots—further buttressing the trunk and improving moisture uptake to boost future above-ground growth. Thus the ability to adjust oneself under duress plainly becomes a matter of focused inclination. Whosoever will may come to the light.

Anxious to return to the symphony site, Jusdyn stood with the men at the far end of the lunch table, discussing what needed to be done next. Loren had called Mannie, requesting his truck and chain saw to aid the recovery effort. On a notepad borrowed from the nurse's station, he had started a sign-in list for the children. When the Newcombs endorsed it, he realized the wisdom of it and scribbled *Storm Victims* across the top.

Loren rose from the table, searching the group with a sweeping gaze. "Guess we need to get back out there and take our medics with us."

Muriel finished the last bite of her lunch, wiped her mouth with a napkin, and then kissed the top of Valor's head.

Ready to move out, he stood at one end of the table while Arie popped up from the other.

A bit unsure, Virgil stood from the children's section and received a nod from his father.

Loren paced over to the nurse's station to speak with the staff, lending them with a few extra minutes of preparation.

Muriel searched the faces of the remaining adults. "Who volunteers to take care of this brave crew?"

"Ruby and I will," Morrill replied. "Don't worry about a thing."

Vernis pointed to the adjoining room. "Erskine and I figure to start a checkers tournament in the rec room. There are other games and puzzles, too. And we aren't turning on the TV." His gaze darted to Bobby Dean Hale, the pudgy driver of his truck at the rescue scene.

Drooping in her chair, Opal stared into her cup of hot tea. The offer of games and puzzles failed to stir her interest.

Sympathetic, Muriel stopped to squeeze her hand on the way out.

Dread dried the back of his throat, as the day continued to affect victims in less obvious ways. Despite his constant prayers to thwart a total takeover, the storm had reset their normal routines—almost to the extreme.

Arms crossed, Valor knelt in her chair to gain authority. "Don't you dare forget about my bullfrogs, Virgil. Look under the seat of the Jeep—inside a violin case."

"There might be a tad more important finds out there than your silly frogs." The teen took his next breath in a huff.

Her demeanor softened as she rounded the table to approach the redheaded youth, placing her hands on his forearm. "I hope and pray you find your mother, Virgil." She paused to punctuate her claim with a single bat of her gold eyelashes. "But if not for you, those innocent frogs are going to die locked inside my violin case. I never meant to bring them any harm." Her countenance saddened over the discourse, leaving the youth genuinely affected.

"You know what, Valor?" Arie leaned over the table. "You might have just saved their rubbery necks."

He caught onto Arie's ploy and wanted to lend it some added punch. "Yeah, like putting their soft flesh in a sturdy vault for safekeeping during the twister."

Virgil dropped his folded arms to break her grip on him. "Look, I'll be glad to unlock the violin case if I can find it."

"Down by Big John Creek, if at all possible," Valor whispered.

Virgil hopped to his feet and grabbed her by the shoulders, peering straight into her eyes. "Tell the truth. Did you heal that bad cut on Bobby Dean's forehead while we were in the tube?" He stood at point blank range as if to disallow any squirming around his question.

Valor stood stone-faced in total silence.

With the air crackling with tension, Jusdyn questioned whether he should intervene to keep the fireworks down.

Valor finally flinched, crinkling her nose as if to taunt him further. "If you already know I did it, then why'd you have to ask?"

"Well, I couldn't see everything going on. It was dark in that tube."

"Faith is all about believing what you don't see, right?" She turned and walked away.

Jusdyn's jaw dropped, thinking that the preacher couldn't have done a better job at putting legs and lips on scripture to make it walk and talk.

Virgil glanced over at him in total puzzlement.

"Welcome to the club, speaking for the fraternity of irreconcilable gender differences."

"Glad that's all clear as mud." Virgil shoved his hands in his pockets and muttered something indiscernible.

Loren walked back into the room, stopping behind the chair of the solemn-eyed Jenna Baker. "Are we all set to go?" He motioned in a circle as if to round up his helpers.

Jusdyn nudged Virgil to fall in behind his father.

Arie hugged Valor as she passed, smoothing the girl's hair. "Keep the kids occupied so they don't think sad thoughts."

"I suppose we could have a talent show. I could play some songs on my violin."

"Perfect, Valor. Tell Uncle Morrill about your idea. He'll let you be in charge."

Muriel hesitated as the team began to exit to the parking lot. "Does anyone know where Darlene took off to?"

"Deke and Darlene went to check on Merrilee and Doug." Loren dialed his borrowed phone. "We need to head back over. Have the volunteer firemen been brought in yet? Okay, we'll meet them on the east side. Send Deke and Darlene out, will you, Mabel?" The phone clipped closed as they walked to the cars.

"What did Mabel say?" Muriel fell behind a step.

"Doug's still in surgery, so there's no further news yet. Hey, listen up everyone. This next round isn't going to be as fun. Fortify yourselves for the grim aftermath, and lend help wherever you can." Loren shifted his stance as if to offset his message.

Virgil turn a bit green behind the gills as the gravity of the situation set in.

"You don't have to come with us." He held up his hands to suggest an opt out.

"Yes, I do." Virgil dug his heels in and rocked back. "You can't expect me to leave my mom out there unaccounted for. Besides, there's a case full of bullfrogs calling my name. Heaven help me if I come back to Valor without a good report in that department."

He muted a chuckle at the youth's passionate delivery in the face of a daunting task.

Loren stuck a thumb in his chest to assume ownership. "You're with me, Virgil. I'll be responsible for your whereabouts, if anyone should ask."

Muriel reached into the floorboard for her nursing bag and headed for the passenger seat of Darlene's car.

Upon opening the truck door, Arie paused to brush off tart crumbs and came to rest by her old gearshift friend. She punched the silver button releasing the glove box lid and retrieved her oilskin bag, clutching it to her lap.

He crossed over to the driver's side, sorting through his rescue options. "What's in that bag anyway?"

"Gold powder."

"You used that when the calf got shackled in the barbed wire, didn't you?"

"That's right."

"Okay. I'll call that good medicine. Glad you're on my team." He turned the ignition and the truck rumbled into active duty. The same instant that Arie gave him a peck on the cheek, a raucous howl sounded from outside the cab.

Deke gestured through the open window like a mime. "Hey, can I ride with you guys?"

"Oh, get in. This is a rescue mission, not a date."

Arie gave Deke a protracted look as he entered the cab. "Yeah, the date portion ended when the storm left the calaboose."

"Someday, you've got to tell me about that one. I'll trade you for the story of how I went two-for-two in the baby birthing department." Deke mimicked a catcher working the pocket of his mitt.

As the truck eased from the lot, Darlene trotted out of the hospital to her car, the last of the rescue caravan.

"Two women and a little bad news." Deke checked the side-view mirror as the Subaru slid behind them. "That equals a rainstorm on the inside."

"Heartache lurks all around." He pulled the gearshift into second gear, trying not to let negative thinking deter him from his mission.

Arie twisted the drawstring around her fingers, pulling it taut. "The strong know how to survive."

He claimed her statement as pure truth. He had to, as they were heading back east to the destruction zone where a tornado had extracted all signs of life from the land.

~

TJ found the cluttered library in the rear of Henry's house held all the trappings of a seamstress, complete with sewing machine, multicolored threads on a bobbin rack, and a calico pincushion that had been accepting donations since Elvis had been crowned king. When Henry cleared a magazine-covered chair, he took a seat.

Seconds passed before a timid woman with large brown eyes entered the room, clutching a pad of matches. Without a word, she pulled up her sewing chair, grabbed the pincushion, and started searching for the proper spool of thread. Opting for a tan specimen similar to his hair color, she cut a length and threaded the needle. The slightly curved tool gleamed under the bare light bulb. Short of making landfall on his lip, the seamstress hesitated.

"What is it, Tilly?"

"I think it's too messy up there. I'm not real sure how to start."

"Wait. Would it help if I shaved?" TJ held that his moustache might be more of a nuisance than stylish nuance now anyway.

Tilly lowered the needle into her lap. "Yes, though I hate to ask you."

"We'll be back." TJ nudged Henry toward the door. "I'm going to need some help with this operation."

Henry led the way to the restroom sink. "I used to shave my grandpa's head when he got older."

"How'd that go?"

"Not all that smooth, as I recall."

"Just pretend it's a hayfield then." TJ yielded at the sink, giving up yet one more trace of his previous good life.

~

Three more patients had been brought in from south of town, diverting the ER intern with new territory in which to apply his blood pressure cuff. Across the room, the doctor threw another bloodied tool onto the surgical steel tray.

"Almost done here." The doctor bent to suture the final segment of the incision closed. After his wrist made several swift passes over the site, he stood erect, cut the dissolving thread, and surrendered the needle to the tray. "Say, my stitch job looks like a fishhook. Sure hope Mr. McLauren is an angler." He pulled off the skin-tight gloves, threw them through a hole in the counter, and headed for the sink.

The intern crossed the room to retrieve alcohol wipes from the far cabinet and glanced at the back of their first storm survivor. There, plain as the print in a first-grade primer, was the letter J branded into the man's muscular back, puckered like the red stitching on a baseball.

~

Loren scanned the town for any signs of damage and saw several awnings mangled along a desolate Main Street.

Virgil stared straight ahead. "Sir, can I ask you a question?"

"Go ahead. What's on your mind, son?"

"Can you tell me what makes Valor seem so special?"

"Well, some people have the knack of walking away from adversity, unaffected by all the bad that comes with it. Valor manages to rise above her troubling situation."

"Could you tell me what kind of trouble?"

"Over a year ago, her mother was arrested for operating a meth lab from a shed in their backyard. She's doing jail time now."

"My father abandoned our family when I was eight years old. Mom claimed we were better off, as he'd go missing for days on end. Things were hard for her at first, since I was too young to earn money to help out. That's when she joined the symphony. But I can tell you, she truly loves playing."

Loren grew encouraged that the boy felt he could talk about

such personal matters. "What instrument?"

"Clarinet. She's played since fifth grade. Claims she never wanted to try anything else. That's one of the things I'll be searching for out there, because I know she'll want her instrument back. It has a fancy embossed S in gold on the bell. I bought that decal for her out of my own mowing money."

"Got a picture of your mother on you by any chance? I'd be glad to keep a special lookout for her as we go." Loren gripped and released the steering wheel.

The youth dug into his back pocket and produced a leather wallet with an eagle on the cover. He flipped it open and shoved it toward him.

"Wow, she's a nice-looking woman."

"Meet Nancy Sinclair, the clarinet player." Virgil offered up a smile that was altogether too short-lived.

"If she hasn't left the symphony grounds, we'll find her, son." Loren had no earthly idea how to make good on the promise aside from checking every square inch of what the storm left behind, which appeared none too promising based on his earlier assessment. Still, he'd been wrong many times before, so maybe he could add to that list today.

~

"Ever walk into a place surrounded by a feeling you should have been there all along?" Darlene shot a glance at her passenger.

Muriel sensed a soul-purge coming with the serendipitous question. "Mine was more of a person, not a place. But the day I met Loren, I felt something deep inside that I knew would usher in change for me."

"I'll never forget how beaten down Doug looked that first morning when he answered the door and saw me standing there."

"You probably scared him half to death. He's out there hiding away from the entire world, and you come buzzing around like a bee trying to stir up something."

"He felt so guilty about me having to come out, really. It struck me as precious. And he refused to let me lift anything heavy. He kept an eye on me, taking out the trash when the can got full, emptying the vacuum, and helping make the beds. Let me tell you, in all my years cleaning people's houses, I never got the attention that Doug gave me. In fact, I usually get ignored."

"My cousin has a heart of gold. Not everyone down in the valley as long as he's been can remain a gentle person. I worry about Doug though. All that time alone isn't good for anyone. And the girls never come out to see him. That's a real sore spot. He works around it as best he can, going into town twice a week just to pay visits to his dad and Uncle Morrill in hopes of seeing the rest."

"Well, that's destined to change once Vernis returns home tomorrow. Things definitely have to change."

"I don't know if Doug mentioned it to you, but there's a big McLauren family meeting tomorrow at two o'clock in the Cordiality Room of the senior care facility. The entire meeting centers on changes coming for the family. This storm adds another layer of consideration to the agenda. I don't know how Doug's going to attend, quite honestly."

"If it's important to the family, I predict he'll make it there, one way or another."

"You're going to be good for him, Darlene."

"At the ranch, Doug and I watched the horses run across the corral while we drank coffee and planned our day. He said the scene was too beautiful for words. Not to be too assuming, I hope my profile got thrown into the forefront of his landscape commentary."

"Time will tell." Muriel closed her eyes to shut out the storm-ravaged details.

~

TJ grew restless in his seat, surprised how the row of cottonwood trees leading back to the cabin confirmed his plan. A receiving line to checkpoint number two, the tree row masked his hideout from discovery by the society he aimed to shut out. The El Camino bottomed out on the uneven lane, loosening a worrisome thought about the governor stuck down the abandoned well. *Not my problem anymore.* Then he set the care of it free like a helium balloon from the top seat of a Ferris wheel. When the bunker came into sight, he could hardly wait to get inside and begin his encore existence.

Without a word, he opened the car door and approached the cabin, locating the key ring in his duffel bag. When the old lock gave way, he threw open the hasp and set his bag inside.

Henry retrieved the rest of his things, surreptitiously taken from his house after the mending job. His accomplice handed over the remaining bags and stood before him with open palms. "Guess this is it then."

"Wait in the car." TJ stepped back inside. One thing could be said of his new line of work. He never lacked having cash on hand. He exited the cabin with a wad of uncounted bills folded over his fist and jabbed them through the open window of the cab. "You never saw me."

Henry took the money with a crooked smile. "No sir, sheriff. I haven't seen TJ McLauren in a couple of weeks."

TJ nodded and turned toward the cabin, never looking back. Checkpoint number two had been accomplished. He glanced at the portal, ignoring the rust. *Home sweet home at last.*

~

With a swarm of volunteer firemen crawling over its length, Jusdyn noticed the fallen walnut had lost some of its majesty. He pulled up in the 4-H fairgrounds and parked out of the main access corridor. Once Loren and Darlene pulled in beside his truck, they all gathered.

Loren approached the walnut impasse with Virgil in his wake. "Let's check in and find out where they need us."

Arie secured the oilskin pouch to a belt loop and fell in with Muriel and Darlene. Several rescuers filed onto the site up ahead.

Loren managed to catch the last man crossing the tree. "Who's in charge here?"

"Everyone's meeting up by the stone barn, sir. We don't even know who's here to help us yet, let alone who's in charge."

"Fair enough. Our group has already been here once, and we're back to help. We'll just follow you up to the barn."

The young volunteer fireman began to run up the access road, leaving them to devise their own plans. As Jusdyn helped Muriel over the roadblock, Mannie pulled up in their two-ton farm truck.

Loren closed in as his neighbor descended from the cab. "Hey, Mannie. Am I ever glad to see you." As the men shook hands, Sam dashed out of the truck and ran straight to Jusdyn.

"I messed up letting the dog out in the farmyard after the storm." Mannie shrugged his shoulders. "Sam jumped in the truck, and I couldn't get him out."

"That's okay, my friend. Maybe he'll be useful out here, since I don't know exactly what we're up against."

Jusdyn slipped his fingers under the farm dog's collar. "I've got a lead line in the truck, in case Sam decides not to be friendly."

"Guess we need to divide up from here." Loren glanced over the symphony scene. "Who'll stay here with Mannie and get the bulk of this walnut trunk off the road?"

Deke stepped up ready for duty. "I'll stay. Then I can catch up to Jusdyn and Arie."

"Okay. Muriel, you and Darlene are definitely needed up at the stone barn. Virgil and I will escort you up there and then we can branch out, depending on what's needed. Mannie, don't stop until you get this roadway cleared. The ambulances will need access in and out once we start finding survivors."

"You've got it, boss." Mannie turned and headed to the rear of the truck.

"Deke, we're going west to look for survivors." He gestured toward a tree line. "We'll stop at Big John Creek and then head north. Bring my truck and come find us."

"Roger that, scouting party." Deke held his hand out for the keys making him gesture back at the truck.

Darlene distributed a reusable grocery bag to each member. "These are for anything valuable that you might find. You know—keepsakes and the like. We'll start a lost-and-found with it." She tried to hand him one, but deferred to Arie instead.

"Son, try to make a quick loop and end up back at the stone barn where we are. We'll run the emergency vehicles from there."

"Got it, Dad. Good luck." Jusdyn offered the shallow sentiment without much thought.

"Something tells me we'll need more than luck." Loren glanced north into the ravaged zone, his expression grim with anticipation.

~

Taking the heavy medic bag from his wife, Loren led his group up the access road to the stone barn. Half a dozen volunteer firemen walked aimlessly through the rubble scattered around the edge of the building. He stepped uphill past the southern wall to get a better perspective and grew horrified by the scene. The entire northeastern portion of the building had vanished, torn away by the twister. He could hardly believe his eyes.

He climbed a rubble pile from the northwest corner on his way to assess the damage inside. The interior resembled an ancient burial chamber. He hung his head as the agonizing realization overtook him. In the haste of the exodus, what had appeared a safe refuge from the storm had collapsed, becoming a mausoleum for the masses instead. He stepped back, trying to mask his reaction for the sake of the others. "Hold up, Virgil. I need you to branch off from here. There's a jumble of cars over in the ravine to the east. Can you search for survivors over there?"

"Yes, sir. I'll head right over there. Should I just come back here afterwards?"

"No. Try to find us along the perimeter, son. This structure looks pretty unstable so I'd rather not have you inside. Stay clear, do you hear me?"

"Sure. Can you tell me where Big John Creek is, in case I find the Jeep with those bullfrogs in it?" Virgil gave him a look of honest inquiry.

Loren's heart twisted in his chest at the youth's dedication. "Head west beyond the rodeo grounds there. You should see Jusdyn and Arie walking along the creek's edge. And Virgil, if you find a human survivor, go get an adult to help you."

"Got it. You can count on me, sir. Don't worry."

"I'm worried about all of us. This place is an absolute wreck." Loren watched stone-faced as the youth walk out to the ravine and then motioned for the women to come closer.

"What was that all about?" Muriel checked her position with a half-step. "I thought you wanted Virgil to work with us."

"What I don't want—is for him to witness this." He led the women around the rubble pile straight into the heart of the disaster zone.

Darlene scanned the limestone jumble. "Good Lord, have mercy."

Muriel struggled to inhale. "Tell me they all didn't end up in here."

"Let's hope and pray they didn't." He stepped down into the carnage. It resembled ground zero of an explosion site, with limestone rocks from the barn walls serving as hastily scattered headstones.

"Look for survivors first. We'll deal with the less fortunate later." Loren reached for the cell phone and dialed his main connection. "I need the coroner to come on over. And Mabel, tell him he's going to be here awhile."

~

Opal sat comfortably in the top-dollar seats beside Ruby and the McLauren men, ready to view the impromptu performance. She wished she could muster up some of the children's enthusiasm for the show, as her energy level seemed to have ebbed ever since the cemetery.

TJ's little girl took the stage. "Welcome to the first annual Prairie People Talent Show. I'm your emcee this afternoon, Valor

McLauren. Let's get right to our program, which I sure hope you're going to enjoy. Here's Jenna Baker, our first act, bringing you a piano solo of the lovely song, 'This Side of Heaven.' Okay, Jenna, take it away."

The ten-year old blonde readily displayed more than a passing acquaintance with the piano, playing with flourish from total memory.

Perhaps I haven't lost anything to the symphony performance after all. Opal sat and soaked in the lively melody.

Morrill reached over and took Ruby's hand, sharing mutual enjoyment for the show. Vernis leaned toward the music, satisfying his strained hearing while tapping his foot to the rhythm. When the piece ended, Jenna stood and couldn't bow enough in recognition of their ample applause, to which Opal generously contributed.

Patient through the first several bows, Valor finally had to escort the pianist back to her seat to clear the stage. "Next, we have Bobby Dean Hale reciting his favorite poem. Come on up here, Bobby Dean." The emcee waited for the lumbering boy to make his way to the front. "Tell everybody how old you are."

"I'm eight years old." The boy showed his dimples in a full-faced smile.

"And what are you bringing for us today?"

"This is a poem that I wrote. I call it 'Just for Awhile—The Light' and it goes like this:

Just for awhile, the light shall shine among us,
Just for awhile, the darkness will have to flee;
Just for awhile, those in dark will lose direction,
Just for awhile, the light leads us to believe.

The Bible says that the light you trust in will shine through you when you walk as children of light." The stocky schoolboy finished the recitation with a stone-sober expression and bowed deeply from the waist.

"Amen," Morrill chanted over the audience's applause.

Valor retained him on stage for further entertainment. "Aren't you going to tell us who that light is, Bobby Dean?"

"Jesus said, 'I am the light of the world. Anyone who follows me will have light aplenty.' Do you get that, Valor?"

"I think we all got it, Bobby Dean. I'm not sure folks, but I think we may be looking at the next preacher out of Council Grove." Valor winked as she nodded for him to be dismissed.

Her heart warming, Opal couldn't stop clapping for the mention of Jesus, tickled pink for the child's enthusiasm despite the circumstance. A few hoots broke into the applause to encourage the boy.

Valor led him back to his seat on the front row with the other storm children since the poet seemed to be fixated on the crowd's accolades. She tucked the boy into his seat. "Remember, Bobby Dean, they don't clap like this in church."

"Well, why not?" The boy stood halfway up in protest. That won him another laugh from the audience.

Valor shooed him back and retook the front stage. "Next up will be the twins, Hope and Faith Laramie, performing 'Let There Be Peace on Earth' vocally without accompaniment. Ready, girls?"

When she motioned for their approach, the crumpled ribbon-wearers stepped forward in spotless black patent leather shoes. With each clasping their fingers about bodice height, the girls began blending their voices around the musical challenge.

Opal received their song like the voice of angels, pure and delicate. As the song ended, she found herself unable to clap. A strange tingle worked its way down her right arm. She slapped her left hand against her thigh, not giving the pesky sensation a second thought.

"Maybe it should be my turn now." Valor clasped her hands under her chin. "For those of you unable to make today's symphony performance, I'll now play the second piece of the afternoon on my new violin. This instrument has become dear to me already, as my teacher entrusted it to my safekeeping when the storm came up and I was snatched away to safety. So, this song is dedicated to him, my violin teacher Dr. Anton Vorchenski. I'm hoping they find him safe real soon." She took the violin from on top of the piano and grabbed the slender bow.

Opal adjusted herself on the folding chair with heightened expectation. Beside her, Ruby snuggled up against Morrill and welcomed his arm around her shoulder. A slide of the bow transfixed the crowd in the rec room, as one note seemed to follow another across the unhindered space. By the end of the first line, several more staff members gathered in the doorway. Valor held nothing back as she played, a rare treat for all within hearing distance.

When the room went silent, Opal joined the crowd in showing appreciation. *What joy to hear a bit of heaven here on earth.* The instant she clapped, something seized inside her core. She rapidly went from clapping to pressing her sternum. A sharp sensation pierced her front to back. Losing control as the seconds ticked past, she slumped sideways in the chair from a massive chest squeeze.

"Someone help Opal," Ruby shouted, standing in alarm. The staff rushed toward the front row. "Hurry. Move the children to another room."

Morrill held up his arms and herded the storm survivors out like chicks in a barnyard.

Their exodus was the closing scene before Opal began to float away. The urge to hang onto consciousness overwhelmed her ever-weakening shell. *One last favor Lord, a mere word.*

~

"The soil itself is gone." Jusdyn walked toward the creek across what had been open prairie. "This had to have been an EF Five tornado, with everything sheared to the ground like this. Never thought I'd see the land raked so completely bare."

"Could we look at it more like a clean slate?" Arie squeezed his waist and clung to him for her next step. "You could make a plan for throw-back here, just like the hayfield at Deke's."

The mere suggestion of restoration released a torrent of ideas for what it would take to get the land restored, given the absence of topsoil. He shook his head. "We'd have to rebuild this upper soil horizon to get anything worthwhile to grow. Otherwise, you'll have a nice crop of ragweed and horse nettles."

"Just like the heart, you have to be purposeful in what you cultivate after cleaning the slate." Arie kicked at the dirt left behind. "You remember, whatsoever things are pure, noble, and of good report. I'm referring to all that stuff."

He looked at her, trying to adjust up to her level of thinking, from soil to soul. "How about some manure to go along with that virtuous fodder? I'll need to rebuild the organic layer here." He kissed her forehead and kept his pace through the storm-plowed zone.

"I bet if every ranch in the county cleaned out their corrals, you'd have plenty of organic layer to go around." She stooped to bury the exposed roots of a shrub.

He tried to imagine a fleet of manure spreaders operating in synchrony like a mechanical ballet. Something told him the recovery would more likely resemble gritty hard work.

"Hey. I may have just found the first item for our lost-and-found bag." Bending, she dug a silver oval from the dirt.

"Wow. That's a rodeo belt buckle. Someone's really going to miss that."

Arie dropped the heavy trophy into their shopping bag. "Next, we need to find the cowboy that goes with it."

"Be careful what you ask for." Uncertain what the creek bed would hold, Jusdyn upped his caution quota as he strode forth. Most of the debris fell a mile short of keepsake status, so he kept walking.

~

The cars that had once been parked so ordered and parallel now mingled pell-mell in a gully at the base of a flint-rock hill. Virgil tried to wiggle through them and finally jumped up on a sedan's trunk to make better progress. He crouched and stared through the back glass looking for a survivor. "What if I actually find someone trapped inside? I mean, someone in need of help should matter more than my being afraid of what I'll find." He switched to walking on hoods, getting a better view of the driver's seat through the front windshield.

After half an hour of search with no rescue, he'd almost completed his circuit of the crumpled parking lot. His feet found the ground and he threaded through the last section of mangled vehicles. There, closest to the stone barn with its passenger side crunched against the hillside, sat a Jeep.

"Whoa. Now I can actually keep my promise to Valor—and a promise is a promise." Excitement building, he swiped his hair back off his forehead. "She sure managed to get worked up about such a lowly treasure and didn't seem to mind begging for my help." Bolstered by the thought, he tugged at the driver's door and forced it open. He thrust his arm behind the driver's seat and came up empty-handed. To check the passenger seat, he had to climb inside the vehicle, which already tipped into the hill.

Proceeding with the stealth of a cat, he scattered cracked windshield glass with every move. After one unguarded step toward the rear of the vehicle the floorboard rocked, flipping the Jeep end-on-end. A shower of glass rained down on him, and at the same instant, the violin case slipped out from under the seat. In nimble reaction, he held the case up to shield his face and quickly paid for it with cut knuckles. When the tumble halted, the vehicle settled on its side.

"So much for a simple game of hide-and-seek." The case responded to his quip with a series of uneven thumps, which brought an instantaneous smile to his face despite the dilemma of a world out of balance. He'd found living creatures that survived, a timely reassurance.

~

Jusdyn kicked a dirt ridge as they approached the creek bed.

"Mom's going to want custody of Valor after all this."

"I think Valor would be happy in Wilsey, and get the attention she deserves." Arie swung the lost-and-found bag and stopped when something caught her eye.

"Yeah, the only downside is that TJ may not take it like a good sport. He thinks he's doing an adequate job." His stomach tightened as he wrestled with the issue.

She looked up from her stoop, dismissing the discovery as worthless. "Well, we haven't found TJ yet, have we?"

"At any rate, we'll have extra company in Wilsey tonight, if this day will ever end."

"I hope your day ends at my porch swing, Jusdyn. My heart is counting on it."

Weighed by a sense of duty for the immediate catastrophe, it seemed like a nebulous request. "Keep the lamp on for me." At the rim of the creek bed, he stopped and gazed upstream.

Arie gasped trying to take in the scene. "Have you ever seen the likes of this?"

Jusdyn barely trusted his own eyes. "The tornado has erased the creek." Before them, the once-constant waters of Big John Creek were nowhere to be found.

~

Valor came out and stood with Ruby, following the attendants as they rolled the cot toward the ambulance. Miss Opal looked frail, almost blue-skinned against the white sheets. The attendant bent over the patient before he loaded her inside.

Reaching back to close the door, the man turned and rendered her request. "Get Muriel. She wants someone to get Muriel."

"I'll do it!" Valor ran out across the front lawn and tracked down the head nurse at the hospital before the ambulance could depart the nursing home parking lot. "Please, I have to get to my Aunt Muriel at the symphony grounds." She stared at the nurse with considerable sincerity and drew several deep breaths.

Mabel gave her a long look and nodded. "There's your ride

over, leaving right now." She pointed to a skinny man in black pants who was exiting the building. "Hey, Mort. This girl's riding over with you." When the man threw a melting glance back at Mabel, she shrugged it off her white-clad exterior.

Valor ran and locked her hand on the man's bag labeled *Coroner*. "Sir, thank you so much. My mission is a matter of life or death."

"Mine, too." He headed straight to his car without so much as giving her another look.

~

"There's a deer or something even larger moving in those trees up ahead." With the unexpected spotting, the skin crept up the back of Arie's neck.

"You mean what used to be trees." Jusdyn stood stock still and stared at the shredded mess. When Arie ran ahead, Sam pulled at the lead line so he trotted to catch up.

The trees had stood their ground, raking the wind like tines of a fork through a soup bowl. Scrap metal, large sheets of roofing materials, automobile fenders, and unrecognizable trash littered the riparian woodland. How intensive would the labor have to be to clear a mere quarter-mile section?

Movement tripped up ahead and she angled toward it on instinct. Once close enough to make sense out of the distorted shape, she covered her mouth to trap her shriek. Unprepared for this level of injury, her stomach flipped. Nausea soon filled her throat.

"What'd you find?"

"A suffering horse. Don't bring Sam any closer." She folded an arm across her stomach. A struggling appaloosa knelt before them, its front legs mangled from its coerced collision with the creek bank.

He tied the dog to a stump. "That horse belongs to Junior Yates, which means he might be close by."

"I don't think my little pouch has enough mineral powder to fix this horse." She soothed the animal's speckled rear flank as its agony registered deeper in her chest.

He knelt down beside her to commiserate. "Let's look for Junior. Maybe he had a chance at survival since his horse ran away from the storm." He worked to loosen the cinch belt and free the horse's breathing. The saddle soon slumped off, startling the horse. It made a pitiful attempt to stand. "Easy boy." He steadied the animal as it crouched, broken in front yet buck-strong in back. "Could you try running your hands down its front legs, just in case?"

"It must have been Valor back at the cherry orchard, not me." Her gut-wrench seemed to double at the admission. When he begged with a lingering glance, she capitulated and caressed the animal's crushed front limbs.

The horse quieted as he backed away. At the dog's whimper, he grabbed the saddle blanket and brought it over. The blue heeler sniffed and lunged up-creek as if impatient for its master to release the tether. "We're on a hunt." He gave the dog full rein up the empty creek bed.

She stood and began running behind him. Not fifteen yards from the horse, the dog jumped the bank and nosed into a fairly steep rise. At the edge of the woods, she spotted two denim-clad legs wedged into a badger hole.

Jusdyn shook the half-man by his belt. "Junior, is that you?"

"What's left of me, anyway," a muffled voice replied.

"He's alive." Relieved, she caressed the cattle dog turned bloodhound. Once she positioned opposite Jusdyn, the two of them began to ease the survivor from his refuge.

"Don't want to alarm anybody, but I had a run-in with the resident badger while I was a-visiting and the critter held its ground right well." Face down and matted with dirt, the cowboy's warning brought a new prickle of apprehension with it. They pulled his torso out of the burrow and sat him upright, revealing the shredded remains of his face. His forearms hung limp, bloodied in clawed streaks.

"Thank the Good Lord above." Jusdyn began to tend the survivor, straightening his shirt collar and dusting off his chest.

"Junior, this is Arie Henning. She's a pretty fair medic and is going to work on cleaning up your scrapes while I run get us some help." With a wink, he took off across the prairie.

Hands trembling, she untied the oilcloth sack and pulled a tissue out of her pocket. Once a measure of light bronze powder poured from the pouch, she began to dab the victim's forehead.

"Ouch," Junior exclaimed under the pressure of her touch.

"So sorry. I'll be gentler." Arie made softer dabs across his cheekbone.

"Guess I should relish how it feels to be alive. That's more than I can say for the badger."

"Oh? What happened to the badger?"

"Well, there wasn't room down there for the both of us." He attempted a cocked smile, but released it right away. "That's why they call it survival of the fittest, I reckon."

She grimaced and focused on her work for several agonizing moments. "Do cowboys know what it means to be a burrow commensal? You know, sharing life down a hole to the mutual benefit of all?"

"No ma'am. We cowboys are solitary creatures by nature. We must be missing that particular get-along gene." He tightened the skin across his jaw as her work progressed.

While she dabbed, the gold powder started healing the striated wounds and escorting the scratch victim back into the grateful-to-be-alive category. A glimmer of hope birthed in her heart for more rescues, though she couldn't imagine anyone being more messed up than this survivor.

~

Virgil inched forward through the carcass of the Jeep, plowing chards of glass with the violin case held firmly in both hands. Positioned on the back of the driver's seat, he lunged against the door panel. The door flexed open allowing him to roll and strike the ground. He stood, shook off the glass, and then attempted to orient in the wreckage.

A caravan of vehicles made its way up to the stone barn, now freed from the walnut tree's blockade. Help of every imaginable kind poured onto the symphony grounds including fire trucks, ambulances, private vehicles, and even the Sheriff's Department had arrived. Charged by the advance, Virgil ran for the stone barn.

His pace slowed as he approached the rescue site and took note of an infinitely long line of lifeless symphony goers laid parallel to the south wall of the barn. His legs began to tremble as if he was running through a sonic boom. A black sedan eased onto the scene as he stepped into the surreal setting. Without warning, a girl with long legs bolted from the car and ran straight for him. Unable to look at anyone's face, he focused on the violin case, his bloody fingers a blur.

"You found it!" Valor hugged him, case and all. "Virgil— you're phenomenal." In her happiness, she planted a kiss on his cheek. "Now, let me have them."

The embrace made him snap to, the pain in his hands pulsing. He released his grip on the case, surrendering the refugees inside.

Valor shook her head. "Not the frogs. I meant your hands." She stooped, laying the case aside with care.

He stretched out the damaged appendages, nicked in a hundred blood-marked places. This time no questionable circumstances obscured the unfolding miracle. He clearly observed her heal by touch in the full light of day. The pain vanished and the nicked skin of his knuckles smoothed again, as good as new. He gazed down at the girl, fortified with trusting belief. "You are remarkable."

Muriel appeared from the rescue scene nearby at the barn. "Valor? What in the world are you doing here?"

"Aunt Muriel!" The girl threw herself into the woman's arms in dramatic fashion. "Something awful has happened back in town. While we were having our talent show, Miss Opal had a heart attack right there on the spot. They loaded her up in the ambulance for the hospital, but she told the man, 'Get Muriel.' So, they sent me to come fetch you."

"Virgil, go tell Loren everything. I'll take Valor back with me. We'll use my car."

"Ma'am, if you don't mind me saying so, we need Valor here a bunch more than they need another kid back at the care facility." Virgil didn't want to challenge her authority, but angling for more medical help for the survivors was worth the confrontation.

Her expression froze as she gazed between them.

"Please, Aunt Muriel. I promise to be helpful."

"Oh, all right." She stepped toward the access road. "Please don't make me regret this."

Valor turned toward him expectantly as Muriel departed. "First, we have to go—"

"No! Quiet down and listen to me." Virgil stared down at the uppity girl. "We're going to dump these frogs back into the creek first, and then you've got a bunch of healing to do."

"That's exactly what I was going to say." She lifted her chin in defiance and struck out across an expanse of open grass.

Virgil picked up the violin case and followed, determined to part ways with the case of frog flesh at the creek. Striding past her in no time, he could hear her footsteps plod behind him. The sound somehow lent reassurance, even though girls typically complicated things.

~

Jusdyn surveyed the in-coming caravan and relief washed over him to spot his truck in their number. He ran halfway out, criss-crossing his arms to waylay the driver. The antique truck broke from the formation like a maverick steer, making a mad dash toward him.

With devilish haste, the brakes soon seized and brought the runaway vehicle to a halt at his feet. "What's cooking, Just-man?"

"Deke, we've found Junior Yates. He's alive." He slipped into the passenger seat. "Up there by the twin stumps." He pointed toward the creek.

"Wait up," a voice called across the prairie. He twisted around to see Valor and Virgil running toward the truck.

Deke goosed the gas pedal to pick up the kids and then veered back on course to get Junior.

The cab felt crowded in a good way. "How's the frog population?" He tapped the case in the youth's hands.

"About three too many." Virgil fought to suppress a grin while Valor sat between them, beaming.

As the truck approached the rescue site, he studied the progress with Junior. Now working on his hands, Arie tried to spread the powder over them. He caught Virgil staring at his own ruddy hands and sensed something must have transpired earlier.

Virgil twitched in his seat, restless. "Make sure you touch his hands."

He had a more powerful suggestion. "Make sure both you and Arie touch his hands." At earliest opportunity, he popped open the door handle and sprang to her side. Even at first glance, he could see measurable improvement in the patient.

Deke squatted nearby. "Hey there, cowpoke. What kind of bull have you been riding?"

"The low down, dirty kind," Junior replied with obvious soreness.

Virgil and Valor approached with slow, deliberate steps. Valor knelt and stuck her head down the badger burrow. "Uh-oh. I think we've got company." Her tone had a distant ring to it.

"Now what?" Virgil lifted the case full of bullfrogs out of the gaping new hazard zone.

Valor waited motionless by the burrow entrance as twin squinty-eyed badger pups slinked from the hole. Their noses twitched in sensory assessment.

"Be careful with those." He felt the need to couch the child's animal rescue tendencies with caution. They could hardly afford a setback at this juncture.

The critter magnet scooped the pups into her skirt and wrapped them in a cotton corral.

Arie pulled out the silver oval to clear the tote. "Here, Valor.

Put your pups inside this bag for safe handling."

"My belt buckle," Junior exclaimed as he snatched the trophy from Arie. His eyes soon watered at reconnecting with the sentimental token of his roping and riding pinnacle. "Why, this must be my lucky day." He kissed the buckle and stuck it in his shirt pocket.

A reluctant rescuer at best, Jusdyn burst out laughing. Luck lived a country mile from this disastrous day, but insignificant reconnections still had a place. He took a mental picture of Junior's elated expression, a rarity amid the jumbled mess left on the symphony grounds.

~

Morrill followed Ruby's interactions with the children across the room and shuddered under the grim realization that the Lord often closes a door when he opens another. The life Ruby shared with her dear sister since the day she was born was drawing to an abrupt end. Everything would be changing without Opal. Since the inclination came so clearly ordained by the hand of the Almighty, he would have to make sure she did not resist one element of the divine turn-of-fate, lest he forfeit a single blessing meant to accompany it.

It ached to watch the sweetheart of his lengthy life wade through a quagmire of a major life transition. Still, he couldn't resist the impulse to set things right. He rose and floated across the room to fulfill his rightful—yet much-delayed—destiny. When she produced a faint smile upon his approach, he took her hand and lowered onto one knee.

The children became drawn in by the spectacle of a fairytale moment. One by one, they crowded around. When Bobby Dean started to say something, Jenna hushed him.

"Ruby Litke, with God and these children as our witnesses, I ask you with the most genuine of intentions. Will you marry me?" The tidal wave of love he beamed at her must have reached its intended target, as her violet eyes filled with tears and began to overflow.

"I'd be most honored to, Morrill McLauren, today for each day forward." Ruby took his hand and sobbed with a demure smile. The children moved closer into the healing moment.

Resourceful, Jenna removed her hair tie and placed it in his free hand.

He doubled the elastic band and slipped it onto his fiancée's finger.

Ruby glanced at the pink plastic daisy on the band and giggled.

With the children helping him stand, he lifted Ruby to swirl her through the air in celebration. Somehow, under the grace of God, he managed to banish the hurt from the room in the magical moment. Time stood still until Ruby kissed his lips, and then he became a much younger man.

Chapter 21

In the natural world, death becomes merely an allegory for the end of one creature. Only through the advent of death may decay and decomposition occur. The end of life on the macroscopic level becomes a bountiful feast for the microscopic decomposers whose role is to recycle the elements for the next user to absorb. Not so with humankind, whose spirit becomes liberated with death from the circle of elemental life to a place where moth and rust can no longer corrupt. In this greater sense, there is no end in death, though there is a parting for a brief time. Such temporary separation creates a longing heavenward and helps remove the stinger of bereavement from the tender-soled.

Jusdyn assumed the driver's position while Deke rode shotgun, accompanied by a traumatized cowboy with a grizzled-tempered dog underfoot. He zeroed in on the sheriff's car, spirited to report a survivor amid the ruins.

Jimmy John Wilson stood bleak-faced beside his patrol car with radio in hand, surveying the land. The damage seemed to suck life's vitality right out of him.

Deke pounded the door panel as the truck slowed to a halt. "Sheriff Wilson, can you stand a good report?"

"Say on, Purple Cat," the sheriff replied. "I haven't heard much good news today."

"We just found Junior Yates alive," Jusdyn announced across the cab. "His head was stuffed down a badger's hole."

The sheriff turned toward the truck as Junior sat forward and pretended to tip his missing cowboy hat. Though slashed up, his face brought a hint of good-natured reaction from his long-time friend. "It's great to have you still with us, Junior." The lawman struggled through the reunion. "Why don't you come let the EMTs have a look at those scratches? If you pass their inspection, I could use your help identifying the less fortunate."

"Sure thing, Jimmy John." The cowboy nudged Deke to open the truck door and release him. In three gimpy steps, he approached the patrol car.

He switched off the truck as the sheriff lowered Junior into his car and shut the door. "We're here for the long haul. What needs looking after next?"

The sheriff returned, scratching his forehead beneath his hat rim. "The worse matter at hand is our governor hasn't been found yet." His gaze swept the panoramic hills. "Plans were for her to use the north gate to come and go. TJ had that assignment on the perimeter."

Jusdyn gave Deke a look that meant trouble understood, not expecting Jimmy John to read it like a rookie logbook entry.

"He knew that land to the north like the back of his hand in our high school days. There's a root cellar and similar cover on the grounds of the old Metzgers homestead. Knowing TJ, he's plenty cocky enough to try outrunning the storm."

"We're taking the governor assignment then, Jimmy John." He restarted the truck, grinding the drive train into gear. "At least we know she's wearing red."

Jimmy John held up his palm as a radio transmission began. He stiffened as if anticipating more bad news. "Roger that, I'm on my way over." As he straightened, he fired a laser glance right through the truck cab. "A tornado's bearing down on the campground at Richey Cove. There's not an inch of storm shelter over there to house the campers. What am I supposed to do, pull off a miracle?" With that pronouncement, the sheriff folded his height into the patrol car to depart for another ruinous destination.

"No way," Junior protested from the back seat. "Leave me here, for pity's sake."

Jusdyn understood the cowboy's determination not to relive the catastrophe and sympathized as he slipped out, diverting to the stone barn.

Deke squeezed his eyes closed and leaned his head back on the rear glass. "Will this day ever end?" A low groan followed.

The dog whined and jump between them on the seat. He reached out and stroked Sam's salt-and-pepper coat, looking up into the hills of the north pasture as the truck eased forward. He knew dread had already camped out up ahead. How could he possibly dodge it? Maybe Deke's shut-eyed approach had merit. "Want to find another stray, boy?" The dog barked sharply in response, bringing Deke temporarily back into the land of the wakeful alert, bloodshot eyes notwithstanding.

~

Arie stared at the broken appaloosa. "Surely this creature can be spared this misery." She read the astonishment on Virgil's colorless face, both at the horse's predicament and her suggested remedy. "Jusdyn thinks if we join together, the power to heal might somehow be greater."

Silent for once, Valor stood rigid in her resistance.

"The earth is the Lord's and all it contains," Virgil quoted in tranquil pacification, as if yielded to the divine.

Valor turned her gaze on him, clearly unconvinced.

"Then consider this," Arie added, determined to make her case. "Each step of recovery is part of the greater restoration of the prairie. We're only required to heal what's broken, so focus on that."

The girl deliberated a moment longer, stooped to place the bag of baby badgers at Virgil's feet and then walked toward Arie. "But didn't this horse try to outrun God?"

Waffling under the intensity of her objection, Virgil glanced back to Arie.

"What if this horse heeded God's warning and ran away to save its rider? Sometimes you can't base your decision on how things appear. You have to sense things from a deeper level."

"I believe you can do it, Valor." Virgil opened his stance, the frogs bumping inside the case he held. "Isn't that what you told me? Faith helps you believe what you can't see, right?"

Arie watched as the far-away look overcame Valor, the deep-in-thought look she'd witnessed in the cherry orchard once before. She led the girl to the horse's shattered front limbs, placing her hands on both legs.

Eyes closed, Arie soon found a pastel mix of restorative power swirling across the darkened inner screen. This time, she registered the power surge as her hands overlaid Valor's. The movement of the horse rising from the prairie floor signaled an end to the divine provision. When she opened her eyes, there stood the appaloosa, shifting its weight from one foot to the other. It seemed anxious to run the hillside once again.

"To God be the glory," Virgil exclaimed over the scene, his voice filled with awe. He stepped forward to grab the reins with his free hand.

As the youth's expression grew exuberant, Arie no longer sensed fear for the reconstructed animal. In fact, she felt drawn to its restored strength.

"Who let my badgers go?" Valor slung the empty bag through the air, reclaiming her usual testy resolve. The next instant, she scampered to catch one of the escaping pups.

Arie stifled a laugh and took possession of the reins.

"Guess I'm guilty." Virgil cornered the second critter with his right foot while clutching the violin case ever closer. "Excuse me for feeling a little like Noah's attendant. Honestly, we've got to get to that creek in a hurry."

"Welcome to our next problem," Arie stroked the horse's nose and led it forward with a gentle tug. "You might want to start praying for a bit of water in Big John Creek."

"How about a little water for three amphibians to share?" Virgil pointed at the sky. "Is that too much to ask?" His voice cracked as the question ascended into his upper range.

Valor slung the badger bag over her shoulder and started out for the nearby creek. "It's definitely your turn." She chided him with a leer as she passed.

The faith-filled youth plodded down the embankment, acting as if he might be able to somehow draw the water downstream on request.

Trailing her amateur rescue team, Arie knew one thing for certain. The junction of maybe and maybe not served as the ideal place to fling up a prayer. So with horse in hand, she did.

~

Opal stirred and opened her eyes, taking strength that Muriel had been brought to her side. A back porch sit-a-spell friend to three generations of McLaurens, it felt fitting that life should ebb away in the company of one. When she lifted her hand ever so slightly, Muriel met it with her own. Prompting her spent flesh through the weakness of a leaky heart, she rendered the commissioning required of her. "Daughter." Her whisper echoed up a torturously dry throat.

Muriel nodded and leaned closer, her thumb rubbing across the top of her hand.

"You must now take this secret role of mine." She stopped, laboring to breathe.

Muriel tilted her head as if to question, her tears spilling freely.

"The Lord's work." Opal continued, fighting to draw a breath. "You'll be guardian."

Muriel shook her head as if she didn't understand, clearing her wet cheek with the back of her hand.

"The grass must not vanish. Protect them all, to aid the Lord's acquisition."

"This duty comes to me through a glass darkly," Muriel replied, "but I may be familiar with some of the players involved. Their acts appear miraculous."

Opal nodded as the strength ebbed from her core. "They'll help Jusdyn." A peace overtook her as the spiritual endowment transferred.

Muriel squeezed her hand as if grasping her new duty.

Languishing, the elder saint pulled her hand away, having delivered her message and transferred her divine role. *To God be the glory.* A shallow breath left her chest.

~

On the east shore of Council Grove Reservoir, a sandy beach that had been abandoned by its users began to quiver under the atmospheric vibration of the approaching tornado. Campers had been rushed into the lower level of the ranger's quarters up the road, a partially enclosed garage open to the south. Hushed from their trivial banter by the train roar of the tornadic winds, the mixed group watched helplessly as the storm advanced. The next instant, rain pelted the ground, lashed sideways by the wind. Uniformed rangers stood in front, clasping heroic hands in a makeshift human barrier to protect the campers. Moving across the rock-walled valley of Richey Cove, a stovepipe tornado's swirling winds banked off the flint-rock reservoir liner, retreated up into the unstable sky that had birthed it, and inexplicably disappeared.

Unable to see for the line of bur oak trees along the lane, the rangers never flinched from their position guarding the group. Not half a minute after the storm left the ground, the sheriff's patrol car rolled into the recreation area, its high-beam headlights piercing the vertical rain. Jimmy John Wilson stepped out into the watershed of a driving rain and found nothing left of the swirling stovepipe.

With the brim of his hat shielding his eyes, he took a sober look at the helpless mass of humanity under the inadequate shelter. "Folks, I sure can't explain this, but the tornado lifted when it hit the waters of Ritchey Cove. It's gone." Jimmy John stared at the head ranger he had known for fifteen years. As the rangers dropped their arms, the campers gave a spirited cheer.

"Thank God Almighty." The head ranger stepped forward to confer with him. "We would have been caught in a right vulnerable position here under the house."

"If you only knew what a tornado left in its wake back in town, you'd all be on your knees thanking God for sparing your lives. No campfires this evening. I can't afford to send the firemen away from town."

"Got it, sheriff. I think we'll stay put until the rain slackens a bit. This would be a great time to address the powerful forces of nature with my captive audience."

"Oh, this storm has life lesson written all over it." With a tip of his hat, Jimmy John folded himself back into the patrol car and completed a three-point turn back to the disaster zone.

~

Muriel received the revelation of her assignment with a quieted spirit and the typical feeling of utter unworthiness that accompanies such divine appointment. Her mind raced through a litany of pictures of her family and its dedication to the land. *A lineage is birthed with a melding of time, heart, and devotion.*

"Bring the baby," Opal whispered.

Muriel hastened to the door only to find Merrilee entering with Beryl in her arms. The elder and the babe touched one another for an infinitesimal moment, framed in inspired silence. "The Lord is good."

Within moments, Opal's head slumped to one side in the finishing fade of life.

Muriel lifted the baby, sensing her spiritual potential with heightened awareness. Close by, Merrilee became the first to grieve the death of the beloved town matriarch, weeping into Beryl's blanket. Muriel put her arm around the new mother and ushered the next generation of prairie warrior back to the nursery for safekeeping.

~

Jusdyn and Deke walked across the edge of Metzgers pasture, its fence and gate ripped from place. Only the stones of the old dry-stack rock walls remained, haphazardly slung far and wide across the hillside. Sam worked the rubble pile fronting the stone arch of the root cellar, his nose to the ground.

"Anybody in there?" he called through the cracks. They listened, ears pricked for the faintest response. Sam traced scents on the ground, then slicked back his ears and bolted north. He tracked with the canine toward the northern gully, spotting a rescue flare of sorts that made him punch Deke's side.

"Wahoo!" Deke exploded over the root cellar rubble to give ready chase.

He broke into a full run as Sam froze over a hole in the ground with his haunches hackled up like a wild animal, filling the hole with loud barks. The tree branch bearing a red jacket stopped bobbing and lowered into the shaft. Seconds later, he stood poised on the edge of the hole, staring down at Topeka's reigning monarch, alive and well. "Afternoon, Governor." He lowered on the rim, relieved by the find.

Deke's muscular shoulder soon nudged his. His jaw dropped at the sight of their quarry.

A soaked governor held her arms up toward the clearing sky. "Heaven help me, you guys are a sight for sore eyes." She twisted her wrists with the impatience of a three year-old. "Would you ever so kindly get us out of here?"

"Yes, ma'am. Give us a second." He unclasped the dog's lead line and dangled the looped end down the well shaft.

The governor maneuvered up to her husband's shoulders, gripped the loop with a white-knuckled handhold, and held her breath as they hoisted her up to ground level. Standing, she assayed the storm-strewn land, turning in every direction. "Tell me. How bad are the casualties?" Though disheveled, she still clung to duty.

He shook his head. "More dead than not, I'm afraid. The stone barn collapsed under the force of the wind, crushing the symphony-goers inside. But we did find all the children, safe and sound in a drainage culvert under the road." He bit back any more commentary, unsure how much she could take.

The governor struggled through a labored inhalation, seemingly ready to balance the weight of the state back on her shoulders. "I won't leave until some semblance of order has been restored, you have my word. Could I ask your names?"

"I'm Jusdyn Linquist, and this is my cousin Deke, who just became a first-time father as the storm hit."

"Bet you'll enjoy telling this story to the grandkids one day, Deke. Sure will be a day for this community to remember."

Deke looked down. "Tell you the truth, ma'am, I hope to only recall parts of it."

"Yeah, like the humorous part where you left the governor's husband down the hidey-hole," a masculine voice added in a jesting tone.

"Hold on, sir." He bent over the opening, assessing his approach. With nothing for the man to climb up on, the distance seemed unfathomable. "Looks like we'll need to borrow a ladder to get you out."

"Even that will likely require some extra help, as I've got a bum ankle down here that's going to make for a difficult ascent. So what are a few more minutes anyway? Actually, I was just starting to like the place."

Saluting the first man's positive spirit, he turned his attention back to the governor. Taking her elbow, he led the way back to the truck.

"Have mercy. My guards hid inside that cellar," the governor said, pointing to the arched stones marking the root cellar as they walked past.

Deke turned to him hollow-eyed.

"We'll get a team and come right back." He helped her up into the cab, attempting to sound confident.

Deke loaded Sam into the truck bed and then slid in the

passenger side.

The governor placed her hand atop the gearshift. "Do either one of you know TJ McLauren?"

"Yeah, he's my cousin." At a loss for something more constructive to say, he fired up the truck's engine.

"TJ hasn't been found yet," Deke added.

The governor set her jaw and silently weighed out the matter.

Determined to complete the rescue, he eased the truck from the pasture.

"I promised I would remember him to Valor." She cut the sentiment short, choked with emotion.

"She's around here somewhere," Deke replied, "helping with the rescue."

"Actually, she's kind of hard to miss with her animal collection." With three bullfrogs still tucked under her wing, Valor should be plenty easy to locate. Confident the meet-up would transpire, he aimed the truck down the lane toward the old stone barn.

~

Arie approached the familiar creek bed and could tell nothing had changed. Recovery took time, and they appeared too early for Big John Creek.

Virgil took several plodding steps down into the waterless bed and summoned them in, trading Valor the violin case for her bag of badgers. "You should be the one to let them out Valor, since you caught them in the first place."

The girl unlatched the case and cracked some airspace around its perimeter. The contents shifted with a thump.

Virgil held out his arm. "Wait for the water. Oh, Lord, we stand in a scarred land that needs to heal." His prayer rose with earnestness. "In the power of your son Jesus Christ, we ask you to start restoring this land right here by cranking some water back to its muddy spots again."

Arie pinched her eyes closed, willing the restoration to start with such intensity it made her dizzy. She envisioned pools of rain being released from the wind, set free to re-explore the drainage system carved into the land by ancient forces over time. Opening her eyes, the bed of Big John Creek sat empty, still awaiting restitution of water from its upstream source. Moments passed and then, in a slow cohesive slink, water slipped into the upper creek bed, arriving as a thin reflective sheet.

At the sight of water, Virgil shucked off his shoes and flung them onto the far bank. In unity, his frog-toting assistant rattled the bank with her shoes as well and, barefoot, the two animal tenders waited in the mud for the clear advance of recovery to wash across them. Virgil kept his arms up until the moment water first lapped at his ankles. "Release the bullfrogs."

Valor lowered the case and the ex-patriots readily entered the rehydrated ecosystem with a leggy plunge.

A deep satisfaction overcame Arie so she began to applaud the team effort.

"Hey—take a look at this bonus." Valor held the case wide open for their inspection. A gelatinous mass covered a symphony program, its slimy addition spilling onto the red velvet lining of the case.

Peering inside, Arie translated the contents as pure joy. "Oh, wow. Eggs. What better way to repopulate the creek?" She smiled at the jubilant violinist.

Virgil found a stand of sedges along the flat rocks and scooped the clear clump out of the case. Sliding the cache into place between the wet blades of the nut sedges, he wiped the program cover clean and stared at it. The bullfrogs remained visible for a few splish-splashing hops and disappeared into the aquatic habitat.

Virgil slapped the program against his free hand. He scanned the creek and then looked up at his companions. "I think I know what my next assignment should be. No one else here knows the symphony members like I do."

Valor glanced up at him and her quizzical look melted into

admiration.

"Great. That makes our next stop the coroner's station." Impatient, Arie motioned them out of the creek.

Valor stepped onto the bank, retrieved her shoes and took possession of the badger pups.

Virgil lingered at the creek's edge for a brief moment, visibly savoring the encounter.

"I'll get the horse." Arie appreciated her newfound lack of fear for the creature. With gentle hands, she untied the reins to lead the resilient appaloosa back to a world torn apart.

~

Jusdyn brought the governor to the epicenter of the devastation by the stone barn where his parents labored. Multiple lines of bodies extended past the corner of the stone barn. Volunteer firemen and EMTs took turns escorting survivors to the hospital.

After helping the governor from the cab, Deke pointed toward the sheriff's car returning at a rapid speed.

He checked west across the barrenness toward Big John Creek and spotted Arie bringing the kids back, along with Junior's horse. A notable convergence of survivors was occurring in the aftermath of this storm, but he sensed even more discoveries ahead. First, he had to make a notable deposit. "Governor, we've got to let Sheriff Wilson know you've been found." Adhering to protocol, he hoped the discovery might buoy the lawman's spirits. "He'll authorize the crew that goes back for your husband and searches for your guards. First, I'd like you to meet my father, Loren Linquist."

Loren approached, extending his hand which she readily received. "Madam Governor, we're relieved that you're safe and unhurt—which puts you in the minority right now."

"It seems I have your family members to thank for that, Mr. Linquist. TJ put me in that hole for safekeeping, and then Jusdyn and Deke pulled me out."

"TJ?" Loren failed to hide his surprise.

Jimmy John stepped into the collecting group and extended his hand to the governor who met it with her own.

"Sheriff, I was just telling Mr. Linquist how I'm doubly indebted to his family, both for putting me down the well shaft and for retrieving me out."

"For once, I'm grateful TJ's quick on his feet."The sheriff's genial admission stirred laughter from the group.

"I think my husband would be ever so appreciative if you could send some men with a ladder to spring him out. And my guards are unaccounted for in the root cellar close by."

"We'll give it top priority, ma'am." Jimmy John singled out Deke for his next assignment. "Let's send the fire truck up the lane. They're equipped with ladders and a wench, so use them as necessary."

"I'd be glad to show them the exact spot, Jimmy John."

"That'd be handy, Deke. But before you go, let me update everyone on the storm. The tornado banked off the rock ravine at Richey Cove and—for reasons that defy mortal explanation— disappeared into thin air. That means it missed the huddled masses under the ranger's house by a quarter mile, if that."

"Thank God for the end to that killing machine." Loren wiped his brow in relief.

"I've lived all my life in Tornado Alley and never seen the likes of something as destructive as that," The governor pulled her shirttail back in place as if resetting her resolve.

"Level EF-Five, don't you think, Dad?"

"Most likely Jusdyn, and at the top of the category probably, judging from the damage."

The coroner wheedled his way into the group, slouch-shouldered from his consuming work. "Sheriff, do I have your permission to start transporting bodies from the wet ground into the morgue and funeral home, wherever we can accommodate them?"

"How do you plan to get an I.D. on everyone?" The sheriff crossed his arms and waited for an answer. A commotion stirred which ended up being the other half of the family team.

Virgil stepped into the group. "I'd like to help with that, sir."

Jusdyn slipped his arm around Arie's waist and nodded at the horse. When she raised her brow and smiled a secretive response, it lifted his spirits.

"How can *you* possibly help *me*?" The coroner ladled on condescension thicker than his Oklahoma accent.

The youth flashed the symphony program toward them without a flinch. "I'm Virgil Sinclair. My mother has played for the symphony for years. I know almost every one of those individuals. They'd all be wearing black, so it's easy to single them out. And I have this program listing all the members performing today. Would that be of any help?"

The sheriff scorched an authoritative look at the coroner. "Wagon-loads. I'd like identification of each victim before they're moved. Let this young man take a crack at the symphony members, and I've asked Junior Yates to look at the attendees. Got that, Mort?"

"Just as you please." The coroner bowed out of group and headed toward the stone barn.

Virgil stroked the badger bag in Valor's possession and then shadowed the official with gangly, determined strides.

"I could come with you." Valor lurched forward only to be blocked by Loren's arm.

"Governor, this is Valor McLauren, the girl you wanted to meet." Jusdyn added extra emphasis on her name to help redirect the headstrong girl.

"Yes, Miss McLauren. I'd like to spend a few moments talking with you, if your family wouldn't mind." She beckoned to the girl making Valor turn sheepish.

"Be our guest, Governor." Loren addressed her with gracious overtones. He stooped to deliver his next message to Valor with direct expectations. "On your best behavior, young lady."

"Okay, Uncle Loren." Valor shifted the badger bag into the crook of her arm. "Do you know my Dad?" She looked quizzical as the governor took her by the shoulders and led her away from the group.

"Your father is my hero," the governor replied, "and I'd like to tell you why."

Jimmy John gave them an uncomfortable look as the pair walked off for their private exchange. He shot a business-like glare toward Jusdyn and Loren, nodding in the opposite direction for a private consultation. "Deke, can you get that rescue of the governor's husband underway while I chat with Jusdyn here for a minute?"

"Sure thing, sheriff. How about it, Arie? Want some hilltop rescue action next?"

"Count me in."

"Take at least four firemen and a truck. Give that area a good combing for any other survivors, too." The sheriff traced the hillside with the flat of his hand.

Deke nodded and took the reins from Arie, escorting the resurrected appaloosa.

As the two walked shoulder-to-shoulder into their next adventure, Jusdyn wished he could break away to accompany them.

The sheriff waited until they moved out of earshot. "Gentlemen, let me say that I'm more than a little uneasy about the governor vaulting TJ up on a hero's platform regarding her rescue from the storm."

"What part of it bothers you the most, sheriff?" Loren asked.

He felt a swarm of negativity riding his father's elevated blood pressure, but resolved to remain objective over the situation. Maybe TJ deserved the benefit of the doubt.

Jimmy John stared at Loren and then turned his gaze to him. "We've had some indication that TJ is involved in a local meth ring. Some plea bargains from the Junction City raid started the finger-pointing his way, which bears up some other feedback we've been receiving from the state-wide Meth Shield program. We know there's been a major producer in the area, but haven't been able to ferret him out."

The sheriff's disclosure dumbfounded him. "And you think it's TJ?" He glanced at his father whose agony rode the deep lines carved into his face.

Jimmy John flinched and nodded. "We had surveillance lined up for tomorrow, but with this storm hitting, it could be months before we can tighten down those screws. You both know TJ. He's wily and will likely operate full steam ahead, knowing we have our hands full."

"You sound as if you're confident that TJ survived the storm, sheriff." Loren waged a credible protest.

Though weary, he knew his father meant no offense by the insinuation. To his credit, the rescue work had left him with higher priorities than playing the role of devil's advocate for TJ.

Jimmy John gave them a sharp look and then dropped his gaze down to the ravaged ground. "Surveillance tells us he made a call from his cell phone sometime after the time the weather service pinpointed the tornado in this area. Given that evidence, we believe he not only survived the tornado, but is likely operating on the lam from here on out. I'm going to ask you both to cooperate as much as possible with this investigation. Can I count on that?"

"Linquists are straight-shooting, law-abiding citizens." Loren's tone came laden with defensive protection for the family. "We serve a higher law—and live accordingly."

He raised both hands with open palms. "We both agree to cooperate."

"Right now, we'll just play along that we don't know anything about TJ's status. We'll keep him on the missing list, but not memorialize him with the dead. And by no means will we vaunt him as the hero of this tragic day, is that clear?"

"We understand, Jimmy John. Do your job, and we'll protect his family."

"Muriel and I will be taking little Valor to Wilsey with us." Loren jabbed a thumb into his chest as if to claim ownership of the girl.

"Go right ahead, for now. As long as we know where she is, we're agreeable."

"And for decency's sake, can we leave her out of this as much as possible?" Loren's cheeks reddened as he made the request.

"You bet, Mr. Linquist. Sorry it has to come down to this."

"TJ brings it on himself, Jimmy John." Jusdyn had no problem conceding the point. "You're on the right side of the law. We all recognize that."

The sheriff toed the dirt with his once-polished boot. "This meth grows like a rural cancer, though we're digging deep to eradicate it. Sometimes the disease pops up behind a familiar face, which makes it more personal in a small town. TJ and I go way back, so don't imagine for one minute that this has been easy for me."

"I appreciate that, Jimmy John. TJ's made some bad choices that no one in our family supports." A lump formed in his throat, but he fought to regain control. "He's running from more than what's obvious."

"Somebody's got to catch him and get him turned around, so it may as well be me."

"I'll stay and help with the rescue work until my wife returns from the hospital, and then I'm taking the girl and going back to Wilsey." Loren's shoulders slumped as he walked back toward the stone barn.

He hesitated, unsure of his next destination.

"Hey, who's the pretty lady with Junior's horse?" Jimmy John's voice struck a more upbeat tone.

"Arie Henning, Doug McLauren's niece—and someone special to me."

"At the end of the day, could the two of you make sure that speckled horse gets back to Wilsey? I'm sure Junior would count it as a personal favor."

"I'll probably bring Junior back with us, too, since his rig took a hit in the tornado. Let me find out if there's a decent trailer left in these parts while Junior's helping you."

"Sounds like a deal, Jusdyn. I sure appreciate being able to count on you." The sheriff tipped his hat and returned to the melee.

He stood there, unable to speak as his throat parched despite the prevalence of water all around. Out of necessity, he'd add Junior to his entourage. Matters grew more entangled by the minute. After surveying his position, certain essentials became clear. *I gotta have that trailer.*

~

Muriel entered the rec room at the senior care facility with leaden steps surprised to find something of a celebration occurring. Cupcakes and punch resuscitated the storm children while Jenna played lively songs on the piano without any sheet music. A circle of activity gyrated from the checkerboard, with Morrill and Ruby standing at the hub. She tucked a soaked tissue behind her back. "What on earth is going on here?"

Vernis motioned above the merrymaking. "You're looking at an engagement party." He moved a red checker forward with an arthritic finger. Mr. Newcomb switched a toothpick to the opposite side of his mouth and began his black countermove. Mrs. Newcomb saluted her with a green cast.

When the piano playing stopped, Jenna ran up to her short of breath. "Mr. Morrill is going to marry Miss Ruby. And we children get to be their witnesses."

Muriel involuntarily let out a sob that turned into a chuckle and then migrated into a full laugh as her arms surrounded the engaged couple to share their joy. Shrugging off the weariness from lack of sleep, the pleasure of acknowledging love's pending culmination took center stage. Jenna presented her a cupcake with a slight curtsey and Bobby Dean sloshed a cup of punch toward her other hand.

The room seemed to pause for her response. In the lull, she received a refilling of appreciation for the little things of life. "Thank you so much, children." She shifted the cup in her grip and elevated it, moving toward an appropriate outcome. "Shall we pose a toast to this handsome engaged couple?"

A rush to refill cups ensued at the punchbowl, which solicited warm smiles from Ruby and Morrill. The children reassembled in front of the couple, some with wet knuckles.

Muriel cleared her throat. "Now then, I salute a young-at-heart couple who finally acknowledged their love for one another. May you have many more years to delight in your discovery, and may you always be surrounded by those who truly love you."

"Like us," Jenna added, smiling before she sipped her punch.

"Just like you, sweetheart," Morrill replied with a wink. "Goodness, Ruby. In our haste to get hitched, we haven't even discussed the possibility of having a family."

Her violet eyes twinkled at the prospect. "I'm certain we'll have children if the Lord blesses us with some."

Morrill lifted his palm high as if taking a formal oath. "Well, no one here need fear being abandoned for even a moment. We'll watch over each of you not reclaimed by your parents."

Bobby Dean shuddered and sobbed, "Heaven's giving us a family-away-from-family." He stepped toward the committed couple without any hesitation.

Ruby opened her arms to embrace him and several other children responded.

So overwhelmed by the tidal wave of love cresting in the room, Muriel completely forgot the real reason she had come over from the hospital until the soaked tissue fell from her hand.

Ruby tracked its fall and her gaze hesitated before glancing back at her.

Muriel nodded to confirm the passing and the tears began to flow again. This time, joy mingled with sadness, acknowledging both gain and loss.

~

Awakening in a fog, TJ turned stiffly in his cot, trying to find a comfortable position between the bruises from his pelting by storm debris. The overhanging hood of darkness could be attributed to a lack of windows in the cabin, but he couldn't shake the irony of how it evoked his mental state as well. *This must be what it feels like to turn your back on everything you know and love.* Before regaining sleep, the solitude of his cabin bore him an illegitimate companion. The specter called loneliness slipped under the threshold, shapeless yet suffocating.

~

Loren had worked his way into a corner of rubble that held little hope for survivors. He lifted a neatly hewn limestone rock and tossed it into the building's interior. Another crushed body of a symphony member became apparent, and he bent his aching back to free it for removal. Something about the hair color seemed a trifle familiar, though he had grown too weary to make the immediate connection. Securing his load, he staggered out to the infinite line of similarly crumpled victims, walking past the coroner and his junior assistant.

"Anton Vorchenski, violin player." Virgil forced a checkmark into the margin of the program book. When the coroner made his counter notation on the body tag, the pair stood to regroup and shift one victim down the line.

"Nancy Sinclair, clarinet player," Loren said with difficulty, the similarities now ever apparent between the mother-son pair. His heart broke for the youth, whose hand now would be forced to make the mark he'd hoped to avoid at all cost.

The boy's first sob sounded like more of a cough, chased by a crackle vented from the soul. Virgil bent double to support his quivering knees, the program pressed against his thigh.

"Nancy Sinclair," he repeated. "She was the best clarinet player ever." His eyes began misting with tears.

Ever so gently, Loren laid her body next to the iconic violinist and reached for his shoulders with rock-scraped hands. The boy heaved as Loren clutched his frame.

The coroner straightened at the break and drifted to the trunk of the Crown Victoria.

Loren attempted steadfastness despite his weariness. "You'll never be alone, son—rest assured of that."

Virgil shuddered several times, as if digging for enough composure to respond. "No place for me to go." His voice turned airy as he became orphaned by the storm in a free-fall of tears. His thumb dug across his cheek as if trying to divest his face of emotion.

"We always have room for one more in Wilsey." Loren knew the vast prairie would extend its horizon for inclusion of the youth. His family would welcome him, too.

~

Jimmy John directed the EMT crew to escort the governor's husband to the hospital for treatment of his broken ankle. While the head-of-state showered her affections on the lame man, Valor seemed compelled to touch the man at the site of his infraction. Arie had delivered a bag full of items found in the north pasture, including one slightly smashed cell phone. He flipped it open with limited expectation of it working, only to be pleasantly surprised by an inwardly lit picture of the prairie in full bloom. He retrieved the contact list and scanned down the alphabetical entries to If Found. Cueing it up, the line read *TJ McLauren* followed by the Conservation District number. "Gotcha," he said, acknowledging the direct hit of evidence his case needed. He closed the phone and slid it into his pocket. When the radio blared from the console, he snatched it from the dashboard. "Sheriff Wilson here. Go ahead."

"We've got a report of people raining out of the sky up Ritchey Cove way." The dispatcher's voice crackled and halted.

Jimmy John held his head in his hand and braced for the jarring details. "Are we talking about bodies, or living, breathing human beings?" He couched his wafer-thin optimism with late-in-the-day caution. A pause followed while the dispatcher tried to gain a clarification.

"According to the ranger, they're wet, screaming human beings," the dispatcher replied.

A wry smile hooked up the sheriff's cheek as he gazed out over the symphony site turned cemetery. "Well, now. That's just how I like 'em. I'll be right up." Such favor from God came to him as unmistakable manna. No matter what unexpected form it took, he felt immersed in the blessing head to toe. "Thank you, Lord, for landing those folks in the water." Slipping back into his car, he acknowledged that the flint rock rimming the cove would have made for a painful reception committee.

Chapter 22

Nature is not averse to recovering from catastrophe. In short order, scars formed by standing water, slaking fire, or slithering lava begin the process of healing with impressive immediacy. Long-dormant seeds and spores that have escaped rotting in the standing water of a flood now have the chance of a lifetime to germinate in the rich silt it imported. Serotinous cones that have shielded the seed stash from damage by the fire are now signaled to release the hope of the next generation amid the charred forest remains. Pioneer plants with rock-drilling roots now creep confidently atop the pumiced substrate to unabashedly claim their new territory where once a volcano flowed. For nature, time heals all wounds in vegetated forays, rebuilding the damaged ecosystem brick-by-botanical-brick, and then re-raising her flag in resilient green to attract the wildlife back once again.

Guiding the old truck down the familiar ruts of Road Z, Jusdyn sensed sleep must have fallen on his companion who hadn't stirred since reuniting Junior and his horse with their ranch a few miles back. Bone-deep contentment accentuated his weariness because he and Arie remained together at the close of the day. Turning into the driveway, he saw the lights on in the big house and could imagine his father's satisfaction sheltering his loved ones at long last as the cloak of night fell upon the land.

With Arie's cottage waiting peacefully to the left and his boyhood home beckoning on the right, an ultimatum of the heart resurrected—one he had sensed coming for some time. While the truck crept forward out of gear, he evaluated the two housing options and searched for insight. Should he retreat to his lifelong sanctuary again tonight? Or should he face a greater calling—one that involved Arie and so much more?

He nosed the truck beside the front porch and cut the ignition, pressing his forehead onto the steering wheel. *Two roads diverge into the woods so I must choose one.* His father's voice echoed back to him assuring him that there's a right way to do everything, which came quickly chased down memory lane by his earlier admission that he loved only the land.

"Lord, help me with this choice," he whispered into the night. "Please help me get it right." The post-storm prairie spoke back, solidifying which road he should take.

Arie began to awaken, stirring by his side. "Are we home?"

"Yes, we're home." He opened the cab door and carried her toward the cottage as if she were the final victim of the day he had the privilege of helping. As he opened the screen door to bring her inside, the truth dawned on him. He represented the one getting rescued, despite all appearances otherwise.

~

Loren stood in front of the open doors to the storm cellar, initiating Virgil on its whereabouts and reliable contents should the unpredictable night sky drive them into the shelter. He peered down the steps to see a neatened version of the shelter poised for occupancy and felt a quick indebtedness to Arie for all her trouble. "This is where I thought we should have been."

The boy took several steps into the throat of the shelter and paused. He glanced back up at him as if weighing the safety forfeited against the unknowns risked at the symphony grounds. "We needed you more in town." Honesty flashed in his blue eyes.

He leveled his gaze at the youth with the evaluative stare of a guardian.

"Really, sir. I can't imagine how the day could have gone without you, or think about where I'd be right now if you had stayed home."

He chose his words with deliberateness. "I heard a higher calling, all right." A smile rippled out of his weary core. "Looks like I gained a new son to show for it."

Jusdyn stepped into the brittle illumination of the back porch light. "Finally, I get the little brother I always wanted, but never had."

Virgil rose from the shelter and they shook hands, sealing the new relationship.

Loren put a hand of blessing on each son's shoulder and looked overhead to find some indication the storm had passed. The faintest of constellations peered back, offering him a firmament full of assurances.

"And Virgil can have my old room." Jusdyn turned and headed up the deck steps. "I've decided not to come back home."

~

Though the tranquility of rest induced by the anesthesia drifted over his being, Doug sensed a distinct chill piercing the hot haze and managed to rally toward it. From his last train of thought, he recognized his current state of captivity by the relentless desert-dwelling enemy. He'd somehow lost use of his arms, as they had been tethered to the austerity of the cot.

Willing his body to regain consciousness, he opened his eyes in time to witness an angel pressing ice cubes to his sand-dry lips. He struggled to place her face, and then melted in the awareness that she represented the angel sent to rescue him from the annihilation of abandonment. A heart-message strained up his throat, determined for expression lest she be sent away before he could fully awaken. "Is this heaven?"

The angel bent over him to administer the complete provision of her blessing on his motionless form. "Only if you want it to be," she whispered.

"I do," he replied. A kiss fell upon his lips, one that hung like a healing garden, and then a lilting song began to lure him back to sleep. The shackles he fought gave way, and he floated up in weightless release.

~

Morrill tucked the last of the children into bed and whispered the Lord's care upon them. He found Ruby waiting in the back hall when he stepped out and they clasped hands in silence. He eased into a smile and placed his arm around her shoulder. "I gave up my bed, so now I'm homeless."

"That's almost fitting for your last night of bachelorhood. The nurses have roll-away cots made up for you and Vernis in the corner of the rec room."

"Do you think we could we ask the preacher to marry us in the morning? I see they're planning an ecumenical memorial service for the community down by the river at eleven o'clock. Maybe our hitching could tag along afterwards."

"But we haven't any civil license to marry yet, Morrill."

"Let's put matters in the right order. The things of God should come first, and then the things of man. We'll have our union ordained by the sacrament of marriage in God's cathedral on Sunday, and then repeat our vows to the justice-of-the-peace come Monday." When Ruby's violet eyes clouded, another consideration occurred to him. "And for you, I'll bear one more night on that cot, so the honeymoon can begin both blessed—and legal—come Monday night, if I have to." As her blush plummeted beyond the cameo clasping the neckline of her dress, he found himself enjoying every square inch of her reaction. "Would you like for me to wear my best suit to the service tomorrow?"

"Yes, if you would, please, and I have a little something put away, too." She stopped outside the rec room door.

"Should that dress smell of mothballs, you may blame that part on me."

"It will have the aroma of a late-blooming prairie rose—a held-back answer to the hope of a lifetime."

"Do you think we need a reception afterward to celebrate?"

"No, it wouldn't seem right, with Opal just passing, plus all the storm victims are still mourning. Muriel has offered to throw us a party next Saturday out in Wilsey, so let that serve as our reception. I'll ask her to extend the invitation to the community tomorrow at the river."

"Oh, I imagine the children will simply love Wilsey."

Ruby jerked from his arms. "The children? Dear me, oh my. I need clean clothes for all the children." She gave him a quick peck on the cheek and hastened out to the parking lot.

Morrill walked soundlessly into the room and kicked off his shoes by the bedside. With Vernis already in the arms of sleep, his snoring came as a welcome rhythm to blot out the other night noises. He lowered himself into the sheets and rested his weary head on the pillow. His brother's regular breathing provided solace like days of old, ushering him into a deep sleep.

~

Jusdyn burst through the back door as Muriel placed a plate of cold cuts out for a late snack. Seated at the bar, Valor nibbled cubes of cheese balanced on round crackers and sipped milk. Four sandwiches laid in various stages of readiness on the counter. "Hey, Guardian of the Bullfrogs." When he leaned toward her, Valor flashed an appreciative smile in return.

Loren and Virgil slipped inside from the porch, making the country kitchen fill with life.

Muriel opened the cabinet and reached for an additional plate. "Hey, Jusdyn. I can make another sandwich if you'd like."

"No thanks. Mom and Dad, I came back over to share some news with you." He paused, glancing at the new family members and wondering if they needed more privacy.

"Go ahead, son," Loren said. "We'll have no secrets here among family."

He nodded, obliged to get this admission out in the open and off his chest. "Every day since Arie moved in next door, I've come up that driveway having to make a choice. Do I turn this direction to the only home I've ever known, and with it, all the comforts of the familiar? Or do I go where my heart has been leading me, to Arie and a life together?"

Loren made a throaty noise and moved closer to Muriel.

"Earlier today, while we hunkered in the calaboose while the storm raked by us, I felt the future opening up in front of me. Right when I needed to know if God meant for Arie to come along with me, she admitted she had been sent back here so I wouldn't have to go alone. That's the closest I've ever come to hearing God speak directly to me—and it was unmistakable."

Muriel nodded, a countenance of peace making her face glow.

"I plan to clean up and go ask Arie to marry me. God willing, she'll say yes."

Valor slipped off the stool to wrap him in a hug. "Oh, I think I can guess Arie's answer to that question."

His father extended a congratulatory hand while Virgil's face cracked with a slim smile.

Muriel dried her hands on her apron. "You'll need Grandma's ring, won't you?"

He leaned into a cheek peck as she passed by toward the desk. "How'd you know?"

"Because engagement is a rite of passage." She reached for an old cigar box in the overhead cabinet. "The mother has to pay off the future daughter-in-law so she'll accept kitchen duty for the rest of her life." Laughter rang out as she opened a hinged velvet box to reveal the diamond that captured the light and released it back in a shower of color.

He choked up at seeing the ring, the direction of his intent now taking shape.

"Tell Arie that we're holding a reception party for Morrill and Ruby here Saturday, if that gathering can work into your plans."

Muriel raised one eyebrow as if to prompt a response.

He nodded, his throat constricted from accepting the heritage piece.

"We release you with our full blessing." Loren slapped his back as if to launch him on his way with added momentum.

Emotionally speaking, he had already left that dock, fortified by faith and floating on a shaky sea. Still, his choice had been made. The distance he had to navigate equated to the width of one dusty driveway. Too bad his knees were already shaking.

~

TJ's hands knew the motions, the formula, the sequence, and the steps. The rote process worked across the lab like a second-shift laborer, detached from his inner being and the fire that singed his upper lip. By tomorrow night, he'd have enough products to complete his weekly disbursement, blazing a traceless trail as a spirit of ill repute. Remembering the key to that portion of the plan, he took a union break and walked to the rear of the cabin where the silo hatches securely held their age-old secret. He tore away the canvas cover to reveal a gleaming black-and-chrome motorcycle, his stealth delivery vehicle.

In a moment of self-aggrandizement, TJ reached up to stroke his moustache and rekindled the blazing pain splitting his bare upper lip. With a curse fomenting under his breath, he sidestepped into the cabin's latrine to check the damage. In the reflection of a standard issue mirror, he examined the hastily repaired gash. Between the neat, even stitches, a feather-fine red line radiated beneath the skin's surface. Even with his limited medical knowledge, the tale-tell evidence of a complicating infection gave him pause for concern.

Finding his duffel bag, he reached in and drew out two anti-inflammatory tablets. Tossing them into his mouth like life rings, he searched for a water bottle to flush them down the pike. The irony of this self-professed carefree life presented itself with such stark reality not even a chemist could miss it. He'd become his own worst enemy, bearing out proof in weak flesh.

~

Responding to a bare-knuckled knock at the front door, Arie slipped the oil lamp off the mantle and accompanied its glow toward the caller. A familiar purple-clad icon waited outside the screened panel. She stood inside, savoring the blessing of receiving his visit to the porch swing on a day turned upside-down.

Jusdyn beckoned beyond the screen. "Come on out."

She pressed the door latch and stepped out into the night, bringing the essence of fresh honeysuckle with her. She set the lamp in its customary place and took his hand, allowing him to lead the way to the swing. Alighting on her side, she patted the pillow beside her. "Would the Wildcat like to swing?" She remembered their first night in this identical setting. When his gaze rested on her in a purposeful way, she grew self-conscious. Dressed in her white nightgown, she tucked her bare legs beneath the swaying courtship platform and gazed up.

"I'll sit in a minute." He swallowed hard and put both hands behind his back.

Something about his hesitation hinted that this might not be an ordinary goodnight exchange. A nervous butterfly made a pass under her ribs. "I know it's been a hard day, but surely we can spare a few minutes more to simply be together." She waited, hands folded in her lap, in hopes he could collect himself. From beyond the porch, sounds of the nocturnal prairie surrounded them with a hundred faceless witnesses.

"Today I saw a piece of heaven open up and show me a path to the future." He held his hand skyward. "I can't and won't travel down that path alone. And I believe God doesn't intend that for me." At this admission, he knelt on one knee in the unhurried gesture of gallant men in days of old. Then he reached for her hand and held it.

She felt a rush of love pulse through her, but kept her place on the swing. Her free hand rose to wipe the first tear from her cheek.

He caught that hand to trap it with the other. "Let those tears flow. Arie Henning, with everything you are and will be—would you marry me—for all I am and hope to be?" He fumbled retrieving a small box from his back pocket and then opened it, releasing a diamond solitaire to twinkle in the lantern light. The prairie wooed from afar.

Slipping from the swing, her gown overlaid his bent knee as she knelt before him in equal submission before the Lord. She gazed into his eyes, reveling in the joy of the moment. When his pulse matched hers in the palm of her hand, she somehow began to experience the mystery of two souls becoming one. "Yes, with all that I am and ever hope to be—I will marry you, Jusdyn Linquist." Unable to suppress her joy any longer, tears fell to the front of her gown, completing the cycle up from her heart and back down again.

He fitted the ring to her finger, allowed her an admiring glance, and then sealed the promise of life together with a lingering kiss.

She tugged at his hand and situated onto her side of their favorite perch. "You suppose the Wildcat can come settle into the swing now?"

"Actually, not until I do this." He leaned over the porch railing and let out a rousing yell. A spattering of applause trickled up the driveway from the main house.

She giggled at the conspiracy, and then pushed back the porch swing to send her own message. "Love you guys."

"Goodnight, Mrs. Linquist-to-be," Valor shouted.

Jusdyn assumed his rightful half of the swing and beckoned her over for an imbalanced trespass into his territory. "Want to talk over some plans for the wedding?"

"Oh, let's not ruin the night with a bunch of needless chatter." She turned to face him not wanting to miss a second of his satisfied expression.

He brought his feet up off the uneven planking with a push, refueling the swing and propping her up against his knees, a mere breath from his lips. "How do you always manage to say the right thing?" He bent over her as if to search for the answer in her eyes.

Compliant, Arie met him halfway as his arm slid around her shoulders. Secure in his embrace, she inhaled against his cheek. *May love feel like this forever*. Their next kiss held the promise of a good deal more.

~

"Am I calling too late?" Jimmy John regretted having forgotten to check the time before dialing his deputy. "Okay then. Let's go ahead with the stakeout tomorrow. Watch the house for awhile, and then go to the door for the questioning. We're only trying to gather information at this point, and give them something to think about—like telling the truth." His children romped by in their cute matching pajamas, following his wife to their favorite reading spot. "You too, get some rest."

He hung up the receiver and forced himself out of the recliner, following the parade into the breakfast nook. He picked up his youngest like a precious puppy and spun him around for a gauntlet of kisses. "Say, can I get in on this episode?"

"Sure, Dad." His oldest girl turned and gave him a snaggletooth smile. "You can be the zookeeper."

"Oh, I love that part." He set the puppy free. "Now, tell me. Who has my keys?"

Their youngest son ran to retrieve the plastic ring of keys that hung beside his real ones.

His petite wife opened the cover of the book to begin the dearly loved procession of *Goodnight, Gorilla* while flashing a treasured look at him.

He touched his heart, right about badge level, and arrowed it back to her. He loved his life with every ounce of his being, mainly because it was made of little nights like this one.

~

Valor checked the fluid level in the pilfered bottle. "Almost done."

"Hurry up." Virgil adjusted the flashlight to illuminate the second pup.

After an empty suck, she detached the badger, placed it beside the sleeping sibling, and stroked its flattened head until it shared the same blissful destiny. "Who's going to teach these babies how to be badgers?"

"Nobody silly. They just know how. It comes from the inside. They have extinct."

"You mean instinct, sleepyhead." She removed her hand from the pup and rubbed her eyes, yawning.

"Yeah, well. We need to go to bed, too. Go on. I'll listen for your door to latch." He closed the laundry chute door.

"Isn't it funny how you can know something, even before it happens?"

Virgil stood. "You mean, like Jusdyn asking Arie to marry him?"

She shook her head and stuck out her tongue.

"With the Good Lord as my witness, will I ever understand you, girl?" The flashlight clicked off in protest, forcing a parting of ways.

"Goodnight, brother." She padded down the hallway barefoot.

"I'm *not* your brother."

"What then?"

"Let's try friend," he whispered into the darkness.

"Valor's new friend Virgil," she repeated louder than necessary to try it out.

"You two go to bed this instant," Muriel shouted up the stairwell.

Valor suppressed a giggle as her door crimped a lid on a pivotal day on the prairie.

~

The sleepy-eyed proprietor of the Redone Consignment Shop worked the coffee pot behind the checkout counter as Ruby flitted about the children's section, checking sizes and examining the condition of an entire brigade's wardrobe. Two mounds formed on the counter, a frilly pile of feminine clothing and a denim-dominated stack for the boys.

Ruby consulted the dress rack again, looking for matching outfits for the twins. She stood back and scanned the perimeter of the shop when the front window display caught her attention. At her insistence, the proprietor obligingly revisited the front ledge, stripped the mannequins of their butterfly ensembles, and topped the feminine stack with the final selection.

When the register rang a total, Ruby proffered a nest egg of cash across the counter. Sighing in relief as her plans began to take shape, she could at least dress the children in suitable attire tomorrow. The Good Lord would have to manage the other details.

~

Made milder by the passage of the storm, the summer night called out to Jusdyn in restless nocturnal activity. An exchange of cackling howls from a family of coyotes awakened him as he slept on the front porch. Arie had insisted that he use the cushion off the fainting couch to soften his outpost, for which he gave repeated thanks. In the faint light of the moon, he noticed a reclining figure stir nearby. Camped inside the screen door, Arie had knotted the ribbon from her gown around the far corner of his pillow, connecting them with a tie of abiding love. Lending additional comfort, he succumbed to the draw of sleep.

An alarm clock of guinea fowl went off without warning, bringing him into the land of the wakeful much too early. Looking eastward, he noted the first light of dawn and praised God for his sovereign rule over all the land. Glancing through the mesh of the screen door, he spotted an empty mattress. A reactive worry shot through his chest. Sounds from the kitchen soon quelled the sensation. He snatched to his feet to go find his hostess.

Arie stood unharmed by the sink. "Go ahead. You first in the bathroom." Her voice rose in harmony with the morning. "I've already put your bag in there."

He smiled, running his fingers through his bed-head hair. Whatever this promised land of togetherness held, it would be a far better place than where he'd come from. Plus, it held an angel in the kitchen.

~

Deke brought Merrilee and Beryl out to be granted discharge by the powers-that-be behind the main nurses' station, surrendering their room to those in dire need of it. Patient beds lined the halls, filled the break room, and leaked out every serviceable space as the injured sought help.

At their approach, Mabel glanced up and stopped in mid-sentence to attend them. She motioned for the baby causing Merrilee to pass her with a smile. No sign of the pushy nurse could be evidenced now, only a grandmotherly saint who wanted to marvel at God's creative genius. "She shined as our little darling during the storm, didn't she?"

Mabel checked the match between mother-daughter bracelets. Turning to the replacement nurse, she nodded toward the discharge log. "Linquist. Merrilee, with infant Beryl Leigh." The bun-topped nurse searched and found the proper ledger entry and made swift note of the discharge time.

Mabel handed the sleeping baby back to Deke, her gaze steady on him. "I couldn't have done it without you." Humility filled her tone as her chin trembled.

Sensing a ton of weariness on the aging woman, he reached across the counter and threw a compassionate strike across the medical fortress.

"By the way, your neighbor Doug is taking callers if you're up to it." She nodded, her eyes shifting back to the debriefing at hand.

Deke hoisted the baby like a prize while guiding Merrilee toward post-op. "I wouldn't let him miss this for the world." Leaving held a feel-good sensation. He chose to wear the changes ushered by the storm like a decorated veteran. The baby spit on his shoulder was the best medal of all.

~

Behind a flimsily drawn curtain, Doug received his beautiful visitor, now washed free of the mud plaster that once defined her exterior. Her auburn hair had been pulled up on one side and secured with an ornate hair comb, which struck Doug like exotic scenery as he transitioned into the wakeful world.

Darlene approached, wearing a form-fitted dress that boasted a bold geometric pattern. "A fine good morning."

"How's my corn crib mate?" He fished for a clue, wondering if she felt equally blessed having survived the day together.

"None the worse for wear." She placed a hand on his forearm. "Better in fact. All the richer for it."

He closed his eyes, relishing the comfort of her touch. "I've been on a battlefield." He shifted toward her, trying to make sense of his inward journey. "The enemy overwhelmed me and took me prisoner."

She leaned over him, seeming content to listen. "What did you do?"

"I had no strength to fight back—until you appeared—and then I somehow found my fortitude." His free hand drew her down, applying her like a healing compress to his fragmented self. Her geometric print merged with the faded stripes of his hospital gown in a truce, declaring a new alliance.

Deke appeared through the curtain, looking sheepish. "Wait. Is this a private recovery party, or can anyone crash it?"

"Absolutely anyone. The more, the merrier." Doug chuckled to prove it.

Darlene straightened and adjusted her outfit, blushing at her compromised position.

Merrilee wrapped her in a hug while Deke placed a baby bundle in the crook of his arm.

"Would you look at all this hair?" A stab of back pain penalized his exuberance, but he refused to be bound by it. "She can ride ponies at my house any day."

Darlene looked ill at ease. "If you have any ponies left, that is."

"If nothing's left, we'll restock." He refused to give up the pleasure of his horses.

Deke slapped his hands together. "Tell you what. Once we get settled back in Wilsey this morning, I'll go by your place and check on things. I promise to feed whatever I find."

"There's still corn in the crib—and that's all I can guarantee." Darlene shrugged her shoulders.

Doug reached for her hand at the mention of their refuge, completing the circle between his angel and the baby. He felt imbibed with the fullness of life and a future that had not been his before the storm. How ironic that such an erratic force of nature could usher in so much purpose.

"Thank you. Thank you all." His voice cracked with emotion. "I'm blessed through and through."

Merrilee stepped forward to place a kiss on his forehead. "You just get better and come back to God's country real soon."

When Deke took the baby, Doug noticed the he looked a little rough around the edges.

"I'm looking forward to getting back, too." Deke reached for the rancher's hand.

Doug upped his fence-fixing grip, letting the younger man know he'd be back in the saddle before the flood waters went down. When Darlene started to escort the threesome out, he caught her arm and held her back. Merrilee smiled and winked farewell, releasing the spellbinding grip of courtship to continue. Though torn up and stitched back together, he'd landed in a good place.

~

Jusdyn drove his mother's car toward the river with the men seated in front and the women in back. He chose a parking spot on Main Street and exited to the delightful aroma of beef brisket cooking at the Hayes House. As he held the car door for Arie, he looked down Main Street and noticed that the bonnet atop the Conestoga wagon at the foot of the bridge had been shredded by the storm. Reminded of the chronic threat of tornados for Kansans over the ages, the state's motto *To the stars through difficulties* didn't begin to cover half of it.

A shuttle van from the senior care facility pulled in beside the corner store and opened its doors to a younger-than-usual patronage. The Linquist party caught up to this familiar group and soon had to help herd the strays. Bobby Dean jumped off the bottom step and headed right for the river, but Virgil caught his belt loop and corralled him toward the outdoor theater. Next, a pair of butterfly girls flitted down the cottonwood trail behind Valor, their hair neatly braided. Morrill and Ruby stepped off last, looking sharper than usual in their wedding suits.

Loren reached for Morrill's hand. "What a great day to be alive and in love."

Jusdyn joined the men as they trailed the children while Arie gravitated toward the women. Morrill clapped his hands across the strong shoulders of the Linquist men and seemed to be savoring every moment leading up to their big day. They walked into a buzzing crowd that held everyone in town.

Restlessness filled the open-air amphitheater, typical of a loosely planned event. With the ecumenical memorial service scheduled to be underway in minutes, presenters huddled at the stage, working out kinks in the last-minute agenda. He'd heard rumor that a reading of a list of deceased and missing would be made, information to be released for the first time. He hoped such a weighty task would steer the content heavenward for proper perspective. He stepped up the riser of the grandstands as the McLauren/Linquist party began to fill their row. Unease alighted the moment he sat down.

"Ladies and Gentlemen, thank you for gathering here today in this opportunity to raise our faith above our circumstance." The preacher from the Christian Church shifted his stance to include an overflow area of people standing to the north. "Ours is the distinct privilege to be born, to live abundantly, and to die right here on the tallgrass prairie—with God Almighty overseeing it all. We celebrate every aspect of this existence, so we should not count it overly remorseful to lay the dead to rest in the shadow of this most recent storm—which we must do for the community today. But first, and my blessing to read, is the list of surviving families here ready to reclaim their precious children."

He glanced down the row and saw nothing but tense expressions, both young and old. Jenna's jaw dropped open and Bobby Dean pinched his eyes closed as if to brace for the truth. A prayer sprouted straight from his heart in the moment, though it sounded more like clearing his throat.

~

Alarmed by the pending dissolution of their tossed-together family, Morrill placed a calming arm around Ruby's back, pulling her toward him for strength. She managed a thin smile, and then began mouthing a silent prayer.

"If the children would come to the police department's table here under the cottonweed tree when their names are called," the preacher said, "then the authorities will validate the pairings and send them on their precious way."

Poised on yet another coerced transition, the children grew unsettled and one by one linked hands down the line to steady one another. Vernis linked hands with Bobby Dean who sat closer to tears than Ruby, and the boy in turn clutched his hand.

Morrill glanced up and down the link-up. "God's will be done," he offered aloud. Though he sensed a divine element in the pending sort-out, the wide-eyed children sat uncertain of their fate, voiceless on the verge of yet another separation.

~

Surveillance in the small town of Americus seemed conspicuously over-the-top to the deputy, having been recently imported from Ottawa to shore up a rural law enforcement effort. The El Camino had been parked in place up the driveway for the entire duration of his watch. So far, two dragonflies and a red-tailed hawk had moved across the target zone. Maybe the time had come for the front door Q and A exchange that he'd rehearsed.

He started the patrol car and eased it into gear, calling in his intent to the dispatcher as a matter of procedure. With no traffic for miles, he pulled into the driveway and inched toward the house. Stepping out of the vehicle, he adjusted his equipment belt and came up the front walk.

"Good morning, Mr. And Mrs. Bessler," he said under his breath. "Sorry to disrupt your peaceful day on the prairie." Glancing through the picture window, the deputy spied the petite body of Tilly Bessler clear the sofa shoulders first, landing awkwardly with her feet splayed across the coffee table. Instantly alert, he reached for the door knob and overheard Henry Bessler screaming slurred threats in an uncontrolled rage. In a matter of seconds, he had the door kicked in, the perpetrator knocked down, and the handcuffs snapped into place.

He forced the man to his wobbly feet. "A little early to be drinking isn't it, Mr. Bessler?"

"This time, he never put the bottle down," Tilly replied, dabbing the corner of her bloody mouth with her apron. She had a determined look in her eye, one that would serve them well.

"I can call in for back-up, ma'am. Should I have them send out an ambulance? Either way, I'll need you to come into town for questioning."

"No need for an ambulance, deputy. I'll be glad to talk to Sheriff Wilson about the whole ugly mess."

He nodded, mindful to show her some compassion as the victim. "Mr. Bessler, I have to read you your rights." He opened the door and stepped out into the tranquility of the prairie, prisoner well in hand. His morning had just accelerated from zero to sixty in nothing flat, which was exactly what he loved about his job.

~

"Jenna Baker," the preacher said, setting off every paternal alarm Morrill had been bequeathed.

Trembling, Jenna peered out over the group waiting under the cottonwood tree and looked up at him with searching eyes. Down below, a dark-haired woman paced around, spotted her up in the crowd, and beckoned for the girl to descend. Jenna's expression escalated to fear.

"Who is that, child?" he whispered down the row.

"My father's legal assistant," Jenna replied in a shaky tone. "She barely knows me. Why would I go anywhere with her?"

Ruby threw Morrill a heart-tugging look, as if requesting proper representation of their joint interest down in the vicinity of the cottonwood tree.

Morrill placed Bobby Dean's hand in Ruby's as he stood. "Let's go get to the bottom of this together." He hooked hands with the thin pianist and sidestepped down the row.

As Jenna passed Ruby, she threw her arm around the aged bride's neck and sobbed out loud. When Ruby whispered something reassuring to the child, she collected herself enough to follow him the remainder of the distance.

During the descent, Morrill experienced an inner flame of fire welding a bond with the precious child. Clearly a new arena for him as advocate for an orphan, he had no idea what words would have to accompany the validation of supervised legal exchange. Despite his inexperience, a confidence alighted on him, certain and calming like the cottonwood's shade.

As they approached, two officials manning the security table picked up on the child's apprehension right away. Morrill gave them an extra moment to make full note of it.

The petitioning woman approached the table, her arms cocked in arrogance. With a flick of her wrist, she proffered a photograph as evidence to corroborate their relationship.

"The company picnic this spring?" Jenna shot a puzzled look up at Morrill.

The closest law enforcement officer waved a sheet listing the claim criteria at her. "Don't you have something more official, ma'am? We like to see birth certificates, school photo IDs, custody forms, and the like."

When Jenna started to speak, Morrill raised a finger to his lips.

The second officer looked up from his note writing to regard the girl. "Young lady, can you tell us why you're so uncomfortable leaving in the custody of this individual?"

"I'm Jenna Baker. But she's not my family at all. In fact, I barely know her—other than she works for my dad. He's a lawyer." Jenna's response caused the second officer to lay his pen aside and fold his hands.

Morrill chose to enter the fray. "A legal assistant, I believe."

The woman rolled her eyes. "I can assure you that I am more than a work associate of her father's." The claimant snatched the photo off the table. One hand traced her budding abdomen to infer the nature of their true relationship, elevating her allegation to the level of far-fetched.

He had to intervene. "Jenna, did you come to the symphony with both of your parents?"

"Yes, Mr. Morrill, I did." The girl pressed into his side.

At this, the two officers exchanged weighty looks.

"Then I suppose they would be the ones to come claim you—if and when they are able." Morrill paused for effect, taking a breath. "Perhaps we can wait and check the victims' list and the missing persons' list—exhaust every possible option—before releasing this precious child to someone with whom she's so visibly uncomfortable." He stood towering above the rest, hoping his line of reasoning would convince the custody officers.

"Ha. So, you fancy yourself a more credible guardian than I would be for the girl?" the woman asked.

Jenna cringed and grabbed his hand.

"Absolutely, because I care about her well-being, and I dare say you do *not*. Jenna, please write down the names of your parents for the officers so they can check them against the other lists. I hereby request that she be allowed to stay with Ruby and I until the parents can be accounted for and the proper next of kin duly notified."

"Yes, sir, Mr. McLauren. I'm in agreement with you." The second officer then turned to the woman. "Ma'am, I'm only willing to make a side note on your claim today, and nothing more. May I see your driver's license, please?" He pushed a blank paper in front of them.

Jenna neatly printed two names on the notepad, never inching away from his side.

In moments, he turned toward the bleachers with the child in tow and saw Ruby rise from her seat, straining to see. On impulse, he raised the girl to his shoulders and held out her arms, swirling out of the shade into the victorious light of day. The remainder of the row stood with Ruby, cheering the ten-year-old back to the safety of the group.

"Way to go, Mr. Morrill!" Bobby Dean shouted before Vernis clamped a hand over the boy's mouth.

Ruby squeezed the little fellow's hand. "Yes, way to go Morrill," she called.

Playing father to the fatherless with selfless abandon, he never parted his gaze from his intended bride until they were standing side by side. He presented Jenna to her like a small gift.

After two more minutes of agonizing anticipation, the preacher announced the final name on his list. Morrill surveyed what remained of their group—Jenna Baker, Bobby Dean Hale, the twins Hope and Faith Laramie, and little Tucker Marshall. Like a mother hen locating her chicks, Ruby counted and held up five fingers to confirm his total. He smiled and reached past Jenna to weave his fingers into hers, acknowledging their mutual commitment. When five little hands joined their grip, he crowned them with his free hand.

Next, he needed to validate their legitimacy by marrying their adoptive mother down by the river. Blessings cascaded under the morning sun as if providence had opened its storehouse and sent them spilling forth like a waterfall. His heart swam unrestricted in the current.

Chapter 23

Once pioneer plants have adequately colonized a recovering area, the phased reestablishment of botanical assemblages traverses nature's timeline. On the eastern coastal plain, succession begins as pine seedlings overtake mixed grasses, eventually competing with, but unable to outwit, the full-force invasion of deciduous hardwoods. Left to its own progression, the succession of any biotic community culminates in its climax form, held to be the most stable cover type for the land. Because of the abiotic variables of episodic wind, rain, and fire, the prairie is held in place botanically, arresting nature's timeline mid-sequence. Thus the prairie's mix of grasses and flowering forbs comprises a tribute to halted succession, with the constant threat of invasion by shrubs and trees ever present. Over generations, the edaphic grassland maintains a constancy of low-key cover, in its humility having foregone the quest for climax community eons ago.

Jusdyn stood behind Arie at the base of the dike, nuzzling into the honeysuckle of her hair while they waited for the central characters to take their positions. He smiled as the children fought for a place closest to the bride and groom.

Vernis stood beside Morrill, patting his breast pocket to confirm the ring.

Muriel held a domed bouquet of ribbon-wrapped lipstick roses and waved down to them. Arie waved back as Valor picked her own bouquet of wildflowers along the riverbank.

Nearby, Virgil threw stones into the water below.

"Six more nights of sleeping on that hard porch," he whispered through her hair. His hand slipped around her waist.

Arie responded by overlaying her hand on his. "Most women have six months to plan their weddings, not six days."

"Well, we're plain folks from the prairie so we don't need that long."

"You're right, we don't." She smiled over her shoulder.

He kissed her cheek and listened to the cottonwood tree play the wind through its heart-shaped leaves like nature's musical prelude to the wedding on the elevated dike. "What would you say if I told you I'm considering asking for TJ's job with the Conservation Service tomorrow morning? Does that sound crazy or what?"

She turned to face him. "Sounds like you'd be taking the next logical step—on the prairie and for the prairie—just like we pledged."

"So you'll be there to help me identify the plants when I need you?"

"I'll be there." Her assurance came without hesitation.

Somehow, even standing still he sensed the gaining of traction in his plans for their future together. "Okay then. I'll need to teach you how to drive the truck."

"Oh, I'm sure that task will be much easier than the horse."

"Well, the horse doesn't have a clutch." He turned her frame back toward the wedding platform to quell any possible objection.

~

Ruby refused to take the document in hand. "Wait a minute. What's this I'm signing?"

Morrill smoothed the official-looking paper that had been folded into the sanctum of his breast pocket. "Our marriage license, that's all." A smile broke onto his face. He offered her a pen while the clerk from the telephone co-op looked on with notary seal in hand. Ever helpful, the preacher extended his Bible as a writing surface, which made the pact all the more legal and binding.

Ruby capitulated after some hesitation and signed her maiden name. When Morrill signed his name, Vernis and Muriel joined as their witnesses. The notary crimped the page and stuck it in the Bible, blew a kiss to the bride and groom, and then exited the dike. The haste of matters left Ruby dizzy.

Morrill held her gaze and planted a hand on the small of her back. "Now who's not ready? Sixty years isn't long enough?"

She feigned formality and adjusted her jacket. "Plenty long, thank you."

Vernis leaned toward her. "I'm taking babysitting duty tonight for your kids."

"And these flowers aren't going to stay fresh forever." Muriel shoved the lovely arrangement toward her.

Ruby glanced at the children and they were all nodding. "Okay, I suppose I'm ready." She looked straight into Morrill's eyes. Everything she'd ever wanted was about to transpire.

He took her hand, keeping her at arm's length like something fragile. "We both are ready. Preacher, start the show."

The ceremony unfolded in alternating pulses of heartfelt recitation and nervous jitters. The state of matrimony had finally arrived at Ruby's doorstep, a wondrous destination though latent in timing. When the preacher paused to prompt her with a thump on his Bible, she remembered to interject her wifely pledge. "I do, so help me God."

~

TJ named the still life image portrayed in the mirror *Face on Fire*. He tipped the anti-inflammatory tablets out and swallowed three, ever hopeful to keep the fire contained. The last of the product sat curing, the motorcycle stood ready, and now he only needed the cover of night. The feather-thin red line of inflammation had lengthened and turned down the side of his mouth. With its source now swollen, the thread pulled taut against his puffy skin, tender to the touch. He cursed the bad luck and yanked the pull-chain on the latrine's solitary light bulb.

Walking into the cabin's disarrayed front room, a wayward thought drifted to his family. A glance at his watch told him they would all be together in less than half an hour, discussing McLauren family business and making plans for the future. For a fleeting second, he visualized racing into town on the motorcycle and walking in as the storm-saved prodigal son. But the meth became a tainted crystalline wedge between the decent and the despicable. He had already chosen the darker side, vanquishing any hope of such a respectable return. No, the black sheep had shed its wolf's clothing in its final metamorphosis. He had become what he was meant to be.

~

Jusdyn sat on the front row of seats in the Cordiality Room beside his McLauren connection—his mother. He couldn't deny the feeling of being blessed to be a Linquist, generational ranchers on the tallgrass prairie, and to live it out alongside the McLaurens, a family that enjoyed a parallel existence. All of his life experience distilled down to his next endeavor, and he felt more than ready for the challenge. Having Arie's support elevated him beyond his ability to express—a divine gift.

"Never would I have imagined a week ago that I would be standing before you a happily married man." Morrill opened the meeting with a nod to his bride. "And I surely would not have been able to predict the storm our community has just survived. But welcome McLauren clan, one and all, to what Vernis and I hope will become our annual family meeting. This kickoff session will certainly be one we long remember, given this weekend's circumstances. Before we get started on our agenda today, we're missing a couple of key family members due to the tornado. I want us to stop and lean on our faith a minute as we pray for Doug's full recovery and for TJ to be found. I've asked our newest family member to come up and pray over these missing individuals."

Ruby stood before the group and held Morrill's hand, then led the family in a heartfelt prayer.

Jusdyn reached and found Arie's hand, uniting them before the Lord. Several cousins echoed 'amen' when Ruby finished. A commotion arose from the doorway.

"Don't count me out yet." A force to be reckoned with, Doug rolled into the room in a wheelchair pushed by Darlene. Without hesitating, Vernis approached and embraced his son in a rare display of affection. Lettie led the three-daughter parade that arrived next, and the ensuing tearful reunion stalled the meeting.

Muriel wept without restraint, so Loren captured her in his arms, once again providing the stability for which the Linquists were known.

Arie took her turn, hugging Darlene and kissing her uncle's cheek, whispering her recovery sentiment into his ear. When Darlene pushed Doug to the end of the front row, Jusdyn slipped his chair alongside the wheelchair for her use.

Morrill quieted the guests and beckoned his brother to join him up front. The two aged patriarchs gazed upon the adult members of three generations of the McLauren family.

Jusdyn sensed something memorable about to happen and collected a new chair.

"We McLaurens have always been people of the prairie." As Morrill spoke, Vernis gave a nod to show that the point sat well with him. "We never minded a hard day's work because the land somehow always gave us back more than we gave it. After a lifetime of modest living, we McLaurens can stand proud of our accomplishments.

"Today, we have more land than any generation before," Morrill continued. "But, we haven't always had a clear vision where to go with all our efforts. And we haven't safeguarded our investment from others down the road that might be of a different mindset. For these reasons, Vernis and I are pleased to announce the placement of all family lands into the McLauren Family Limited

Partnership."

The tactic resonating, Jusdyn leaned forward and gave his father a knowing look as a murmur swept the room. Loren returned his glance and flashed a thumbs-up to Morrill. When Arie whispered a question, he clarified it in a few words as best he could.

"In doing so as one of the two general partners, I've had to revoke the Power-of-Attorney from my son," Vernis said. "In no way does this fall as a commentary on how good a job Douglas was doing, and I'd like to make that clear to the entire family."

From the front row, Doug nodded in receipt of the recognition.

"Our plan right now is to oversee the implementation of the FLP and watch it for a five-year period, and then turn its administration over to the next generation of McLaurens," Morrill added. "Doug, you and Muriel would transition from limited partners to the general partners at that time. This should have been a three-member team, but we lost Dale in Iran so his branch will set out a sequence in the FLP, with TJ set to pick up leadership with Jusdyn and Doug's three daughters in approximately twenty years. That may seem like a lot of long-term planning, but that's the strength of the FLP—making the ranch work today and preserving it into the future."

"Now, we know this is going to generate a lot of questions, so we've prepared handouts for everyone," Vernis replied. "Let's go through the structure and expectations together."

On cue, Ruby stood and passed out the packets of information, waving sweetly at Valor who had come to the door. The girl hovered until Muriel motioned her away.

Jusdyn held nothing but admiration for the McLaurens as the founding brothers began laying out the specifics of the FLP. Never again would the family lands be threatened by misuse or sale outside of the family's majority vote and wishes. Morrill appeared committed to its inaugural launch, keeping a spirited watch over the family's best interests while bringing insightful understanding of the working plan to the group.

"Before we take questions, I'm going to present one more aspect of the FLP that Vernis and I have decided to include." Morrill took several long strides back up front. "Since so many family members are scattered around the county now, we need to have a way to equitably reward efforts invested in the ranch. Some will put in more work than others, so it stands to reason that those individuals should get more of a percentage back from the FLP in the form of annual pay-outs." That announcement created another wave of murmurs.

"To accomplish this, we are going to implement a work bank for the upkeep of the McLauren lands," Vernis said. "Any time you come out and work on fencing, weed removal, crop planting or harvest, and livestock tending, that time will go into your account. Since Douglas manages the ranch, we're going to ask him to keep track of the work bank ledger. Think you can make that a priority, son?"

"If it means I'm going to have a lot more company out there, you bet I can." Doug's zeal generated congenial laughter among the extended family.

"Just trying to set a minimum quota to start out, I'm going to ask for fifteen hours a quarter. That's the equivalent of two Saturdays of ranch work every three months." Morrill held up two fingers. "Let's test this through the remainder of the year. We can revise as necessary."

"It's time for questions." Vernis looked around for raised hands from the group.

Loren hesitated, and then indicated a pending concern by standing. "What about the Helmick land? Does it fall under the protection of the FLP now—or are you too late to get it included?" Loren sat slowly as Morrill nodded at Vernis to respond.

"Because it represents part of the heritage lands Morrill and I acquired from the generation before us, we were able to nullify the recent transfer of ownership and add Helmick back into the family holdings going into the FLP. Parts of that reversion are still in process and will be complicated if TJ is—let's say unavailable—to co-sign the paperwork."

Doug rolled forward seeking recognition. "Dad? Could I say a few words about the Helmick land?"

Vernis nodded and motioned him to the front of the room. Darlene maneuvered the wheelchair to place Doug in front of the group and returned to her seat.

A lump formed in Jusdyn's throat, knowing that honest regret had taken the podium.

"I'd like you all to know what motivated my selling that land to TJ in the first place." Doug looked down into his lap, but soon regained his fortitude and regarded them as a group. "Ever since we lost Dale in the war, I've made a point of trying to be there for TJ, even though he seemed hell-bent to distance himself." Several cousins looked uncomfortable because the difficult situation had been a touch-point for a long time.

"In this day and age, it can be challenging for a young family to get ahead. TJ led his family as best he could, had a good-paying job, and thought he could afford to live in Americus away from the family. That location didn't please many of us when he made that decision, but I stood by TJ and even loaned him some money for the down payment. After Jesse got in her troubles and went to jail, again I felt like I needed to stand by TJ. When he came up with the Helmick land idea for the county landfill, I agreed to sell him the land." A murmur ensued from the more uninformed family members.

Jusdyn gave Arie a knowing look.

"I need to apologize to Dad for that," Doug admitted, "as I'm sure it wounded him to the core. Dad, I was wrong and I know it. Could you ever forgive me for not discussing it with you first?" Laboring for his next breath, he began to slump in his wheelchair. With bandages evident beneath his shirt collar, his emotional wounds now seemed equally exposed.

Vernis stood up, walked over, and placed his arms around the broken man. "This is my dear son, who never did a spiteful thing in his life. I couldn't be prouder of him." His voice broke as the forces of restoration took control. They gripped each other in sobs, a wordless acknowledgment of forgiveness.

The lump in Jusdyn's throat swelled with the sudden show of emotion. The meeting ascended above his expectations.

Loren stood again, looking more tentative this time. "While we're speaking about family difficulties with TJ, may I make a comment to the family?"

Morrill motioned him toward the front while Vernis labored to shove Doug's wheelchair back into the seating area.

Jusdyn found his feet before Darlene could respond and helped the aging man with his precious cargo. When Loren flashed a signal to accompany him up front, he forced his feet to obey. He hadn't planned on taking an active part in the meeting.

"If I could find a way to speak out in love, I would have to be truthful about the pain of paternal forfeiture and how it has affected TJ. Dale was gone before he even left for the war, and most of us here over the age of thirty-five are keenly aware of that." Loren paused and looked at Muriel, who bit her upper lip but nodded for him to continue.

Vernis hung his head as if pierced by an inability to reach his own son, a failure that still seemed to sting long after the rebellious heir's death.

"Now, I can't blame Doug one ounce for going out on a limb for TJ. We all bent over backwards to give him a fighting chance at success in life. The truth is TJ didn't want to live on the land and work hard for success. He wanted to take shortcuts. In doing so, he made decisions against his family, against the land, and against God. That's what made his world cave in. He brought his own doom in a chain of bad decisions. No degree of bailout could possibly rectify his life of compromise, Doug, not even the Helmick land where he hoped to make a quick fortune."

Loren waited out the murmur for a few seconds and then raised his hand to settle it. "What many of you do not know right now is this—if we haven't already lost TJ to the storm, he's in trouble with the law. For that reason, Muriel and I can no longer sit back and watch TJ keep shortchanging his daughter from the wholesome upbringing she deserves, which is why we have initiated legal action to take custody of Valor. Muriel and the child share a tender bond—no doubt their McLauren bloodline—that will serve this arrangement well. As for my part, I'm just hoping to be able to keep up with the two of them." Loren smiled and nudged Jusdyn.

Free to speak of the future, Jusdyn glanced at the familiar faces in the audience. "And I want everyone to know that tomorrow morning I plan to show up at the Conservation Service to ask for TJ's job." When he glanced at Arie for validation, she beamed it back to him in a smile. "I suppose I could merely fill it for TJ until he can return, but in truth, TJ's hated this job for some time. Even so, the higher truth is, I feel called to the work for the sake of the prairie. If Mom and Dad could use my salary to help raise Valor, they're welcome to any part of the money. This storm, as destructive as it's been, has caused me to re-evaluate the things that are most important to me. The old Jusdyn could have sat in a storm cellar in Wilsey and been plenty satisfied."

"Amen, son." Loren quipped, his tone light.

Apparently touched by the honesty in his speech, Arie had begun to cry.

Instead of inhibiting him, he felt emboldened, and opened his heart further. "For me, hiding like that would have been taking a shortcut like Dad referred to earlier. I feel called by God to bring the vanishing tallgrass prairie back, it's as simple as that. I'll plan to use some of the tried and true land management practices that Dad taught me on our ranch, plus go above-and-beyond to return what's been taken from the landscape and restore it back. As family, I'd sure appreciate your prayers because—like the virgin prairie—some of this restoration work will be unbroken ground."

Morrill stood to his full height, a venerable rancher. "Son, if anybody on God's noble earth can bring it back, you can. And why not have it start right here in rural Morris County? You're the fifth generation of Linquists and McLaurens to live on the land. Now, the prairie becomes both your heritage and your destiny. Ruby and I would be honored to pray for you."

Doug wheeled toward him. "Darlene and I will too, Jusdyn."

Lettie stood from the middle row. "I'll add you to the kids' prayers every night."

"Please, don't just pray for me. I've asked Arie to marry me, and for some crazy reason, she said yes. She's part of how God is equipping me for such a big challenge and, believe me, I couldn't face this work without her."

"It might help that she's a good cook, too." Doug's tease came chased by laughter and well-wishing that soon filled the room, with handshaking and hugs ensuing for the next several minutes.

Morrill glanced at his agenda and then flashed a thumbs-up to Vernis who seemed more than ready to pack up and leave. "Were there any more questions?" he asked over the hubbub. "Any more questions at all?" Silence filled the room for a few gracious seconds. There appeared to be no further inquiries.

"What about the lamb of stone in the cemetery, Uncle Morrill?" A small voice echoed from the doorway. There Valor stood in all her innocence, hoping for some closure to a painfully open McLauren family story. "Great-grandpa Vernis said you knew who the A stood for, so could you tell us—please?"

The skin prickled up the back of Jusdyn's neck in auspicious anticipation. When he glanced at his great-uncle, Vernis had turned a sickly pale green. The question seemed to suck the very air from the room. No one dared speak a word.

~

Sheriff Wilson faced the fragile woman seated in front of his desk, attempting to make his questions sound routine. "What did you do when your husband brought TJ into your home?"

Tilly Bessler gave the wadded tissue in her palm a squeeze. "I went into the sewing room, where the men waited for me."

"What were they doing back there?"

"TJ showed up hurt. He gashed open his top lip in the storm. They wanted me to fix it."

The sheriff gave a swift look at his deputy who nodded back. "So what did you do?"

"Well, nothing at first. I couldn't figure out how to get started, it was such a jangled mess. Then TJ offered to shave off his moustache."

"And did he?" Jimmy John swallowed to offset his growing anticipation.

The petite woman reached into her handbag and pulled out a swatch of cellophane tape looped around a clump of reddish blond whiskers.

Recognizing the hair color of his high school sparring partner, he opened a plastic evidence bag and nodded for her to drop in the sample. "Were you able to successfully dress the wound after that?"

"Yes, I used an upholstery needle and stitched it up fairly well." A meditative moment passed that raised a furrow on her bruised brow.

"Was there something more, Mrs. Bessler?"

"I just remembered having matches in my hand, but I don't recall using them."

"Matches for what purpose, Mrs. Bessler?" He truly hated to press, but had to insist.

The woman looked back at him with a vacant stare that dropped to her lap with a fearful recognition. "Oh, my gosh. I forgot to sterilize the needle." She covered her mouth with the postponed dread of a coerced, incompetent accomplice.

~

The fever came like a stowaway on the midafternoon nap that TJ had chartered to compensate for the late delivery planned for Fort Riley. Cloaked as a fiery dream sequence, the fever made the silo flash into flames. He tried to outrun the fire, but his feet bogged down in an invisible quagmire, making forward progress impossible. All at once, a wispy cottonwood leaf landed in his hand and emblazoned its heart shape onto his palm. The fire extinguished as he stirred, awakening from the nap. Barely able to raise his feverish head, the fine line between real and imagined blurred. For all intents and purposes, the silo had indeed caught fire.

~

When Morrill motioned for Valor to come in, Virgil bobbed into the room as if connected. They took the seats Jusdyn and Arie had vacated. As the eldest, he walked with deliberate steps to the front to unfurl the ancient tale.

Vernis sought refuge on the far side of Doug's wheelchair, as if still hiding from the age-old memories.

His gaze panned across the faces in the room, validating their right to hear the full truth of the unspoken story as he knew it. *This is what makes the resurgence worth the effort, these precious people and the land.* The story somehow loosened in his mind and he corralled it scene by scene, though it felt like someone else's life.

"Mother's younger sister Fannie moved to Denver and started her family about a decade later than Mother had started ours. The Currys managed a new birth in the family just about every other summer. Each time, Mother would go out and tend the family for about two weeks, despite Father's mild objection. When Dorothy turned eleven, she was allowed to accompany Mother as well, helping with her younger cousins. The two traveled by rail, and it became a girls' getaway of sorts.

"Father was a devoted Free Mason, and that Denver trip invariably conflicted with his quarterly lodge meeting. Instead of allowing her trip to inconvenience him, Father began a practice of loading the remaining crew in a wagon and taking us into Council Grove with him. Because of the late hour of the meeting, we had to stay in town overnight. Needless to say, it posed quite the adventure for the Wilsey boys' club to go to town.

"Evidently, on the last trip before Vernis was born, my older brothers Lloyd, Willard, and Burton proved to be too much for Father to handle. He missed half the meeting trying to rectify their misbehavior. Not quite two years old and mild of temperament, I posed nary a trouble like the rest, except for my complete inability to feed myself or find a necessary facility when that time came. Father recognized his need for assistance and vowed to bring a sitter with us from then on, both to free himself for the meeting and maintain control of us all the while."

Vernis stood, warming to the rhythm of the tale. "Don't miss the cute baby in the next part of the story."

"Was that you, Great-grandpa?" Valor pointed to Vernis, needing clarification.

Virgil's gaze shifted between the two of them as if processing the possibilities.

His younger brother nodded and winked at the girl.

"Yes, Vernis came about a year later, so when Father made plans for the trip into town that spring, he asked the farm foreman if he could borrow their oldest daughter as a sitter. Thrilled to be going to town, the girl begged him for permission, so the foreman yielded."

"Who were the people living in the tenant house, Uncle Morrill?" Muriel joined Valor with her inquisitive nature.

"Our closest and dearest friends, the Good family."

Valor stood as if shocked at the connection. "That's why you wrote *good* across the top of my artwork, isn't it?"

"You're exactly right, honey. Sorry my tongue was too tied up to tell you, which is why I tried to write it down. Reed and Anna Good lived there with their children—almost too much family for that little tenant house. We children played happily together."

~

Eyes closed, Arie leaned against the wall as she listened to the story unfold. An image flashed into her mind of the pine trees shading the loafing shed, the view falling away into the valley toward Diamond Springs. Her little cottage tucked into the vista, with children playing about the yard in full contentment. A smile spread across her lips as its tranquility drew her in.

"Proud that he had planned for everything, Father set into town with his wagonload. We'd no more made it to Helmick when the rain started." Morrill's even tone turned to gravel.

"Oh, no! Please—not the big flood, Uncle Morrill," Valor protested in earnest.

Muriel reached for her rigid frame and drew the child to her side.

"Yes, we were to get a month's worth of rainfall in one night. Father's stubborn streak wouldn't allow him to turn back, so we arrived at the Hays House wet and shivering under the oiled tarp. Some nice folks sat us by the hearth and fed us soup while our clothes dried. Then it came time for the Masons to meet upstairs."

Arie opened her eyes and glanced around the room at the spellbound audience. A difficult history cascaded down the core of the Cordiality Room and soon they would all be awash in the tragic ending. She caught Muriel's gaze and noted that the fourth generation McLauren appeared on the verge of her own recollection, her eyes hollow and sullen.

"Back then, the Hays House operator kept a bunkroom across the hall from the dining room for drovers and cowboys just passing through. Father managed to secure that room for our use and ushered in his brood, then hastened upstairs to the meeting. As for our part, we were dry, fed and happy, so we commenced turning the room into a circus of games and activities. Burton claimed the faded rug and played us all in marbles, but no one could beat him. Lloyd and Willard became gymnasts, performing handstands on everyone's bunk and climbing the potbellied stove like a diving platform, then somersaulting down. Our babysitter permitted the ruckus, all the while holding baby Vernis on her shoulder. If the constant rain worried her, she never let on."

Valor sat up on her knees, trying to get comfortable. "Were the boys happy?"

"Yes, honey—so very happy. That's one of my fondest memories, the antics of that early evening. We enjoyed a special time together unmarred by hardship or chores, just lighthearted play." He smiled with honest emotion at the tender recollection.

"Would the floodwaters come soon?"

"Much too soon, honey." Morrill begin to struggle under the emotional weight of the tale.

Arie tried to make eye contact with Jusdyn, but he sat transfixed on Morrill like the rest.

Ruby stepped up in support, the pair resembling figurines atop a wedding cake. "Those of us living higher on the hill in Council Grove never knew what was happening down by the river that night." She wiped at the lipstick smear below her lower lip. "Papa used to say that it was the worst natural catastrophe ever to hit Council Grove—although I do believe the tornado yesterday may now have that ominous claim to fame."

Muriel stood as if to press for a positive resolution. "Uncle Morrill, don't you think it would bring a healing if you could just lay out the rest of the tragedy and thereby conquer it?" While others nodded in consensus, several had begun to cry.

Vernis gestured at his older brother, rebounding from the comment. "You don't have to."

Arie began to feel a pit widening in her stomach from the tension in the room. She closed her eyes to see the cottage again, but the children had vanished and a solitary figure stood looking out into the pouring rain of a grim night. When her attention returned to the room, Muriel held her in a questioning stare.

"Yes, it's high time I conquer this." Morrill's admission came in a strained tone.

Ruby wrapped her arm in his as if to sturdy him for the tale's bitter end.

"Father returned when the meeting adjourned and took us boys to the back porch for our last relief while the sitter put the baby in sleep clothes. She padded a drawer from the oak dresser and placed

Vernis by her bunk. We came back and stood inside the door as Father gave us his last admonishments for good behavior. Without further explanation, he closed the door and locked it from the outside, unwittingly trapping us in the bunkroom to await our fate. I still remember hearing his footsteps on the stairs as we pressed against the door, wondering what we had done that could be so bad as to make him leave us like that."

Pierced with a prick of authentic anxiety at the pivotal point of the story, Arie pressed against the wall in helpless apprehension.

Doug slumped in the wheelchair, experiencing deeper agony than most, having inherited its weighty pallor from his father, the baby. Though Darlene made an attempt to straighten his shoulders to keep him from pulling against the stitches on his back, she may as well have held back the tide from the Bay of Fundy.

The air quivered with electric current. Then from somewhere in darkness of the aqueous remembrance, a woman began to laugh. Arie responded with unmitigated offense. So vivid, her next breath hitched in her chest. Catching Muriel's gaze, her unease must have been evident, as her hostess became much more attentive.

"We were in bed asleep when the waters came, the Neosho River exceeding its bank and roiling against the batten board and brick of downtown Council Grove. Standing less than half a block from the Main Street Bridge, the Hays House laid directly in its flood path." Morrill paused and inhaled.

Arie began to quell another type of uprising, mostly birthed from the tension on her diaphragm. Though she sat captivated by the story, the content became too potent to handle.

"The sitter heard the rushing waters and called out to us in the dark. Lloyd shook Willard and we all met by the stove where she stood. There, a coal bin opened overhead that could be filled at street level from the alley behind. Frantic, she worked the door loose. Then Lloyd handed her the baby. As she tucked Vernis up into the coal crib, the flood struck in a crash."

Morrill paused as if regaining his composure while Vernis

could be heard weeping in breathless agony on Doug's shoulder.

In the lull, the floodwaters rose up against Arie's midsection, swirling down an unknown corridor in her mind. Panicked, she had to retreat. Stepping around Jusdyn and heading out the door, she ran for the nearby restroom, struggling to survive the overwhelming sensation that she was perishing. *What's happening to me?*

~

"Willard, of course, couldn't hear the water's threat and kept a firm grip on me," Morrill continued, rallying his strength. "As she lifted me up, the waters roared about us, and I noticed something being placed in my hand. Though the coal bin frame proved too tight for me, she shoved me up there anyway, determined I should survive. That's when my collarbone broke. In less than a minute, the rest were gone—washed down the river along with the eastern half of the Hays House.

"In the morning, Father came down to find only the locked door intact on that lower level. He must have been horror-struck at what the river had taken. About then, Vernis began to cry so I rocked him in my good arm, striking the coal pile by accident. Hearing the ruckus, the adults crawled in through the street opening and found the two of us covered in soot but very much alive."

Ruby delivered a hug as if acknowledging the privilege of life continued.

Valor slipped from her seat and approached her great uncle. When she reached up to feel his broken spot, he stooped to allow her to find his collarbone inside his dress shirt placket.

Unhurried, the girl traced the overlapped rift-and-mend line with her delicate fingers as Virgil smiled from the second row.

Morrill felt the electric warmth she rendered, though the spot had no sensitivity.

Valor began to pat his chest with her palm. "What did they put in your hand that night, Uncle Morrill? I'm curious to know."

He hesitated, and then made his way to the suitcases waiting in the corner. Upon unzipping the outer flap, he pulled out a worn cigar box filled with aged treasures. With a gentle touch, he lifted the lid and retrieved a small leather pouch cinched by a cotton string on top.

Without a word, Valor cupped her hands and the family treasure changed hands between generations. Kneeling, she loosened the drawstring and poured its contents onto the floor. Two handfuls of color-swirled orbs escaped and fanned out on the carpet. "Burton's marbles!"

Virgil soon stood by her side, smiling at the enduring emblem.

She jumped for joy as family members surrounded her ready to celebrate the ray of remembrance that shone beyond the dark night of family tragedy.

When Ruby slid a hand up to caress his shoulder, Morrill realized the lump left by the old rough-hewn collarbone repair had simply vanished.

~

Muriel shoved open the restroom door to detect the sound of a retching stomach coming from the first stall. Once inside, she held Arie with all the maternal instinct she could muster, and then assisted her out to a padded bench by the sinks. Clearly dealing with something deeper than a weak constitution, she assumed the flood story might hold a clue. She handed the shaken woman several paper towels and gave her half a minute to settle down.

Arie made a kitten-like noise and then blew her nose.

To close the gap, she perched beside her. "What could you possibly know about the flood situation that is causing you so much grief?"

Arie tried to stone-face her, but couldn't fully collect her emotions.

"What would Opal think of our non-communication? I'm supposed to be some kind of guardian, though it's unclear what that entails. But I do know we need to be honest with each other. God expects that much."

Arie capitulated, leaning into her offer of sanctuary like a bruised reed against the mud bank.

The warming spark of acceptance filled her core. After a while, the agony abated into manageable dread. She thought they could press ahead. "Now, can you please tell me what has your spirit so broken?"

"That night of the flood, two sets of footsteps sounded on those stairs, and a woman's flirting laughter sifted through the keyhole. The McLauren boys were young and naïve, but it wasn't hard to discern the truth. Their father was done with family obligations because he had something else in mind."

Muriel rocked back on the bench sucker-punched, undone by the hidden moral failure that had led to the family's untimely destruction. The needlessness of such devastating loss flowed through her veins like an internal river.

Arie's frame shivered as she dried her eyes with finality.

"I'll need to tell this part to Uncle Morrill and Uncle Vernis. In doing so, we'll set them free of the guilt that it was somehow the children's fault they'd gotten locked in that night."

Arie shook her head, refusing to look up. "That's going to be a difficult admission."

Muriel took her hand, stood on shaky legs, and headed for the door. "Though the path may seem bleak at first glance, love always finds the right way." The hallway back to the Cordiality Room seemed awash with fresh opportunities for restoration. How to pose the hidden truth became her next monumental challenge.

~

The good-natured sheriff teased the compliant patient lying motionless on the cot. "No more rodeo riding for you, I reckon."

The fractured cowboy grimaced with the pronouncement. "You can save that for the younger boys."

A bun-haired nurse affixed a teetering rack to his drip line and unlocked the cot wheels for transport. "We're moving him into a semi-private room, sheriff. Can you give me a hand?"

"You bet." Jimmy John secured a hold on the mattress,

clamping it to the metal frame. "This here part will be a cakewalk, compared to where you've been, Keeter."

"Don't you know it." The patient exhaled in a whistle.

All at once, the nurse pulled the cot forward and the noble hands that once corralled a culvert-full of children now clung to the padded edge of tolerable existence. Jimmy John shook his head over the transformation. At least his buddy was alive, showered down into Richey Cove like a tornadic discard. *How lucky can a guy get?*

~

"Could we excuse the children for a moment?" Muriel asked from the doorway. With a meek glance, Valor scooped up the last of the marbles. Virgil offered her a hand up off the floor. Muriel smiled as they reached the door. "Why don't you two stop by the dining room on your way? I'm pretty sure I smell popcorn."

Jusdyn touched Valor's shoulder as she exited and flashed Virgil a thumbs-up.

Arie slid back into the room and soon sought refuge in his arms.

Muriel made her way to the front and gestured for Vernis to join her. Loren came up from behind her and took his post by her side. Morrill clung to Ruby, seemingly exhausted from his storytelling.

"As a family, we must allow ourselves to live in the healing freedom which exists beyond this tragedy." Muriel paused to make sure she held everyone's attention. "Because we must trust each day to the sovereignty of God, we can never know what's around the next bend of life's river. Our challenge is to take what we've been blessed with and follow God downstream to the best of our abilities. As we navigate these channels, what we really don't need are guilt and regret weighing us down. In that light, I need to share with you a remembrance beyond what Uncle Morrill has been able to recall about the flood story."

Morrill straightened to full attention as if piqued by her inference.

Ruby stood arm-in-arm with the brothers, bracing for the

disclosure.

Arie glanced up at Jusdyn, so he planted a conciliatory kiss in her hair.

"That night, after you children got locked in the bunkroom, there were two sets of footsteps headed up the stairs. Your father had not been retreating from the shame of your misbehavior as wayward children. He selfishly pursued his own gratification up those stairs." She focused on the elder survivor as he appeared to retreat. "Can you hear a woman laughing through the keyhole, Uncle Morrill?"

"She laughed once—and my poor mother never laughed again." Morrill came to the final admission at long last. "I thought that losing three boys had saddened my mother's heart beyond repair, but it was really the death of her marriage. All those years of living in a house with no love resurrected for the two of us, what a shame." He stared at Vernis. "With you, only a baby yet starved of everything you really needed. And me with my cowardly self, choosing to lock my mind away to somehow cope."

Doug rolled the wheelchair up to his father's trembling legs. "But love has free reign on the McLauren river now. We choose to let go of all those past hurts from here on out." He wrapped the frail patriarch in his arms and soon became surrounded by Lettie, Laynie, and Lorene.

Caught in the loving press of Jusdyn's sudden embrace, Muriel linked with Arie and then entwined Loren. Next, the Linquist huddle moved past Doug's clan and found Morrill and his bride, engulfing them in a raft of earth's highest emotion. Soon, everyone present found an affiliation, connecting to the restorative flow of life-giving waters. She celebrated through tears as the heritage rift between the ranches evaporated in divine forgiveness.

"Hold on a second," Morrill called above the din. "I never answered the original question. Can someone bring the children back?"

Jusdyn and Arie volunteered together, sweeping out of the door with quick steps. Like a refreshing tide, seven children soon flooded into the room with popcorn bags in hand and were received into a host of loving arms.

Like a drought ending, Muriel stood tall and basked in the fullness of love's completed work. They had found a place to heal at last. Best of all, she had her resilient family all around.

Morrill straightened, somehow looking like a younger man. "Now, as to the lamb of stone which marks the unselfish effort making this day possible, I've just remembered what the A stands for."

Valor clapped her hands in excitement, spilling waves of popcorn in every direction.

"Except for my sister Dorothy's line through Muriel, we all can thank this angel for the gift of our lives. Our farm foreman's daughter was buried with the rest and marked with the lamb of stone. Our sitter, Arabella Good, represents the saving saint of the McLauren clan."

Now inseparable, Muriel stood strong, her arms locked with Arie's in the revelation of the moment. The younger woman's eyes became resplendent beyond explanation. Having recognized the similarity in names between the saving saint and her future daughter-in-law, she gained a foothold for another inexplicable step in faith, readily choosing to press onward and advance beyond the erosive hindrance of doubt.

~

Jusdyn spotted Jimmy John Wilson standing outside the front door tossing his hat into the wind and catching it again like a canine unit lacking any dog. The McLauren family emerged next, locking elbows and pulling suitcases in the happiest patient discharge on record. Laughter preceded the rest of the Linquist branch out of the automatic door, and the butterfly twins frolicked on the classic tractor situated in the front flowerbed.

Lightheartedness caught like contagion across the sheriff's brow and untied a few troublesome knots the lawman had been hauling around as unnecessary ballast. "Howdy, Mr. and Mrs. McLauren." The sheriff nodded to Morrill and replaced his hat only to tip it to Ruby. "Congratulations on getting hitched this morning."

"Thank you kindly, sheriff." Morrill shook his hand. "What brings you out our way?"

"Well, I thought you folks might be interested to know that Keeter Grant was recovered up Richey Cove way. He's been tossed around by the twister's meat grinder once or twice, and now resides over at the hospital yonder contemplating the meaning of life with his body locked in traction. I kept telling myself what a shame it would be for him to feel all forgotten and alone after what he did for all these children."

Jusdyn exchanged glances with Arie who found it impossible to conceal her delight.

"Do you mean that cowboy who put us in the tube?" Valor couldn't control her escalating excitement.

Jimmy John toed at the grass. "Yup. That'd be Keeter all right."

With a nod from her aunt, the girl took off running across the grass between the two facilities with Virgil trailing mere steps behind.

Ruby attempted to corral the butterflies perched on the rusted seat of the M tractor. "Hope and Faith, do you feel like singing today?"

"Yes, ma'am," they replied in unison.

Jenna pulled little Tucker alongside the plummeting twins. "Count us in, too."

Morrill stepped away so as not to get left out. "You're a good-hearted man, Sheriff Wilson. Thanks for letting us know about Keeter."

His pudgy eight-year-old cornered the lawman on the sidewalk. "Say there, sheriff. Can I wear your hat?" Bobby Dean twitched his mouth side-to-side waiting for an answer.

"Oh, why not?" Jimmy John popped the oversized hat onto the precocious boy's head.

Bobby Dean inflated his chest with importance as he assumed the lawman's role. "I'll make sure everybody obeys all the hospital rules while we're inside." With a salute, the boy ran to catch up with the rest.

"You do that, deputy." Jimmy John passed his fingers through his hair. "Mr. Linquist, can I have a minute with you and Jusdyn?"

Loren stepped closer. "Sure thing, sheriff."

Jusdyn released Arie and she connected with Doug's wheelchair as Darlene followed the pavement apron back to the hospital.

"I understand you were on the opening end of that tube full of children, Jusdyn." Jimmy John produced a rare smile that reflected how tenderhearted he was for children.

At this positive line of questioning, Jusdyn's spirit buoyed within his chest. "Arie and I heard Valor playing violin over the drum of the rain and bird-dogged it over to the culvert." He grinned at the remembrance. "About the time I got my truck cab loaded with the refugees, Dad pulled up followed by Darlene, and that's how we got all twenty-three transported over here safe and sound."

A genuine look of gratitude radiated from the lawman's face. "I'll make sure that gets into the official report, if I ever have a few free minutes to write the thing." He shifted his shoulders and gave a furtive look around. "Listen, I wanted you both to know we got some new information on TJ. He had a neighbor out Americus way pick him up, but that accomplice is sealed tight. His wife, however, has been most cooperative. Seems she performed some first aid work on TJ's lip. Sounds like he gashed it pretty bad. Anyway, he had to shave off his moustache to get her to stitch up the damage, and you know how attached he was to that thing."

Jusdyn couldn't suppress a smirk. "You're right, that does sound serious." He turned and noticed his father's deadpan demeanor.

"What's worrying you the most?" Loren asked with guarded candor.

The lawman shifted his weight from one foot to the other and gazed across the landscape. "She gave us reason to believe the wound might get infected, given the unsanitary conditions. You both know what's worse than a wild animal on the run."

Jusdyn's throat tightened with a familiar dread. "An animal with a festering wound?"

Jimmy John's gaze froze on them one at a time. "We've got to find TJ, gentlemen—the sooner, the better."

Loren struggled to cooperate. "Muriel wanted to stop by Americus and pick up some things for Valor tomorrow. I could take a look around the house."

"In their line of work, nothing typically gets written down because they don't want to leave a paper trail. Instead, look for something that might tip us off as to where he's been hanging out. Maybe fast-food wrappers or gas receipts. Little clues like that."

He sensed the need to be forthright. "I'll be at the Conservation Service office in the morning asking for TJ's job. If they take me, I'll try to comb through his desk looking for tips. There's got to be something incriminating at one place or the other."

The sheriff nodded his approval. "We're going to notify every walkin clinic within a sixty-mile area, in case TJ tries to get treated. Who knows, we just might get lucky."

"And trap the animal before he gnaws off his infected paw?" Loren asked.

"His—or possibly someone else's." Jimmy John's expression turned dead serious. "Population dynamics are never well-served by its most desperate member."

Jusdyn felt a sinking sensation in the pit of his stomach again. Not only was the dog barking up the wrong tree, it now had an insidious case of rabies. *I have to stop TJ.*

~

Another banked turn challenged TJ's ability to maintain control of the motorcycle as he returned on the back roads from Fort Riley. Weak, he should have never made the trip out, and now was forced to make the requisite return trip home. *Isn't this the epitome of my dream, riding free in the night wind, making drop-and-go encounters and returning all the richer?*

A huge raccoon snuck out of the far ditch and wandered into the beam of his headlight, posing an added threat for which he had no reaction. His vision blurred, but the right foot peg filed an honest report—a glancing blow to the skuzzy-backed looter. The bike wobbled, but he regained control. *Which is worse, to be undone by a backcountry coon or to waste away in bed from a mutinous lip?* Either way, a loser's mentality beset him as his dream to be a modern-day pirate became nothing more than a sickbed sham. Sobered by the strike, he slowed his speed to better maintain control which multiplied the road's length by a factor of ten.

Chapter 24

Part of nature's beauty is the randomness with which plants are scattered about the landscape. A spring seeps between two rocks in a gully, watering a lush garden of nut grass and sedges. Crown vetch hangs from the rock ledge above, while the secretive cliff brake fern seals the crevices with its diminutive lace. From there, the meadow spreads out, spacious in its allocation of non-patterned plant life where both prairie grasses and flowering forbs are welcome wherever. The farmer's straight-lined insistence on a monoculture crop brings a sharp contrast across the fence. Should the velvetleaf sprout amid the soybeans, he deems it 'cheat' and longs to pull it up. Blessed are the pure in heart that are able to see the weed as a misplaced plant and, with tender hands, nurture it back to the prairie.

"I'm Jusdyn Linquist, TJ McLauren's cousin." He faced the Natural Resources Conservation Service director who barely blinked. "TJ's still missing from the tornado Saturday, so I'm here to ask for his job." He managed to hand over his resume before two phones started ringing at the same time.

The director reached for the phone on the back desk, pointing to the closer one for Jusdyn to handle.

He found a notepad on the desktop and jotted down the caller's name. "Yes, sir. Give me a few hours to see what help we can come up with. You have my word on it." After hanging up, he made several more notes. Upon further consideration, he placed a heading across the top that read *Help Needed*. Before the director could clear the other line to continue their conversation, he heard another ring and answered the next call, soon adding a second entry onto the page.

The director waved the resume back at him with an inquiring look. "Could you at least hang here with the phones and give me a chance to look this over?"

"Yes, sir, I'm planning to stay all day, if you'll have me." The phone rang again as they squared each other up. Jusdyn reached for the phone and then paused one ring to let the director assess his options.

"I'm Bob Compton, Regional Director. To be honest, I'm more than glad to have you in this morning." He shook his hand, released it, and then gestured to the persistent phone.

"Conservation Service, Jusdyn speaking. How can I help you?" Another request for help unfolded, this time for fencing repair. The familiar task made its way onto the notepad. By midmorning, he had seven substantive requests for assistance from storm-ravaged landowners. Used to being more self-sufficient, he came in slightly under-connected in the resource department. The phone rang again so he grabbed it.

"This is Shawn Allen from Alta Vista. I'm the Farm Bureau representative serving on a coalition team with TJ McLauren from your office. I'm calling this morning and see what kind of assistance you guys might need."

"Hey, Shawn. Jusdyn Linquist here. TJ's my cousin so I'm filling in this morning. He got caught in the tornado at the symphony and hasn't been found yet. Listen, I've got a list here of some fairly major needs, fence repairs, equipment loans, and some straight-out manpower requests. Any help you can bring to bear would be great. In terms of size, the storm path turns out fairly significant, leaving a whole string of damage in an arcing band from south Wilsey northeast to Richey Cove."

"I've heard that Big John Creek disappeared up at the symphony site." Shawn's disbelief was evident in his tone.

"You've never seen anything like it, I can assure you. And the topsoil out there is gone. I mean it vanished everywhere the wedge touched down."

"Why don't you read down that list for me and let me see what I can come up with?"

Shawn's offer had a leveling effect, lending Jusdyn his first ray of hope that morning. One by one, he detailed the requests, giving specific locations and contact names. When the coalition representative asked relevant questions, he readily discussed the issues and offered his recommendations until they had worked through the entire list.

"You know, TJ never had anything positive to say about being a member of a multi-agency coalition." Shawn chased his confession with a tight laugh.

He found a wry truth to the admission. "Guess I'm here to prove him wrong. Hey, how about we take a tour of the symphony site when you come to town?"

"You're reading my mind, Jusdyn. I'm truly looking forward to meeting you."

"Thanks, Shawn. Call back when you have some resources for me." He lowered the phone and began scribbling notes on a second sheet of the notepad. He thought of a heading and then scrawled *Help Offered* across the top. After holding the two lists side by side, he made blanks on the second page to align with the requests. Looking up, he caught the director staring.

"I like your go-get-em attitude, Jusdyn. For that reason, I'm sending your resume on up the line to Human Resources by fax. Let's wait and see what Topeka says about the actual hiring. As far as I'm concerned, the job's yours if you want it."

"I do, sir. Thank you very much." He stood to accept the offer, shaking hands with his new boss to seal the deal. The phone beckoned with urgency. This time, he answered it with an added measure of confidence.

~

Arie placed two more cherry pies into the double ovens and made a crosshatched tally totaling ten pastries ready to send to town. Remembering the sugar canister ran low, she added the staple to a shopping list resting on the counter. Sounds of the prairie filtered through the screen door which provided only half the company she really needed. Thinking about Jusdyn and his quest to get the job this morning, she wished the cottage had phone service.

She walked out into the short hallway looking for any evidence it may have been wired for telephone at some point in time. Unable to find any signs of a jack along its walls, she stepped into the living room and continued her search. A cool morning breeze wafted through the front room, offering a respite from the kitchen's heat. She caught the hem of the lace curtain and pleated it in her fingers, placing it over her wavy hair as if trying on a veil. When she turned to glimpse her image in the vanity mirror, her bridal reflection melted into a faraway scene.

A corrugated tin building stood out in the quiet of nowhere. Only a row of cottonwood trees along the ditch bank across the front made any motion at all. The rustle of leaves became more and more pronounced as the building loomed closer. Writing appeared beside the doorframe as the leaf noise rose to a crescendo. The print read *Property of the US Government: Trespassers Will Be Prosecuted.*

Arie had no sooner deciphered the stenciled message when the whole scene exploded with a flash, leaving only the cottonwoods, leafless and disarmingly still. Stunned, she dropped the curtain. *What kind of bride dreams of world destruction five days before her wedding?*

~

Morrill approached the kitchen doorway with moccasin-quiet feet and stood there marveling at his energetic wife.

At the counter, Ruby scrambled the eggs and commanded the

toaster into service. She hummed her morning meditations while starting a new routine, all a prelude to bringing her children home.

"Aha. My favorite combo—bacon and eggs." He sent her a devilish look.

She came to him and gave him a short peck on the cheek, her violet eyes dancing.

"First things first. Let's enjoy a shared moment for the two of us this morning and save the rest of the day for our new family."

"Our time together should only include the most intimate of tasks, like writing an obituary for your sister." He cocked his brow to enlist her cooperation. "It has to make tomorrow's paper. Otherwise, no one will know the funeral is Wednesday."

"Could you be a dear and help me?" Her chin started to quiver as she produced a notepad from her pocket that read *Opal Eunice Litke* across the top.

He took the notepad in one hand and cradled his struggling mate with the other while he contemplated the solemn duty. When the toaster sprang, an idea popped to mind. "How about I interview you, and we write it from that?" He planted the notepad on the table.

Ruby scraped the knife laden with margarine across the crusty slices. Next, she loaded fried eggs, bacon, and toast on two china plates and brought them to the table. Taking her seat, she motioned for him to join her.

He sat and bowed, asking God to bless the food.

Ruby glanced at him as she placed a napkin in her lap. "First question, please."

"When did this wonderful life that Opal led get its start?" He posed his question trying to stimulate more than a dated response.

"Well, Father used to say it was the snowiest winter on record." She forked her egg around the plate. "Claims he had to throw a rope down the hill for old Doc Watkins to make the climb. That was the fourteenth of January in nineteen-thirty. She must have made quite an entrance." She took a bite and chewed.

"I can only imagine." He recorded the date on the page with

several other embellishing details. Perhaps a great life story harkens from such subtle beginnings, like a baby crying from a hilltop in a silencing snowstorm. He allowed a bite of bacon to be his just reward in attempting to capture an enigmatic life on mere paper.

~

Loren regarded the sleepy-eyed fourteen-year-old across the breakfast table from him. "How inclined are you to farm work?"

Muriel raised an eyebrow from her post at the stove where she had pancakes bubbling on the griddle.

Valor walked between them, raiding the refrigerator for milk and poured two glasses without having to be asked.

Virgil took an orange quarter in one hand and picked at its peel. "Well, I like the outdoors, but never lived on a farm before. Guess I could learn how to help out. Plus, I know how to mow the yard."

Valor brought over the milk and returned to the kitchen to retrieve the maple syrup.

"We mow with a tractor out here." Loren planted his forearms on the table's edge, staring at the boy to see how that revelation would strike his confidence level.

Virgil popped the orange section into his mouth and ripped the pulp away from the rind. He chewed for a thoughtful moment, and then grinned. "Sounds like a promotion to me."

"All right then. It looks like I have my replacement for Jusdyn right here at the table. Tractor driving lessons start right after we check on the herd."

"Don't forget we're headed to town at eleven-thirty to take Jusdyn his lunch, followed by a stop in Americus for Valor's things, and then to Emporia for Virgil's clothes and some wedding shopping." Muriel rattled the spatula into the sink. "Arie wants to come with us if she can get her baking done in time." She brought breakfast in on a platter.

Virgil studied the heaping stack of pancakes being loaded onto his plate. "Can I just ask a simple question?"

"Go ahead, son." Loren inhaled with robust anticipation,

grateful for the identical stack finding its way to his plate.

"On the farm, why does everything have to start so early?" The teen gestured with his fork, carving a question mark out of midair.

Valor used the syrup and passed it to Virgil.

Loren exchanged an amused look with his wife. "When you work for yourself out on the land, there's never any end to it." He added some mock cheerfulness to his tone for effect. "Ain't that great?"

"Just swell," Virgil replied, the sarcasm dripping like syrup down his pancake stack.

Muriel set a second platter onto the table, this one bearing sausage patties. "At least we don't muzzle the ox while he's treading the threshing floor."

"I so get that." Virgil reached with effort to snare a patty on his fork.

Valor cleared her mouth with a sip of milk. "You could always go to bed earlier if you need more sleep." Her meek suggestion seemed to hang between them.

Muriel sat down at her place and folded her hands for the prayer.

His brow furrowed. "Guess I could if it wasn't for you and those suckling badgers in the laundry chute."

Muriel's eyes grew wide. "Do you mean my laundry chute?"

"We'd better pray now, Aunt Muriel." Valor bowed her head as if to dodge the issue.

Loren pronounced a brief prayer thanking God for the food and caught the girl arching one eye open to spy on her accomplice. For his part, Virgil stared at her straight on, not fearful of confrontation.

"Amen." Valor chimed in saint-like, a true choir member.

"Those critters go into the laundry room right after breakfast." Muriel grabbed her coffee cup for reinforcement. "We have to keep them away from Sam."

"Yes, ma'am." Valor straightened in her seat. "Thanks for letting me keep them. They need me, you know."

Loren intended to end the critter discussion. "Only for a few days. Wild things need to stay wild, after all." Though right, getting her to let go would be the hard part.

~

Fever cultivated its hydroponic crop of pain, seeping from his lip across his face and dripping from his brow. TJ threw the empty bottle of anti-inflammatory medicine, making it skip across the lab table, finding a beaker to object with. Overtaken by exhaustion upon his late return last night, he had parked the motorcycle in the cabin's front room. Now, everything reeked of a heady gasoline fumes. He pushed open the front door to let in some fresh air. The brightness of midmorning assaulted his eyes.

"Oh, great. I've gone nocturnal. Guess that's what happens when you choose to walk in darkness." He retreated to the cabin's interior, opting to check his lip in the mirror. Entering the latrine, he pulled the light chain and stood aghast at the pustulated creature his upper lip had become. Arachnid-like, eight red legs now radiated from the swollen body of the purplish beast, one for each stitch taken across the original gash. He stared at his image in full disbelief.

"Great Mother of Betsy Ross." Oh, so obvious, the seamstress had delivered the fire with the fix. For the first time, he allowed the demoralization to erode his attraction toward the dark shortcut he'd chosen. Victimized by fate, he pressed his forehead onto the mirror, refusing to identify with the desperate person reflected in its frame.

~

"Well, it's about high time." Vernis pretended austerity, and then broke into a hearty laugh as his brother and new bride came up the front walkway of the care facility. "We've already been through breakfast and two pans of Jell-O."

Ruby scanned the rumpled group. "Was the Jell-o green, Little Tucker?"

The tyke brushed off the front of his stain-dappled shirt. "How'd you know?"

Jenna hugged her new father figure and Morrill gave the thin girl a bear hug in return.

The twins had Bobby Dean cornered and were teaching him a new song.

"Are we ready to go home yet?" Morrill's voice resonated across the room.

"Yes we are." Jenna gave a little jump to fuel her reconnection. Bobby Dean grabbed her hand and copied her hopping, which generated a game the rest had to enter.

Rita Fieldcrest approached the group. "What's going on out here?" The facility director stood tapping the papers in her hand, scowling at the children. A slow smile spread across her face as they quieted down. Then she produced the paper to Morrill. "Turnabout is fair play, Mr. McLauren. Now, you can do the springing out."

"I'm thrilled to do so." He made quick work of the signature.

Rita turned to Vernis, nodding to his packed suitcases. "What about you, Baby Brother?"

He seemed to be losing both his audience and his sense of purpose at the same time. "I reckon nobody wants me."

"Oh, I wouldn't be too sure of that." Rita nodded toward the front doors. A familiar green Subaru pulled into the temporary parking space, its youthful driver stepping out with a wave. Her much-improved passenger leaned on his helpmate as they made the short walk into the nursing home.

"Children, I want you to meet your Uncle Doug." Morrill introduced the wounded man with tenderness.

Doug attempted to stand straight to make a good first impression, but his stitches insisted otherwise.

"Nice to meet you, Uncle Doug." Jenna found her poise and curtsied in a brief bob. "This is Bobby Dean. He's good at memorizing things like poems and verses. Beside him are the twins Hope and Faith. They like to sing and climb on things, like tractors."

Doug smiled at this admission and Darlene came to him, locking her arm around his waist.

"Lastly, this is Tucker." Jenna twitched her nose sideways. The boy stood straight and tall as a big, green-stained mess. "We haven't figured out what he's good at yet."

Doug knelt down to his level. "Would you like to ride horses like a cowboy, Tucker?"

"And how," the preschooler replied, his face brightening. The other children clamored for inclusion, stepping toward Doug as if to be the first in line for a pony ride.

Vernis smiled at their enthusiasm and grew misty-eyed at the target of their affection.

Doug peered over at him above the ruckus. "How about you, Dad? Would you like to come home and see the horses?"

Vernis glanced at Rita and then turned, viewing his former facility of incarceration circumspectly. There was nothing endearing to cling to here.

Rita nodded her permission, handed Doug the dismissal papers, and kissed Darlene on the cheek, wishing them all well.

Vernis' gaze rested on the precious children spared from the jaws of death by a lowly culvert and turned back to Doug. "And how." Though scratchy-throated, he attempted to reply with as much enthusiasm as the four-year old had, possibly even more. When Doug motioned toward the door, Vernis took his first step toward freedom in over a decade.

~

Arie peeked into the NRCS office door. "Anyone allowed a lunch break in here?"

Jusdyn glanced up from his accumulating desktop and smiled.

The director grabbed a stack of papers from the adjoining desk and proceeded to sweep Jusdyn out with them. "Go ahead and take your break."

"Mr. Compton, I'd like you to meet my fiancée, Arie Henning." He crooked a finger in her direction with a smile.

"My pleasure, Miss Henning. Are you two getting married anytime soon?"

"This Saturday." The admission heated her cheeks.

"Arie's my in-house plant expert. We may have to use the team approach until I can come up to speed in that department." He slid his hands in hers at the admission.

"That's fine with me. Don't be too tough on him though. I still lose my way through some of the milkweeds."

"We'll start with my bridal bouquet." Arie gave him a wave, pulling her fiancé toward the door to go purchase their marriage license.

"Take an hour, Jusdyn. You deserve to be away from these phones at least that long."

"Thank you, sir. Thanks for everything."

With one final tug, she stole her accomplice and disappeared out the door to keep the jam-packed day in forward motion.

~

Jimmy John stepped toward the phone on his desk with spirited enthusiasm. Things were beginning to resume a pattern of normalcy around town despite the proliferation of funerals and requests for sturdy pallbearers.

"Sheriff Wilson here," he said into the phone. "Riley County Hospital? Six cases of meth overdose in one night? Sound like we have some bad crystal out there. Yes, let's press charges, if the suffering victims live through it. Thanks for keeping me posted. I'll be in touch." He replaced the receiver with a thud.

"Okay, TJ. I've got to find you before you poison half the drug users in the tri-county area." He growled like a bear, weighing out his game plan against the concealed producer. He thought about the irony of being terminally wasted by your own drug habit—such an unintended, self-inflicted wound. What a reduction in crime would result if only law-abiding citizens remained. "Or maybe I should wait." Unconvinced, he grabbed his hat and headed out the door.

~

Morrill paused on the stair landing to catch his breath as the piano-playing oldest adoptee brushed by him on her way up.

"My room at last!" Jenna raced into the first room she came to at the top of the stairs.

Ever patient, Ruby led the girl on down the hall with a gentle nudge until they stood in front of Opal's old room.

Jenna peeked in and found the massive walnut sleigh bed covered with a colorful floral comforter. "This room is beautiful."

He forced his way up three more stairs.

Ruby motioned toward the room. "Go ahead, sweetie."

Jenna entered and twirled around, viewing the panorama of its elegance.

"I'm so tickled you like it, Jenna."

"Oh, I do. I truly love it." Her fingertips traced the graceful bed with its curving headboard and matching footboard.

He cleared the last tread and hugged the upstairs newel post. "Let's save the word *love* for other people, shall we?"

"Yes, sir. I truly, completely like my new room. If anyone ever has a bad dream or is afraid of the storm, they're welcome to join me on this big bed. We can ride out the fright together."

He could hardly let the opportunity to encourage her pass. "See, the Lord made you to be a firstborn, Jenna. You're protective by nature and always have a thought for the others. Tell me Ruby. Where can these two butterflies alight?"

"The first room we passed, but they'll have to share a bed for now. The boys need the twin beds at the end of the hall."

Faith and Hope hugged each other and ran in claiming sides of the bed.

He backtracked down the hall, mumbling his praise for a spacious second story.

"All I want is a window in my room, so I can see the clouds from up here." Bobby Dean spoke his rendering in a melancholy tone as he came up the stairs with leaden feet.

Unease shortened his next breath as he ushered easy-going Tucker down the full length of the hallway.

Ruby winked and locked her elbow through his while the twins remained behind to christen their bed with a fervent trampoline routine.

Bobby Dean found the bedroom first and halted at the doorway.

Fearful that the boy might be on the verge of rejecting the only available accommodation left in the house, he tried to think of something redeeming to say. Standing at the end of the hall, they had run out of options.

Tucker broke from his grip, squeezed under Bobby Dean's outstretched arms, and sucked in his breath.

Morrill clasped Ruby's hand and braced for the potential rejection. At her touch, he sensed a fortification of sorts.

Little Tucker pointed with his stubby finger. "Why, this room has a window straight up to heaven."

Intrigued at the unusual comment, he peered past the door jamb to find an arched window gracing the front of the Victorian house, the edges trimmed with cobalt blue stained glass.

"It's like God is watching over me," Bobby Dean said with emotion. He walked in on stiffened legs and took the twin bed on the far side of heaven's window.

"Well, that's because he *is* watching over you." He had never felt more certain of his words. "God watches over all of us, in fact."

The girls found their way down the hall and collected in front of the stained-glass window, standing close enough to have the midday sun cast blue streaks across their faces. So enthralled with the color filtering into the room's interior, the children missed the crystal tear streaming out of the violet eyes of the only woman in town both brave enough—and worthy enough—to be their mother. He, however, captured every aspect of the precious image.

~

Doug struggled into the doorway, trying to adjust his hindered gait to the thick carpet.

Vernis stood in the middle of the family room of the ranch house. "Boy, this place is a sight for sore eyes." He walked up to the hearth and touched the double-barreled shotgun that adorned the mantle. "Here's my Old Smokepole."

"She never left the rocks on the hearth." He eased into in the leather chair facing the fireplace.

Darlene stopped beside him, adding a soft pillow behind his back.

He nodded and continued to take joy in watching his father get reacquainted around the house. "Your room is neat as a pin, Dad. Darlene made doubly sure of that."

Vernis stepped back into the hallway to make eye contact with him, grinning like a possum after having crossed the road. "There's my hat hanging on the footboard, as if I walked out and left it only yesterday."

"Welcome home, Dad. It hasn't been the same without you."

"It sure feels good to be back out here, let me tell you." Vernis gestured and turned to inhabit his room.

Darlene rustled a few things around on the counter. "Does anyone want anything from the kitchen?"

"Just the cook." Doug cranked the footrest up on the recliner and melted into the soft leather for a long moment. Prompted by snoring that soon resonated from the guest room and Darlene's sustained humming from the kitchen, he dozed off in total comfort, content that his ranch had filled with life once again.

~

Driving home after a stimulating day, Jusdyn considered what a rush it had been working from his strength—a love for the land. Today that had meant putting out a few fires and making connections between people standing in need with others positioned to help. Tomorrow would be a whole different scenario from the same office. By week's end, he hoped to have spent some time in the field parting somebody's bluestem with the toe of his boot. The truck ambled down Road Z and turned into the driveway between his two favorite houses. As he parked by the garage, Sam trotted over carrying his favorite rock-ball.

"Hey, boy." He scratched the old canine behind his ears. "Miss me?"

"I sure did." Valor appeared, riding her bike up from the pond's edge.

Virgil skipped one more flat rock across the pond surface and ran up to join in the welcome home.

"Hey, little brother. Where are your wheels?"

"We didn't have room for my bike this trip." Virgil shrugged his shoulders. "Your dad said he could bring the trailer next time, so I only grabbed the essentials."

"Arie bought a ton of stuff today." Valor pedaled ahead toward the back deck. "She hogged all the trunk space."

"Oh, great." He fought off a sudden sense of dread at the cost associated with her shopping. Breaking into a jog, he headed toward the cottage. "Tell Dad I'll come over later, Virgil. And remind me to show you where the fishing poles are kept."

He burst into the back screen door and found the kitchen empty, though the smell of cherry pies still lingered. In two steps he maneuvered through the hall and into the front room, where Arie laid motionless on the fainting couch, the victim of excessive shopping.

"Tell me where it hurts, my beautiful bride-to-be." He bent and planted kisses up her dangling arm.

"Oh, my aching feet." She remained motionless, though dimples popped up on her cheeks when his calf-wrangling hands kneaded her feet back from numbness.

"Valor squealed on your shopping spree, saying you hogged all the trunk space. Do I need to know what you bought?"

"No, I think you only need to know how much money you owe Dad. My pie money ran out after the third stop. You didn't expect me to pay for the entire wedding, did you?"

When a smile crept across her face, he seized the moment to plant a kiss on top of it. "Wait a minute before you pack me up and send me on a guilt trip. I paid for the marriage license earlier today, didn't I?"

"Okay, I'll credit you for that one."

"I'll take my payment right now." He closed the gap between them, enjoying her playful mood. She didn't kiss too badly for a sore-footed fiancée. "So how much do I owe Dad?"

"Oh, I'll let you men hash that out. We've been invited over tonight for pizza."

"A round pie for a square meal? That doesn't make any sense, does it?" He entwined his fingers between hers, trapping her like a prisoner.

"Does that mean I should forget to serve the cherry pie I saved back for you this morning? Because it's round, too." Her eyelashes fluttered in exaggerated blinks.

He considered her ultimatum. "No need for such extreme measures. Last time I checked my geometry, two rounds do make a square. Bring on the cherry pie so we can celebrate my first day on the job."

"Did you hear back from Human Resources?"

"They called just before we closed for the day. Looks like I'm a keeper."

"I'll say." She caught him in a body lock and wrestled him onto the chaise.

After an agreeable three-count, he pulled back to catch his breath which he accomplished through her sweet-scented hair. "See anything on the vision screen today?" He nodded toward the antique vanity.

"Why yes, this morning." Arie turned sober and alert. "A tin building stood out by itself on the prairie. It had a line of cottonwood trees planted in front and their leaves were blowing in the wind."

He frowned and tilted his head. "You just described half the outbuildings in the county."

"The vision zoomed in as the tree leaves shook all the harder. Then I could read a sign by the door. It read 'Property of US Government: Trespassers Will Be Prosecuted.' The instant I finished reading the sign, the entire building exploded, leaving nothing except the poor cottonwood trees stripped bare."

"Do you think this has to do with TJ?" He stretched, trying to unravel the message. "Mind if I run this by Dad? He might have some insight."

"Go ahead, I think it's meant to help us. The more brain power we have on it, the sooner we can get this mystery resolved."

"Preferably before the explosion." He imagined the meth lab, full of volatile unknowns.

"You know, it could mean more of a figurative explosion."

He hopped off the chaise and lifted her back onto sore feet. "Or it might not."

~

"This is why I quit my day job so I'm sticking with it." TJ clenched his teeth, close to delirium from the infection and its shadowing fever. Even if his mind had clouded a bit, he could still trust his highly skilled hands to carry out the formula. Like a victim of walking pneumonia, he intended to carry on as long as he could stand. Even leaning on the edge of the table, the survival period on his feet comprised less than fifteen minutes. A deathbed would have been a relief at this point, as the concrete floor where he soon landed proved less than accommodating.

~

Jusdyn picked up a carrot stick from the leftovers on the bar and focused on his father's reaction. The vision's federal connotation meant nothing to him.

"I'd guess Delevan. It's got to mean the old prison camp at Delevan." Loren glanced at his watch and seemed restless. "We have a couple of hours before sunset. Want to drive over?"

"Sure, I'm up for it. Arie should come so she can check the setting against the vision."

Deke shot through the back screen door. "Anybody home?"

"Well, look who's here." Muriel retreated from the kitchen sink, putting the last clean dish in the draining rack.

Valor ran to the back door as Merrilee lowered the baby carrier. "So how does the new mama feel?"

"Euphoric, sleep-deprived, cozy and cranky. Sometimes all at once." Merrilee gave her a fleeting smile, and then pointed to a chair. Once Valor sat still, she transferred the sleepy baby into her arms.

The girl studied the petite features of Beryl's face and blew puffs of breath into her wispy dark hair.

Virgil positioned his lanky frame across the table and looked uninterested.

Muriel wiped her hands and came into the eating area, hugging Merrilee.

Jusdyn greeted Deke with a handshake and passed him to his dad while he took a peek at Little Miss Sleep-a-lot.

Looking down at the ladder-back chair, Muriel departed toward the front room and returned with a seat cushion for Merrilee, motioning for her to sit.

Deke frowned with mock sternness. "What's this about an engagement?"

"Guess I forgot my booster shot this spring and the marriage ailment caught up with me." To drive the analogy deeper, he covered a weak spot, his heart.

"A sickness, is it?" Arie walked away from him to hug Merrilee. "Listen, I have an urgent request for a maid of honor this Saturday evening. Would a certain new mother be up for that kind of challenge?"

"Why, yes. I'd be more than happy to. Deke can hold the baby while I'm standing up front with the beautiful people."

"Except I need Deke up there by me on the groom's side." He planted a fist against his cousin's arm. "How about it?"

"Count me in. No bow ties, though. They make my ears look big." Deke waggled his ears causing Loren to snicker so loud the baby stirred and everyone got to see a flash of her blue eyes.

"Okay then, I'll hold the baby at the wedding." Valor adjusted her skinny arm under Beryl's head.

"Well, I was sort of hoping you might carry this instead." Arie pulled a moss-lined twig basket out of her shopping bag.

Valor's eyes flashed at the prospect.

Muriel nodded and pretended to toss flower petals in the air.

"A flower girl at last. Does that mean I get a fancy dress?"

"You both do, if I can get them made in time." Arie's tone carried a touch of chagrin.

"I'll help you as much as I can." Muriel fished in a drawer and produced a cloth tape measure. "Want me to get some measurements while I have everyone right here?"

"Yes. Great idea."

"Listen, Deke. We were just headed out for a drive to Delevan." He proceeded with caution. "We might need your help on this. Could we borrow you for about an hour or so?"

"Sounds mysterious. I'm in."

Jusdyn motioned toward the door. "Sorry ladies. We need to take Arie with us this time, but I promise to have her back soon." He guided her out, uncertain why he felt so committed to find the family's missing black sheep. He exchanged a look with Deke that mixed futility and frustration as they hastened down the back porch steps elbow to elbow.

~

Brain fog began to set in as TJ fought the effects of the high fever. He managed to pull his body upright and wandered into the back portion of the facility. *A breath of fresh air would be nice.* Mistaking them for windows, he unlatched the missile silo hatches and shoved them open. A cesspool of groundwater contamination lofted its vaporous influence upward, assaulting his nose. He stumbled back into the bunkhouse and fell onto the cot, heeding neither the chemical reaction going awry on the tabletop nor the volatility of his bunker. His hand fell around the neck of a water bottle. He lifted it, dousing his upper lip, lending momentary relief to the fire within.

~

Arie dropped her arms to her sides in disappointment. "This place isn't right."

Jusdyn drove a circle around the abandoned base.

She kept a tense vigil, but nothing seemed to match the vision.

Deke shivered. "Talk about the creeps. This place seems haunted with suffering."

Arie began to sense something other than pain. "What was this base used for anyway?"

"Delevan served as an interment camp for German-Americans during the second world war." Loren's hand traced the scarred landscape. "They considered such imprisonment a necessary evil in its day." The truck halted in front of an old barracks and they slid out. After checking several buildings for printed signs, they found no wording anywhere.

Arie rubbed at the goose bumps tickling her arm. "Does anyone else hear that?"

"Tell us what it sounds like." Jusdyn fixed his gaze on hers.

She ducked and then peered up as if something hovered immediately overhead. "I hear helicopter blades slapping, only with a more rhythmic beat that's less threatening."

"Could be a drone," Deke offered.

"Or perhaps wind turbines." Loren stepped up beside them. "She could be hearing the future of wind power right here where the prairie is already impacted by man. That would be a downright brilliant retrofit for this dilapidated camp. I'll recommend it first chance I get."

Arie looked over the barracks to imagine a host of white propellers churning in the Kansas wind, but soon retreated to more familiar territory in Jusdyn's truck. As night fell across the windshield on the trip home, she rode in silence, knowing she'd let the search party down. Darkness robbed them of the one commodity they couldn't spare—more time.

~

Jusdyn's second day on the job focused more on the land than putting out fires. The task of reviewing files helped him determine what needed to be done—or redone—due to TJ's lax performance.

A great opportunity to search for clues as to his cousin's whereabouts, he tried to blend his personal mission with his day's work. The thickness of the US Government file folder seemed daunting at first glance. After all, his agency fell under the auspices of the Department of the Interior. He spent the morning reading through historic files and existing management plans, establishing an order he could more readily access.

Just before noon, he stumbled on a page that seemed out of place. It appeared to be some type of land lease for a sixteen-acre hayfield in Lyon County. Examining it further, he noted the raised pattern of a notary seal on the lower corner. *What business would the government have leasing hay grounds to the likes of TJ?* An uncanny sense of wariness permeated his core as he reached for the phone. As he dialed his home number, he glanced back up at the seal identifying the branch of government involved in the transaction. His mind went numb. The gold and black seal read Department of Defense. Arie's vision flashed to the forefront of his thoughts.

"Dad, I've just found something in TJ's files. It's a land lease from the feds in Lyon County. Nothing about it makes sense, so I think we'd better check it out. Can you come to town? I'll call Jimmy John next and clue him in. And Dad, bring along the plat book, as the location of the lease is written in legalese. I stumbled onto the document because the hayfield is government property. How ironic is that?"

Jusdyn slipped his thumb over the DOD seal as if to snuff out a bomb. He released the receiver and opened the cover of the Council Grove phone book where the emergency numbers emblazed the opening flyleaf. Most definitely in the throes of an emergency, he could hardly wait to share the situation.

~

Surely someone would come for him, someone like Henry or possibly one of his customers. *Who comes to the rescue of a persona non grata?* His morale sunk lower than low. He glanced up in a daze and noticed his motorcycle, looking like a means of escape. If he had enough strength left to wheel it outside, he could drive to town and save himself. Formulating the vague plan lent him the motivation to try. He had to crawl on his hands and knees to close the distance to the bike. He stood only to collapse across the leather seat as the cabin fazed in and out of black.

He struggled with the heavy bike. "Must get outside." Fumes had striated in hazy layers over the lab table, burning the back of his throat. The bike resisted his initial efforts when the sudden sound of shattering glass on the tabletop convinced him to abandon the burdensome scheme. Shrinking to his knees, he crawled for the door in pathetic retreat.

He raised a hand and managed to depress the latch, springing the door wide open. A fresh supply of oxygen stretched across his lab, fanning the fire. The midday sun pierced his unshielded eyes, forcing him low to the ground. A precarious position, he crept forward on his belly like a snake, heading for cover under the distant cottonwoods. A high-pitched siren went off in his head and bled out his last ounce of strength. He collapsed face-down in the dirt.

~

Red and blue lights twirled in anger from the lead car's roof, sickening Arie and the other peace-loving occupants of the vehicles that followed. The sheriff's car threw up a rooster tail of dust as he targeted the cottonwoods at the end of the access road. Jusdyn's truck shadowed Jimmy John, with Loren right behind him and then Doug riding in Darlene's car. The whole family had come to rescue their black sheep, praying as they arrived.

They pulled up to the clearing in front of the bunker where a gray-black plume of smoke billowed from the door like a grass fire crossing the prairie. Arie traced the smoke plume back to the entrance and saw the stenciled sign identifying the government property, exactly like the vision had warned. She glanced at the leaves of the cottonwood to judge how far along in the detonation sequence they might be.

Jimmy John jumped out of his patrol car and raced toward TJ's body, with Jusdyn trailing steps behind. The two men lifted the runaway and spread his arms across their shoulders. When Valor broke away from Muriel and tried to embrace her father, Arie caught her and held her back. Amid the mayhem, a low rumble came from the back room of the bunkhouse.

Her blood ran cold. "Everybody take shelter behind the cottonwoods." She motioned toward the tree line, fueled by outright panic.

The support team members responded. Muriel came and took Valor, retreating toward the trees. Darlene hooked Doug's arm and insisted on his cooperation. Jimmy John and Jusdyn struggled past Arie, heading for the patrol car with TJ's limp body. A steam-driven scream suddenly joined the rumble from behind the structure.

"No. It's too late." Arie pulled at Jusdyn's free arm, determined to save him.

TJ slid off his shoulder and reached into Jimmy John's holster on the sly, pulling out the revolver. With liquid quickness, he grabbed her hair and jabbed the gun into her ribs like a madman.

"Don't do it, son," Doug begged, hunching over the hood of the patrol car for support. "We came back to save you—all of us. Don't throw your family away again."

Arie searched for support. "Loren, please. Make them get back." Of all the family members, he would listen to reason.

The rancher extended both arms and shielded Jusdyn and Deke from the hostage scene, pulling them back a safe distance.

In seconds, Darlene grabbed Doug's waist and pulled him away.

Only Jimmy John remained to confront them, refusing to yield.

TJ began to lean on her so heavily she thought her knees would buckle. The final scene of her vision began to transpire right before her eyes, and she could feel the elemental rawness of the surrender. The cottonwood trees shook their leaves in an inconsolable quiver as the sky filled with tension. All at once, a martyr's peace came upon her as she stood as an outsider on an acquired land—the tallgrass prairie. When the siren's warbling crescendo matched her pulse, she sensed the end was near.

~

Restless electricity tore through Jusdyn as he viewed his family members, now hunkered in safety in stark contrast to Arie, still out there at risk. His feet tingled against the ground as he backed further away from the danger.

"Take us out of here," TJ shouted through his teeth, his wild eyes fixed on the lawman.

Feet spread, the sheriff held his ground. "You're not going anywhere—but the hospital."

When TJ jerked Arie's hair in response, Jusdyn's core ripped in half. *I can't live without her.* His back-pedaling halted. Bolstered in the moment, he broke from the protection of the trees determined to save Arie or die trying. "The land's not enough, Lord." His confession floated over his shoulder as he sprinted toward the impasse.

~

Vernis somehow had known it would come down to this. A mulish moral failure ran through the McLauren lineage like a crack in a dam. What had started with his father had perpetuated through one son. Now, his grandson had hit rock bottom, planning to take as many decent folks with him as he could. That scenario had already played out once with the flood victims, but history would not repeat itself here—not twice in his lifetime.

Ignored by the rest, the backseat rider positioned his helper front and center, poised for a means to end the travesty. With his feeble hands gripping Old Smokepole, he aimed out of the right rear window, both barrels gleaming in the sun. He marked the mutineer with the center notch and waited for his chance to end the weakness.

~

"Can't you stop yourself?" Arie confronted TJ directly. "Can't you stop running away from God?" Distracted by movement, she caught sight of Jusdyn running straight toward the pending inferno.

"Don't," she protested, her knees buckling beneath her.

Jimmy John lunged at TJ, knocking the handgun away. A split second later, an explosion ripped from the Subaru, arresting the fugitive in a scattershot of resistance.

As a high-pitched screech echoed up the throat of the missile silo, Jusdyn grabbed her waist and forced her toward safety, ending with a running leap into the ditch behind the trees. A massive explosion rocked the ground and sent up a fireball, the shockwave stripping the sentinel trees bare. Having felt the ground heave, Arie shuddered to regain control. Seconds into the aftermath, the surrounding land held an eerie quiet while heart-shaped leaves fluttered down on the hunkered survivors. Like a peace offering, they alighted on her shoulders. She glanced down only to discover Jusdyn's protective arms wrapped around her midsection.

~

Through the inferno's last hiss and diminishing shower of leaves, Jusdyn heard a solitary voice weakly crying up to God. Beyond consolation, his mother wept passionately, calling TJ's name over and over.

Loren, who had shielded the children in the swale, now rose on rigid legs to salvage what was left.

Jusdyn clung to Arie, still silent from her hostage ordeal, determined to protect her from further trauma.

The back door of the Subaru swung open and Vernis stumbled out. He threw the shotgun to the ground in protest. Then the bent rancher faced into the bunker's residual heat and stepped over to reclaim what remained of his grandson.

"Won't you send someone?" A brittle voice repeated, torment evident in every word. "God, please—send someone to bring me back."

Moved to forgiveness at last, he separated from Arie and responded to the plea by closing the distance between them. The resistance he felt in that first step ebbed with each pace he took.

"Here I am, grandson," Vernis said with guttural resolve. "I've come to bring you back."

Doug stepped into the smoking debris next. "TJ—I'm here for you, too." Weak, he knelt by the shot victim.

Loren came forward and took a knee beside his ranching neighbor, his expression taut. When the downed sheriff struggled to his feet, he lent a strong arm for support.

Jusdyn stooped to lift the fugitive out of the explosion's ashes and was relieved to discover he had Deke's ready assistance. "We're all here, TJ. You left us, but we never left you."

Virgil led Valor past her father and made her kneel beside the wounded sheriff being tended by Loren. He gave a silent nod for the start of her healing touch, engaging a fourth generation in the rescue.

Bent and broken, Vernis clung to Doug and wept like the coal bin baby once again.

Shed of emotion, Muriel began to affix a tourniquet on TJ's left thigh. The lower leg had been pulverized. Her attempt to bring the blood loss under control gained limited traction.

Wrapped by Arie's arms, Jusdyn surveyed the scene with his feet planted firmly on the land. Breath by breath, he sensed God restoring his soot-stained relatives like the prairie rises out of the spring burn with miraculous newness of life. Here in the bittersweet aftermath of near-destruction, they stood reconciled as a family once again. He bent and planted a kiss in Arie's smoke-scented hair, holding her close to assure they would travel restoration's lengthy road together.

Chapter 25

In the days to come when the crystalline river flows in the land of God, the striving between predator and prey will cease at last. The wolf and the lamb shall feed together, and the lion will eat straw like the ox. A never-failing light will shine, forever lending its splendor to the land. Standing by that pure-flowing river and basking in the radiant light is the Tree of Life, bearing fruit in every season. Likewise, the prairie shall be perfected in the blessing of eternity, restored in all its vastness—open and treeless—with ample food for the coyote and badger. And when the old order has passed away and the new earth has come, men will walk with the Lord and he will dwell with them, in a land where big bluestem forever grows shoulder high.

"I tell you, he's always throwing something." Jusdyn nodded as Virgil fished out another green apple rejected by the oldest tree in the orchard. The youth released the orb with well-paced precision and tracked it as the discard landed behind the corral.

Deke turned evaluative. "Yeah. Good shoulder movement." He loosened the top button of his dress shirt and began shucking the matching vest that linked them as bridegroom and best man. Hanging his satin on the pump handle at the implement garden, he made a few hasty steps toward his truck.

"Merrilee's going to have your hide if you get messed up before the ceremony." Jusdyn laced the threat with an ounce of good humor. Another green apple whizzed through the air, landing with a crack on the back fence of the corral.

Deke backpedaled, his palms flexed up. "Methinks an hour or so lends more than enough time for a tutorial on the finer art of pitching." Within seconds, he had retrieved the baseball wrapped in the leather rag of a glove he kept stowed behind the driver's seat.

Jusdyn wandered toward the pond where Valor and Tia led horseback rides for the McLauren storm orphans and the younger Hernandez kids. Valor's hair had been braided into a crown that would soon cradle a halo of lazy daisies and black-eyed Susans, two wildflowers he now knew by sight. Laughter rippled across the pond, making the scene all the more idyllic.

Looking up the driveway, he caught a glimpse of the silver truck pulling in, heavy with horse trailer. Curiosity propelled him past a cluster of men under the bur oak scrutinizing blueprints for the new McLauren barn. Not until the appaloosa stepped out of the stall-on-wheels did Jusdyn recognize storm survivor Junior Yates, who hid his healing façade under the broad brim of his best Sunday hat.

"Howdy, Jusdyn. I heard there were some goings-on out this way."

"Good to see you coming back to your old self, Junior." He extended his hand into a firm handshake. "We're celebrating Uncle Morrill's marriage to Ruby earlier this week."

"Love never shows up late. I've come on personal business myself, and hope I can see to it today, if you'll let me."

"I suppose this has something to do with this piece of horseflesh following you down the driveway." He stroked the appaloosa's nose and it blinked.

Junior nodded and swallowed hard as emotion seemed to tighten the collar of his shirt. "Doc Corbett came over to take a look at Lightning and doesn't think he should bear up the weight of a full-sized cowboy like me. I thought I could just turn him out to pasture, but that would be a cryin' shame. He's full of life and has a lot more to give. When I started thinking about somebody smaller than me, that sprig of a healing girl came to mind." Junior gave him a questioning look.

A smile birthed at the idea of pairing the two spirited creatures together. "Can I buy the appaloosa from you, Junior?"

"You can't buy a blessing when someone needs to give one. Reckon she'd have him?"

"How about we find out?" He motioned toward the backyard. "Hey, why don't you consider staying awhile, Junior? Arie and I have a surprise planned for everyone around twilight. There's plenty of food and festivities in the meantime."

"Much obliged for the invite, Jusdyn. I'd love to stay." He clicked the horse forward and walked down to the backyard.

Curious at seeing the horse, the older men fell in behind the traders. Deke hooked Virgil with his teaching arm and moseyed over from the implement garden pitcher's mound as they debated the trading of free agents in the majors.

Jusdyn beckoned to Valor, hopeful for optimal results.

The attendant-to-be pulled on Chica's reins and trotted right over.

He gave Junior a quick wink. Generosity always landed in the right place. In this case, he delighted in being the middleman.

~

Passing the picture window on the stair landing, Arie caught a glimpse of the gathering as it transpired down below. Excited, she called up to the ladies who were dressing in the guest room. In a rustle of silk and petticoats, they soon huddled on the landing with her. Below, the two parties approach each other, both with a horse in-hand resembling a treaty signing from days of old. She pressed the lace curtain against the glass to search for Jusdyn.

Junior waved a demonstrative arm toward the forelegs of the speckled-rump horse and shook his head. In the next moment, he extended the reins toward Valor and removed his hat in a gracious sweep, landing it against his chest. Valor stood frozen for the briefest of moments, then handed Chica's reins to Jusdyn and received the appaloosa's reins from Junior. The girl stroked the horse's muzzle and placed a kiss upon its jagged white blaze.

Arie clapped in delight at the blessing returned to Valor for a good deed done in healing the storm-crushed stallion. Muriel covered her mouth in a private hush, but allowed the tears to flow as Loren hoisted the slender child into the saddle. Merrilee gasped when the horse shied sideways upon her arrival, but Valor seemed to anticipate the move and leaned with it in perfect synchrony. As the crowd below began to applaud, giggles filled the stairwell in unanimous approval.

"Lord, keep Valor safe on the back of that fidgety horse," Ruby prayed instinctively. A round of amens followed, punctuated by a flurry of petticoats rustling back up the stairs.

Muriel disappeared into Jusdyn's old room and reappeared with an aging baseball glove. "You want to deliver this?" She gestured to Merrilee through the doorway. Baby Beryl responded by bobbing her face against her mother's bare shoulder like a woodpecker, begging to nurse.

"Would you, Aunt Muriel? And give Deke my blessing. I better feed the baby one more time before the ceremony." Merrilee headed for the rocking chair with Beryl.

She looked over from her perch on the dressing stool and recalled another point of closure prime for addressing. "Mom?" She rose to address her new mother-in-law. When Muriel stopped and turned to her, the time to confess had arrived. "I have something to tell you. My secret piecrust ingredient is vinegar. I don't want anything to come between us, even the trivial matters." Her cheeks heated at the silliness of the disclosure.

Muriel smiled as if to say the secret was safe with her. "Well, who would have guessed vinegar for such a flaky pastry crust?"

"Could you please give Valor a fifteen-minute warning for me? And tell her she cannot throw her flower petals from horseback."

"Oh, speaking of throwing flowers." Ruby clasped her empty hands. "I brought my bouquet because I've always dreamed of throwing it to bequeath the bride's good fortune to our next matrimony candidate. Besides, I need the refrigerator space for a second gallon of milk. Let me go down with you, Muriel."

Arie smiled as the two matriarchs locked elbows and descended toward the backyard together, appreciating how wonderfully remarkable the day had become.

~

Beneath the bur oak, Doug checked his watch face for the fourth time in half an hour and then rolled the well-reviewed barn plans up for storing behind the truck seat. A streak of forest green glinted in the late afternoon sun, catching his eye and allowing him to exhale.

Darlene pulled up in front of the cottage and was soon approached by the riders' club. "Well, well. Who's this?" She placed her manicured hand on the appaloosa's velvety nose.

"Meet my new horse, Lightning." Valor's tone carried an obvious pride of ownership. "Mr. Junior brought him to me because the vet doesn't want a grown man riding him anymore, on account of his front legs being shattered by the storm."

"I must admit, you two are a perfect match." Darlene stepped back to allow them to continue the ride. When Jimmy John Wilson drove up into the yard, his three children spilled out of the van and raced toward the horses, too. Valor yielded the saddle for more rides. In the right vicinity, Darlene stooped to lift the oldest girl into the saddle.

"Please allow me." Doug made the offer with his eyes riveted on Darlene's scenery. Their gazes met in mutual attraction. Weak at the knees, he could barely lift the child in place.

~

"Sheriff Wilson?" Loren walked past the horse riders to greet his guests.

"Today, it's simply Jimmy John." The lawman gestured toward

the petite woman beside him. "Loren, have you met my wife, Amy?"

"Yes, we run into each other in the Apple Market every now and again. We're pleased to have you both at the Linquist ranch today. It means a great deal to me, Jimmy John, so thank you for accepting our invitation."

"How's TJ coming along?" The man shifted from one foot to the other. A squeal from one of the children sent Amy drifting off to help supervise the riding line that had detoured to the front porch swing.

"Doctor Montgomery removed his left foot in a five-hour surgery Wednesday morning. But the right foot cleaned up nicely and the skin graft on his lip took just fine. He ought to be in good shape by his court date."

"I'm pretty sure the governor will intervene early on in that process. She called to tell me she's pressing the state attorney's office for a lesser charge, since the explosion left us a bit empty-handed in the evidence department. TJ might be given a stiff probation period, but I can't imagine him having any objections over that."

"He's overdue to take a hard look inside to find out who he truly is, but at least he's talking it over with the Good Lord now."

"And he'll still be able to drive with his accelerator foot intact." Jimmy John tapped his right leg.

Loren stopped walking and looked the sheriff straight in the eye. "I hope there are no hard feelings between the two of you." He knew better than to allow old wounds to fester.

Jimmy John stood still for a few thoughtful seconds and placed his hand on his backside where the buckshot had been extracted. "No, not an ounce." He placed his gun hand across his host's shoulders as if to prove it.

"Good deal. TJ will need all the positive influences he can get at this juncture. Thanks for coming out to Wilsey today as the McLaurens and the Linquists rebuild to fortify the future." When the giggly horseback riders tossed them a wave, Loren gestured to the side yard beyond the bur oak tree.

~

"Hope nothing kept you from coming out today." Doug stared at the ground as they walked down the drive. When Darlene propped her fancy sunglasses up into her hair, he noticed puffy red rims surrounding her brown eyes. A pang of guilt pierced his midsection, guessing that redness might hint at a hitch-up of the introspective kind.

She cleared her throat and looked away. "Oh, I guess I had to do some soul-searching earlier this afternoon."

Doug held his peace and examined the puzzle of a woman standing before him. Assessing her youthful cut sundress dappled with morning glories that trailed vines down the hem, he gained confidence that he could be a sturdy trellis for her bloom—if only she were of a mind to let him. "When you ride in on a crest of a storm, I reckon you forfeit the gradual progression of getting acquainted like a regular courtship."

"Still, I wouldn't have changed a minute of that day." Her words bore a deflated tone, and her eyes remained downcast.

Doug searched her face, his heart breaking at her reluctance.

"Don't you see, Doug? In the storm, the situation was crystal clear. You needed me. I cannot begin to tell you how good that felt. But now, you don't anymore." She sobbed and lowered the sunglasses in place to hide the pending tears.

"But now that I'm stronger, you think I don't need you anymore. Is that what you're thinking?" He grappled for a constructive direction for this unexpected derailment. A beam of hope came to mind, so he stepped to the truck and removed the blueprint roll. "Miss Cosgrove, could you please join me over here?"

She stepped over to the truck a bit tight-faced, awash in her quandary.

"Here's my future hope and direction." He traced the lettering on the header bar labeled *McLauren Barn*.

Blinking the tears back, she reviewed the graceful rendering of a Midwest prairie-style barn. "It's going to be lovely." She fought to speak the words.

His fingertip traced the interior layout next. "Eight stalls will come off the central hay mow, with a handy tack room, a foreman's bunkroom, and storage to the rear."

"It seems to have everything."

"Not everything," he corrected, moving his fingertip back up to the front elevation. His index finger tapped on the neat lettering centered over the twin barn doors. *Double D Riding Stables* was printed over the entrance. "Right now, I seem to be missing one D, but this is only a draft which may be subject to revision."

A bell began to ring on the back porch of the big house, calling the party attendees to gather. He rolled up the blueprints and secured the rubber band with a wordless snap, then stored them back in the cab. As he took a few steps toward the back porch, he paused to impart a final comment. "Any worthwhile gain has an element of sacrifice to it. There comes a point where you have to step forward if you truly hope to achieve something greater. Any sacrifice you might feel at the moment becomes secondary to the greater dream."

When Darlene shoved the sunglasses back into her hair in dubious response, his stomach wrenched. Man enough to step aside and give her room, he left her standing by the truck. That made for a lonely walk over to the back deck, but he didn't regret a single word.

~

Jusdyn sensed a sudden camaraderie with his elderly great uncle, both being green in the wedded department. Muriel welcomed the guests from her post on the porch while Ruby stepped down and flushed Morrill out of the gentlemen's club under the bur oak. His father stepped up beside his mother and amicably surveyed their guests. Ruby flashed one finger requesting a few moments while she straightened Morrill's tie.

Loren pressed against the porch rail seeming to relish the gathering. "Since I have an extra moment, allow me to share a few updates with our family and friends. The storm has certainly stirred things up around Morris County. I'm happy to report that TJ is stable and resting comfortably at the hospital in Emporia. I'm sure he'd appreciate any visitors if you're headed out that way. The Linquist and McLauren families would like to express their sincere gratitude to Sheriff Jimmy John Wilson for standing with us to bring TJ back from the dark detour he'd chosen. Thank you so much, Jimmy John, and sorry about that stray buckshot."

Jusdyn started a round of applause for their heroic law enforcement friend and their guests joined in.

Jimmy John humbly threw a hand in the air to acknowledge their appreciation. His children ran up to him full of hugs as he bent to kiss his sweet wife. When Bobby Dean stood in front of the lawman, he took off his cowboy hat and gave it to the presumptuous boy.

"Muriel and I want you to know we'll be pursuing custody of Valor to both take the load off TJ and bless ourselves, to boot." Valor ran up from the corral and arrived on the porch bright faced but winded, which met with lighthearted laughter and additional applause.

Muriel opened the screen door and ushered the little busybody into the waiting arms of the maid of honor.

"We are also privileged to have the opportunity to adopt Virgil Sinclair, a fourteen-year-old orphan of the storm. That is, if he'll have us." Loren held his hand up until the youth appeared.

Virgil tossed the baseball to Deke without a trace of rotation, and then clomped his way up the porch steps. "You bet I will."

Loren placed his fatherly arm across the boy's shoulder as if to symbolize his merger.

Jusdyn shoved a fist toward his kid brother who bumped it with his own in masculine welcome.

"Here's another change to announce. As of yesterday, I've been asked to be a replacement Morris County commissioner backed by the farmers' co-op as the rural-interest representative." When the applause started, Loren waved it off.

Jusdyn beamed a look of sheer admiration up to his father, realizing he had not been alone in his willingness to step out from the safety of Wilsey.

Loren tapped his temple. "In fact, I'm thinking of a new hole in the ground out toward Allen that would make one dandy of a landfill site."

Jimmy John thrust a thumbs-up into the air. "I second that motion."

Vernis swung little Bobby Dean's arm. "That'll sure save our Helmick land."

Loren glanced at the commotion behind the kitchen door and hurried his presentation. "Well, I see Ruby's got Morrill ready, so I'll end with this. Our son Jusdyn took a job in town this week that will challenge him to promote the land and preserve the prairie all across the county with the conservation service. It's a big task, and I'm sure Jusdyn would appreciate knowing he's got our support. What do you say, folks?"

Deke spoke up without hesitation. "Count on me, Just-man."

Virgil hammed it up like a true brother. "I'll take your old job and your bedroom."

"You've got my help anytime," Mannie Hernandez added.

"Minc, too," Junior said, accompanied by a hoot from Jimmy John.

"We've got you covered back home," Doug replied, his arm latched around Vernis.

Moved by the groundswell of support, Jusdyn removed his hat, tipping it in every direction.

Muriel exited back onto the porch and nodded to her officiating husband.

"Ladies and gentlemen." Loren motioned for the couple to join him. "I now present our guests of honor, the newlyweds Morrill and Ruby McLauren." A hearty applause greeted the pair, causing Ruby to blush at all the attention. Morrill kissed her on the cheek, raising some catcalls amid the clapping.

"Been in the doghouse yet, Morrill?" Jimmy John called from the right side of the crowd. Amy tapped his back pocket in reprimand making him wince.

"Not yet, sheriff," the groom replied. "I just say 'Yes Ruby' and do what I'm told."

When Ruby feigned a swat to his lapel, Vernis chuckled at his brother's fate.

"We're going to ask the bride and groom to cut the cake in just a minute," Muriel said. "But first, Ruby has requested a tradition that's near and dear to her heart."

The bride lifted her bouquet. "Yes, thank you, Muriel. I've always dreamed of tossing my bouquet and passing the matrimonial honors to the next maiden in line."

"That's right. So unmarried ladies, if you'll humor us. Come gather off the railing here, and we'll get Ruby ready to throw." Muriel made the request with a hand flourish before darting inside. "Bouquet time," she called upstairs.

With a gaggle of young girls below ready to make the catch, Ruby inhaled the fragrant roses once last time, whispered a prayer, and launched an arching trajectory toward the maidens.

Jusdyn rose on tiptoe to track the bouquet and see who the lucky recipient would be. Jenna's eyes widened as the floral prize seemed to be descending right toward her extended arms. At the last second, the well-manicured hand of a height-advantaged maiden reached out and claimed the bundle, her white sunglasses slipping from their tucked position.

"Sorry dearie," Darlene said to the crestfallen girl, "but I think this particular bouquet was meant for me."

Ruby clapped in anticipation, looking down as her intuitive dream took shape.

Doug locked gazes with Darlene and approached with intention, extending his right hand.

In the overhead window, the lace curtain moved under the

giddiness of the flower girl hidden behind it. Deke elbowed him in the ribs and nodded toward the window.

He looked up with expectation, feeling lonesome though standing in the crowd. The curtain hung like a veil between them, responding to the exhalations of the breeze. For a moment, he could see Arie peering down at him like an angel bestowing a blessing, but then she'd vanish with the following breeze. He whispered a longing prayer and laced it into the wind.

Arie placed her open palm onto the glass pane as if to reach for him.

He touched his fingers to his lips and pressed a kiss on them, then flung it up toward the angel in white.

"I know you felt I had everything." Doug's voice resonated above the quieted crowd. "But the truth is, when a man who seems to have everything is lonesome deep in his bones, he really doesn't have anything. Here are two things I'm grateful for at this moment. One is a father who fought the onset of age and had the good sense to come back to the ranch. And two is a tornado that swept away some of the old me and blew a fanciful songbird to my doorstep."

The bouquet holder smiled and bit her trembling lower lip.

"Darlene Cosgrove?" Doug began the pronouncement and then paused to fold his body toward the ground.

When Muriel lifted a hand to block a tear, Loren wrapped her into his steady arms.

Seeing his parents' rare show of affection made him long for Arie all the more. In his ache, he glanced up at the window and saw her second palm press against the pane, reaching across the infinity of space—straight toward him.

Doug bowed his head. "Would you be so kindhearted as to hang your 'D' next to mine over the barn door as my partner, the love of my life, and my wife?"

Darlene looked at the recovering rancher and dropped her left hand down to him in a graceful gesture. "Yes, take my 'D' and hitch it next to yours," she sang out in clear-voiced surety. "I will… I do…

I'm yours for life."

Doug rose with difficulty, yet refused assistance. Jenna snatched the daisy band from her hair and placed it into his hand. "With everything to gain," he said, slipping the daisy in place.

"Everything, indeed," she replied, meeting him halfway for the celebratory kiss. The children made a spontaneous circle around the couple and skipped about, adding to the merriment of the occasion.

"Cake, everyone," Ruby announced, openly thrilled with the outcome.

He looked up with heightened expectation at the window on the landing, but only the lifeless curtain remained. For a final time, the hollow core of bachelorhood rumbled down the full length of his frame as he stood there alone and empty-handed.

"You're next," Deke said, his eyebrows bobbing in jocularity.

He wiped sweaty palms on his dress slacks and reached to straighten Deke's tie. "From what I could see up there, she's looking one hundred percent woman in that dress of hers." He gave the comment further thought and exhaled with a slight whistle. When he tried to step up onto the deck to get a piece of his great uncle's cake, his feet refused. "Oh, thunder," he whispered under his breath.

Deke locked a strong arm around his quaking shoulders and escorted him up to their place in the reception line. "It's a little too late to hang on the verge."

Jusdyn relaxed with a smile and gazed out over the farmyard beyond the familiar landscape, wondering what kind of discoveries would be waiting for the two of them as husband and wife, after the curtain was no more.

Twilight falls across the evening sky while a violin plays to coax the constellations out of hiding. Tiny white lights twinkle over the implement garden, arching toward the arms of the cherry tree to mark the place of matrimonial vows. The leader of the Lord's movement for prairie restoration stands under the arch, moment by moment becoming more fully imbued with expectation. Where once only darkness awaited him from the perimeter of the unknown, a radiant bride now appears, casting the assurance of her countenance in the purity of white. Her uncle ushers her in with tender temperance, one step of faith at a time. With anointed blessing, he releases her arm and she comes forward to her groom of her own free will. Mourning doves coo their angelic blessing from the catalpa canopy as the horizon collapses in a crown of vermilion rays. The bridegroom reaches out for her and takes her hand. Kneeling before the Lord, they vow devotion to one another and to the land. Rising, he begins the journey down the less trodden path to restore the prairie, and she—rising beside him enjoined by his embrace—will name the plants and name his children.

AUTHOR BIO

Cindy M. Amos writes inspirational fiction from Wichita, Kansas and ranches on the Amos family's heritage lands around Council Grove, a stopover along the historic Santa Fe Trail. With a background in field ecology from the Mid-Atlantic coast, she views the mid-continental tallgrass prairie as the hub from which a major restoration may take seed. Working to inspire the fifth generation of Amos laborers as well as fellow ranchers, Ms. Amos weaves a complex tale of family devotion and enduring commitment to caring for the land. Ecological subheadings are included to lend the prairie an active yet distinctive voice throughout this series.

Cindy M. Amos is an Amazon best-selling author and member of American Christian Fiction Writers. "Acquired Land" is her 52nd release with Editor Cynthia Hickey at Winged Publications.

Her website can be found at
http://cindymamos.wixsite.com/natureink

Her Amazon author page can be found at
https://www.amazon.com/Cindy-M.-Amos

OTHER BOOKS BY CINDY M. AMOS
Landscapes of Mercy Series
Redeeming River Rancher
Saving Bicycle Man
Justifying Sound Strider
Sanctifying Ace Aerialist
Lifting Lock Runner
Salvaging Doctor Junk

National Parks 100th Anniversary Romance

Collection
Everglades Entanglement
Mesa Verde Meltdown

Holiday 3-in-1 Collection
Running Out of Christmastime

Taming the Cowboy's Heart Collection
Warming Stone Cold Lodge

50 States Collection
Secondhand Flower Stand (Kansas)
Red Cloud Retreat (Nebraska)
Tidewater Lowlands (North Carolina)
Canyon Country Courtship (Utah)

John Denver 20th Anniversary Collection
Calypso Reimagined

Loving the Town Hero Collection
Cascading Waterworks

Cowboy Brides Collection
Renegade Restoration

America's Fabulous Fifties Series
Oil Field Maven
Airfield Aptitude
Camp Field Capable

Small Town Christmas Collection 2018
Gift Tag Tree

Romancing the Rancher's Daughter Collection
Waylaying the Hauler

Romancing the Farmer Collection
Furrowed Hearts

Adventure Brides Collection
Ocean's Edge

Romancing the Bachelor Collection
Impasse to Springtime

Romancing the Boy Next Door Collection
Forty Acres on Loan

Romancing the Doctor Collection
X-Raying the Doctor

Vote for Love Collection
Ballot Box Rumors

A Secret Santa Romance Collection
Sweet Regrets from Sourwood

Christmas Cookie Brides Collection
Pizzelles for Elves

Romancing the Drifter Collection
Derailing the Drifter

A Family to Love Collection

Skinny Ranch Romance

Nonfiction Little Lift Gift Books
Signs of the Seasons: Hints from Nature

The Men of Mustang Pass Series
Silver Lining at Mustang Pass
Copper Halo at Mustang Pass
Sapphire Skies at Mustang Pass
Holiday Hitches at Mustang Pass

Horizons of Hidden Promise Series
Rekindled from Ashes
Reconciled from Heartache
Recaptured from Oblivion

Cape Pointe Series
Salt-Stung on Cape Hatteras
Current-Ripped on Cape Lookout
Tide-Trapped on Cape Fear

A Christmas Secret Collection 2021
Ocracoke by Christmas

Romance at Riverfront Stadium Series
Home Run Hunter
Season Two Snafu
Yuletide Grand Slam

That Merry Season Collection 2022
Upload Christmas

Summer Junket Series 2023

Hoard Haul-Out
Kitsch Kick-Out

Once Upon a Christmas Romance Collection 2024
Come Again Christmas